PAUL PREUSS

STARFIRE

TOR

STARFIRE

From "Little Gidding" in FOUR QUARTETS by T. S. Eliot, copyright 1943 by T. S. Eliot; renewed 1971 by Esme Valerie Eliot. Reprinted by permission of Harcourt Brace Jovanovich, Inc. in the United States. Reprinted by permission of Faber and Faber in Canada.

A TOR Book

Published by Tom Doherty Associates, Inc.
49 West 24 Street
New York, N.Y. 10010

Jacket art by Vincent DiFate

Printed in the United States of America

for the gang
at Colossal Pictures
and USFX

Nature cannot be fooled.
    —RICHARD P. FEYNMAN,
        independent report on
        the destruction of *Challenger*

THE
SUN

Seconds before impact, Travis realized the pilot was unconscious. Too late. The station loomed in the windows of the little satellite tender; the screech of metal on metal drowned his surprised yelp. Even as he bounced his head off the deck he noted with amazement the brilliant flares that spewed past the window, aluminum shrapnel burning in an outrush of pure oxygen from the ruptured air lock.

In the Newtonian exchange—one slow billiard ball against the rack—the several-thousand-tonne space station was nudged into an imperceptibly different orbit. The satellite tender that had smacked it, in which Travis was a passenger, was now skidding away at a flat angle, its cabin air whistling through a thin rupture in the gasket of its docking collar.

Inside the little tender Travis struggled to get the unconscious pilot's helmet over his head and seal it to his suit. Travis was taking big gulping breaths as he did so, filling his lungs from what air remained in the cramped cabin. As the whistle dwindled to nothing, a suspiciously giggly sense of what-the-hell crept up on him, warning him that he had to get his own helmet on. That took about four seconds, longer than it should have in the tender's lazy spin. He punched his chest valve, and air hissed into his suit.

Travis allowed himself a quick sigh. It was going to be one of those ODTAA days, just one damn thing after another.

He dragged the pilot free of his straps and quickly taped

him to the wall with tape from the roll he kept at his waist. He wrestled his wide shoulders forward and clambered into the single control seat, buckling down, slapping at the panel switches to douse the hysterical alarm blinkers.

"Uh, Euclid, this is Twinkletoes. Do you read?"

"Copy, UT-two. Trav, this is Takumi. Everybody's in the cellar but me and George and Lizzy. What's your ES?"

"Let's see, looks like we got total loss of cabin pressure. Max passed out, I don't know what's wrong. He's suited up, and air's flowing in his suit."

The star field outside the trapezoidal windows wobbled drunkenly, then was sliced away by the brilliance of the blue North Atlantic 400 kilometers beneath the ship. It was a beautiful, almost cloudless early fall day down there, but Travis had no time to appreciate it. While he talked, Travis wiggled the joy stick. In the absence of air to carry sound, he heard—if you could call it that—the hiss of the attitude jets through the seat of his pants. Like a series of long, low farts after a bowl of Uncle Albert's industrial-strength chili. Comforting.

"Travis, do you have control of your vehicle?"

The blue ocean went away and the white-painted space station swam into view—*pooot*—and out again—*poot, poot*—and in again, each time staying a little longer.

"Give me about five more seconds."

Euclid Station was a small, ungainly thing, a confusion of spidery trusses and flimsy panels and random spheres and cylinders, feebly floodlit against the brute glare of subarctic September. The station housed a score of astronauts, engineers, scientists, and government busybodies; all but the short-timers among them were presently huddled in the big "storm cellar," a tube of sheet iron surrounded by many cubic yards of plain sand. Ten minutes ago Houston had relayed warning of a major solar flare from sun-watching satellite sensors. Euclid was sliding toward the blue-white polar region, pursued by a hail of lethal protons incoming at a quarter of light speed.

Caught outside the station with Travis and his pilot in the satellite tender was another ship and the six people in its crew, a high-orbit shuttle that was at this moment urgently trying to redock at the main launch bay.

In the tender's windows the ocean and the stars stopped contending. Travis eased the joy stick forward, and the tender moved slowly toward the station. He spoke cheerfully into his suit mike: "Takumi, my friend, my updated ES is that I've got a pilot out of commission and a piss-ant little tin can of a spacecraft with no air in it, but it'll still fly. I reckon we're ready to come in out of the heat now."

A few seconds passed before he got an answer. "Travis, I'm trying to figure out how we can help you. We have severed gas lines in the utility air lock."

"No sweat, we'll use the launch bay, soon as you evacuate that high orbit choo-choo and shove it out of the way."

"We've run that option. Estimate is a minimum one hour to dock and clear the hatch. She's loaded, Trav. We've got to off-load some of that fuel to vent overpressure."

Travis didn't bother asking for details. The big shuttle had been interrupted in its launch sequence, and like an airliner lifting from the runway, it was a flying bomb, bloated with toxic and explosive fuel. It had to be secured in place in the launch bay until excess fuel could be bled off into the station's holding tanks, blocking the only remaining pressurized entrance to the station.

The ratio was cold and simple. Six lives in the shuttle to two in the satellite tender.

"An hour, huh?"

"Yeah, Trav. Houston's putting a tiger team on your situation. We ought to have some fresh options for you soon."

Euclid Station completely circled the Earth every ninety minutes, sixteen times in a day; now heading north to the

Arctic Circle, in forty-five minutes it would be approaching the Antarctic. At both poles the Earth's magnetic field lines curve down to the ground, steering captured charged particles into the atmosphere—producing delicate auroras below but leaving orbiting objects naked to the electromagnetic storm. Unlike its sister, Archimedes Station, whose orbit never took it outside the magnetically shielded middle latitudes, Euclid was exposed to radiation eight hours in every twenty-four.

"Patch me into Houston, okay?" Travis requested.

"Wilco."

". . . investigating opening the weld in Corridor Z. That's in the schedule for next week anyway." Caught in midsentence, the relaxed, gently concerned female voice of Houston's mission communicator, the Capcom, sounded in Travis's headset. "Another alternative is to put all hands in pressure suits and blow one of the emergency hatches. Aside from the inherent risk, however, we have to calculate how long it will take to resupply your oxygen. First approximation is not promising."

"Houston, this is Travis Hill."

"Go ahead, Travis."

"What are the likely dose numbers?"

"Current estimates are that you and your pilot will have taken approximately twenty-five rads from early fast protons by the time you get over the hill. You could collect another hundred rads on each pass over the poles, as long as the flare lasts."

"Good-sized flare."

"That's a roger."

If exposed to 500 rads in a short time, a human stands a fifty-fifty chance of dying within thirty days. Two hundred rads produces serious illness, although the chances of recovery are favorable. Workers on Euclid were monitored and sent home if they got seventy-five rads in a year. After three years they were retired in any event.

The Capcom spoke again. "Travis?"

"I'm listening."

"It doesn't look like we can get you inside the station in this nightside pass. Suggest that when the shuttle is in the launch bay, you tuck up Earthside of its number three tank. The liquid H-two in the tank will give you some shielding, with minimum secondary radiation risk. That could reduce the dose to about seventy-five rads over the Antarctic."

"Gee, I feel better already."

"There's a reasonable certainty they can move the shuttle out of the way within this orbit."

Takumi, aboard Euclid, chimed in. "We'll do it, Trav."

"We're pretty confident they can do it," said Houston.

Travis was being told to give in, to stop thinking of escape. He was being told to exceed his career limits for radiation exposure. They would never let him go into space again. "What kind of retirement benefits you offerin'?"

The woman in Houston tried to put a smile into her voice. "We can't do miracles with physics, Travis. But we'll see what we can do with Uncle Sam's red tape."

For a long moment Travis was silent. The ungainly station was directly over his head now, slipping past by millimeters each second. The high-orbit shuttle was settling into the launch bay, its three bloated fuel tanks clustered like a clutch of ostrich eggs beneath its stubby torso.

Travis wiggled the joy stick. The satellite tender responded instantly. "Houston, I am proceeding to dock the UT-two under the shuttle's number three tank, per your advice."

"Copy."

"Say if we can assist," said Euclid.

"Thanks, Takumi, this is the easy part."

Minutes passed as the tender approached and scraped gently across the orange fiber-glass skin of the fuel tank. Travis manipulated the tender's articulated arms with practiced skill, hooking the claws through D-ring hard points in the tank's surface until the tender clung fast to the shuttle with a steel grip.

Travis twisted in his seat and studied Max's peaceful face through his lightly misted faceplate. He poked at the pilot's shoulder, where blinking biomedical monitors were clustered for display. "Houston and Euclid, copy this for the record. Max's biomeds show a normal and stable heart rate, normal and stable blood pressure, normal and stable respiration, brain-wave pattern consistent with ordinary sleep, no signs of distress"—talk about wearing your heart on your sleeve— "and I don't know what the hell's the matter with him, but I can't do anything about it while he's inside that suit. Euclid, assure me you will be able to reach Max if I am incapacitated."

"No sweat. Soon's we move the shuttle out of the way, we'll come get both of you."

"Copy that, Euclid." Travis slapped the chest plate to release his suit harness. "You come get Max as quick as you can, Takumi. Don't bother about me, I'm bailing out."

"Say again, Travis?" Euclid spoke first; Houston's nearly simultaneous reply was delayed by distance.

Travis was already yanking at the tender's ruined docking collar. He shoved hard against sprung hinges, moving the hatch aside with effort, squeezing through. He floated free of the little ship, under the orange belly of the shuttle tank.

He spoke in bursts into his communications cap radio, spacing his words for economy. "I figure if I can launch an escape pod . . . in the next five minutes . . . I can hit air a couple of minutes after that . . . be in the water in half an hour."

The orbital escape pods distributed at various handy points on the exterior of Euclid Station were generally regarded by astronauts with amused contempt—another inept safety gesture on the part of ground-bound bureaucrats, sops less practical than an airliner's floating seat cushions.

"Hill, this is not a life-threatening situation."

Travis recognized Taylor Stith's voice in his headset, querulous, trembling on the edge of temper—the *Wunderkind* flight director had just violated etiquette by grabbing the Capcom's mike. "Those pods have not been operationally tested," said Stith.

"Copy." Travis continued his progress around the outside of the shuttle's bulging hydrogen tank, flying hand to hand from D-ring to D-ring; behind him the abandoned tender, with Max inside, looked very small, like a mosquito poised on an oversized female breast. Travis was breaking the rules even more grandly than that ground pounder Stith, of course, maneuvering freely in space without an umbilical, without a maneuvering unit, without even a safety tether.

Bright dots of ice floating in water the color of Aqua Velva formed the convex sky above Travis's head, while beneath him the flimsy raft of Euclid Station floated in a bowl of unblinking stars. A brief leap across the open space between the shuttle's tank and the edge of the station's launch bay took him to the nearest pod storage bin. He flipped its barn doors open.

The escape pods were lenticular ceramic heat shields with thermoplastic covers, hardly bigger than Porta Potties. Stored inside each was a parachute and an inflatable raft in an ejection rig and—the only really specialized gadget—a hand-aimed, gyro-stabilized, solid-fuel retrorocket. An astronaut who had to leave orbit in a hurry was supposed to climb in, lie back, clutch the retrorocket to his or her chest, adjust position and attitude with its gas jets, then take aim at an easily identifiable star specified by mission control and pull the trigger.

The impulse from the solid-fuel rocket would gradually slow the pod until orbital velocity was lost, whereupon the astronaut threw away the rocket, closed the flimsy hatch with its little bubble window, and tried to relax while falling through the atmosphere, on fire, decelerating at five gees plus. Below about 7,000 meters or so the pod's cover would pop off, spilling the astronaut and deploying the chute.

Simple.

In seconds he had the nearer pod free of its straps. Lifting the thermoplastic lid, he found all the neat packages of equipment nestled where they should be. He ripped open Velcro fastenings of yellow webbing, yanked at cotter pins festooned with red warning strips. One of them activated a SARSAT radar beacon.

"Hill, we just ran some quick numbers and we want you to consider that the calculated uncertainties in your re-entry show a damn poor chance of getting any helicopter ship near you in less than two days from Hawaii. Assuming you land in water."

"It's gonna be dark soon. How about giving me a star?"

"Astronaut, this is a direct order. I'm ordering you not to attempt to use that escape pod. We can't be responsible for your safety." While no one had ever used a pod, it was not strictly true that none had been tested. What was true was that in no test had an unmanned pod ever been seen again.

"You can't fire me, Taylor . . . and I won't quit." The pod drifted free of its mooring. Travis kicked off and went with it. For a moment he had a bizarre image of himself as a surfer launching a surfboard while standing on his head. It made him irritable. "Give me something to aim at, dammit. Or I'll shoot from the hip."

Flipping over to squat on the pod, he shrugged off his life-support backpack and hooked into the pod's portable emergency oxygen supply. He wrestled himself onto his back and tugged the parachute straps across his chest and shoulders, pulling the life raft package up under his rump. The strap edges scrunched thick layers of suit material into an oppressive lump in his crotch. It was exhausting work, and he heated up fast without the coolant flow from his abandoned backpack, but it had to be done right; parachutists had dismembered themselves with loose harnesses.

Now Euclid was overhead, and the dazzle of the north Greenland ice pack was rolling unseen below him. Euclid's orbit was inclined several degrees from true polar coordinates, and within moments the whole orbiting miscellany—station, shuttle, pod, and all—would be heading south across the Northwest Territories of Canada.

"Travis, this is Houston." The voice was Capcom's again. Flight director Mr. Taylor Stith had evidently realized that ambition was not to be served by putting himself in the front lines on this one. Travis imagined the newsheads. SPACE STATION CRISIS MISMANAGED: ASTRONAUT LOST/ASTRONAUT INCINERATES SELF/ASTRONAUT DROWNS/ASTRONAUT EATEN BY SHARKS. He forced a grin. His mother was always telling him that acting scared scares you, that acting brave makes you brave. "Go ahead, Houston."

"We have acquired your beacon. When you are secure, we want you to aim on Altair and do a one-second gas burst to separate from the station."

He nudged the rocket canister into place with his knees, deflecting it at a low angle, and aimed across its verniers through its wide cross hairs. Altair was one of the brightest stars in the sky, the brightest star in the constellation Aquila, now just rising in the southwest above the twilight rim of the world. "I have it." Like all pilot astronauts and countless mariners before him, Travis had long ago committed Altair's position to memory.

"Whenever you're ready, Travis."

"Firing." The gas cylinder on the barrel of the bulky rocket pack puffed compressed gas into space. Travis saw nothing but the indicator light on the butt of the rocket pack, but he felt feathery pressure against his diaphragm from fractional gee forces. "One, one thousand," he murmured, and lifted his thumb from the gas button.

The stars had shifted. Euclid Station had rotated perceptibly to his right. There was silence in Travis's headset. "Still with me, Houston?"

"We're with you. Give us a moment before we finalize."

"Copy, Houston. Thanks for the help."

The pause was a fraction of a second longer than it had to be. "We aim to please, Travis. You do likewise."

Travis ignored the implied rebuke and took comfort in the promise. He really wasn't ready to think about what state his life must be in, that he'd rather stake it on this desperate chance than allow himself to be barred from space forever. It wasn't the time for that kind of introspection, anyway.

"Travis, assuming you're lying down in that thing, you should find Beta Aquarius straight ahead. Do you have any question about its identity?"

"No. I have Beta Aquarius in the verniers."

"Copy."

Again there was silence. He lay supine in a cockleshell raft, adrift on the river of night, judging its current by the stars and nebulae that washed over the gunwales.

"Travis, we want you to take aim on Beta Aquarius and initiate the preset charge precisely on our mark, T minus thirty seconds. Do you copy?"

"Copy." Again he nudged the fat barrel of the retrorocket and sighted through the open cross hairs at the white star.

"Travis, I have a note here from Guidance. Says the common name of Beta Aquarius is Sadalsuud, if I'm pronouncing that correctly. It means the Luckiest of the Lucky." The Capcom's voice was without emotion, as if she were afraid to jinx the omen by regarding it as anything other than a useful datum.

He would need the luck. The first unmanned test pods had had an attitude problem. The pods were meant to skitter across the top of the atmosphere like a pebble on a pond, until they slowed enough to sink straight in. With the wrong attitude, a pod didn't even bounce before tumbling into meteoric ruin. After NASA had licked that, the test pods began making it into the atmosphere, their beacons beeping right up until ionization blackout—but after that, nothing.

"Ten seconds to de-orbit burn . . ."

He listened to the numbers and thought of nothing but keeping the retrorocket braced, the star in his cross hairs. When the count ran all the way down, he squeezed the trigger.

This time flame spurted between his toes. His stomach sank. The impulse was gentle, but it seemed to go on forever. The stars slowed, and Euclid wheeled away into darkness before the rocket flickered out.

"A good burn, Travis. Now all you've got to do is roll into eyeballs-in position."

"Roger." With quick bursts of gas he rotated the pod until the surface of the planet was rolling away beneath his feet. Below him the Earth was darkening, and scattered lights winked on in the great glacier-planed desolation of central Canada. The regions of middle air were hung with milky veils of northern light. He unlatched the spent rocket and gave it just enough of a shove over the side to ensure that it wouldn't re-enter on top of him.

"We're scrambling ASR from Johnson Island. See you in Waikiki."

He knew this communicator, a red-haired kid, pretty and smart and tough as nails. "You meet me in person and I'll buy you a mai tai."

"Can't pass up an offer like that." She paused. "Go with God."

Choked good wishes from other voices in Houston and aboard Euclid joined in, whispering in his headset—writing him off, he thought.

He kept his amen to himself.

Like a tetherball wrapping around a pole, the escape pod accelerated as it dove toward Earth. The first widely spaced molecules of air offered resistance. Travis began to feel a bit sludgy. He pulled the thermoplastic cover over his head and peered through its fishbowl window; between his helmet and the window there was so much refraction that he could no longer make out the stars.

A bead of sweat trickled from the inside of his brow, down the side of his nose, into his eye. Stung like hell— that's gravity for you. He could feel his weight now, pressing against all the ridges and wrinkles of his clammy suit. The wad between his legs was as oppressive as a loaded diaper.

Something whispered in his ears, and a flicker of red licked over the glass, inches from his eyes. Perhaps he was imagining it, but the pod seemed to vibrate with febrile energy, nervy as a wet fingertip sliding around the rim of a glass.

The window was all red, tending to orange—not the red of flame, but the diffuse red of a neon sign, glowing with gas discharge. The abused air molecules outside the pod were hot, excited enough to glow, but too far from one another to transfer much heat to the pod.

That proved to be a temporary state: molecules swiftly swarmed closer as the diving pod continued to accelerate against the braking force of the air. The window was ablaze with pearly light, and inside Travis's spacesuit the air was getting unmanageably hot. Vapor clouded his faceplate. Sweat poured into his eyes.

Steady white flame outside the window, and a banshee's wail rattling his eardrums . . . he hadn't been prepared for the noise, inexpressibly louder than the controlled bellow of a returning space shuttle, a painful shriek drilling into his head, straight through his solid helmet. He groaned but couldn't hear himself. Neither could anyone else, for by now the falling pod was deep inside the cone of ionized gas that blocked the passage of radio waves.

Each second was a minute, each minute a year. Ten minutes in real time he basted in his juices in the howling furnace, waiting for death. The gee forces increased as fiery air slowed the onrush of the escape pod from 29,000 kilometers an hour to 19,000, to 9,000, all the while piling stones on his collapsing belly.

His brain force-fed on blood, and black flecks swam before his eyes; his oppressed guts threatened to heave. He closed his eyes, but that was worse: he began sliding dizzily toward unconsciousness as an inner voice said calmly, as if it had no stake in the matter, *this may have been a mistake.*

The white glow flickered again, fell back through pearl to pink to red, and once more to black. The shriek subtly altered, and groggily he perceived that he was hearing not just the vibration of metal and plastic but the sound of wind. A drop of condensed moisture fell from his faceplate onto his cheek.

The ride got bumpy; the pod encountered seemingly solid layers of air, then dropped into wells of vacuum. He was slammed from one side to the other as the pod bucked in the turbulence. He knew he had five minutes to fall before he got down to air thick enough to grab his chute, but his time sense had been destroyed. Was the blackness outside the window due to high altitude or merely to night? He had no choice but to trust the pod's altimeter.

The turbulence increased; his helmet bounced painfully off the useless window. For a moment he was sure he was traveling up, not down, and he heard a rattle of hail like a handful of birdshot thrown against the pod cover. Lightning glared through his window. Thunderhead! He had to suppress momentary panic—a primitive fear, left over from student pilot days.

Not that a thunderstorm couldn't still destroy him.

Suddenly the ride was smooth again. As his throat relaxed into the beginning of a sigh, the pod's cover ripped away and the mortar shell he was sitting on blew him into the night. He tumbled like a rag doll through the air. The unsecured oxygen package slammed into his face, shattering his faceplate, and he pawed at it and tore it from its connection.

Somewhere deep in the back of his skull the self-that-refused-to-get-involved noted another useful design change.

The drogue caught and the chute spilled and streamed out behind, tugging him upright just before it blossomed and braked him with a bruising jerk. He craned his head back to check the shroud lines. His shattered helmet got in the way; he twisted it, dragged it off his head, hurled it aside. He saw that the shrouds ran taut up to a small round canopy high above his head, darkly silhouetted against a sky of blue-black clouds and moist stars.

He twisted the wrist locks on his gloves and consigned them to the air. He lifted his waist flap and worked at the waist ring until the top and bottom of his suit were detached, but the parachute harness prevented him from shedding more weight. He hung there, swinging in the night, with a fragrant breeze pushing into his nostrils and a wad of fabric crushing his balls, and he began to worry.

He could not yet see the surface below him, but he imagined the rolling immensity of the ocean. Already he was faint from the effort of pulling off his helmet and gloves—a few weeks in microgravity is sufficient to decondition the hardiest body—and he dreaded what was to come.

Inky ripples resolved out of the darkness beneath his white-booted feet, liquid black running on gray, teasing the eye to imagine a curve of moonless sea. Travis fidgeted with the parachute harness release. The ripples became swells; waves textured the swells. A tang of salt mist . . .

He pulled up his knees and flipped the releases as the heaving floor of black water rushed up and struck him. All was dense and ringing darkness, with something yanking hard at his foot, tumbling him into boiling confusion. There were bubbles all around him, he could feel them bulging and slithering between his inner and outer suit and wobbling over the skin of his face, but he could not see them.

Whatever it was still dragged at his foot, but his attention was completely focused on the mass of aluminum and nylon that swaddled his upper body. With a deliberation born of terror he held firmly to his open left sleeve while withdrawing the arm inside it, inevitably also pulling the garment over his face, where it clung. He did not panic—he had moved through panic to a place where the universe was reduced to a single dimension, a straight space-time line, allowing one act only, and then another—but reached outside with his free left arm and taking hold of the right sleeve, forcing his reach against the rigid metal of the upper waistband now levering into his neck, pulled those arms apart . . . until the smothering whiteness of the upper suit was gone.

The lower half next: he pushed at its waist ring to no effect; his feet were stuck in his boots. He tucked himself as if doing a sit-up, but his abdominal muscles were so much spent elastic. He could reach to his boots, but he had no strength to pull at them.

He lay back then, and almost inhaled ocean. It seemed much the easiest solution, not only the easiest but really the only sensible course, because he was so very tired, and after all he had done his best . . . after all . . .

. . . his all . . . over . . .

That damned thing tugged on his leg again *his shoulders slammed into the dirt a rock pounded into his ribs an oak thicket tore the side of his face and his ankle was about to snap the hooves were slamming into the caliche throwing yellow dust up his nose no goddam horse is gonna do that to me you sonofabitch all he had to do was reach up and grab that stirrup strap and haul himself up to where he could grab the saddle horn and grab that fancy long mane and he'd kill that fucking bonehead animal by God he'd put a .45 slug right in its ear if it was dumb enough to run all the way back to the barn with him still on it my Daddy'll give me the gun to do it too you'll see*

His arm was over the side of the raft and his right leg was out of the spacesuit bottom. The floating parachute harness still tugged at the empty boot. Irritably Travis kicked at the other leg, and the garment slithered off and silently sank.

There was a lot of stuff he was supposed to do now. Flares. Radio. Salvage the chute and all that. He'd get to it. Right now he needed rest, with his cheek snugged against this hard rough bosom smelling of rubber cement, the salt water dribbling into his mouth. . . .

He gagged and choked. He raised himself and screamed an obscenity—against the night, against his weakness and cowardice—and with strength he got from some unknown place he pulled himself into the bottom of the raft.

He had passed out before he knew he was safely aboard. When he woke he felt nothing but his own immense weight, and something punching him rudely in the stomach. The sea. Six inches from his face was a curved wall of textured yellow, brilliant in sunlight—the raft's inflated gunwale. His soggy Snoopy hat, its radio dead and worse than useless, muffled his hearing, but beyond the lap and gurgle of water under his ear he could make out another sound, a distant rhythmic hiss and sharp intermittent crack, which puzzled him. Until he recognized it.

Surf.

Travis rolled carefully onto his back. The sky was soft blue, the clouds were benign billows of vapor, high and white, and the sun on his face was a warm caress. He dragged off the communications cap and hauled himself up, half sitting, half lying against the gunwale. The water beside the raft was of a startling blue—not the royal blue of the deep sea but the turquoise blue of a sandy lagoon.

A meter away, floating belly up just beneath the surface, was a three-meter-long hammerhead shark, dead as a plank. Did I land on it? Travis wondered, and started to giggle.

Repeatedly jumping up over the jagged horizon formed by the little nearby waves he saw, on the farther horizon, a long curl of white water curving away to the right and a flat strip of yellow sand beyond, surmounted by a uniform fringe of coconut palms. And on this side of the surf, coming toward him, were two palm-log canoes powered by outboard motors, driven by fat brown young men in orange and purple undershirts.

Travis tried to stifle his giggles, but it was really too funny. This wasn't Johnson Island. He wondered what the boatmen would think when they found this guy in a raft wearing this ridiculous suit of long underwear. . . .

Still snorting and chuckling, he went back to sleep.

Later, waking in the bottom of a canoe to the racket of a two-cycle engine and the smell of unburned motor oil and fish, he did ask, but he couldn't understand the answer. He had never taken French.

Later still, in Houston, after they'd pumped him full of electrolytes and nutrients and reassured him that everybody on Euclid was in good health and fine spirits, including his friend Max, the pilot of the tender, whose undetected neurological aberrations would have grounded him even if he hadn't OD'd on solar protons, a bureaucrat who was still trying to decide whether to treat Travis as a hero or a dangerous madman showed him on a map the exact point where he'd impacted: twenty-seven miles east-northeast of Manihi atoll in the Tuamotu Archipelago.

He'd drifted for half a day, asleep the whole time, while search planes homed on his beacon. He was not implicated in the death of the shark.

DEATH-DEFYING BAIL-OUT FROM NEAR-EARTH ORBIT
(New York–Los Angeles Times)

AMERICAN COSMONAUT-SPY ABANDONS STRICKEN COM-
PANION, PLUNGES TO EARTH IN FIERY SPACE ESCAPE
(Pravda)

ORBITAL ESCAPE SYSTEM PROVES ITS METTLE *(London
Times–Monitor)*

TRAVIS TO NASA: LOOK MA, NO WIRES *(Us People)*

The verdict, in the West anyway, was "hero." The newsheads saw to that.

NASA bit its collective lip and went along with the gag.
As ever, the agency was desperate for good publicity. As
ever, it was paranoid schizophrenic on the question of what
sort of publicity was good.

Safety-conscious to the point of absurdity for the first
quarter century of its existence (to so absurd a point, in fact,
that at first NASA had wanted to make its systems pi-
lotproof), by the advent of the shuttle era the agency had
fallen victim to its own propaganda. Estimates of risk were
based on engineers' choices of adjectives. One guy would
say "occasional," and that got written down as ten thousand
to one; another guy would say "remote," and that came out

a hundred thousand to one. We are safety-conscious, therefore we are safe, they thought—the sort of logic that proves fatal.

Which was one reason why, deep down, NASA still hated its heroes. NASA's engineers turned managers had never stopped resenting individual initiative when it bucked the system. As an eloquent defender of the profession once phrased it, engineering has its existential pleasures. But it seems they are more likely to be found on the CADD screen or in the shop. Hell, as an earlier, more cynical existentialist had pointed out, is other people. And individuals with initiative have an alarming tendency to reveal the system for what it is—an assemblage of ordinary folks whose judgment is sometimes questionable and who rather frequently make mistakes.

Worst of all, NASA hated to remind the tax-paying public that men and women would die in space, inevitably, even when the system was functioning perfectly—if only because the work was inherently, irremediably dangerous.

That Travis. He could have died right out there in front of everybody. NASA resented him for making a personal choice, even when no other lives were at risk, and secretly some of them resented him even more for *surviving* his personal choice, for who knew how many others might be tempted to pull the same kind of dumb stunt?

Through some fluke he was a hero, though, and they had to treat him that way until it all blew over. The public affairs people obligingly facilitated numerous video and fax interviews with Travis and his mates aboard Euclid, and the Polynesian fishermen who had beaten the search planes to the rescue and plucked him out of the raft, and his mother and brothers and uncle; they supplied animated reconstructions of his re-entry trajectory, plus background sheets on orbital mechanics and escape pod design; they talked about the importance of the research he had been doing aboard Euclid, searching the skies for eccentric Earth-crossing comets and asteroids.

Higher up, the administrators reluctantly decided they had to let Travis go back into space one more time. They played up his colorful remark about how his ma had always made him get right back on the horse after he'd been bucked off, but they kept him to a short tour on Archimedes (little radiation danger there). Not once did anyone ever say to him in so many words, you've had it, Hill, you're washed up with us.

Behind Taylor Stith's gray steel desk a north-facing picture window overlooked an irrigated green lawn—thick Bermuda grass, tough as wire, with a pond full of rocks in the middle of it—the focus of the Johnson Space Center's college-style campus. Fifty years after its planting the Bermuda grass was holding up fine, thriving in fact, but the surrounding buildings, plastered with quartz chips which had once gleamed so pristinely in the sullen Gulf sun, were succumbing to livid rust streaks and tarry black scabs where the wall adhesive had failed. An astute observer might have inferred that NASA was in that stretch of the economic cycle where it found itself tempted to promise too much on too low a budget.

"What can I do for you, Dr. Hill?"

Standing behind his desk, Stith regarded Travis with enforced placidity. Taylor Stith's hair was fine, straight, mousy brown, cut in the boyish, white-sidewalled style of an earnest young Methodist minister, an impression reinforced by pale gray eyes that peered unblinking from beneath sparse eyebrows. Their coldness gave the lie to his smile. On a minister such a combination of features could have been a warning: Brother, I have brought you the Good News, and if you don't like it, eat fire. But Stith's religion was systems analysis; it had less to do with penitence than with PERT, less to do with forgiveness than with Zero Defects, less to do with faith than with Fail-Safe.

"Five minutes of straight talk, Taylor."

"Please, sit down." With his tweed jacket (useful in these frigid air-conditioned interiors) and button-down broadcloth shirt and wool tie, Stith strove to project a classic image. It was a look even more typical of southern fraternities than of the Ivy League—Stith's engineering degrees were from Vanderbilt, his business degree from Purdue.

Travis sat in the hard chair that faced the desk, ignoring the goose bumps that formed on his bare arms below the short sleeves of his plaid sport shirt. Travis was a southern boy too, but the Texas hill country is a different South than central Tennessee. Despite a fondness for tooled leather and flashy belt buckles—and in Travis's particular case, a gold I.D. bracelet on his right wrist, with his first name spelled out in five-point diamonds—the descendants of the Irish and Scottish and German settlers of that dry country tend to grow up stringy and raw, preferring simple issues, holding firm opinions, and keeping their religion firmly and simply in its place. Gilt and incense and crepe paper were for Hispanics, and none of this Deep South ecstasy and paranoia.

Travis was not so stringy as some of his cousins, but there was no fat on his two-meter frame. Much of the twenty-eight years since he'd learned to crawl had been lived in the sun, and the creases around his eyes and beside his mouth would have made him look older if they hadn't fixed in place an appearance of optimism, a cheery mask. His mahogany tan set off green eyes and auburn hair cut close to the scalp in the manner of cowpokes and fighter pilots, of each of which Texas had bred more than its share, but although Travis owned a horse and got on the horse from time to time, he was by inheritance and training a petroleum geologist. The degrees were from the University of Texas and Princeton; the calluses and the sunburn came not from chasing cows but from roughnecking in the Permian Basin. His family owned not a single well, but his father's patented methods for extracting the last reluctant drops of crude from depleted oil fields were worth more than mineral rights.

"Ball's in your court, Trav," said Stith. He was still standing, fussing with the magazines on his credenza.

"My last three research proposals have been stalled, and two of them canceled at the last minute. All but one of the missions I've been scheduled for since my jump have been reshuffled, and somehow I always get assigned off. You got the guts to tell me the truth?"

Stith paused. His lips were set in that pleasant curve which to the unwary suggested good humor. He gazed steadily at Travis out of the window's glare, meaning to convey that he had the guts to say whatever he wanted, and that he had no intention of letting Travis Hill stampede him into statements damaging to the agency.

Recently promoted to assistant administrator for Manned Spaceflight Operations, Johnson Space Center, a title that rated a secretary and a largish space on a middle floor of JCS's Project Management Building, Stith was shrewd enough to keep his decor strictly GI, enlivening the bare walls only with a couple of color photos of launch vehicles, and on the credenza some snaps of the wife and kids and a silver-framed eight-by-ten holo, boldly autographed, of himself shaking hands with Ted Purvis. He now adjusted it minutely—it had been taken three years earlier when Purvis, the president-elect, was a space-enthusiastic Florida senator. Then, at last, Stith sat down.

The message wasn't particularly subtle, but it was clear. Stith was on the first string. Travis, on the other hand, wasn't even a team player. Stith had clout—the soon-to-be-president had pressed his flesh—while as Stith well knew, the strongest card in Travis's hand, now that his notoriety was beginning to fade, was a booze-loving uncle who had been too long in the Texas state senate.

"Travis, we can go into fine detail if you want. The record will show there's nothing personal, not a thing."

"That's what the record will show?"

Stith nodded pleasantly. "As we see it, the way the program has been shaping up over the last couple of years, it looks as if your expertise will be of great value to the folks down here on the training end. Meanwhile we'll continue to welcome your scientific input, of course."

Travis surprised him by showing a row of white teeth in what looked like a genuine grin. "Okay, I guess that's plain enough. Want to hear my offer?"

Stith cocked his head a couple of millimeters. "Your?. . . "

"I sure as hell hate to deprive the training office of my expertise," Travis went on amiably, "considering all the expense the agency has gone to on my behalf and so on—but fact is, I'm thinkin' my work might benefit from a shift to the private sector."

"If that's really the way you see things . . ." Stith's eyes widened with ill-disguised glee.

"Especially if the project I have in mind gets the kind of government support I'm sure you're gonna agree it deserves," added Travis.

Stith's eyes narrowed again. Was he being hustled? He fingered a pressure switch on his lapel comm. "Julie, Dr. Hill and I don't want to be disturbed."

Her voice came through a desk speaker. "Okay, Chief. You're isolated."

"So what's this bullshit about 'support'?" Stith demanded. "What are you trying to pull?"

"I wish you guys weren't all a bunch of chickenshits, Taylor, but you are and there's nothing I can do about it. Okay, I'm getting out, that's what you want. I'm setting up a private center for asteroid study. And I'm going to launch it with NASA's blessing."

Stith sneered. "Christ, another one. Another one of these

little independent hobby club tax write-offs kibitzing Congress to tell us our business."

"A research center. Doing science. Exogeology is the four-bit word, what you hired me for in the first place."

"You can go or you can stay, Dr. Hill, but there will be no agency support for your private schemes." Stith put his palms flat on his green blotter. "I'd say it's been about five minutes."

Travis didn't move. He could look more relaxed than most men, even in a hard steel chair, and his eyes were no stranger to glare, which rather defeated the purpose of Stith's office arrangements. "What I want from NASA is a research contract. I want infrared satellite time—"

"Satellite time!" Aside from launch vehicles, there was no more precious commodity in NASA's coffers than access to its oversubscribed scientific satellites; universities and other agencies were wait-listed years in advance.

"Not a long-term commitment," said Travis. "Just a few minutes a month, for a year or two. And I'll give you an impeccable target list. You won't have to apologize to anybody."

"Impossible."

"It's okay to wait until next fiscal year." Travis was calm, almost comforting. "It will take me that long to get my ducks in a row."

Sullen now, realizing his yelps had served only to encourage Travis, Stith said hoarsely, "Say what you've got to say."

"Well, then. I'll be calling on my new acquaintances in the media, tradin' on whatever meager fame I've got left to get my little center launched." Travis talked as if outlining his plans to an interested investor. "Now there *is* somethin' to be said for the adversary slant"—he nodded, as if the idea had been Stith's—"those reporters and writers really go for a shoutin' match. One side says, 'What are we supposed to do? The guy wouldn't cooperate.' . . . The other side says the first side is, oh, cowardly and incompetent, stuff like that . . . you know how it goes. But personally, I don't think that's smart. What's a little extra publicity weighed against a year's satellite time?"

"Nobody could do that, put you at the head of a list that's three years long already." Stith tried to sound stern, but his objection was a confession of weakness.

Travis, who had not missed the shift from whether to how, abruptly stood. "Hey, looks like I've taken *more* than five minutes. Don't worry about giving me a quick answer. A hard copy of my resignation's in your in-box, but I don't expect anything to be official before the first of the month."

"Travis, for Christ's sake. . . !" Stith swallowed the rest.

Travis's gaze shifted to the holo of Stith and the president-elect grinning past each other, clutching paws. "You got a great reputation for getting things done, Taylor." He sauntered to the door and paused, his crinkled grin stopping just short of a wink. "Don't even bother to tell me if the answer's no."

The atrium bar of Houston's Bolivar Hotel was a meander of potted ficus trees and etched glass panels, crowded with loud conventioneers and singles from downtown office buildings getting an early start on the weekend. But Travis spotted Bonnie within seconds; his radar homed on her frequency.

And hers on his. She was leaning forward, waving eagerly, about to stand when she caught his eye. He moved through the crowd of three-piece English worsteds and fancy-stitched twill ranch jackets, through stifling clouds of perfume—Thai Stick de Montrachet, Sweet Death, and others with similarly inviting monikers—without registering anything except Bonnie's blue eyes, the shaggy blond wings of her cowgirl-style hair, the clinging champagne silk of her tailored blouse.

He got to the table and said, "God, you look so good," just as she was saying, "You're sure lookin' good, Travis," which made both of them laugh. He slid onto the cushioned bench and sat at right angles to her, not quite touching her nyloned knee with his corded one. They gazed at each other a moment, on the verge of laughing again, saying plainly enough in mime what they wouldn't say out loud. Then Bonnie's smile pulled at the corner of her wide mouth and faded away, as she sat back against the bench.

He leaned away too, in time to catch the eye of a harassed, scurrying waitress. "Jack Daniel's, if you'd be so kind. Straight up, water back." Bonnie raised a blond eyebrow. Travis caught the look. "I'm on vacation," he said. "Your husband joining us here?"

"He said he'd catch up at the restaurant. He cornered the mayor of Iraan"—she pronounced it *Ira Ann*, the way the natives did—"up in our hospitality suite."

Travis chuckled. "I know that fella. He's the biggest leaser in the basin. I guess he'll be signin' for a couple of laser pulse drills before he wriggles himself out of Sam's clutches."

"Well, someday we'll make money on those things, Trav."

"Hope so. I hate it when Sam tells me 'I told you so.'"

Travis's drink arrived and he held out a card toward the waitress's tray, but she refused it. "The lady said put it on hers, sir."

He shrugged and withdrew his card. "I guess business *is* good," he said to Bonnie.

"As you'd know if you would read our quarterly reports. Anyhow, it's the same pockets."

"Here's to the family pockets." He clinked his glass against her tulip of champagne and smiled at her. "First time I met you, you were sneezin' your head off on that stuff."

"At that party for the neighbors your daddy threw . . ."

"Which Ma *made* him throw . . ."

"The first time I ever tasted champagne. Sixteen years old."

"The first time I met the girl next door. A real *girl*, my

Lord. The first night I ever laid awake the whole night, hot as a pistol, just thinkin' about—"

"You've recited your lewd adolescent fantasies before." Bonnie laid a cool hand on his, her fingertips brushing his diamond-studded name bracelet. "Maybe once or twice too often."

"That's what comes of puttin' young boys in military schools, they grow up sex maniacs."

Her laugh came from the back of her throat. "They do anyway." She moved her hand away, back to her champagne. "Besides, you always had more important things on your mind. Stars and meteors and stuff."

He sipped his whiskey. "Wish to hell my daddy'd sent Sam off to polish brass for a few years, instead of me." His face darkened. "I respect him for what he can do with the business. But I never did like him always gettin' in first—just because he was born first."

"I've heard this before, too," she said warily.

"He took advantage of my absence."

"Well, you never tried to take advantage of your presence. Until much too late."

"Divorce my brother and marry me." He smiled at her, a wide smile that was meant to be inviting but showed more hunger than he intended.

Her voice was steady. "Travis, you know how I feel about you. But I love Sam and I love my little girl."

"Just kidding."

"Then I guess the subject is ended." Her nylon thighs whispered as she hitched herself sideways on the bench, away from him. "What kind of vacation you on?" Her tanned fair skin was pinker now.

Travis pretended not to hear the question. "Are we expectin' Jim and Manuela at the restaurant?"

"They're invited." She didn't have to say the rest, that Jim, his younger brother, newly out of the medical school at Rice with ambitions to be a heart surgeon, inevitably found pressing business whenever other members of his family were in town.

Travis took another sip of his drink before looking Bonnie in the eye. "Matter of fact I'm not on vacation. I put in my resignation."

"Travis . . ." Her concern was simple and unguarded, but this time her soothing hand kept its place on the oak table top.

"Nothing abrupt. I've been talking with the university folks in Austin for a few months. They're glad to put me on as an associate professor in planetary studies, tenure track, good prospects. And I've raised, uh, private money for a new research center. I believe I'll get NASA's cooperation to get myself started"—he showed his teeth again, within that rictus that passed for a smile—"since I explained it to them so carefully."

"That sounds . . . good," she said, making it sincere. "Something new. A challenge."

"I've been away from real science too long. Fact is, NASA never can put science up front. Not really their fault, it's a structural problem. No big organization can plan for the unexpected."

She looked at him, not understanding from his oblique and choppy remarks precisely what he was talking about, but understanding what he meant. "I just want you to know I . . . support you, Travis."

He drained the bourbon and stared at her. "You'd best support me out of this here saloon, sister-in-law. Before I have another couple of these and make up my mind to try something biblical."

"Biblical?"

"Cain and Abel. David and Bathsheba. Something like that."

She laughed again, that throaty chuckle, genuine and happy. "I doubt you've spent a Sunday in church for quite some time."

*   *   *

On the first day of the following month, August, Travis's sporty white Mistral whirred over a ragged blacktop ranch road that looped through limestone hills north of Bandera, leaving shimmering air in the wake of its turbine.

Travis always liked the homeward drive. To his mind, Houston, with its mosquitoes and skinny pine trees, was barely Texas. In the hill country west of San Antonio the bony yellow Cretaceous seabed is patchy with tough grasses that burst into colorful flower for a month or so in the spring, then wither to brown beneath the mesquite and prickly pear. Twisted live oaks dot the hillsides, and shaggy junipers, known locally as cedars, ooze perfumed resin in the dry heat of summer. In this crusty land the diamondbacks are ancient and sly, the deer quick and delicate, and the buzzards, often found squatting in convocation beside the road, seem almost the size of small aircraft, their dusty black color scheme not intended for stealth but as a morbid reminder, perhaps, of the end of all flesh.

Where the road came down beside the river a grove of stately pecans announced the beginning of Hill Ranch property, the spread his mother had inherited and that his father had insisted on buying from her—independent cuss that he was—with the money actually going into trusts for their sons.

Travis turned off the road where two whitewashed cedar posts supported a wooden crossbar with the name "Hill" scripted in strap iron. His low-slung Mistral bounced over a rusty cattle guard and nosed into a water-sculpted limestone stream bed, dry at this season, but flanked with two-meter-tall black-and-white flash flood markers. The drive to the ranch house wound up and along an aisle of huge cedars draped with Spanish moss.

The new house was long and low, faced with yellow-white fieldstone and roofed with Mexican tile. It sat in a carpet of Bermuda grass bigger than JSC's central campus, three acres of it sloping gently toward the banks of the green Medina River. Beyond the clipped lawn, edged with whitewashed rocks, the ground was bare and stony; a few placid Herefords roamed the oak thicket between the new house and the old one, which had accumulated around the Kreuger's original dog-trot cabin of 1855.

From the vicinity of the half-hidden barns and stables of the working part of the ranch, voices speaking Spanish fitfully disturbed the still, hot air; they belonged to the Martinez family, hereditary residents since before Travis's mother was born, and the only real ranchers left on the place.

Travis left his car between a white Cadillac hydro and a Chevy ATV in the carport, and toted his single canvas bag toward the kitchen door.

"Ma?" The house was cool; an air conditioner hummed somewhere in the shadows. He went through the sunny deserted kitchen and dining room, past shadowed halls, down polished cedar steps to a big room spread with Navajo and Zapotec rugs, furnished in hide-upholstered knotty pine. He dropped his bag beside the steps.

One wall of the room was slatted glass overlooking the back patio and lawn, an overbright backdrop in the afternoon light. His mother was walking across the patio flags, holding garden shears in her right hand, an opulent scarlet rose in her left. Edna May Hill, née Kreuger, was a thin woman of erect carriage who looked taller than her 163 centimeters; knotted silver hair rode like Athena's helmet on her patrician head.

She nodded as she entered through the screen door he held open for her—

"Good to see you, Ma."

"And you, Travis."

—but she did not smile or offer her cheek to be kissed until she had settled the cut rose in the vase of black glass she had prepared for it.

"I trust you had a pleasant trip."

"Sure I did."

"Sit down, then. Ice tea?"

"Thanks." Travis settled into the depths of a calf-hide armchair. Sometimes his mother's moods could only be waited out, and he had learned to let her serve him when she was determined to do so.

Edna May moved to the pine sideboard, where a sweating pitcher of ice tea and two glasses waited, placed there at her order by Maria, the cook. "Lemon, no sugar," she stated, not asking.

"Did I tell you I saw Sam and Bonnie in Houston? There for the drilling and mining convention."

"No, you didn't tell me. Sam did, however." Along with the tea glass, she handed Travis an envelope. "This came by fax. Naturally I read it."

The letter was addressed to Travis Hill, Ph.D., President, Asteroid Resource Center, in care of the Hill Ranch's open code. The originating code block identified NASA headquarters in Washington. It was a request for proposal, tersely inviting the new research corporation to bid on a whole-sky search for undiscovered small bodies of specific orbital characteristics and spectral signatures. The wording of the RFP was familiar; Travis had drafted it himself. Among those few companies invited to bid, only one, his own, would fill the bill.

"That didn't take long," he said, pleased, folding the letter.

"You pulled a fast one, boy. That what you think?" His mother perched on the edge of the couch facing him.

"I got what I wanted."

"In return for a promise to shut your mouth?"

"To shut my mouth?" He smiled, but her glittering eye told him he couldn't bluff the woman who had taught him more than his father had about driving a bargain. "Put it this way—I'll get data they wouldn't let me have when I was inside."

"They'll cut you off when it's too late for you to say anything against them."

"I figured on that. I'll get enough data from these observations to keep a team busy for five years."

She was silent a moment, and he had the uneasy feeling she was listening to that part of his thoughts he himself didn't want to hear. "You shouldn't have quit, Travis," she said quietly. "That's not our way—and it was a blunder. A tactical blunder."

He blushed, his dark face suffusing with blood. "Dammit, Ma—"

"Respect," she said.

"Beg pardon, but listen to me one minute." With effort he kept his voice even. "They canceled my missions. They deliberately tore up my proposals. They were going to assign me to training!"

"So you did what they wanted. You quit."

"I made them give *me* what *I* wanted."

Her eyebrows shot up. "Oh? When do you go back into space?" she asked, as if genuinely interested.

His blush deepened. "There's no way I'm going back into space, Ma. Ever. I got what I could, more than they thought they'd have to give me."

"Maybe they are the damn fools you say they are. I say, you cut a poor deal. You could have stayed inside, made trouble, leaked nasty rumors all over the place, used the good offices of Uncle Albert—"

"Al? That lush!"

"—and waited for the wind to shift, while you still had wings. But you're a civilian now, boy. You're a washout." Her steady look was not without pity, but there was no sympathy in it; her spare bones, clothed in regal blue rayon, were unbending in the hot light. She sat on a throne of calfskin and stared her son down.

Travis, twenty-eight tough years old, capable of being reckless with his life, felt tears burn inside his eyelids. He looked away and swallowed hard against the hot lump in his throat.

"Travis, son," his mother said gently, "I don't want you, or any of my sons, ever to make the mistake their daddy made. Smart, and bold when luck was running his way—"

"Ma, don't."

"—a quitter when things went bad on him." She paused, letting it sink in, the primitive lesson she had forced them all to learn more than once, each time she had judged the matter under discussion to be a matter of survival—not of the individual but of the family and its code. For the Hills had their own version of the system. Its bluntest object lesson was the shotgun Travis's father had used to blow out the back of his skull at a time when oil prices had been down for three years and looked like they were never coming back. They did come back. Therein resided the lesson.

The shotgun itself resided in a rack on the wall behind Travis's head, still pressed into use occasionally whenever the deer became too fond of the roses.

One day, Travis thought—and perhaps that day was near—his mother would realize she could no longer count on her sons accepting her version of the tragedy without their voicing some blunt questions; there had been more to his father's death than economic despair, and they all knew it.

"You don't like what I did. You would have done it differently." He took a long sip of tea; it cooled his panic. "What's your advice?"

"I want what you want, Travis." She pretended not to hear the undercurrent of sarcasm in his question, wasted no energy reprimanding it, for she too recognized the approaching watershed, the last battle between the generations that she could not win. "Starting from now, we're going to make this little company of yours count for something. It may take

ten years. Or twenty. But *by God,* we're going to put you
back into space."

Half a year after Travis Hill walked out of Taylor Stith's
office for what the NASA bureaucrat sincerely hoped was
the last time, a new president ushered in a new administration. Another half a year passed after the inauguration, and
one morning Taylor woke before dawn to confront the grim
reality of a career choice.

The air conditioner in Taylor's bedroom labored hoarsely
but was unequal to the strain of the muggy summer
darkness; Taylor knew he would not sleep again before sun-
rise. He got up in the half-light and went barefoot to his den,
leaving his wife sleeping heavily in their king-size bed, her
lower legs bound in sweaty sheets like a half-wrapped
shroud.

The Stiths' brick ranch house nestled in the piney suburbs
bordering Clear Lake, near the Johnson Space Center, and
through the Oldey Englishey diamond-paned windows of his
darkened den he could see ground fog creeping among the
pines, eerily lit by scattered streetlamps—like dry ice vapor
in a cheap horror movie. He turned on his brass desk lamp
with its green glass shade. The walls of his den were solid
with shelving, dense with collector's items: fine large-scale
working model steam engines made of brass, and fully rigged
sailing ships, and old cars, and gold coins framed under glass
on black velvet, and albums of stamps boxed in acid-free
hardboard portfolios, and picture books—books about crystal, about china, about antique furniture, about guns, about
arms and armor, about jade and netsuke and Cycladic figu-
rines and Uncle Scrooge comic books—about almost every
class of object worth collecting. Taylor's enchantment with
things, severely censored from his public persona, flourished
here.

On his antique green blotter lay a lavishly printed color
folder displaying a holo of President Purvis's newly ap-

pointed NASA administrator—a hard-copy reprint of an interview which had appeared two weeks earlier in *Newstime,* the national weekly newsfax. Office couriers had delivered signed copies of the reprint to everyone in the agency above the rank of G-20; Taylor's was inscribed in a scrawl that was meant to be bold, perhaps, but which looked more nearly incontinent: "Tayler [sic]—glad to have you on Our Team, yours Truly, Rosie."

Taylor was irked by the misspelling of his name, but that's not what had cost him his sleep. It was what "Rosie" had to say about the agency's future, particularly the section helpfully headlined "The Importance of Revolutionary Technologies." Taylor drew his blue terry-cloth robe closer and settled into his mahogany captain's chair, pondering the words.

"While I intend, in general, to pursue the policies honed by my predecessors," the new administrator was quoted as saying, "I won't rule out changes in what football coaches call 'tendencies'—my tendencies might be to decide in favor of exploiting the more revolutionary, rather than evolutionary, approaches to space-vehicle development. I mean, exploiting the advantages of advanced technology by taking a great leap forward."

If there is anything bureaucrats hate it is great leaps forward, for when the leaps fall short of greatness, middle-management heads roll.

Rosie's speech was in bureaucratic code, of course, and Taylor, shivering in the heat, knew exactly what the administrator was talking about. Recently several aerospace firms had submitted conceptual designs for a new kind of spacecraft. Taylor Stith had had nothing to do with the craft's inception or technical development, thank God; still, he knew that NASA's continuing credibility and prominence within the government depended upon developing some kind of solar-system workhorse. In the past decade a half-dozen return visits to the moon, plus a single manned expedition to Mars (in awkward cooperation with the Russians), had all been patched together from miscellaneous bits of hardware, some old, some special-purpose. Congress was showing impatience with NASA's incessant requests for *ad hoc* missions; the alternative was to go to the Hill with one big request—a ship that could fly again and again, to the planets and beyond.

Similar promises had been used in the selling of the first space shuttle a third of a century earlier. One lesson of that flawed program had sunk in: there would be no fleet of ships until an experimental version had rigorously tested and proved the underlying principles. Spaceships were much too expensive for fly-offs between competing designs, as the Air Force and Navy were sometimes privileged to do with their experimental aircraft, so a few people in NASA were going to have to stick their necks out and make a choice—well, since the thing would only be a flying test stand, it was a limited choice—still, a choice on which careers would rise and fall. Given his role in mission planning, Taylor was one of them. He was in a key position to emphasize a new craft's weaknesses or tout its strengths, but whatever he decided, he could not afford to appear wishy-washy.

A dispassionate second-order analysis of institutional politics, suppressing the merits of specific issues, shows that nay sayers are always right: nothing ever works the way it is supposed to. Thus bureaucracies fill with people who are rewarded for doing nothing new, while enthusiasts often get themselves fired. Still, as Taylor understood, the best chance for rapid promotion in any organization is to be *almost* right about something new that looks like it *is* going to work.

Staring at the holo of his polyester-suited boss, Taylor sweated out a decision in the humid dawn. Lockheed-Rockwell-Martin's design, still on the CADD screens, had emerged as a leading contender. Friendly Rosie hadn't actually fingered LRMCo, but scuttlebutt was, he was leaning in their favor.

Reluctantly, Taylor decided he'd do better to gamble his career than to let it stagnate.

THE
SHIP

Five men and women in the blue uniforms of working astronauts were gathered in the ready room of Archimedes Station. Assisted by white-coveralled launch technicians, they donned portable oxygen packs, then moved quietly, in weightless single file, down a long pressurized tube that extended to the spacecraft secured in the launch bay.

Their silent concentration was broken by the thud of an unseen hatch. A technician punched worn steel buttons; air pumps engaged with a whine. Lights flickered from red to yellow to green as air pressure equalized between the station and the ship. The boarding tube's internal hatch swung in and out of the way with a sigh, opening upon an air lock padded in white canvas, big enough to hold two people. The launch technician entered first and popped the ship's inner hatch up and away. He turned back to those waiting. "All set."

"Let's go." The commander's cheeks were rosy, her eyes bright; an astronaut pilot's wings were sewn above her embroidered name patch, which read "Braide." She ran a small, strong hand through strawberry hair cut so short it was almost a brush.

The young man beside her also wore astronaut's wings, although he had an uncharacteristically long body for a pilot; his name patch read "Calder." The commander waved him ahead, and he moved his length with weightless grace through the air lock and into the ship.

A young woman followed close behind him, her tight cap of flyaway curls stirring in the breeze of her passage. "Wooster" read her name tag. At her hip, strapped low like a gunslinger's iron, she carried a submicro video camera.

A fiftyish man with a gray crew cut pushed off past the launch technician, steering from surface to padded surface with practiced applications of pressure, fingertips here, toes there, producing the minimal, minute delta-vees he needed to steer himself against his body's inertia; the name on his uniform was "Deveraux."

The last man was tagged "Giles"; he was tanned, fit, forty, and he turned to wink at the commander—his broad, handsome face folding into ruddly wrinkles—before he dove into the hatch.

Commander Braide followed quickly. Once through the inner hatch she was in a narrow corridor threading the axis of the crew module. Steel staples formed a ladder along one side of the cylindrical corridor; this corridor would be a vertical shaft when the ship was accelerating, opening at its top onto the flight deck, ending below in a second air lock. Below that air lock other, more twisted pathways led to the service module, the fuel tanks, and the propulsion system.

Vertical was a word without meaning just now, but on occasion knowing up from down would become important, so where the walls of the corridor provided enough flat surface, stenciled yellow arrows pointed to the ship's stern. The commander traveled mentally upward, against the arrows' bold thrust, past walls bristling with multiple extrusions of pipes and pumps, fans and filters, worklights and video cameras, air sniffers and fire-suppression nozzles; past sleeping quarters, tiny private closets hung with sleep-restraint bags; past the prissily designated "personal hygiene facility"; through the padded white wardroom with its green plants and galley and wide-screen monitors; past cramped and crowded laboratories and workstations where the other members of the crew were settling in; arriving finally at the flight deck.

Commander Braide slipped into the left-hand couch and pulled her harness over her. To her right the pilot was already strapped in, studying his checkpad.

Two launch technicians in white coveralls arrived—babysitters come to see that everyone was tucked in, that emergency oxygen masks dangled beside each rosy face, that the strap-on escape system was wired for arming, ready to blow the crew and service modules away from the fuel tanks in case of catastrophic accident. Such accidents were less likely to occur in orbit than on Earth, where shuttles astride balloons of explosive were launched in an oxidizing atmosphere, and even less likely to occur in this ship, where coaxing the main engine to start was more problematic than shutting it down. Nevertheless, this was a test flight. Anything that could go wrong . . . could go wrong.

Moments later the main hatch thudded shut as the launch technicians left the ship. There remained many hours of final check and countdown, during which Commander Braide would be busy only occasionally. Unbidden there came the recognition that this was one of those fleeting moments—no matter what unimagined disasters might lurk in the future a second from now, an hour from now, a year from now—when she was perfectly happy. She settled deeper into her couch, inhaling fresh artificial air.

To the commander there was something subtly, inexpressibly arousing about the smell of good machinery, especially new machinery. A brand new spacecraft was far sexier than a new car; there was that citrus aroma of machined brass and welded steel, undulled by oxidation; the spice of machine oil, not yet rancid from heat; the fresh candy odor of vinyl seats as yet unstaled by sweat and intestinal gases; even the clean taste of the oxygen mask's plastic cup, unsoured with spit. The ultimate in sensual pleasure was to hurtle through vacuum at astonishing speed, safely enclosed in a warm, dark, new machine.

The flight deck console in front of her boasted huge "windows" looking fore and aft and to the sides, which were actually high-resolution pixel arrays. Mounted below them was a bank of similar screens, smaller and more numerous, and dials and meters and additional graphic displays. One row of video screens, separate from the others, monitored the ship's interior spaces; on them the commander could look into the televised faces of her crew. Spin Calder. Melinda Wooster. Jimmy Giles. Linwood Deveraux.

"Good morning, everybody. Let's count off." Her voice carried on the comm channels to every corner of the ship.

"Pilot prepared to commence launch preparatory procedure," said Spin Calder, spitting out the exact words of the script written on his checkpad screen.

"I'm ready too," said Melinda Wooster.

"Propulsion control ready," said Linwood Deveraux.

"Ready for prelaunch, Robin," said Jimmy Giles.

"Archimedes launch control, we are go for prelaunch," said Commander Braide.

"Copy, Robin. The count is T minus four hours and counting."

Spin, the pilot (Leroy to his mother, and to no one else), was deep in contemplation of the files in his checkpad. This was a good time to study them, no time more appropriate, but it was what he did with every spare moment anyway: he was refreshing his memory of the precise sequence and wording of the hundreds of steps involved in the launch, not because he was profoundly convinced he needed to memorize the stuff, but because he was afraid NASA would dock him for some nit-picking omission if he didn't. Today's ships mostly flew themselves, but there was always, *always,* that moment when something stalled, broke, got hung up, went haywire. It was at that moment that you had to do the right thing without stopping to think about it; no time then to consult a checkpad, and you couldn't count on the robots. So Spin had already memorized the ship itself in a way that he could not have verbalized.

He was a pilot with a tendency and a preference for flying by the seat of his pants, the sort of thing that flight instructors (and submarine-driver instructors) try hard to train out of their students; the human proprioceptive system is fine-tuned for trees and savanna, not for air, sea, or space, and modern aircraft and undersea craft and spacecraft move too fast, in environments too strange, to function dependably as extensions of the body. But Spin's was more than an intelligence of the muscles and nerves. When he sat in front of a board of screens and switches, took hold of a stick and set his feet on pedals, he and the machine became coextensive in a way that could be described only to those who had no need of the description; the uninitiated were likely to mutter about Zen and the art of spaceship piloting, or about Spin's legendary native American shamanistic origins, or other such nonsense. It was not just the mass, the power, the flex, the speed—which he loved—but the *logic,* the irresistible Q.E.D. of movement through the space-time manifold. To perform a complex maneuver in three dimensions of space and one of time, to pull gees, to thread the eye of a probability needle, this was, for Spin, the triumphant demonstration of the concreteness and rightness of things, the essential reality of the real.

His commander watched Spin's utter concentration on his checklists and momentarily wondered if his mind was really absorbing and filing those dry, abbreviated entries ("(178) BLR N2 SPLY ON, (179) BLR CNTRL PWR/HTR, POS A," etc.) or whether he was daydreaming about something else—about professional advancement, about his intricate and apparently passionless love life, about the last time he had surfed the Banzai Pipeline. She decided it did not matter. When the ship moved, he would be there to fly it with her. Spin was a man whose existence seemed to reside in motion. . . .

Beside the tiny screen with Spin's face on it was the screen showing NAVCOM, the navigation and communication station, immediately below the flight deck. Frizzy-haired, freckled Melinda Wooster, even in repose and with plenty of work to do, managed to look actively bored.

It was not mere physical motion that she needed to excite her, but a challenge of any sort—if necessary, the merely physical would do. In moderate surf, for example, she could outsurf any man, including Spin; like him, she had a high regard for reality, although unlike him, she would not go near the water some days, would not pit her 158 centimeters and forty-four kilograms against storm surges many meters high and many tonnes in crushing power. For analogous reasons her love life was nowhere near as complicated as Spin's. Her affairs tended to be brief contests; having won them, she found herself alone by choice.

With physical needs out of the way, what she liked best was chess, or go, or even Scrabble, despite the latter's propensity to induce schizoid frustration whenever clever wordplay had to be foregone in favor of tactical board position. What Melinda liked best were games that allowed a display of sheer superiority, whether of vocabulary, skill, memory, calculating power, or strategy and tactics. She liked to get the answer before anyone else. She liked to win. Predictably, unless something went wrong on this short test flight, with its routine navigation and communications chores, there would be no new problems to solve, nothing to lick, and Melinda would be bored.

Her commander hoped she stayed bored.

From his mission specialist's post deep in the ship Jimmy Giles looked up at the communications monitor and caught the commander looking back at him. He smiled and held her glance a moment before returning to his own checkpad. Jimmy was the most affable of the crew, but Braide knew very well it was a thin overlay on a seething soul, an attitude more hopeful than real. Jimmy was a man who needed a cause; it had to do with growing up Catholic, perhaps, with attending the Air Force Academy and becoming a career officer, with marrying young and siring a brood of girls, with long unquestioned striving after goals that other, more cynical men and women had erected for him.

Jimmy had nothing much to do on this particular flight except to test a range of secondary systems: cargo bay doors, teleoperators, instrument mounts, and the like. His real responsibilities would come later, when the full-sized descendants of this test ship began operational missions. His rating was mission specialist in satellite guidance and telemetry, but his real specialty was C^3-I—command, control, communications, and intelligence. He hadn't set out to do this; when he'd applied to the Air Force's astronaut program, he'd been a fighter pilot who wanted to fly aerospace planes. The Air Force had needs beyond a few good pilots, however; the Russians were moving into interplanetary space at an alarming rate, had already established a long-term manned base on the moon, and were talking of doing the same on Mars. The Air Force had made Jimmy an astronaut, but not a pilot, for he'd unknowingly revealed an aptitude for dealing with robots and computers. So they made him an expert in electronic surveillance, cryptography, countermeasures, which increasingly meant, as it had ever since Turing conceived the general-purpose computer, the analysis of computer software.

He was disappointed at the assignment, but he believed in his country; he did his job as cheerfully as he could, and he proved somebody right by doing it exceedingly well. Like all men of faith, he had doubts, he had lapses, and he carried with him a mass of guilt. No one knew that better than his present commander.

On the little screen which peered into PROP, propulsion control, the workstation immediately opposite NAVCOM on the deck below, Commander Braide saw Linwood Deveraux tweaking the instruments on a console almost as complex as her own. If Braide was responsible for the ship's brain, Spin its nerves, Melinda its eyes and mouth, and Jimmy its fingertips, Linwood was responsible for its guts.

She did not know what was going on in Linwood's mind right now, but she would have laid even money that he was fussing over instrument readings that were less than optimal. Linwood seemed determined to take everything at face value, although he'd seen plenty of surprises in the course of his checkered career and produced more than a few surprises of his own. Linwood had been in the astronaut corps for almost twenty years now, had not gotten into space until he was forty; his longest tour was two months aboard Archimedes, although he had made several shorter excursions. As a member of a flight crew he was versatile and dependable, and as a scientist he had produced an impressive bibliography of papers on solar physics, but he was only one among some 200 astronauts, pilots, and assorted mission specialists, and he thought that to NASA he was nothing special; Linwood thought there were a dozen men and women who could have done his job as well as he. His commander thought differently.

She had heard the story, unacknowledged by the world at large but true, heard it from him and from half a dozen others who confirmed its key passages: Linwood, though he held no patents, had substantially created the engine that was about to take him and the rest of them for a wild ride. . . .

The world doesn't plunge into the future as fast as the shock merchants would have us believe, but within any couple of decades there are liable to arise one or two differences that really make a difference—steam engines, women's suffrage, quantum theory, that sort of thing. In the first decade of the twenty-first century, engineers were consolidating a technology that physicists had been promising for over half a century but had only recently delivered: controlled nuclear fusion. No individual, not even a single generation of researchers, stood out in the braided history of that struggle. Some years after the turn of the century a thirty-five-year-old nuclear physicist named Linwood Deveraux stumbled upon an amusing technical wrinkle in the design of fusion reactors one quiet evening in the den of his Livermore, California, home.

Since the 1960s one of the leading schemes for controlling fusion, known as inertial confinement, had involved the implosion of tiny spheres of frozen hydrogen, spheres so small that hundreds could fit on the head of a pin—and every sphere a miniature H-bomb. The nation's weapons laboratories, Los Alamos in New Mexico, Livermore in California, Sandia in both states, had a monopoly on the classified knowledge essential to inertial confinement projects; who else regularly set off nuclear bombs and measured their behavior? Who else could generate mathematical models of nuclear explosions on the world's fastest computers?

These diminutive superbombs were to be triggered by an array of powerful lasers or particle accelerators—ray guns, that is—arranged in a circle, pointing inward. Firing simultaneously, the beams would hit each frozen pellet as it fell into their midst. As the flash-heated surface expanded it would crush the sphere's interior until the hydrogen nuclei were fused into new elemental combinations—ideally releasing some three orders of magnitude more energy than that used to trigger the blast. Provided that it did not instantly melt the machine or blow it to pieces, this thousandfold increase in energy could be used to produce electrical power. Or to do other things. Fusion research had long been entangled with the military's yen for Buck Rogers–style death rays.

That was okay with Linwood Deveraux. As reticent and gentle and genuinely polite as his soft Louisiana accent and his long-nosed, sad face suggested he was, Linwood never-theless loved things that went zap and boom.

His job, as one member of a brainy team at Livermore that called itself Q Branch, was to build an inertial confine-ment chamber that would convert thermonuclear explosions into directed beams of energy—ray guns thousands of times more powerful than those used as the spark plugs to ignite their hydrogen-pellet fuel.

In his basement den at home Linwood had a slim com-puterized drawing pad equipped with a nice fat CADD ROM chip, but he didn't use it much. In Linwood's opinion, computer-aided design and drafting systems, for all their power, were lumbering dinosaurs compared to a pencil and a scrap of paper during those critical stages of creation when ideas came quick and loose, when the less extraneous circui-try there was between brain, hand, and eye, the better.

Some of the things Linwood drew by hand on his table of varnished birch—its surface nebulous with rubbery Dandy Rub Cleaning Powder—he had no business drawing there. At the lab they used much bigger CADD machines, and it was bothersome to let light fall on the screens. At the lab the lighting was soft and indirect. At the lab the windows were covered with steel plates, and all transmitting and receiving devices were forbidden. At the lab the air was always filled with Muzak to discourage electronic eavesdroppers; the lab's security consultants had correctly suggested that Muzak would drive spies crazy.

Linwood had his more useful ideas at home, in the morn-ing shower, or after dinner sipping a glass of the local Wente Riesling, or lying in bed watching a favorite chip from his large collection of old Creature Features while his wife, Jeri, snored lightly beside him. Sometimes, after the movie had disintegrated into electronic snow, he'd get up and go down-stairs to make sketches on his home drawing table. He'd smuggle them into work the next day, disguised as sandwich wrappings; there he could elaborate upon them even while listening to Muzak.

On this particular summer afternoon Linwood was sitting at his drawing table, his stiff eyebrows arched in quizzical alertness, his long, narrow beak quivering in anticipation of inspiration, while he savored unaccustomed quiet. Jeri and the girls had been gone for a week, driving east to a family reunion in Baton Rouge. He would join them by plane in a couple of days, assuming he survived that long on his bachelor's diet of Coke, canned chili, and Fritos.

Bars of orange light penetrated the converted half basement. On the sill of the room's only window, light collected under the chines of a small blue pot in which two lithops burrowed. Linwood put water in the pot perhaps once a month, and then only a spoonful. "Stone plants," desert plants from southern Africa, the lithops thrived on deprivation. Their visible parts were their mottled tops, each about as big around as a marble, deeply creased in the center, as smooth and bisymmetric as a baby's bum. Fleshy windows conducted sunlight down cellular light pipes to the plant's photosynthesizing organs, sheltered an inch beneath the insulating soil. A lithops was Linwood's kind of plant, efficient, private, and deep, content to live its life half under the ground.

At the precise hour when the late afternoon photons came screaming through the westward window, bouncing off the neighbor's asparagus fern in a blaze of light, tickling the shy lithops, punching him in the eye, Lindwood got his modest idea.

Several tricks were needed to design any fusion reactor, but they all required an intimate knowledge of the behavior of atoms and subatomic particles in the presence of strong electric and magnetic fields. That sort of knowledge, in turn, rested partly on a powerful intuition of geometry, and there is no useful theorem in geometry that cannot be at least

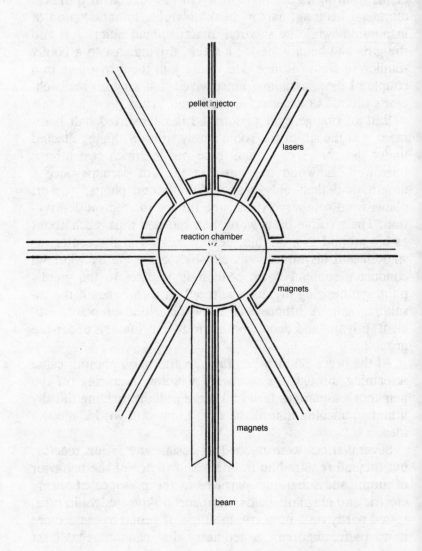

pellet injector

lasers

reaction chamber

magnets

magnets

beam

qualitatively suggested with a paper and pencil. He sketched the lab's current test machine, with its ring of lasers firing inward toward the tiny hydrogen pellet target, and the strong magnetic "nozzle" that contained and directed the resulting explosion.

What is the heart of a thermonuclear explosion? Provided it starts and ends clean—uncontaminated by heavy elements like plutonium or uranium, which are intrinsic to the brute force of real H-bombs—a thermonuclear explosion is a clear hot soup, a plasma of protons, electrons, ionized helium, free neutrons, un-ionized hydrogen atoms and leftover neutrinos and such. All the electrically charged particles will stay in the soup, if it is confined and shaped by electric and magnetic fields.

Most of the energy of the explosion, more than three quarters, is in the form of speeding neutrons. Neutrons aren't significantly affected by electric or magnetic fields, but they can be slowed in a materially dense "blanket"—liquid lithium or some such substance—their energy thus converted to heat.

What happens to the heat depends on what the reactor is designed to do. A power reactor uses it to make steam, and eventually electricity, but in ray guns most of the heat is a waste and a nuisance. Over the decades ray gun designers had played with various ways of using the energy of a thermonuclear explosion, for example, by letting it squeeze magnetic fields to produce huge electrostatic charges, or by opening one end of the magnetic bottle to let the products spew out, or by focusing some of the energy into x-ray beams, and so on—but no matter what the scheme, most of the thermonuclear reactor's energy was wasted as heat.

On his sketch pad, Linwood roughed in the liquid blanket and the circulating coolant systems required to dispose of the waste heat. There he paused.

To Linwood, with his passion for efficiency, wasting so

much heat had always seemed criminal. Surely something clever could be done with those copious neutrons!

In power reactors, neutrons were intrinsic to the fusion fuel cycle; they were captured to breed radioactive tritium, the rarer (because of its short half-life) of the two isotopes of hydrogen that composed the fusion fuel, the other being the more common deuterium. Tritium breeding was a secondary process, however, a civilian process. A ray gun orbiting in space would be supplied with all the tritium it was ever likely to need.

Linwood wondered about other neutron-capture scenarios. In the heart of the sun, neutron capture contributed to the formation of heavier elements . . . but to take advantage of stellar fusion processes was a dream of the far future, awaiting the day when truly monstrous magnetic fields could be generated, capable of rivaling gravity at the heart of a star.

Linwood thought about all this a long time and drew nothing. Applying the old creative principle that when the going gets tough the smart go somewhere else, he balled up his rough sketch and threw it away.

He stared morosely at the lithops, now faintly glowing in the setting sun's last light.

At the lab his discarded sketch would have been sucked into a high-temperature furnace and instantly reduced to fine ash, but at home Linwood had an open wastebasket beside his table, the contents of which he conscientiously burned . . . whenever he remembered to. The security disadvantages of this practice were offset by certain practicalities, one of which Linwood now demonstrated to himself—

—by changing his mind. He fished the crumpled wad of paper out of the basket and flattened it on his table. Now what if, instead . . .

The lithium-neutron reaction that yields tritium is quite efficient: a neutron entering a blanket of liquid lithium travels ten or twenty centimeters and scatters from a few lithium atoms, heating up the neighborhood before strongly interacting with one of them to create a helium nucleus and a tritium nucleus. A typical power reactor circulates the liquid metal lithium through heat exchangers, meanwhile tapping a small side flow from which the tritium is chemically extracted.

Instead of thinking of the lithium blanket as a coolant, optional for his purposes, Linwood tried thinking of it as an extra fuel tank. He imagined introducing lithium into an annular ring around the reaction chamber at a steady rate, letting it circulate long enough to be bombarded by sufficient neutrons to produce a good proportion of tritium. He imagined mixing this tritium-enriched fluid with a separate supply of deuterium. He imagined injecting the lithium-tritium-deuterium mix into a magnetically confined and compressed outflow of hot plasma from the primary reactor—in such a manner that it burst into a secondary fusion reaction, additionally heating an outgoing beam.

Hot stuff. Not all that efficient in the long run—only a small fraction of the injected fuel would fuse, even under ideal circumstances, and a great deal of waste heat would still have to be disposed of by radiators—but Linwood was satisfied that at least he had salvaged some neutrons.

It was dark outside when Linwood happily finished his sketching. Not that he made an improvement on the Q Branch beam projector; he knew that what he'd drawn had little or nothing to do with death rays. That was fine with him. He turned out the light and went upstairs, made himself a wiener sandwich, and lay down in bed, after popping a chip into the viddie—that classic British thriller from the 1950s, *X the Unknown,* starring Dean Jagger; it had a great monster, a puddle of smart, ravenous, radioactive mud.

The next day, when Linwood displayed a suitably gussied-up draft of his idea to his coworkers in Q Branch, the youngest of them, a kid on summer loan from MIT, had an attack of giggles. What Linwood had drawn had nothing to do with

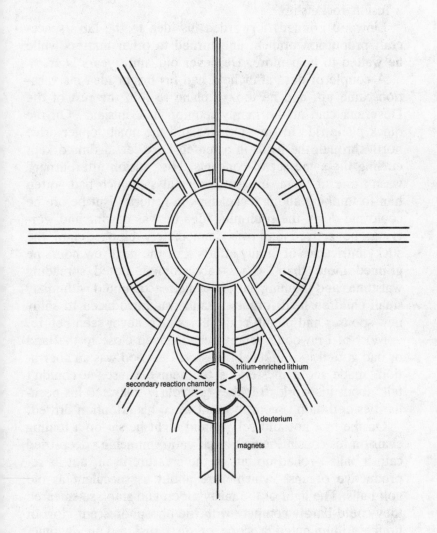

tritium-enriched lithium

secondary reaction chamber

deuterium

magnets

ray guns, said the pimpled kid—who spoke as an authority
on ray guns, having read in his short life a great deal of
space opera and very little else—and it wasn't even all that
original. What ol' Linwood had here was an afterburner for
a fusion rocketship.

Linwood grinned, forwarded his idea to the lab's spacecraft propulsion branch, and turned to other matters while
he waited to hear more. He never did, until years later.

A couple of days after he'd had his bright idea his vacation came up, and he took a plane to join the rest of the
Deveraux clan at the family reunion in Louisiana. On the
quick plane ride to New Orleans and the much longer drive
north through the fields in a rented Ford jet, his mind kept
circling the same set of concepts. His "fusion afterburner"
wasn't one of them, except as a catalyst, which had gotten
him to thinking about rocketships in general. But before he
could pin down the squirming idea he was pawing and worrying, he arrived and was immediately plunged into the
sticky intricacies of family affairs. For the next few hours he
grinned more than he was accustomed, noted spreading
waistlines and thinning hair, became reacquainted with many
small children he'd forgotten, and was introduced to shiny
new spouses and plump pink babies he'd never seen before.

Most of Linwood's relatives had stayed close to the land
or had gotten jobs in local industry; Linwood was an aberra-
tion, made more mysterious to them because he couldn't
talk about his work. But they graciously tolerated his pecu-
liarities and didn't seem to mind when his attention drifted.

On the first hot and very humid night he sat on a folding
chair on his cousin Pierre's brick patio, munching deep-fried
catfish balls—rolled up bits of the creature itself, not its re-
productive organs—which were about as succulent as old
golf balls. The light of the misty moon and stars, so smeared
they could hardly compete with the phosphorescent glow of
fireflies, illuminated a slope of dirt, rust red in daytime,

which led down to a cattle tank. After a while Linwood's attention drifted—

—away from the men's talk of church politics and cotton to memories of the year he was fifteen years old, the year *Challenger* had exploded while he and the other kids in his high school class were watching it on TV.

That was the same year the debate over a new antimissile system, strategic-defense-something—he couldn't recall the acronym, everybody had called it Star Wars—had reached a crescendo of sorts, sad in retrospect. The president of the United States had promised an impenetrable shield against nuclear weapons to cover every American city, a sort of bombproof Astrodome, but his supporters kept trying to explain that he hadn't really meant to put it quite that way. Perhaps, at unspecifiable cost, it would be possible to defend some of our missile sites—not our cities.

At age fifteen, while Linwood easily absorbed the technical arguments for and against Star Wars, he modeled his opinions on those expressed at the dinner table by his father, a computer programmer at a local pump manufacturing plant that had recently acquired an army contract. A devout deacon in an offshoot fundamentalist congregation, the senior Deveraux stressed the innate moral superiority of any kind of *defensive* weapon over any kind of *offensive* weapon. This seemed a strong and reasonable stance to young Linwood; it did not occur to him at the time to ask whether "defense" that was dedicated solely to the defense of offense shared this ethical superiority.

He never had asked that question, during all the years of college and the Marine Corps—he had made a particularly thin, tough, quiet marine—or during the years of graduate-school grind that followed, or during the many steady hours at Livermore Lab, working first on miniature bombs, graduating at last to these damned innately morally superior ray guns that still would not function the way they were supposed to.

Occasionally Linwood would catch a newsbite about how NASA was putting itself back together, securing its technical base, making fitful strides in scientific exploration, laying the foundation for human colonization of space. And about how the Europeans and Japanese and Russians were doing it better, maybe. He would experience a fleeting moment of regret that NASA's confusion following *Challenger* had deflected his teenage enthusiasm from what had been his goal until that moment: to be an astronaut.

But not until after he had almost subconsciously designed a hot-rod rocket engine, not until he was sitting on a dark sweltering patio in his home town listening to the judicious Christian murmur of his farmer relatives harmonizing with the drone of the cicadas, their slow sentences punctuated by the blue flash of fireflies, had it occurred to him that he was only thirty-five years old, that he was in excellent physical condition, and that it was not too late.

He applied to NASA. A year later, somewhat bemused, Linwood found himself bent over in an Air Force doctor's office with a plastic rod stuck up his behind, the white-coated M.D. behind him shoving the thing this way and that, whistling while he worked. There was nothing abnormal about Linwood's plumbing; this was simply the final indignity in that long *rite de passage* endured by all astronaut candidates.

He went home to Livermore, and within a couple of days he got a call saying he'd made the cut. He was happy and sad at the same time. Sad because he'd wasted a lot of his life doing stuff he wished he hadn't. But he hoped in his quiet way to start compensating for that.

An astronaut, for his conscience's sake . . .

"The count is at T minus two hours and fifteen minutes and counting," said launch control.

Commander Braide scrutinized her console. Some of the little screens showed computer-generated diagrams; others displayed live TV pictures of the ship's systems—its fuel pellet "factory," where spheres of deuterium and tritium were continually cast in free fall; the bulky glass lasers, with their mirrors and frequency-amplifying crystals; the capacitors and transformers of the power storage subassemblies; the field magnet coils and their cryogenics; the magnetohydrodynamic generators; the tanks and pumps and motors of the maneuvering system; the thermonuclear propulsion core.

"We have a hold at T minus two hours and twelve minutes," said launch control.

"What do you show, Linwood?" the commander asked.

His voice returned over the comm system: "Capacitors fully charged, pellet injector primed and ready, nozzle field strength optimum—a green board in propulsion."

"Not your problem, *Starfire*," said launch control. "We have a sticky tracking antenna."

Braide switched the main pixel array over to the view from the station, seeing the ship as launch control saw her: long and sleek, gleaming in the sunlight, a stack of stainless steel cylinders hanging in starry space, attached by umbilicals to Archimedes Station: *Starfire*.

Starfire. The name had seen use at least a couple of times before: once for one of Lockheed Aircraft's slow and ugly jet fighter planes of the 1950s, once for an inelegant lump of a tokamak, an early design-study fusion reactor of the 1970s not worth building. This time it fit.

The simple shape was embellished at its base with more intricate constructions. Here a cage of glass bars embraced a steel spheroid; the glass bars split a master laser's beam and directed it through mirrors and crystals to the heart of the fusion reaction chamber. Rooted to the reactor were three great black fins, as big as wings. This deceptively streamlined craft would never feel atmosphere, however; its wings were radiators of carbon-carbon and molybdenum tubing through which liquid lithium flowed to carry off the reactor's excess heat.

The ship's narrow fuel tanks were packed tight and tall to provide maximum shielding between engine and crew. Its main engine exhaust nozzle was not the solid bell of a chemical rocket but an openwork of lacy pipes and coils in steel and bronze, generating invisible magnetic forces.

For two years the ship had been growing like a bud from the side of Archimedes. Its vital components had been preassembled and pretested on Earth for five years before that, then disassembled and carried into orbit, there to be reassembled and tested again. But as a whole system *Starfire* had never been tested. Until today.

Starfire was an X-ship, an experimental model, but its descendants would open the solar system as the railroads had opened the American West, as jet airplanes had contracted the globe. The commander believed that *Starfire*'s fusion-powered grandchildren and great-grandchildren would penetrate the Galaxy. Simply to be members of its crew would earn them all footnotes in history.

As the hold on the count stretched, the commander fingered a platinum cross that hung close to her neck on a strong chain, centered it on her throat, let herself slip into daydreams. . . .

"What do *you* know about other worlds?" said Ransom. ". . . Your roof is so dense that your people cannot see through into Deep Heaven and look at the other worlds."

When she was of an age to be read stories, her mother and father had taken turns reading her all of C. S. Lewis's Narnia fantasy series, and a little later, *Out of the Silent Planet* and its sequels. Only much later did she realize what her parents, agnostics both, had been trying too subtly to convey. It was a passage from *Perelandra* that came back to her now:

> "Oh, I see it," she said. "I am older now. *Your* world has no roof. You look right out into the high place and see the great dance with your own eyes. You live always in that terror and in that delight, and what we must only believe, you can behold. . . ."

Robin Braide had turned seventeen a few weeks before the accident that took her mother's life. The Saturday had started as one of those startlingly clear, hot, blue Seattle summer days that people greet with mixed emotions: some northwesterners consider them a well-earned reward for enduring months of dark drizzle, but many also feel an upwelling of guilt, as if dark drizzle were all they deserved.

Guilt was not congenital to Robin. Stubbornness was. Her father, a physics professor at the University of Washington, and her mother, a landscape architect, had held firm (if oxymoronic) notions about discipline: they believed people were responsible only to themselves for their behavior, so long as they did not impinge on the rights of others. But long before their firstborn daughter could speak, she had found a means to subvert their tolerance.

When disgruntled, she held food in her mouth. Splurting would have been okay—messy, but a healthy expression of independence and easy to deal with: the kid doesn't want to eat, let her go hungry, clean up the mess. Simple. But a baby can't be forced to swallow, nor can she be allowed to fall asleep with a wad of mashed prunes poised on the threshold of her windpipe. The first time it happened Robin's parents tried to wait her out; Robin sat in her battle-stained high chair for two hours, cheeks bloated and eyes crossed, until she began to nod off. Then Mom and Dad went in with fingers to dig out the food. She woke up; she fought and bit. And thus it continued . . . for months.

Robin's father had a horror of biological explanations and proposed that some early experience, however trivial, must have been the source of the quirk. After their second daughter was born and quickly developed into a placid and laughing baby, her parents decided that Robin wasn't so much stubborn as *determined,* a trait more worthy of praise. Meanwhile the example of a younger and very much beloved sibling, possessed of much less determination, led shrewd Robin to temper her own displays.

Her childhood was in fact unusually happy. She excelled in school. She excelled in sports. As a teenager she excelled in car repair, and by the age of fifteen she owned a souped-up secondhand Mustang jet. But by sixteen she was spending all of her spare time sailing, and boys, while interesting, were not worth much of her time unless they virtually lived, as she did that year, on the water.

The day her mother died Robin was captaining one of Portage Bay Yacht Club's twenty-two-foot Carlsen Comets against the Bellevue YC. Her mother, who lacked Robin's passion for things nautical but knew her way around a boat, was serving as her crew.

The first leg of the race, east across Lake Washington, was all tedious tacking, with barely enough wind to keep headway and no significant advantage gained by any in the field; ski boat drivers roared past, sneering at the frustrated sailors. But rounding the buoy the wind freshened; a glance at the sky showed hazy clouds gathering rapidly, already obscuring distant Mount Rainier—sudden contrary weather, and the promise of a squall.

Still, the north leg was slow and unexciting; only by sailing wing and wing, with constant nervous trimming of a lolling spinnaker, did Robin gain even a few feet over the second boat.

At the second buoy Robin held a precarious lead. Her mother got the spinnaker stowed smartly just as Robin came about and headed southwest for the finish line. A wayward dollop of spray pasted her cotton jersey to her chest as she hauled in the mainsheet; Robin smelled the tang of hemlock and spruce. The windward rail rose clear of the chop; she hitched her butt highside as her mother scrambled to set the jib.

The sudden brisk wind, the spray, the thrill of the boat heeling over exulted them. Her mother turned to grin at her. As Robin was grinning back, the prow rammed driftwood; Robin yanked in the tiller to let the floating log roll by, but the still-taut sails threatened to knock the boat down. She came into the wind again and her mother overbalanced, lost her grip, and pitched over the side, shrieking with embarrassed laughter.

For a few seconds the disappointed Robin thought she might still win the race—the sails were well trimmed, and if the wind held steady on course she might get across the line without another tack . . . but of course she'd forfeit anyway. So the unworthy thought passed, and she loosed the sheets.

Her mother was grinning apologetically from the waves, her blond head framed in her orange life vest, as Robin's boat hissed by a few feet to leeward, barely clearing the path of the oncoming pack. The skippers of the next boats in line called out dutifully, offering assistance, but Robin and her mother called back that they were fine, they didn't need help. The sun-warmed water was warm enough, and even without a vest her mother was a strong swimmer. They had all the time in the world.

Robin planned to come about again, drive crosswind slowly with the jib luffing like loose laundry, ease up beside her mother, pull her over the side, then haul in—and *still* pass the last of the pack. As she was plotting her moves she felt cold air moving overhead and saw the sparkling water in front of her turn dull green. Clouds had covered the sun. She came about into a solid gray wall of rain. Her mother was nowhere to be seen.

Within seconds Robin was blinded by sheets of water

pouring out of the sky, thundering against the mainsail, pouring over the rail in freak waves. In the cockpit her white canvas shoes glimmered under a foot of water.

The boat wouldn't sink, no matter how much water it took—the trick was to keep it from capsizing. The wind came in driving gusts from all quarters, randomly. The waves seemed impossibly high and close together. Robin recognized the effects of wave interference but it was of no help to her; it took all her strength and quickness to dodge the swinging boom, to haul on wet lines until her fingers were white and stinging, to whipsaw the tiller until the sluggish hull responded. The minutes stretched interminably; the squall was squatting on top of her boat.

Then it moved on again, as rapidly as it had arrived. Excited gulls wheeled and screamed as the sun filtered through filaments of cloud. The lake was littered with bright flotsam and capsized hulls; of the squadron of Comets, Robin's was one of only three still upright. She began crossing the water back and forth, searching, and because there were no flares aboard the day sailer, she took a few seconds to raise her pennant, upside down, to the top of the mast. Somebody onshore spotted the distress signal with binoculars and sent a launch out. Shortly before it drew alongside, Robin came upon an orange life vest with frayed and broken straps.

Her mother's body was never found. Eventually it was assumed that some trick of inversion had carried it to the bottom of the deep lake and trapped it there, likely forever. Robin did not cry as long as they were searching, for she had persuaded herself that her mother was not dead; it surprised her that she could not cry even when the search was abandoned.

She did not cry at the memorial service, and when she overheard a murmur she was meant to hear—about time healing all wounds—her lips tightened in determination. Not this wound. No amount of time. Something of her mother lived as long as Robin refused to forget. She did not cry when her father took her into his arms and clung tightly to her, pleading with her to let go, as tears rolled down his own cheeks and dripped into her hair; sadly she realized that she did not feel closer to him for that, but more distant.

On her seventeenth birthday Robin's mother had given her a pendant cross of platinum set with a single irregular pearl. Robin's thanks had been sincere but unenthusiastic; she wore it for a few days, then put it in her jewelry box. The day of the service she hung the cross around her neck again.

It had stayed there ever since, removed only temporarily, only when necessary. Now she wore it on a fine choker of titanium steel.

"Hold released. Counting from T minus two hours eleven minutes."

Starfire began to hum with contained electromagnetic energies seeking release. Soon the commander was very busy. . . .

"T minus one hour and counting."

Heavy couplings beat against the hull, ringing it like a bell. The ship lurched sideways. Everywhere there was a shriek of escaping gases, quickly squelched. . . .

"Umbilicals away. Separation fifty meters . . . two hundred meters . . . approaching launch radius."

"T minus forty minutes and counting."

On the feed from Archimedes Station they had time to gaze upon the dwindling winged needle of their ship, floating free and clear in space. . . .

"T minus ten minutes and counting."

Communications channels crackled between *Starfire* and launch control on Archimedes Station; overeager Houston waited on the sidelines, itching to grab the ball.

"Nine minutes . . ."

Like a head of water behind a tall dam, *Starfire*'s bank of seventy-two squat black capacitors constrained an enormous electrostatic potential, uncounted electrons eager to cascade freely when the spillways were opened . . .

"Eight minutes . . ."

. . . to be shaped into hundred-billion-watt pulses, each ten nanoseconds in duration . . . ,

"Seven minutes . . ."

. . . each fed to flash lamps surrounding the master laser . . . ,

"Six minutes . . ."

. . . each lamp exciting a discharge of coherent infrared photons inside the laser's glass . . . ,

"Five minutes . . ."

. . . each coherent wave refracting and dividing, channeled down twenty-four separate columns of glass . . . ,

"Four minutes . . ."

. . . each wave crest encountering crystal wafers that filtered the polarized light . . .

"Three minutes . . ."

. . . and amplified it . . .

"Two minutes . . ."

. . . so that each pulse of light, now ultraviolet, bounced from mirrors and simultaneously converged . . . ,

"One minute . . ."

. . . traveling through the apexes of an imaginary solid resembling a soccer ball . . . ,

"Thirty seconds . . ."

. . . speeding radially inward toward an emptiness, where any nanosecond now there would appear . . .

"Ten . . ."

. . . a small sphere, recently bubbled out of liquid isotopes of hydrogen . . . ,

"Five . . ."

. . . having fallen freely through vacuum to be enclosed in a perfect jacket of plastic film . . .

"Three . . ."

. . . then to be gently seized, this ringed sphere, by electric fields . . .

"Two . . ."

. . . and propelled to the very center of an empty hemispherical chamber, plated with gold . . . ,

"One . . ."

. . . arriving just as twenty-four pulses of light converged . . .

"Power."

. . . to crush it . . .

"Ignition."

. . . and slash the night with fire.

"Damn fine! Damn fine!" Senator Albert Kreuger slammed a heavy glass, empty but for its still fresh ice cubes, down on the pecan-wood surface of his desk.

A big pixel-array screen was mounted on the senator's paneled wall, and on it *Starfire* was visibly dwinding, its steady one-gee acceleration piling on velocity at the rate a stone would fall toward an airless Earth.

But *Starfire* was falling away from Earth. Falling for minutes. So crisp were the electronic sensors of NASA's remote cameras and the emitters in the office screen that the sunbright ship and its much brighter trail of glowing exhaust were held in visual equilibrium against faint stars and velvet night. "Damn, damn, damn, look at that son of a bitch go!"

An aide turned from the sideboard, Jack Daniel's bottle in hand. "Sir?"

"Why thank you, Bob, I believe I will. Just a splash." The silver-haired senator cocked an eye at his visitor, standing rigid in the shadows. "Help yourself, Travis. Don't be shy."

Travis grunted his thanks and unbent enough to hold out his hand. Bottle clinked against glass.

On the screen, as the angle between ship and line of sight declined, bright exhaust overwhelmed the ship's outline, and its image became that of a rival planet, a wanderer among the stars.

"You would have given somethin' to be on that ship,

70

wouldn't you, son? Makes a man proud to be an American. Hell, I woulda given a lot, too." The senator's pride seemed oddly soured. With a sudden slap of his hand, Kreuger cut off the video replay; the video chip popped out of the desk-top player. No one reached to retrieve it. "Thanks for show-ing it to me," Kreuger growled. An oil portrait of hill coun-try bluebells descended to cover the blank television screen. The only light in the room was from the senator's desk lamp and, through the blinds, from the brilliantly illuminated Cap-itol dome a block away.

Travis watched his uncle's once handsome face, his dull eyes teary with emotion and alcohol.

The senator swung around in his leather chair. "Sit down, son, you make me nervous stalkin' around like that."

Travis perched on the edge of the matching leather couch opposite the desk.

Kreuger grinned, disconcertingly. "How ya like the of-fice?"

"Looks good, Al," said Travis. "Didn't take you long to get settled."

"Bob here's right efficient."

Travis glanced at the blond aide, whose expression was inscrutable. He looked back at his uncle, tried to put on a bright and friendly expression. "Had a chance to look over that report I brought by, sir?"

The senator looked at the aide. "Bobby?"

"The staff is making an evaluation, sir."

Travis kept his eyes on the senator. "If this isn't a good time . . ."

"Good as any. Details ain't important. What we need to discuss is political realities."

Travis hesitated, then gulped a mouthful of bourbon. "I'm not much of a politician, Al."

"Oh, you're a quick study, son." Kreuger smiled at him, that foxy-grandpa grin some politicians hope implies that they can think faster than they talk. "I confess I was a might overwhelmed when the governor informed me he was appointin' me to fill out poor Manny Castro's term. 'Bout the only advantage in it for him I could see was, well, nobody had nothin' against *me*. Not much to argue about in my corner of the state. Long as the price of oil's up."

"Things are busier here in Washington, I reckon."

"It's a sure bet I'm gonna' make more enemies than friends, no matter what I do."

Travis said quietly, "Still, you've got a chance to leave your mark. Fight for what you believe in."

"I swear my sister, your esteemed mother, used much the same words to me, not one week ago." Kreuger took a gulp of his drink. His grin slid. "You know, Travis, I had no *idea* what a substantial contribution your father's estate had made to our governor's last election campaign."

Melting ice cubes clinked in Travis's glass. Kreuger eyed the glass. "Bob, I wonder if you would be so good as to freshen my guest's drink one last time. And my own. Then I don't think I'll be needing anything more from you tonight."

The aide moved efficiently to do as he was asked, and Kreuger bestowed a warm smile upon him as he reached the door. "Thank you, Bobby. Get a good night's sleep, you hear?"

Travis and his uncle sat quietly until they heard the door of the outer office close. Kreuger's patter lost its folksy charm. "Edna May never consulted me about this, Travis. She found out—from me, and I regret openin' my trap—that Manny was sick, and she started right then puttin' the governor in her debt. God knows I can't get elected to this seat. Morales and Polonski between 'em will chop me into dog food. And that's just the primaries."

"Then why did you accept, Al?"

"*Why?* I'll tell you. You can't think of anything bigger than ridin' around in outer space, nephew, in your world. In mine . . . hell, I'm a U.S. senator, boy. I'm at the top. Today, and for the next three years."

"You're not going to run for re-election?"

Kreuger took a long sip, then guided the glass back to the desk top. "Well, could be I'll get to like it here."

Travis studied him. "I suppose it could hook you."

"Maybe there's ways to keep the options open," said Kreuger languidly. "Old Jack Fassio, now there's a popular fellow." He let out a sigh that was half a groan. "Not that folks from my old district care much for him."

"Chairman of the space committee. A good friend of NASA."

Kreuger snorted. "Any Texas senator in the last half century ain't supported space?"

"Some people think what NASA spends at home is all there is to the space program." Travis paused to sip his drink, then rattled the ice in his glass. "Fassio's been courteous to me over the years. Barely courteous."

Kreuger nodded. "He's up for re-election. I could identify myself with the guy. Support him on every single issue, campaign for him. Maybe arrange for funds."

"He'd surely be obliged to you."

"I do believe that's what Edna May has in mind." In the lamp's glow Kreuger eyed Travis with something close to malice. "You're a popular fella too. And nobody could object to askin' NASA to devote part of that fancy new rocketship's time to asteroid research—hell, they're already makin' noises about doin' it themselves. That part's easy."

Travis waited. Uncle Albert had never shown much spine, but he'd always been transparent, even naive. It kept him almost honest. And unpredictable.

"Gettin' you a *ride* on it . . ." The senator leaned back in his chair. "You gotta bring me somethin' special, Travis. Somethin' completely out of the ordinary."

"Say what you need, Al."

"I don't *know* what I need, dammit. What I know is, all the relatives workin' together can't buy Jack Fassio's committee without an excuse that'll persuade the voters. Even if he wanted to sell."

"Al . . ."

"You just heard my offer." Kreuger leaned forward abruptly, planting his forearms on the desk. "Now go away. Before I stop actin' like your uncle and start actin' like a real senator."

Travis stood and laid his glass on the sideboard, harder than he meant to. "Thanks for the drink."

Kreuger eyed the glass. "One more thing. From your uncle."

Travis was already at the door. He waited, one hand on the heavy knob.

"This whiskey business. I've had occasion to study it. There's drunks who admit it and quit. Others admit it, try to keep goin' anyway"—he put on a twisted smirk—"yours truly, fer example. Then there's the real dumb ones, who don't admit it even to themselves."

"Jesus, Al. Do I need a lecture from you on this?"

"Who better? I knew your daddy pretty well. And I'm your ma's brother. They say it's in the blood."

"I don't drink when I'm in training."

"Maybe it's time you started trainin'."

Back in Austin, Travis found a fax from NASA on his desk at the Asteroid Resource Center. Still depressed from his interview with Texas's newest U.S. senator, he picked up the fax in anticipation that it would boost his spirits, if only a little.

Travis had achieved tenure at the University of Texas in the five years since he'd left NASA and, when it was convenient to be so known, he was Professor Hill. He owned a restored nineteenth-century house within walking distance of the state capitol building and the university; the Asteroid Resource Center occupied the ground floor of the house, and he had his living quarters upstairs.

The airy and fashionable offices of ARC housed a secretary and a programmer, who sat in the outer office, and a full-time postdoctoral fellow of planetary sciences who rated a private cubicle like Travis's own. The center also had the half-time services of an astrophysics graduate student who was pursuing her Ph.D., with Travis as one of her advisors.

To the surprise of a great many people, the center had made substantial contributions to planetary science in its short life, through its ingenious computer-programmed exploitation of disparate data on meteorite geology, asteroid spectrometry, orbital mechanics, and a dozen other scattered disciplines from equally scattered laboratories and academic offices around the world. Travis and his colleagues had authored notable papers in the area of meteorite parent-body identification, providing surprising insights into the early history of the solar system and into the far from simple relationship between comets and asteroids.

The university administration had bargained for nothing more than Travis's notorious name and the access it implied to Hill Foundation funds. As a bonus, the center's solid science brought honor to the Texas faculty. Not only did Travis produce results, he cultivated his departmental colleagues. His reward was his youthful professorship.

Even NASA was happy with ARC. The original research contract, granted on a grudge, had been extended twice. The first time the contract was renewed Travis was surprised; the second time he was pleased and a little smug. He fully expected the fax from NASA on his desk to be still another extension of ARC's satellite infrared observation program—

"We regret to inform you that your request, while upholding the high standard of scientific inquiry your organization has established in the past, cannot be met at present owing to a backlog of other urgent research needs. . . ."

Shit.

It was a blow, but he supposed—after a moment's thought—that he should not have been surprised. The elevation of Uncle Albert to the U.S. Senate had brought Hill family affairs under NASA scrutiny; this cancellation was just as likely a bit of judicious distancing on the part of some NASA bureaucrat as it was an act of spite.

The outer office was unusually quiet; Travis stuck his head around the corner of his partition to see his secretary and programmer working at their consoles with uncharacteristic concentration. Quickly shifting his glance, Travis caught Don Sloane, the bearded postdoc, peering out of his own cubicle. Sloane shrank back, realized it was too late, then tried to pretend he had merely stumbled on his way to the water cooler.

Travis waved the fax at them. "Okay, you've all read this already. It's not the end of the world."

The guilty trio exchanged glances. Sloane was the first to fess up. "Right. Not so bad," he said, filling a paper cup with water. "Hey, there's lots of meteorites around, right? Poor man's space probes."

"And ground telescopes," Ruben, the programmer, added brightly. "When you can get time on *them*."

"Yes, and that's exactly the way we've made our reputation," Travis said, "analyzing other people's data."

The secretary, Irenie Su, gazed at him in silent admiration.

"Actually," Sloane began, pausing momentarily, "we have always been able to confirm our hypotheses with our own observations. That is the *real* basis of our reputation." He swallowed the water in one gulp. "Face it, Trav, things are going to slow way down around here."

"Don, I don't agree. We'll do a little horse tradin', get some of these other teams to expand their programs and let us piggyback. It's done all the time. Meantime, I don't want anybody to worry."

"What are we gonna trade 'em?" asked Ruben, hooking his long silky black hair out of his eyes; his split ends hung so low they threatened to get tangled in his keyboard when he leaned over it.

"Prestige. Expertise," said Travis. "Ahh . . . mmm."

Three pairs of eyes gazed at him in polite silence. Not too convincing a speech, he thought. He focused on his secretary; she had black hair and blue eyes and a pout that said talk-to-me-if-you-dare, stranger, and she thought she had a date with Travis tonight and was probably, he figured, trying to do him a favor when she asked, "How'd it go in Washington? With the senator?"

He winced. "We've got a deal," he answered firmly.

Don Sloane's eyes widened. "Travis! Why didn't you say so? Kreuger's really going to help get you on that ship? To go pick up rocks?"

"The deal's not final. But he'll work to move an asteroid flyby to the top of *Starfire*'s mission list."

Sloane's grin faded into politeness. "Hey, well . . ." He crumpled his paper cup and tossed it into the designer-provided woven Indian wastebasket. "Great."

"The main thing is, I don't want anybody worrying about their jobs." Travis wondered why he was displaying his doubts. Certainly money wasn't an issue; he had access to plenty, and besides, it wasn't exactly fabulous amounts of money that lured people into studying the small bodies of the solar system in the first place.

But he stood to lose Don . . . and Doris, the graduate student . . . and maybe even Ruben, his star-struck programmer, if he couldn't keep them interested in the program. He didn't want to lose them.

Nobody'd ever warned him that starting a small business is like marrying a woman with kids of her own. Instant family. He grinned with all his teeth—"Things are gonna be busy. So don't worry, okay?"—and retreated into his cubicle.

Travis managed to keep himself busy with scheming and paperwork until the sunlight got long and yellow through the spade-leafed tallow trees outside his windows. Finally, Don and Ruben called their good evenings; the front door closed behind them. Irenie Su appeared at his cubicle doorway, smiling languidly, fingering her string of Egyptian beads.

"Hey, Irenie Su." He grinned up at her. "Say, you been to that new Hoof 'n Claw out on Airport Road? Near your place?"

Her smile developed a dubious kink. "Yeah. . . ."

"What say we go on out that way? I'll follow you."

She blinked and thrust out a lip. "Wouldn't mind stayin' right here, Trav . . . in town."

"I'm headin' on out to the ranch, hon. Tonight. Plenty of time to treat you to steak and lobster first."

She recovered nicely. "Let me just call up my roommate before we go. Make sure she's got other plans."

The sun hadn't yet risen when Travis's Mistral whispered into the carport at the Hill Ranch. He got out of the low seat and stood up, groaning involuntarily; he arched his back and splayed his hands over his kidneys. His lifestyle was getting to him.

A blue white light gleamed far off among the black and twisted live oaks, like Venus newly risen: it was a bare bulb over a barn door. As he walked toward it, two mangy half German shepherd mongrels came out, growling deep in their throats, but he clucked at them and they sniffed his jeans fore and aft and licked his hands and walked beside him, panting and interested, as he went into the barn.

The barn was dark except for a single yellow low-wattage bulb splotched with fried insects. It was warm and smelly in here, the smell of fresh and fermenting hay and fresh horse manure, which was pretty much the same smell as used beer and chili beans. Smelling so much like raunchy, rub-your-nose-in-it, honest-to-God home, in fact, that Travis smiled and sighed and for a moment felt very sad.

He had a pony named Riptide, a plain old bay gelding. Travis hadn't seen the animal in a while, but he found him in the third stall on the right, alert and familiar. Riptide was a tad small, but he'd been a good quarter horse in his day, with a good deep chest and powerful hindquarters and no-nonsense knees. Travis talked to him now, gave him sweet hay from a bale in the front of the barn, rubbed his muzzle. Then Travis went to the tack room and came back with a threadbare saddle blanket and a cracked and sweat-blackened saddle. He brought Riptide out of the stable, slung the creaking harness over him, buckled it and cinched it. He swung a leg over and set Riptide off at a slow walk through the predawn gloom. The dogs followed for a few hundred yards, but neither Travis nor the horse paid them any attention, and they found other things to do.

Shattered limestone under Riptide's hooves sounded like splinters of glass. Twisted cedar limbs reached out, strong and stiff, man-on-horseback high, eager to push a rider to the ground. God knew where this broken rocky earth found moisture to make mist, but a thin vapor clung inches above the parched stones, barely visible in the half light of approaching dawn.

The Medina River cut a meander through the Hill Ranch property, an old river fed by an ancient aquifer, springing from the brow of the Cretaceous seabed a few miles to the west. There were dinosaur tracks in this riverbed, not far upstream, the splay-toed tracks of theropod carnivores stalking their prey. As Travis guided Riptide across the broad and mostly dry riverbed of polished limestone, he saw a family of javelinas browsing on the upstream bank: smart, hairy pigs, little changed from the ancestral pig, of a shape familiar from the vase paintings of antiquity and the wall paintings of prehistory. Despite his diminutive size, the boar of this group, with his recurving tusks and fiery eyes and crested shoulders, could have given the Caledonian hunting party a good rough-and-tumble.

Travis watched the javelinas—familiar game and good to eat—and felt himself momentarily unmoored in time.

He questioned what he was about, what it was that drove him to want to climb back into some stinking tin can for the sensation of being a little farther from the planet, a little closer to the stars. There were those who spoke eloquently of the urge to explore space as evolution in action, as the inevitable linear progression of mankind. With apologies, that was bullshit. Evolution had not the slightest idea what it was up to. People hardly ever had the slightest idea what they were up to. They wanted things. They wanted happiness, they wanted satisfaction, and most of all they wanted to discover. They wanted novelty.

Then, after a while, they wanted peace. Humans weren't unlike the others. They were all in this together, all at once, the great reptiles, the hairy pigs, the horse, the man. A swirling sensation came over him but he made it pass, hoping it was an effect of his hangover. Time and eternity—pigs and dinosaurs and other people—were beside the point. The point was, what was he going to do with his own life?

Once upon a time he had driven out to California in an old oil-burning Japanese ATV, sticking to the back roads— the dirt roads, when he could find them on a map—without a chip player or even a radio to relieve the loud grinding of his engine. But his head had never completely shut up during the entire trip. The visual input was rich, the here and now of the road in front of him—sometimes flat, straight asphalt, sometimes a narrow, rutted mining road—and the aural input was that awful engine, and, on pavement, the vibrating whine of the cleated tires. He'd camped out every night, in places like Sitting Bull Falls and the Santa Catalina Mountains and Anza-Borrego, burning a steak and an ear of corn over his campfire and downing a whole bottle of red in slow sips while browsing in Sambursky's *Physical Thought from the Presocratics to the Quantum Physicists* by the light of his hand lamp. He filled his head with historical stuff from the book, stuff enough to silence the noise of his yammering thoughts.

He was five days on his winding road to Pasadena, and only on the fourth day did the yak-yak-yak begin to subside.

By then he'd clearly discerned at least three voices, although he suspected there might be more (perhaps the one that was doing the discerning). One mumbled about choices, about navigating the ATV, buying oil and food, finding a campsite, cooking and sleeping. A second voice kvetched—food mediocre, road too long and rough, oil too expensive—spinning off into grandiose thoughts about science and achievement and all the jerks he had to deal with and the bitterness of his love life. Another voice watched the first two with contempt, affecting detachment.

By the fifth day, Travis had somehow tricked the second voice into shutting up for minutes at a time, and the third voice into cooling it altogether. For those minutes he was merely in the world. But that same afternoon he arrived at the Jet Propulsion Laboratory, his vacation ended, and he plunged back into *stuff*.

Guiding sturdy little Riptide into the trans-Medina, Travis remembered how good it had been to listen to only one voice, the one that dealt with things as they came up, things like hunger and fatigue and the world's occasional sublimity. He doubted he would soon achieve that state again, unless he gave up on everything he thought was worth doing.

The horse carried him deep into the juniper-dotted hills. He watched the sun rise fat and orange in the hazy east; he listened to the yak-yak-yak in his head and tried not to try to make it cease. He succeeded neither in silencing the roar of consciousness nor in confronting the issues that required him to take thought. After two hours he realized he was tired and hungry, and he steered Riptide for home.

He saw Bonnie's hot red Mercedes parked in the drive outside the house. She and Sam had built a house of their own two miles up the road, although they spent most of each week in Austin.

In the kitchen he grinned at plump Maria Martinez and snatched a warm biscuit from a stack cooling under a clean cotton cloth. Maria smiled back, displaying numerous ivory teeth, pretending to take his hunger as a personal compliment. He wolfed the biscuit down before heading into the sitting room. Through the glass he saw his mother and Bonnie in animated conversation in the rose garden. He sank into an armchair and watched them—his mother launched upon some lecture, Bonnie all smiles and enthusiastic nods.

The morning was hot, and Bonnie was wearing the shorts and cotton top she favored when she wasn't horseback riding or being a Texas society girl. Her hair danced and sparkled in the morning sun. Bonnie liked Edna May; her smiles and nods were partly her conception of a daughter-in-law's duty, but mostly genuine. Travis watched her closely—those legs, all long, smooth muscle, the springy bosom—but the feeling that welled up in him wasn't lust, it was a deep, forlorn longing for which he had no explanation and against which he had no defense.

Damn you, brother Sam.

He thought about why he'd come out here today, which was to ask his mother's advice, now that NASA had finally pulled out. It came into his mind that he already knew what it would be. Go to the little people, she would say. Write a book about asteroids, with lots of color pictures. Go on video. Create a constituency.

In fact she'd been saying something like that for years. He'd held back, because he rather enjoyed the staid academic prestige he would inevitably lose when he started hustling in public. He didn't want ARC to become—what had Taylor Stith called it?—a "hobby club tax write-off," even in appearance.

Seduced by respectability.

Out in the rose garden, Bonnie squatted to inspect a plant's roots and her khaki shorts stretched tighter over her buttocks. Travis abruptly rose and walked out of the room, through the kitchen—waving a kiss at Maria as he passed—to his car. The Mistral sped away from the house in a cloud of caliche dust.

*   *   *

Travis landed his drink on the hotel bar and fumbled with the blue-and-white badge that identified him as a member of the astronomers' convention, trying to unpin it from his crumpled tweed jacket. A year and more had passed, and he'd taken the advice he hadn't wanted to hear from his mother: he had a picture book to sell, and he was on the video circuit.

He heard a husky female voice beside him. "Travis Hill? The astronaut?" The woman was young, dark-haired, with the sort of eyes that looked permanently out of focus, possibly because of her smudged mascara. Her wide hips were tightly encased in a blue plastic miniskirt; she held out a hand with nail-bitten fingers. "I'm Charlotte, from *Night Beat*."

He shook her hand. "Pleased to meet you." Her eyes weren't meeting his, they were aimed somewhere lower, at his attaché case or at his crotch. He held up the case. "Stills on a chip. I'd like to talk about these with the director, if I can." Or maybe she was looking at his diamond bracelet.

"You got a cue sheet?" Letting go of his hand, she slid her fingers along his a bit slower than she had to, brushing the bracelet links.

"Yes." He'd done these appearances often enough by now to be prepared. A memorized script. A cue sheet. A video chip that made sense by itself. "Might save some confusion if I could talk to the director," he said. "A couple of minutes." He tried to be firm and reasonable and friendly all at once—because they make a mess of you so fast if they take a disliking to you. Or if they just aren't paying attention, which is more likely.

"He's gonna be pretty busy. . . . You really were an astronaut?"

"Lots of people have been astronauts."

"The other guy's already in the car," she said, turning toward the door.

"The other guy?"

"Cartwright, the writer. The guy you're debating." She headed for the lobby, and he followed.

"Kiki said I was on by myself."

"Your publicist? They'll say anything. Jack says we'll get more viewer interest from a debate."

"Who's Jack?"

"*Night Beat*'s producer. It's his creation." She said "creation" with reverence, as if reading from Genesis.

Charlotte pushed through the glass doors, with Travis close behind her. The Midwest city's summer night was muggy and smelled of badly tuned turbines. Charlotte's tiny Sumitomo jet was standing at the curb under the hotel's marquee; Travis climbed into the back and awkwardly shook hands with Graeme Cartwright, the author, who turned to reach over the front seat.

Travis had seen Cartwright around the convention, but their paths hadn't crossed. He was a red-haired man with soft hands, an Australian astronomy professor who wrote a science-fiction novel every year or two during his summer recesses. Travis had bought one of his novels in an airport once; it was about evil aliens systematically destroying intelligent life in the universe, unwittingly aided in their dire scheme by fuzzy-minded liberal Earthlings. Travis didn't know how it all came out. In Cartwright's code, consciously or otherwise, aliens apparently stood for commies.

Cartwright informed Travis that their "debate" was to be about the Russian presence in space. He nodded. It didn't matter; he would talk about asteroids. They had to give you equal time, and you didn't have to answer their dumb questions. Travis sat back and stared out the window of the car at the passing traffic; half of it seemed to be high-sprung customized ATVs with rows of yellow lights on their cab roofs.

The video half-hour was the usual eighteen minutes long, most of it devoted to the happy talk of the show's two hosts, one of each gender. For half the rest, the science-fiction writer spoke darkly of the Russian menace. Travis spent his fragmentary four or five minutes talking about the urgent need to explore the asteroids, buy his book, and fund his research center. Some of his pictures got on, completely out of sync with what he was saying. But it was all over quickly; he just hoped no one at the convention had been watching.

After the show he felt tired and in need of a shower, but Cartwright had gotten excited about asteroids and wanted to talk about beating the Russians to them. Charlotte's Sumitomo stopped itself in front of the hotel and Travis got out of the car while Cartwright was still in midsentence.

He opened Cartwright's door, and when the Australian paused to say thanks, Travis said, "Dr. Cartwright, I'll be generous and say you're shootin' your mouth off about trivial chickenshit. But I'm not rulin' out the possibility that you're a paranoid schizophrenic. So why don't you stick to fiction, bud?"

Turning his back on the affronted novelist, Travis walked around the car and stuck his head in Charlotte's window. "You want to learn more about astronauts, leave this thing with the doorman. I'll buy you a drink." She gave him a wet-lips stare that lasted a second and a half, then got out of the car, tossing its start card to the nearest guy in a uniform.

He bought her the drink in his room, Jack Daniel's in a bathroom glass with cylindrical ice cubes, and before she finished it he peeled up the blue plastic skirt and worked a long time, three or four times the duration of the video show, it seemed, before he got the little spurt of unconsciousness he was seeking. He told her to call him tomorrow and he would teach her more about astronauts, if she was still interested, and he gave her a hundred-dollar bill to get her car back from the doorman. After she left he went into the bathroom and sat on the toilet lid, swallowing wave after wave of hot spit until the nausea subsided—he refused to vomit, he hadn't vomited since he was eighteen years old and had taken a charging tackle's helmet under his wishbone while he was looking for somewhere to throw the football—and then he packed his bags and went downstairs to pay his bill, and took a cab to the airport.

In the same year, riding on *Starfire*'s glowing wings, NASA's trajectory climbed smoothly upward toward dreams of ever larger programs, ever larger possibilities: an expanded presence on the moon, a permanent Mars base, exploration of the Jovian satellites, and, perhaps somewhere along the way, a visit to an asteroid.

Taylor Stith rose too, by several floors; after the prototype had gone into construction, Taylor had been in on every detail of mission planning and crew selection. By the time the president with whom he had once shaken hands was well started on his second term, Taylor had befriended two or three of his likely successors. Now Taylor was director of the entire Johnson Space Center, and scuttlebutt had it he was soon to be nominated administrator of the agency itself. It was a rumor he squelched firmly, and as often as he could.

Linwood doused a mound of mesquite chunks with half a can of starter fluid and tossed in a match. An orange fireball rose above the kettle, hot enough for Jimmy Giles to feel it six feet away. "One of these days you're going to blow us all to pieces, Linwood."

Linwood lifted a singed eyebrow. "Speaking globally, Colonel, I'd say there's a greater risk of you blowing us all to pieces."

"Why, Linwood. Peace is my profession." He slapped a butcher-paper package down beside the spare ribs and chicken parts on the picnic table, unwrapping it to reveal a stack of slick red sausages.

Linwood eyed them with deep suspicion.

"Homemade, by me," Jimmy explained. "Separate the links. Give 'em about eight minutes, turning frequently. Watch for flare-ups from dripping fat. And let the fire die down first."

Linwood turned his long, quiet stare on Jimmy. "Perhaps I should take notes."

"How did the resident pyromaniac get assigned to be chef, anyway?"

"No one else volunteered."

"Would a beer cool you off?"

"A gracious offer, gratefully accepted."

Jimmy headed off to where the coolers were stacked in

the lee of the dunes a few yards away. He and Linwood were
the oldest members of Robin's crew—Jimmy was forty-two
and Linwood was in his mid-fifties—and unlike the others,
they were old enough to have ridden out career changes and
more than one shift in government policy. Despite their differences, it made for an odd bond between them. Linwood,
the reformed weapons designer, favored new initiatives to
remove a quarter century's accretion of weapons from space,
an attitude Jimmy thought was naive. For his part, the retired if not reformed fighter jock voted the USAF party line,
favoring an increase in space-based defenses, using arguments Linwood regarded as disingenuous. But they managed
to keep their discussion friendly, recognizing that they were
soldiers in the same long campaign, the conquest of space
itself.

Jimmy passed his wife, Eleanor, who was reclining under
a beach umbrella in her one-piece floral-patterned swimsuit,
guarding her freckled white limbs from the sun. He smiled
cheerily, but she didn't look up from her volume of short
stories; she was ostentatiously keeping her own company.

The two Giles daughters, in their early teens, were not so
reserved; they splashed in the sluggish surf nearby and
rooted enthusiastically in the viscous yellow sand after God
knew what living creatures, using the entertainment of Linwood's dark-eyed grandsons, a five-year-old and a three-
year-old, as an excuse to revert to their own earlier child-
hoods.

Jimmy dug a couple of bottles of Pearl out of the ice in
the cooler. A ski boat's jet howled far out on the glassy surface of the Gulf; he glanced up to see Melinda driving the
boat flat out, towing Spin behind her. From the look of the
fancy figure eights she was cutting, she was doing her best to
toss Spin off his slalom ski. Spin was unperturbed; he clattered over the puny waves, sliced the wake, and slid up
alongside the boat at sixty klicks before hauling back, dig-
ging in, and shooting up a ten-meter rooster tail. Before long

they'd trade and he'd be driving the boat just as wildly as she was, trying to throw her. They spent a lot of energy trying to outdo each other.

Robin must have been like that when she first stormed NASA, Jimmy thought, complete with Melinda's legs-braced, Annie Oakley, I-can-do-anything-better-than-you-can stance toward the world. Pintsize Melinda hadn't been blessed with Robin's unshakable inborn determination, but she made up for it with bravado. Luckily for her self-image, Melinda's intellectual quickness meant that she really could do things better, lots of things.

At that physical edge where Melinda's intellect made her cautious, Spin, by contrast, seemed to lack a reasonable sense of self-preservation. He didn't risk other people's lives, but there were times when he seemed to think of himself as a piece of expendable machinery. Jimmy wondered how much that contributed to the fact that Spin was the best pilot Jimmy had ever met.

Two years ago, flying a chase plane, Spin had led a space shuttle with a freaked-out guidance transponder to a night landing in a thunderstorm, precisely duplicating the shuttle's glide rate with his tiny jet while staying close enough in front of the big unpowered glider for the shuttle commander to follow him down visually.

That adventure had passed into legend. Only once had Jimmy seen—on a piece of ancient sixteen-millimeter film transferred to chip—a piloting feat to match it; it was a clip of Neil Armstrong testing an early, crude version of the original lunar lander. Armstrong rode an ejection seat on an open platform, steering by joy stick. The horribly unstable machine rose fifteen or twenty meters above the concrete pad on its rocket exhaust and suddenly flipped upside down and fell. But Armstrong was gone in the millisecond before the thing tilted quite halfway over, ejecting himself sideways to a bone-crushing landing—the kind pilots call good, one he could walk away from. Had he waited to think, Armstrong would have shot himself headfirst into the ground. Spin had reflexes like that—faster than thought. And like Armstrong, he wasn't always very quick with his sentences.

Back at the barbecue kettle, Linwood's wife, Jeri, had joined Linwood beside the still-swirling flames. Jeri was a skinny, tanned woman who often got a mischievous look in her eye when she peeked at Linwood; Jimmy wondered if they really were what they seemed, that mythical rarity, a lasting couple still much in love.

They were talking to one of their daughters and her husband; more precisely, the young husband seemed to be delivering himself of a speech. The younger couple—Jimmy had just met them and had already forgotten their names— were of a different cut than Linwood and Jeri, both of them doughy and pale, their sour expressions reminding Jimmy of his own wife; he knew they disapproved of Linwood zipping about in space at his advanced age.

Jimmy nodded and smiled. "Here you go, maestro," he said, handing Linwood the beer during a second's pause in the lecture. Linwood inclined his head toward Jimmy but said nothing. His close-mouthed expression indicated the discussion in progress was one he intended to stay out of. "If you folks are thirsty, I'll be glad to make another trip to the cooler," Jimmy offered affably.

"Thanks, Colonel, but we're just on our way," said Linwood's chubby daughter, tugging at her husband's arm.

"You're not going to skip dinner!" Jimmy feigned disappointment. "I made enough sausages to feed an army."

The daughter ignored his implied invitation. "Your girls have been wonderful with Jean and Marcel."

"Nice of you to say so. Course, they love it. No boys their age to chase—playing with little kids is the next best thing."

At which the sallow son-in-law appeared affronted. "That seems to suggest that women have a rather limited set of roles to play in life, Colonel Giles."

"Did I say that?" Jimmy recalled too late that the young

man was a newly licensed psychiatrist. He glanced at Linwood. "Maybe I'd better defer this matter to our commanding officer."

"A remark *in itself* suggestive of the peculiar personality dynamics of this group," the son-in-law said vehemently to Linwood, as if scoring a point. "Really, sir—"

"Henry, please," said the daughter.

"Where *is* Robin?" Jeri inquired pertly. "I thought I saw her drive into the parking lot ten minutes ago."

"I'll check," Jimmy said. "Nice to see you folks." He cleared out fast. Jogging up the slip face of the nearest dune, carrying his beer, he trudged through wiregrass to the sand-drifted edge of the asphalt parking lot. Sure enough, there was Robin's silver Porsche with its rear end open, and she with her head stuck under the engine cover.

"That you, James?" she muttered as he joined her behind the car. She already had the turbine's cowling off and was inspecting the compressor rotor.

"What's the trouble?"

"I've been hearing a little whiffle at high r.p.m.'s. Erosion on the blades, I think." She looked up at him as if this were a matter of pressing concern.

"Hold it right there," he ordered. "You have grease on your chin." He fished a linen handkerchief from the hip pocket of his shorts, wet it with beer, and rubbed her face. Then, leaning across the hot metal, he kissed her.

"Mmm," she said. "Now we both smell like a tavern."

Early on, observing Robin from afar, Jimmy had shared in the consensus around JSC that Robin Braide was calculating and hard, an unsmiling pragmatist. Working with her, however, he had found that this impression—while not wholly inaccurate and even, in part, deliberately fostered by Robin herself—missed the point.

Which was that Robin wasted no time trying to get people to like her. Indeed, she sometimes seemed to prefer not to deal with people at all, unless together she and they could make progress on some specific task. Her immediate superiors were essential to that effort, of course, as were the pertinent technicians and managers on any mission—but most important of all was her crew. To understand, to get inside each member of her crew on a deep level was, to her, a primary task, one that made all other tasks doable.

For those in her inner circle Robin's curiosity and warmth and advice could be overpowering, and some privately minded persons assigned to her past crews had proved unequal to the intense demands of the relationship; they got divorced. But Jimmy, to his consternation, responded quite differently. He fell in love. Against every sensible instinct and consideration of logic, so did she.

Jimmy was a Catholic, a serious one, and after the first rush of sensation and emotion he was left with an awful residue of guilt. He considered resigning Robin's crew, resigning his NASA assignment. What could he give as a reason if not the truth? The priest to whom he finally and so desperately confessed was moved to take matters firmly in hand and insist that Jimmy *not* confess to his wife. That he was heartily sorry for his sins and intended not to repeat them was enough for now. Later, when things had cooled off and there was no danger that the marriage would be destroyed, Jimmy could tell all if he felt he must.

The advice was necessary because, as the priest suspected, things were nowhere near cooling off. Robin and Jimmy met in bars in Houston or Galveston to have one-last-mature-adult-conversation, conversations that inevitably ended in hotel rooms. Robin herself began to learn the meaning of guilt, watching its effect on her lover. She had had disastrous affairs before—all her affairs, and marriages, could rightly be called disasters—but never had she foolishly allowed one to so closely approach the center of her professional life.

In Robin Jimmy found a bold and caring sensuality he had

never experienced, a judicious disregard of unexamined values, a celebration of the flesh; in him she found a probing concern that awakened dependencies she had long suppressed. She knew she could not depend on him in the small ways that mates need to depend on each other, even as she knew he would stake his life for hers. What had begun in thoughtless attraction had developed into emotional addiction.

They kissed again, quickly, and she put her head down and started busily remounting the engine cowling. "Good news, James," she said, as if nothing had passed between them.

"What would that be?"

"We're it."

"We're. . . ?"

"We've got the ops flight. Our crew. Taylor called me into his office this morning."

Straightening, he banged his head on the hood. "That's great! That's just great!" He let out a long whoop and holler and jumped up and down. "We showed 'em! We showed 'em all! Good for you!"

She raised her head and shushed him. "Strictly confidential. Pretend I didn't tell you first, okay? I want to tell everybody at once."

"Darn, you're good! Robin, that's the greatest news. The greatest."

"I think so too," she said simply.

His enthusiasm was boundless. "I feel like my life is really going to be *worth* something now, you know what I mean?"

"Jimmy, your life is worth everything." Her response was quick, intense. "Go slow."

At that, he calmed. "Okay, I'm overdoing it."

"Yes, you are. Things can change."

"I know things can change, maybe better than you.

But *Starfire* . . . we're the first string. No matter what happens."

"Yeah." She ducked her head down. "Help me put this two-hundred-thousand-dollar pile of scrap back together, will you?"

"Sure." He stuck his head back under the hood. After five minutes of greasy work he asked, "How *do* you afford German iron, anyway? On your salary."

"I don't eat out much. I wash my uniforms in the sink."

Shadows lengthened, a breeze ruffled the Gulf, and the sun was a broken egg yolk running into the dunes.

The astronauts and their families sat around a campfire in the park-approved fire pit, which was fueled with chemically impregnated, compressed sawdust—there being no significant quantities of driftwood on these shores. Jimmy's daughters made the rounds of the circle showing everyone the treasures they had collected, pebbles that needed to be wet to show their subtle colors, broken crab shells, shattered urchins, one tiny but perfect sand dollar. Their mother sat by herself in the shadows.

Jeri's mood was apprehensive; her attention seemed far away. She and Linwood were huddled beside the fire, clinging silently, like two wet monkeys in a rain forest.

Spin and Melinda sat on opposite sides of the fire, avoiding each other. Spin had inadvertently dragged Melinda over a sandbar, and she was still angry from the fright of looking down and seeing the fin of her slalom ski skidding a centimeter above packed sand that, had it caught, would have sent her flying and likely broken her neck.

They all peered into the flames and sipped at their coffees or beers or sodas and whispered and laughed or thought their private thoughts, until Robin got up and said she had an announcement to make. "But only if everybody here swears to keep the secret." She looked at the Giles girls and they nodded solemnly.

Then she told them that theirs would be the first crew to drive a manned spaceship to the inner solar system, to launch satellites at the sun, to soar above the clouds of Venus. Some were excited by the news, some were made pensive. But Jimmy's exultation was fierce, untrammeled by fear. For months the grip of Earth and its obligations would be loosened. He would leave his guilt behind.

THE
ROCK

The western sky was rosy with the glow of sundown; the lights of the nearest cities, sprawling El Paso and Juarez 200 kilometers to the west, were far beyond the arid horizon. The headlights of a new Mistral convertible swept jackrabbits off the lonely road as it climbed one of the higher of the stumpy volcanic buttes Texans are pleased to call the Davis Mountains.

To escape light—the lights of cars and billboards and all-night hamburger stands and, especially, suburban street-lamps—ground-based observatories in the late twentieth century had fled to the loneliest mountains on Earth, to Hawaii, Chile, Peru, and elsewhere, until only two good optical observatories remained in all of North America: one in lonely Baja; the other, the University of Texas's McDonald Observatory in the Davis Mountains. Mount Locke was a diminutive peak, but one blessed with a transparent sky.

Inside the car, a weary Travis Hill was making an effort to keep his mind on an amiable debate with his passenger, a young science reporter named Harriet Richards, who had been sent out from Washington by National Public Video on a year-end astronomy roundup. Richards had a smooth round face capped with fashionably short black hair; short as it was, her hair still sprouted wayward stiff strands which she was forever swiping at or patting down, gestures that tended to undercut her efforts to play tough. She was new at her job, fresh from six months as a science reporter on a West Coast fax daily, and her news editor at NPV had given her a safe place to start—Travis Hill was a colorful public figure with a pretty picture book on the best-seller list, always a good interview, who never turned down publicity for his Asteroid Resource Center.

Travis had gone down to greet the young woman at the heliport in the dude-ranch resort town of Fort Davis a couple of hours earlier, treating her to a prime rib dinner with persimmon pie for dessert, trying to soften her up with Texas jokes and NASA war stories and a bottle of Rio Grande Valley red. But she was a grinning skeptic, this kid reporter, wise to him, bright and quick to nail anything that smacked of press agentry. "Why waste public money flying to an asteroid?" she persisted in asking, probing the sore spot, phrasing it a little differently each time she asked.

In the car, she phrased it like this: "I read somewhere that the mass of all the asteroids easy to reach from Earth wouldn't amount to the top two or three centimeters of the continents."

"Miz Richards, you got any idea what a layer of Earth dirt two centimeters deep would be worth, if you could process it economically? Or even two centimeters of *ocean*. Processin' the asteroids would be a hell of a lot cheaper and easier. Some are damn near pure nickel and iron, and some are rich in metals, especially in the platinum group, that are rare on Earth's surface but abundant in asteroids."

"How do you know what the asteroids are made of if nobody's been to one?"

"Nobody's visited, in person, an asteroid that's freely orbiting the sun. But we do have samples of Phobos and Deimos from the Mars expeditions—both of Mars's moons are asteroids, captured by the planet. And Navigator II brought back samples of Phaethon. And we've been collectin' meteorites for a couple of centuries now, some of them pretty well protected from the weather—the ones exposed on the

Antarctic glaciers. We look at the spectral characteristics of these samples in the laboratory, and sometimes we see the same spectrum coming through the telescope from an asteroid—bingo, we've got a pretty good idea what it's made of. I'll show you some of that work, by the way, that's what we've been doing up here for the last three days."

"So some of them are valuable. Unique, even. Maybe the asteroids should be preserved, declared a space wilderness area?"

Travis glanced at the crop-headed youngster, whose raised eyebrows suggested mischief. "You moonlightin' for the Sierra Club?"

"Just asking questions," the reporter said primly.

"So happens I agree with you. Certain asteroids should be set aside, left untouched, for historical and scientific reasons. Ceres, the first to be found, and Phaethon, the one that most closely approaches the sun—others like that. Which is not to say that we shouldn't visit them. As for exploitation, what I'm proposin' at this stage is purely exploratory. We need to survey that wilderness."

"I've read that some asteroids are easier to reach than our own moon. If they're so important, why haven't we sent a human expedition to one yet?"

"Excellent question, and I hope you'll address it to the highest levels at NASA. The answer you'll get will be in terms of launch windows and priorities. At times Phaethon is very easy to get to, even with primitive rockets. But somehow there's always been somethin' more important for NASA to do when the launch window comes around."

"You'd like to change those priorities."

"You bet your ass . . . uh, ma'am."

"The major benefit of asteroid mining would not be to Earth," the young woman persisted, unperturbed. "Isn't the principal reason for surveying the wilderness, as you put it, to get ready for expansion into space?"

"Miz Richards, the point is to preserve the environment

of the home planet. We probably oughta stop breedin' and eatin' and diggin' and pollutin', but it might also help to expand into space. So the point is to do both at the same time." Despite his weariness, Travis was getting heated. "And that's why we need to survey the asteroids, dammit!"

Richards was silent a moment, and Travis glanced at her suspiciously. She was fussing with her recorder; caught, she looked up and patted a strand of black hair. "Excuse me, Professor Hill, but that's the first time this evening you've cut the charm. Said how you feel so I believed it. I just wanted to make sure it was on the record."

Travis sighed and settled back. "Call me Travis. Kid."

The first stars gleamed in the clear southwestern sky as Travis parked the Mistral beside a lime green fire truck beneath the biggest dome on the peak. He led the way into the control room of the 272-centimeter reflector, where a man and woman sat, wearing wool shirts and down jackets against the rapidly cooling December night. Travis introduced the man as the observatory's telescope driver and the woman as an associate from the Asteroid Resource Center. Then he excused himself and went back outside.

Doris from ARC was a large blonde who wore pink plastic-rimmed goggles. "We're looking at spectral data from specific Trojan asteroids," she explained, waving at a jagged graph on a flat screen, "for a couple of reasons. Trying to pin down their chemical constituents by comparison with laboratory samples. Also trying to determine their rotational periods. The base-line work on this was done back in the eighties, but a lot of fancy algorithms have come along since then, so we're having another look."

"Why are you interested in rotation rates?" Richards asked.

"We're curious about where these asteroids came from, where they've been, how often they've been hit, the perturbation effects of the gravity of other planets," Doris replied.

"System dynamics. The way the rocks are spinning constitutes a kind of cryptic memory of solar system history, if we can unwind the data. With enough number crunching, we can make a start."

"Sounds tedious," said the reporter.

"I don't agree, and I would if anybody would—I'm supposed to be an astrophysicist. Stars and galaxies were my thing, not puny bits of rock and ice. But the oldest asteroids are made of exactly the same stuff as the stars. And they contain clues to the origin of the solar system and the Earth, and thus to the origin of human life. Also to our future." Her words were energetic, but she'd obviously stated this argument often. "Deciphering those clues *is* time-consuming, but I can't imagine any payoff more exciting."

The young reporter looked at the astronomer's shining, earnest face and nodded politely. "Yeah." Travis came back into the room from whatever he'd been doing outside. Richards glanced at him. "You people give good quotes."

"We aim to please." Travis smiled vaguely; he seemed to have lost interest in the proceedings.

"Travis, did you look at the IAU faxgrams yet?" Doris asked him. There was a playful quality to her voice, as if she'd arranged a surprise party.

He missed her excitement. "Hm? Anything interesting?"

"I think so, yes. Right there on the console."

Travis picked up the curling yellow scrap of paper. It was headed "Central Bureau for Astronomical Faxgrams, International Astronomical Union." Beneath the Cambridge, Massachusetts, fax block was an identifying year and letter code. "The following asteroidal object was discovered by R. Rouse and N. Kline in analysis of CCD recordings taken on the 2.2-m UH telescope at Mauna Kea." Dates, observed coordinates, and a table of calculated orbital elements were appended. Travis's eyes skimmed the fax.

"What's that?" the reporter asked.

Travis rubbed his face. "Notice of a new asteroid. Found

a couple of days ago by Rouse and Kline at Mauna Kea. That pair's the most systematic team of asteroid hunters in the world."

"Isn't that news?" Richards was fumbling with her recorder. "Isn't it pretty rare?"

"No, we get notices like this dozens of times a year." He let the paper fall to the console. "The International notifies all interested parties whenever somebody gets a fix on a new rock."

"Travis, did you look at the elements?" Doris was staring at him, upset now and trying not very well to hold it back.

He heard the edge in her voice and saw the angry emotion. He picked up the fax again. He studied it for half a minute before comprehension dawned. "Son of a bitch." Travis handed the fax to the middle-aged telescope driver. "Can we have those coordinates, Wally?"

"Want 'em now?" With his turquoise eyes and turquoise and silver belt buckle, the weather-beaten technician looked more the Marlboro man than the astronomer.

"If you'd be so kind."

Wally spat something black on the floor and turned to his console. Motors hummed, the data screens scrambled, the massive dome slid, and the tall telescope tilted to new celestial coordinates.

They waited impatiently for the telescope to settle on its target, low in the southern sky. Travis looked at Doris sheepishly. "Thanks. And I owe you an apology."

"No sweat, boss."

"So what's the fuss?" asked Harriet Richards, frustrated.

Travis took the fax and handed it to Doris. "This is yours. Tell her about it."

Doris turned to address Richards, whose sense of timing had told her to aim her pistol-sized video camera and press the record button. "If these orbital elements are correct, this asteroid must have the most eccentric orbit anybody's ever seen. It's practically falling right into the sun."

"Yeah, so what?" Richards pressed. "I mean, why is that important?"

"Lots of reasons. That couldn't be a stable orbit, so this thing might have an interesting history. Practically speaking, it's got a substantial orbital velocity—and it's going to approximate an Earth encounter on the way in."

"Forget hitting the Earth, she was just trying to wake me up." Twelve hours later, Harriet Richards was in an editing suite in the NPV headquarters in Washington, cutting her story together. "Keep the bite where she says it's falling into the sun."

"It's not going to hit the Earth?" the editor asked.

"Not even close—fifty times farther away than the moon." Richards was an authority now; she had the facts and she would happily hit you over the head with them.

"Oh?" the editor murmured.

"Anyway, I mention it in the stand-up at the end. Find me Hill, in front of the dome."

The editor tapped keys; the machine clicked and the screen displayed Travis, dramatically posed in a low-angle shot with the dome of the telescope rising behind him, glowing faintly in starlight.

". . . whether its a rocky asteroid or a burnt-out comet or something in between, still it's certainly one of the most unusual small bodies ever discovered," Travis was saying. "Let me emphasize the excellent work by my colleagues, Rouse and Kline—"

"Want me to cut out this bit about his brilliant colleagues?" the editor asked, freezing the image.

"Yeah. If these guys had their way, every science story would be a list of other people's names—"

Travis unfroze and continued speaking. "Our own preliminary work, which you witnessed just within the last hour here, suggests that the geology of the thing is unique. And we're in great luck—great timing—this country has a ready spacecraft capable of the enormous velocity changes—"

"You want to stick your cut-away question in there? About 'How are we going to get a closer look?'"

"You want I should let you do this yourself?"

"Sorry. Didn't mean to interfere, but it's just another talking-head piece to me," the editor said complacently. "I mean, as long as the thing isn't going to hit the Earth . . ."

"There's more of a story here than you think," said Richards, patting her hair. "That guy Hill would give his left nut to get a ride on *Starfire*—at least he worked hard to give me that impression. Maybe both nuts, considering how much radiation he claims he's taken."

The editor laughed; tough-talking little girls gave him a kick. "Maybe if he threw in a lung and a kidney. I cut a couple of pieces on *Starfire* already. Everybody wants a ride."

Richards looked at the image of Travis on the screen. "I'm not saying he'll make it. I'm just saying it could be fun to watch the fireworks."

The story appeared on home screens across the nation the same evening. Earlier in the day, the science pages of the more comprehensive fax dailies, like the *Global Post* and *New York–Los Angeles Times,* had carried brief mentions of the newly discovered asteroid with the unusual orbit. The science journals, of course, despite their electronic publishing capacities, would not get to the story for days.

Travis Hill found himself on every video screen, in a story filed by NPV reporter Harriet Richards and picked up by the commercial carriers. "The asteroid's not exactly a flying gold mine," he said, in response to his interviewer's question, "but it could be a flying platinum mine. The main thing is, we have the chance to see for ourselves."

Oh, Professor Hill? How would we do that?

"We're in great luck—great timing—this country has a

ready spacecraft capable of the enormous velocity changes needed to actually visit the object."

But *Starfire's* missions are already scheduled for a year or two in advance, Professor Hill.

"That's right. As a matter of fact, *Starfire's* first operational mission, scheduled only eighteen months from now, is to launch a pair of solar satellites—the ship's great power will be used to overcome the Earth's orbital speed and launch these satellites directly into orbit around the sun. That same power can be used to match speed with the new asteroid—*without* impinging on *Starfire's* solar mission. This is a bonus. An opportunity that comes along maybe once in a quarter of a million years—which, incidentally, is about how long the human species has been evolving from its primitive ancestors."

But is NASA prepared to explore the surface of an asteroid, Professor Hill? Is there anyone among the present crews with the necessary expertise?

"No, an experienced exogeologist will have to be added to *Starfire's* crew—virtually the only significant change in the present mission plan at this stage."

An experienced exogeologist such as yourself, Professor Hill?

"There are many good men and women in this field." He grinned his most engaging grin. "I'd hate to say I wasn't one of them."

Cut.

As soon as she said *cut* that night, as soon as he was off camera, Travis swayed with fatigue. He had paid his respects to his fellow astronomers, the asteroid's real discoverers, but he doubted his acknowledgments would ever make it onto the air. He was in danger of becoming one of those scientists who make themselves so famous as to arouse the bitter jealousy of their colleagues. Travis regretted the inevitable fallout, but he didn't let it deter his sales pitch; he hoped that

Rouse and Kline, whom he knew well, would not hold it against him.

He could not have predicted what actually happened. Because of the lucky timing of the newsbite, and perhaps because of his rugged good looks and his practiced video charm, Travis suddenly found himself owning an asteroid.

"Seems a shame to bring you all the way to Washington when I practically live in the next county"—Jack Fassio pounded Taylor Stith's shoulder heartily—"but I just can't seem to get home as often as I should."

"You may be seated right away, Senator, if you wish. Your usual table." The maître d's cheek muscles bunched and his purple lips stretched, but the smile touched his eyes not at all.

Fassio gave Taylor a shove with his right hand and thrust out his left, aiming him toward the back of the crowded restaurant. He followed close behind Taylor, nodding at curious diners on both sides of the narrow room. "Larry . . . Marge," he murmured, throwing in one enthusiastic, "Hey, how're *you*?" when he spotted a young woman reporter whose name escaped him.

The senator's usual table was up against a pink plush banquette in a corner; two waiters jerked it away from the wall so the senator and his guest could slide into their seats. Heavy linen, heavy silver, heavy wall mirrors mottled with black flecks of oxidation, heavy sauces on raw meat—it was the kind of lunch place that thrilled Taylor Stith even as it gave him indigestion. The mirrored walls were functional, for seeing and being seen, the restaurant's raison d'être.

But Taylor had to wait through a drawn-out meal, frequently interrupted by Fassio's kibitzers and fawners, to learn what signal the senator was here to send. After a frothy dessert, Fassio lit up a brown Sherman cigarette and leaned forward over the litter. "Taylor, you ought to know that our committee's put out the word to the president's staff. We insist on being presented with a *quality* nominee when Rosie steps down. You're on our short list."

"I'm honored, sir. Very honored."

"Not surprised, I hope."

"I've heard rumors of Rosie's retirement. I haven't put a lot of credence in them."

"Commendable caution. But a good administrator's got to keep his ear to the ground."

"I certainly appreciate this opportunity to prepare, Senator."

"Hell, nothin' to prepare *for*. Your record speaks. You came out for *Starfire* when everybody else was sticking their heads in the sand. That's leadership. Your innovations—permanent crews, specially—that's brilliant administration, friend. Shuts up the whiners who scream favoritism when the astronauts have too much say in their own assignments." A miasma of sugary smoke spilled from the senator's lips.

"You've looked into this closely." Taylor was turning as pink as the upholstery from basking in flattery, and from the effort of breathing.

"My job." Fassio was a tall man, with the attractiveness of an aging boy. He leaned back and pulled on the brown cigarette, holding the smoke as he rasped, "Enough of that. How's the solar satellite mission shaping up?"

"At this point we seem to be ahead of schedule." Taylor settled deeper into the booth. "JPL and Goddard are nearing completion of the two satellite spacecraft. Our training programs are going into high gear. *Starfire* is in tiptop shape. We've given ourselves a year, but we'll be ready before that."

"Handled those guidance problems?" Fassio asked gruffly.

"Those were minor hardware glitches, sir." Taylor did his best to be as gruff as Fassio, and reassuring; surely the man would have been horrified to hear anything other than that matters were well in hand. "Minor in terms of fixing them. And we're doing extensive simulations."

"And the crew? Made your choice?"

Taylor smirked. "Not officially. Not supposed to let that cat out of the bag quite yet."

Fassio shrugged but did not smile. Smoke trickled from his nostrils.

Noting the impassive face, Taylor added, "But as long as it doesn't get out . . ." He tugged at the skin under his jaw. "Braide and her people handled the initial flight test superbly."

"No doubt. The first operational mission would be a fitting reward."

"A confirmation of their good work, let's say. As a matter of fact, I revealed my decision to Commander Braide last week. In strictest confidence."

Fassio nodded. "Well done, Taylor. Proud you feel you can trust me." He drew on the cigarette. "Knew it already, of course. Keep *my* ear to the ground, too. By the way, what thought have you given to this asteroid rendezvous proposal?" Just as Fassio asked the casual question, he dropped cigarette ashes in his lap. For several seconds his attention was diverted—

—giving Taylor a moment to think. The best he could do when Fassio looked up at him with those handsome, cold eyes, though, was stall. "What's *your* thinking on an asteroid rendezvous, Senator?"

"Damn stupid to miss the chance," Fassio snapped. "Criminal, even." Fassio flicked his lighter at the tip of a fresh Sherman, inhaling slowly and blowing the smoke out his nose. "Some people don't like Professor Hill, he rubs them the wrong way—but nobody in NASA has given the slightest indication that they can think for themselves on

this, come up with their own plan." The cold eyes
flickered toward Taylor. "That's *exactly* why we need a
man like you in the top job. Somebody who's not afraid to
take a risk. And I'd say we're talking about something that
could affect the future of the whole human race here.
Wouldn't you?"

Tiny drops of sweat had appeared on Taylor's forehead,
beneath his fine brown hair. He twisted the heavy crystal
water glass between his fingers. "Senator, I have to take personal responsibility for this." Indeed he did; for the past
week Taylor had adamantly opposed any official commerce
with Travis Hill and had barred discussion of his proposals.
But he risked nothing by assuming that Fassio knew less
than he pretended. "Sometimes we get shortsighted, the
things we have to deal with day in and day out."

"An awesome responsibility."

"But the matter will be vigorously pursued. Starting today."

"Were it not for a few good men such as yourself . . ."
The senator let the rest of the sentence go, busying himself
crushing his cigarette and signaling the waiter for the check.

As Fassio was smearing his signature across the restaurant's bill, the woman reporter he'd hailed earlier approached their table. "Harriet Richards, Senator. National
Public Video."

"Of *course,* Harriet hon. You've met Taylor Stith?
Johnson Space Center?"

"At a distance . . . Sir." She nodded at Taylor, scrutiniz-
ing him. "I was wondering if either of you gentlemen would
care to comment about rumors of a forthcoming shift in
NASA administration."

"On the record or off?" Fassio asked, conveying posses-
sion of the knowledge she sought.

"On, of course. If you can."

"Can't say anything about administration. *Off* the record,

I'd say you can expect some exciting changes at NASA in the
near future. Wouldn't you say so, Taylor?"

Taylor jerked his head. Oh yes.

Fassio placed a phone call when he got back to his office.
"It's Jack. Just did a little mud wrasslin' on behalf of your
boy. . . . My pleasure. And Al, it's damn good to have some
support from the western counties for once. Where the hell
is Travis anyway? Tried to get him today. . . . Baja? Wrong
time to take a vacation. . . . Oh, the observatory. Well, tell
him to drag his ass back here when he can. Things are gonna
start movin'. Listen, you didn't send that reporter around
there at lunch time, did you? From NPV? . . . Didn't think
you'd do that to me. We don't want to push this tall story
about Rosie retirin' *too* hard. It's already back to him, d'ya
know? He's apoplectic"—Fassio chuckled—"thinks the
president is tryin' to send him a message!"

Travis wasn't at the observatory in Baja, although he
wouldn't have been surprised to hear his uncle claim he was.
Upon his return to Austin the week before, he'd been unexpectedly called out of town. . . .

With its bare fieldstone walls and white painted wood-
work, rough wool hangings and raw clay pots and weathered
ranch furniture, the roomy top floor of Travis's house made
for austere, handsome bachelor's quarters—the decorators
his mother had hired had seen to that. Somehow Travis
didn't feel at home there. He didn't spend much time at
home anyway.

On a corner two blocks away was a bar called the Big
Foot, named not for a mythical anthropoid but for a historical Texas Ranger, Big Foot Wallace, who had been real
enough even if the tales they told about him weren't all
strictly true. The Big Foot had once been real itself, having
catered to legislators and visiting ranchers and oilmen and

microchip wranglers for over a century, men who enjoyed the spaciousness of its lofty pressed-tin ceilings, its checkered black-and-white marble floor, its crudely carved bar, its good whiskey and overcooked steaks. Then entrepreneurs got hold of it. The tables got tablecloths, the waiters started wearing Western costumes, and the grub became *cuisine.* Japanese mushrooms. Garlic mayonnaise. A wine list you couldn't pronounce.

Travis used to like to go there anytime, but now he mostly liked to go there when he was in a bad mood. He'd sit at the end of the long bar and complain to Alex, the leathery old bartender who'd been kept on by the new owners because he looked like a cowboy, although he was a reformed pimp. After his fourth or fifth bourbon Travis might start to raise his voice a bit, which could be disturbing to the Big Foot's *nouvelle* clientele of tourists and real estate sales types and young professionals. Usually before that happened, Alex, just to keep his hand in, would have managed to introduce Travis to any unescorted lady who happened to be drinking that night, and everybody would go home happy, or at least quiet.

This night's lady needed no introduction. She was his mother.

"I don't intend to knock that drink out of your hand unless you make me," she said. Under her steel hair her eyes were agates.

"Why'ld you do that?" he asked, querulously, fear and the urge to grin somehow becoming one as he peered at her.

"To keep you from taking one more sip. Ever." She moved closer, until her glittering eyes were inches from his. "The universe gave you what we've been praying for, with a little help from the video. And Al got to Fassio," she whispered. "I tried to call you to tell you that. But it all amounts to horse manure if you're the boozer Al says you are."

"Hell, Ma," he said, his grin jerking at the corners of his

mouth. Maybe to test her, or maybe because he was so far gone, he started to raise the glass.

She stumbled against him with surprising force, and the heavy glass splintered on the marble floor. "Oh, goodness gracious! I'm mortified," she said for the benefit of the bartender, and to Travis, "I'm so terribly sorry, I believe I must have caught my heel. . . ."

Scandalized waiters surrounded them, dabbing at his jacket—twittering like fag ballet dancers in their tight denims and rayon cowboy shirts, so Travis thought, as he considered swinging at somebody. But some reality-tracking portion of his pickled brain urged him to remove himself quietly. He tossed a fifty on the bar—"Thanks furvrthn', Al"—and aimed himself gingerly at the door, supported on one side by a twenty-one-year-old refugee from the road company of *Billy the Kid* and on the other by his sixty-seven-year-old mother, both of them in better physical condition than he was.

They shoved him into the back of her white Cadillac, waiting at the curb with blowers whining. His older brother was at the wheel.

"Drivin' the getaway car, Sam?" Travis demanded. "Whatsamatter, no guts?"

"Ma said you'd probably want to swing on me," Sam said. "Anytime is okay with me, shithead."

Edna May got into the front seat. "Your mouth, Sam," she said. "Close it. There's to be nothing of this in the news."

"How long can you keep *him* out of it?" Sam grumbled, steering the lumbering luxury hydro into the traffic.

"Two weeks," she said. "While he dries out he's going to disappear. After that, if he crawls back into the bottle, no member of this family knows him."

"Hey, Ma," said Travis from the back seat, grinning again

even though nobody was looking or listening. He started to cry.

"And I don't want you talking to him, Sam," she continued, her eyes fixed forward. "Not when he's like this. As long as he's like this, he doesn't exist."

That was two weeks ago. The clinic was on Baja California's coast, north of La Paz, facing east toward nothing at all except salt water and the desiccated mountains of northern Mexico. Here near the beach a palm oasis had stood since prehistory in a cleft of the parched, banded rocks, visited only by iguanas and coyotes and huge black bees and *indígenas,* until taken over a few years back by a silver-haired homeopath with an elegant European accent and a following of ladies from Beverly Hills and Dallas. The suave doctor had built a stucco village, its style vaguely Indian pueblo, vaguely Greek island, astonishingly white in the merciless sun. He'd added a nine-hole golf course, planted a great many more palm trees, and expanded his services to include therapy for drug and alcohol abuse. The clinic did a booming business among those who needed a quick, anonymous boost back onto the wagon and could pay well for it. No statistics were kept on recidivism.

Travis was sweating hard, breathing hard, running hard along pearly sand. The unshaded desert sunlight was a weight on the crown of his unprotected skull. As his pace slowed, a fat drop of perspiration fell into his left eye, stinging mightily. He was put in mind of a time when he had been falling fast through hot thin air in a thermoplastic escape pod, thrilled to be courting death.

The secretly nourished thrill had resurfaced. Philosophers and doctors who had once struggled to make everything rational in terms of the Will would have called it a death wish. Travis thought of it as a parasite, an invasion he could never defeat, although—by exposing it to sunlight—he could perhaps suppress it long enough to keep it from killing him prematurely. He was willing to admit that his longing for elbow room fed his addiction, set him up for escapism, but he was not yet willing to admit that there was nothing to be said for the void.

Still, he had taken a first step away from the abyss. For the time being, he had dropped the booze. But it was easy to stop drinking in a setting so utterly unlike the normal context of his life. How easy would it be when he got back?

Travis's heart pumped fully, strongly, having responded to two weeks of abstinence, exercise, and solar radiation. Rationally, he felt good. Rather sadly good. He slowed to a walk, his chest heaving, hot sand roasting the tips of his toes, and headed for the palm-thatched cabana where one of the staff—white uniformed, quaintly reminding him of a launch technician—was handing out fruit juices and sparkling mineral waters.

A woman was waiting for him in the grove of palms near the cabana. He looked twice to make sure it was really her, his least expected visitor. Why would she come here? Why not overbearing Sam or his mother? But it was Bonnie.

"Hey, you look good," he said softly. And she did, muscular and brown in snug shorts and a yellow halter top, with a floppy straw hat casting a net of shadow over her blue eyes. He leaned forward to kiss her. She let him.

She looked at him seriously. "You too. Best I've seen you in a long time."

"I was stinking for a while."

"That's over," she said firmly.

"Easy for you to say."

"Oh, Travis . . . I'm sorry." She seemed momentarily speechless. "What's it been like? Was it . . . hard?"

"Yes and no. Not the way I expected. I'll tell you about it."

"We're all on your side." It was a fervent avowal.

"I know that. I appreciate it." He raised his eyebrows. "So? How come I'm so lucky?"

"I came to take you home."

"You're not who I expected."

"It had to be me, because there's a reporter been askin' questions about you, tryin' to talk to Sam and Edna May."

"Maybe I should just talk to him."

"Oh, Travis, after all this, everything everybody's done . . ." She stopped, confused. "Sorry. You're what's important."

"I know what you meant. Let's walk."

They took two bottles of water from the white uniformed boy in the cabana and headed down the beach, kicking at hot sand with sandaled feet. To their left aquamarine water scintillated in the hard midmorning light, the Sea of Cortez, across which the conquerors had sailed in search of the mythical golden island of California.

"It's a her," Bonnie said.

"Beg pardon?"

"The reporter. A woman. She's from public video."

"Oh. The one who broke the Apollo-object story. That was sort of a scoop for her, I guess. She's probably trying to do me a favor."

Bonnie looked at him, concerned, from the shadow of her sun hat. "She may already know you're here. She won't be doin' you any favors if she puts that around."

He was quiet again, stooping to pick up a bleached, broken sand dollar. After inspecting it, he tossed it into the surf. Ten meters offshore, on a black volcanic boulder emerging from the blue water, a lean cormorant held its wings delicately open to the sun. "You know what that bird's doing?"

"Looks like it's takin' a sun bath."

"Right. Makes a living catching fish, practically flying underwater. Every once in a while it has to dry out its wings." He gave her a lopsided grin and let her draw the analogy for herself. After a pause, he said, "You asked me what it was like down here. The hard part is, you get to do a lot of thinking. The other folks, uh, encourage it. And I have."

"About?" Apprehensive, she waited for him.

"Hard to get it all out at once." He was quiet a moment. "What I'm wondering is, do I really belong up there in space?" He cut off her nascent protest. "No, listen, that stunt I pulled when I bailed out. It made me kind of a movie hero . . . but by the odds I should have killed myself. It's occurred to me that maybe that's what I had in mind."

"You don't mean that."

"I think I do mean that."

"I don't like to hear that kind of talk. You made a bold choice, took a calculated risk. You acted like a man."

He laughed, genuinely amused. "My mother chose well, sendin' you. You sound just like her."

"Your mother's an admirable woman."

"I do admire her. But is it fitting for a man to arrange his life to suit others? Even his mother?"

"You always wanted to go into space, ever since I first knew you," she argued.

"There's other things I wanted, since I first knew *you*." He stopped and pulled her into his arms. She resisted, and he held her in tension, his gnarled hands clasped across the smooth, sun-warmed small of her back. "But you know something, Bonnie? I finally got it through my head that you really *aren't* gonna divorce Sam and marry me. Ever."

She avoided his eyes. Her voice was a hoarse whisper. "What does that have to do with gettin' you a ride on that rocketship?"

"This: I can stop waiting for you—living that part of my life for your sake. And I can stop tryin' to get back into space just to give my mother another trophy to nail up beside the shotgun. . . ."

"Travis—"

"I can start living for myself—really *do* science. Or hell, maybe even go into the business with Sam, if he'll have me."

She was still in his arms, and he didn't know whether she was deep in thought, or starting to cry, or rigid with fear or anger. Almost imperceptibly she relaxed, and her body grew heavy against his. Suddenly she pushed into him with startling energy. Her face came up, eyes closed, and her mouth sought his, open and wet.

Desire inflamed him—

—but after a moment settled into a kind of aching solidity, and then, as he had half expected would happen should this moment ever come, his desire slowly and completely dissolved, leaving a hollow in his breast. He separated himself from her with surprisingly little effort.

"How did you get here?" he asked.

"Drove to Del Rio and met a company helicopter. Pilot's waiting on the pad."

"Del Rio's a long drive from Austin."

She hesitated. "I don't have to get home tonight."

He gripped her arm and walked her toward the clinic. "Bonnie, I don't know what I'm doing . . . about anything. And I can't see any way out. You oughta go back home by yourself."

"Whether I go or stay, it won't change what just happened, Travis." Her voice was no longer a whisper, but so low he had to bend close to her to hear. "I do love . . . Sam. But I have to set my mind to it. With you, I always had to set my mind against it—ever since that first summer, the day you went back to military school without sayin' a word to me. I thought it would get easier. It gets harder."

"What kind of life could we have if I quit doin' what I do? What kind of life could we have if I keep *on*? Somethin' has to change for me, deep down."

"Somethin' *did* change. You want to be up there, even if you're tryin' to talk yourself out of it. Now you've got the chance."

"I didn't do it for myself." Even as he said it, he was aware of the undercurrent of petulance.

"You didn't bring yourself into the world, either." She stopped and faced him. "Grow up, Travis. Your mother can't make you do what you don't want to. Nobody can."

He studied her, watching minuscule beads of perspiration collect on the almost invisible down of her upper lip, refracting the sunlight into radiant miniature rainbows. He was conscious of the sweat trickling down his own back and arms, and his head felt light—whether with sunstroke or with unfocused possibilities, he would not have bet.

The frown muscles bunched around her transparent eyes. "You think I'm tryin' to bribe you, Travis?"

He flinched. "You know me too well to say that."

"Yeah, I guess." The hardness turned to puzzlement. "I think you are changed. Maybe you put away *too* many dreams."

He took her hand. They walked toward the village, which gleamed an illusory white through the palm grove.

The chopper bored through blue daylight, northeastward toward the Rio Grande. On final approach to Del Rio, Travis turned to Bonnie and asked for her car keys. When she gave them to him, he said he wasn't going back with her; he wanted her to let the chopper pilot take her on to the ranch, and he'd deliver the car later. They had things to talk about, he acknowledged, but he thought it would be better to talk about them later.

"So you're turnin' me down." She looked at him sadly. "Guess I oughta be thankful. What are you gonna do, Trav?"

"As the saying goes, I'm gonna take it one day at a time."

Fidgeting, Robin leaned forward on the beige couch in Stith's outer office to paw through the pile of faxzines on the coffee table: *Newstime, Aerospace Technology Weekly,* JSC's own *Space News Roundup.* Waiting irritated her—this meeting was unscheduled, and it was interfering with training— but she assumed she was here to learn why there had been such a long delay in the official announcement of her crew's appointment.

"You can go in now, Commander," said the secretary.

Stith was leaning against his desk, his arms crossed across his rep tie, studying her morosely. His office was as spare as ever, but wide, as befitted the director of the Johnson Space Center. Among its furnishings was a conference table laid out with yellow pads and fiber-tip pens, and in the middle, a portable CADPAD chartboard. Behind the table, a leathery, suntanned man wearing whipcords and a checkered cowboy shirt was getting to his feet as Robin entered.

"Robin, I'm sure you recognize Travis Hill."

"Oh yes," Robin said, smiling. "I was Capcom the day Professor Hill decided to test the emergency de-orbit system." She leaned across the conference table and thrust out her hand. Travis gripped it hard.

"You gave me a very lucky star, Commander Braide," Travis said, showing his teeth. "Even though it did have a strange name."

"People make their own luck. We were all proud of you, Professor Hill. In the corps."

"Name's Travis, like it was before."

"I'm Robin."

Stith cleared his throat. "Well, since we all know each other . . . please, let's sit down. Coffee?"

Robin and Travis declined the coffee. The three of them sat at the conference table, Stith at its head. "Professor Hill is here to explain his proposal to include a rendezvous with the recently discovered Apollo object, 2021 XA, in *Starfire*'s operational mission," Stith said, in what sounded like a rehearsed speech. "He and I have already discussed this at some length. Since it materially affects the mission plan, Robin, I would like you to get the gist of it at an early stage."

Again Stith studied her with that oddly flat expression, and even as she waited for him to say more he seemed to shrink back, sinking into his chair.

Robin's antennas were quivering; she noted that Stith had not suggested she was here to give advice, but only to listen. "Well, I'd certainly like to hear what, uh, Travis has to propose."

"I'll get right to it, then. Hope you'll go easy on me for repeatin' a lot of stuff you already know." He turned to the CADPAD's control board. "Let's see if I can make this thing move."

Travis pushed his chartboard around so that Robin could see it better: a yellow disk in the CADPAD's meter-square display represented the sun; four tiny white points close to it were the planets Mercury, Venus, Earth, and Mars, and much farther away, almost to the margin, a brighter point was Jupiter.

"I want to stress how peculiarly interesting this rock is. When Rouse and Kline spotted it, it was already well inside the orbit of Jupiter."

A pale orange point appeared between Mars and Jupiter.

"We tracked it for a few days and extrapolated its orbit.

Inclination's only about three degrees, eccentricity's an incredible point nine nine three. The damn thing is falling practically straight into the sun."

An orange line, representing the asteroid's track, reached out to kiss the solar disk.

"It's a pretty big rock, too. We can't get a good image yet, but the estimate is about nine kilometers for the major axis. Somebody surely would've seen it before, if it was in this orbit. It wasn't. Look what happens if we run the trajectory backward."

The orange line, extending out toward the edge of the screen, brushed the point of light that was Jupiter.

"See? Jupiter grabbed that rock out of space, less than a year ago, and threw it practically right at us."

"Now look at this." Travis shoved a set of printed graphs at her. "That's a radar shot. And that's speckle interferometry, and those others are spectroscopic studies, infrared studies. Definite differences between the poles. One end of the rock is real black, blacker than the black velvet they paint those bullfighters on. The other end is kind of blackish red. It looks like we got some kind of complex object here."

He shoved more documents across the conference table. His timing seemed calculated to let Robin study the data he was presenting not quite long enough, before flattering her with the assumption that she had absorbed it fully, then giving her more.

"Rotational period about fifteen hours. Kind of a lazy wobble, suggesting maybe the center of mass is off to one side. That's consistent with the notion that we've got something out of the ordinary here."

She studied the graphs until she felt she understood them, at least on a gut level. Yes, an unusual object. Very tight orbit around the sun. Off center, oddly colored. Interesting indeed. But no more graphs were forthcoming; she looked up at Travis, inquiring. He was staring at her expectantly.

"Hell, it's damned exciting, isn't it?" he said, his green eyes blazing. "We land on an asteroid, we take our samples,

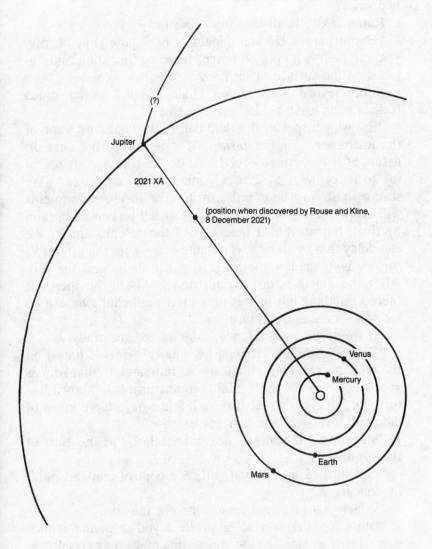

(?)

Jupiter

2021 XA

(position when discovered by Rouse and Kline,
8 December 2021)

Venus

Mercury

Earth

Mars

Detail of Travis's CADPAD, showing approximate position of planets on
December 15, 2020, when Apollo object 2021 XA is thought to have
encountered Jupiter.

we leave our experiments. Seismometers, maybe a gravity wave package, whatever the scientists think of. *Then* what happens?"

Robin said, "It all falls into the sun."

"Damn near!" He was gleeful. "Not quite, but oh my, yes, the heat is gonna be fierce, three or four thousand degrees on the surface. That asteroid's gonna *burn*."

Robin leaned back in her chair. "Which pretty much trashes your leave-behind experiments."

"But we get spectacular data before they go. And some of the instruments we put *inside*." Travis shoved the next diagram at her, a crosshatched oval object with a shaft reaching to its center. "Strictly schematic," he apologized. "We sink a shaft with laser pulse drills. The inside experiments will keep sending—not to Earth—Earth'll be behind the sun by then, but maybe to Mars—until the antennas melt. We can delay that by siting several antennas where the asteroid's surface is in shadow the longest as it rolls around the sun. After the antennas go, the instruments'll still be there. If there's anything left of this rock after perihelion, we can go recover 'em at some future time."

"It would be good science," she agreed, carefully.

"Robin," he said, clasping his sinewy wrinkled hands on the table and looking at her almost intimately, "that rock is gonna come closer to the sun than any object in known history. Leastways any that survived. Some objects we know of didn't survive—comets that got eaten—"

"Starprobe, of course," she interjected, "at the turn of the century."

"Got burned up when its attitude control crapped out," he concurred.

"Which is a principal reason for our mission."

"But even the two solar orbiters you're gonna launch won't come as close to the sun as this rock; they couldn't— and hope to last a year in that inferno."

"How would this asteroid rendezvous of yours fit in with the current mission profile?"

He grinned with all his teeth. "You're gonna like this." He pushed keys to animate the display. "This is your profile as currently planned, accordin' to the design study dated November last year"—Travis glanced at her inquiringly—"which is the latest I could get hold of."

She shrugged. "A few details have been refined. Nothing crucial."

"That's what Taylor said. Anyway . . ."

The lights that were planets moved ponderously in their nearly circular orbits, the Earth approaching that point on its orbit corresponding to early summer. "In June of next year, *Starfire* will do a retro burn to de-orbit Earth." As he spoke, a bright red dot appeared at Earth, quickly lengthening into a red line that curved inward toward the sun. "That puts the ship in free fall toward the sun, which would be about sixty-five days if she went all the way in."

Robin nodded agreement.

The red line lengthened inward, toward the orbit of Venus. "Long before she gets to the sun, a couple of weeks out, as she's approachin' Venus, *Starfire* deploys the two solar satellites," Travis said. "They continue in free fall, eventually usin' their on board engines to go into fixed orbits around the sun—one equatorial, one polar."

Two bright blue pinpoints of light blossomed and continued to fall toward the sun.

"After the launch, *Starfire* does another burn to Venus and gets a gravity boost back to Earth," he said. The red line looped around the bright dot that was Venus and headed back toward Earth. "A final brakin' maneuver and you're home, six weeks after you left." The red line rejoined the dot that was Earth.

Travis froze the completed diagram.

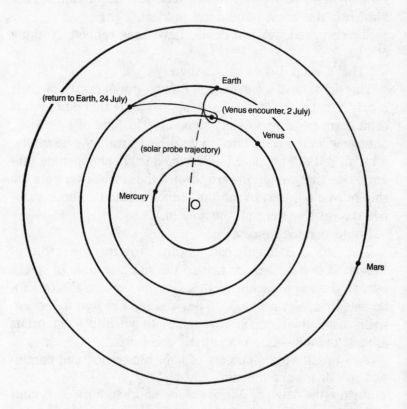

Detail of Travis's CADPAD, showing approximate position of planets on
June 10, 2023, scheduled date of *Starfire*'s mission to launch solar probes.

"You've got the big picture." Robin's tone was noncommittal.

He grinned. "But why am I wastin' your time tellin' you what you already know?" He poked at keys on the CADPAD console. "Excuse the primitive technology—just serves to underscore how beautifully simple this thing really is."

The screen went blank. The sun reappeared, and once more the inner planets were moving in their nearly circular orbits. "Your launch window is determined by free fall to Venus. But *Starfire* is so powerful, you've got considerable leeway in that. Look what happens if you delay launch by five weeks."

On the CADPAD, as the Earth reached the point corresponding to late August, the asteroid's orange line slid in from Jupiter, fast lengthening toward the sun. *Starfire*'s bright red spark appeared at Earth, stretching inward—to kiss the yellow line in tangent. "Now ain't that sweet?"

"The initial burn looks to be fuel-intensive," she said.

"Your initial burn is a couple of minutes longer because the rock has so many vees, incoming. You get four or five days on the asteroid before your delta-vee maneuver to reduce velocity so you can launch your satellites. Then you grab your Venus assist."

Travis was watching his own moving pictures—diagramming the departure from the asteroid, the launch of the solar satellites, the loop around Venus—and his glee seemed genuine, that of a kid who had just brought off a complicated card trick.

Pitching her cheerfully, Travis froze the display. "You get two missions for the price of about one and a half."

Robin glanced at Stith. "Has this been calculated?"

"Oh, yes," he murmured tiredly. "All well within rated margins."

Robin peered closely at Stith, who seemed to have drifted away from the conversation. That bothered her; even if he had already quizzed Travis extensively, it was not like Taylor

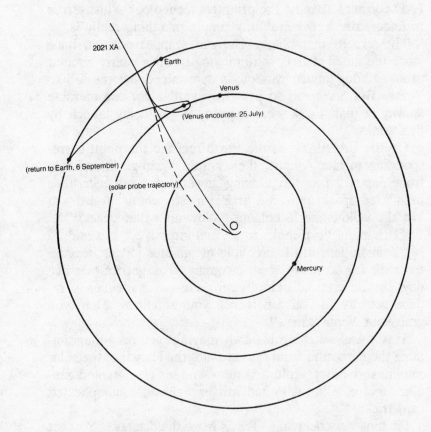

2021 XA

Earth

Venus

(Venus encounter, 25 July)

(return to Earth, 6 September)

(solar probe trajectory)

Mercury

Detail of Travis's CADPAD, showing approximate position of planets on
July 15, 2023, proposed launch date of *Starfire* mission to rendezvous with
Apollo object 2021 XA.

to miss an opportunity to get his criticisms on record in front
of a third party. She had participated in proposal reviews
where Stith had been more eager to prove that a job was
impossible than to talk about how it might succeed.

She turned back to Travis. "You're aware that *Starfire* is
an experimental vehicle—a dragster, a funny car, not a bus
or a truck, not even the family station wagon. It goes like a
bat out of hell over the short course, but total propulsion
mass is a concern in—"

He cut in. "You're sayin' it's overpowered and under-
fueled."

Stith winced at that, but Robin was watching Travis. "Let
me put it this way," she said. "When the Bell X-1 broke the
sound barrier, it shot its wad. It was a rocket engine with
wings, good for nothing except to go fast. We're not quite
that bad. We can carry a little extra weight; we can do some
useful work. But we can't afford to overreach our inherent
limitations."

"I'm not one to advocate overreachin'," Travis assured
her. "The mission profile I'm proposin' involves no risks that
aren't inherent in your current plan."

Robin uncapped a pen and started making notes on a
yellow pad, pretending to study Travis's presentation—although its implications, which went far beyond the paths of
bodies in space, were already clear. She was not the first
woman to command a U.S. spacecraft, but no woman before
her had been assigned so important a mission, or one more
coveted by NASA's cadre of qualified astronaut command-
ers—an assignment that hadn't been confirmed yet. Robin
Braide resembled Taylor Stith in one isolated trait: she combined an active intelligence with an exaggerated respect for
"systems," what some would call office politics, which had
done much to promote her rapid advancement within
NASA. And she knew when the fix was in.

After a moment's pause—for effect, studying her mostly
meaningless notes—she looked at Travis with eyes shining.

"Thanks for letting us see this. This is brilliant work." Then
she turned back to Stith. "The most exciting opportunity
I've seen in a *lifetime*," she said, staring at him, her tone of
certainty enlivened by the thrill vibrating beneath it. What
she said she meant, sort of, or else she could not have
brought herself to say it, but she laid it on thick. "An opportunity to do extraordinary science at virtually no cost beyond
the experiments and an accelerated training schedule. When
can we put Planning and Studies to work? My people will
want to get started on the new routines ASAP."

Stith seemed mildly surprised. "We're still discussing the
proposal."

"Oh, we're past the proposal stage," she said with conviction, taking some satisfaction from Stith's guilty look. Indeed they were. "That's how strongly I feel about it."

"That's . . . excellent, then." Stith glanced at Travis. "I'm
inclined to get this into detailed analysis as soon as possible.
How flexible is your schedule?"

"Put me to work today if you need to," Travis said
cheerily.

"Well, soon, at any rate. Where can we reach you?"

"Next coupla days, King's Inn."

"We'll call you, then."

"Fine, Taylor. Robin, it'll be good to work with you."
Travis stood and swiftly scooped up his diagrams and folded
his CADPAD into its carrying case. He headed for the door,
turning to beam at Stith before he left. "And if you don't
call me, I'll surely be callin' you." The door closed firmly
behind him.

Stith issued an angry groan. "That son of a bitch. Always
has to have the last word." Robin, startled, stifled the urge
to laugh, while Stith recovered his composure. "Sorry. Just
that . . . a few of his mannerisms rub me the wrong way."
Abruptly he pushed his chair back and stood up; he walked
stiffly to the wide windows that looked down on the campus
far below. "I'm relieved, glad I mean, that you're enthusi-

astic about the asteroid rendezvous," he said into the glass. "I'd pretty much made up my mind we ought to go for it, myself."

"Too good to pass up," she agreed.

"There will be a price," he said. He didn't seem eager to elaborate, and she thought it would be a mistake to press him. But after a moment, he went on. "Rendezvousing with an asteroid . . . to get the most out of the opportunity . . . your crew lacks expertise in exo-, uh, exogeology."

"We have time to learn what we need. If we get started soon."

"Well, it's my judgment that a trained exogeologist is essential."

"Let's put one on. Too bad Hill's not still in the astronaut corps, he could have done it himself."

"Well, that's an interesting suggestion about Hill, Robin." Stith's reply was quick. He turned away from the window. "He's experienced. He certainly knows this particular subject better than anyone."

"He *was* good, but he's been gone too long," she said firmly. "He's out of condition. You saw that little pot. That's where guys that shape store the excess booze."

"Yes, that would eliminate him," Stith muttered. "Yes, that would show up right away."

"Why bother with him? There's plenty of younger geoscientists who *are* in the corps."

Stith was pacing the room now, not facing her. "The other thing we have to face is . . . we aren't going to be able to modify *Starfire* for a sixth crew member."

"Why not? That much mass isn't a problem," said Robin.

"The specialist isn't the problem, it's the extra experiments—laser pulse drills, sounding rockets, seismic charges, extra antennas, RTGs, power panels—"

"You have details I don't."

"Hill's recommendations. It all comes out of payload."

"That calls for considerable engineering review—"

"It's easier to train a geologist to launch a satellite," he broke in, "than to train a software guy to do geology."

Robin stopped doodling with the pen. "Taylor . . . whatever you're working up to, I'd like you to give it to me straight."

Stith looked at her over a tweedy shoulder. "If your crew does this mission—"

"If?"

"If your crew does this mission, Giles is out and Hill is in. Can you, personally, live with that?"

In the King's Inn, a rambling two-story motel up the frontage road a couple of miles, Travis Hill was biding his time in a room overlooking a brilliant turquoise blue swimming pool, waiting for the phone to ring.

He hefted the barbells for the fifty-fifth—fifty-sixth—fifty-seventh time, his biceps turning to liquid fire. Sit-ups next; he intended to be rid of that belly flab in days.

A month ago if he'd been sitting around waiting for the phone to ring, he would have been plastered by now, even knowing the stakes. But he'd learned a trick, down there in the lowest depths of lower California. He'd learned that pain could be cultivated, could be made to substitute for chemical oblivion. Except for the hollow place where desire had lived, it made him feel almost as alive.

He knew they didn't want him. He didn't blame them.

Tough on them.

"Okay, the bolts are out, now we just tug on this, right?" Jimmy Giles's intercom-muffled voice reached the instructors at their consoles four meters above his head, where they watched the progress of the training exercise on closed-circuit video.

In the green depths of the pool, a trio of masked and flippered frogmen hovered near Jimmy and Melinda, who were encased in white spacesuits; the big maneuvering units on their backs were dummies, of no use at all, just realistic enough to get in their way. The Weightless Environment Training Facility's deep well of clear, filtered water provided the buoyancy essential to counteract the grosser effects of gravity—although brow sweat and dropped wrenches still fell toward the center of the Earth—and here the astronauts rehearsed their space-walk chores.

A tinny voice sounded in his headset. "That's right, Colonel. That toggle to your left should just slip free."

There was a mockup of one of *Starfire*'s external cargo bays next to one wall of the pool, and inside it, a big sheet-metal construction painted white, a dummy satellite. Bold black stenciled letters labeled it "Solar Probe 1"; its base was spangled with bright yellow radiation warnings, where the real probe's nuclear engines were located. The purpose of this morning's exercise was to practice manually unlocking the probe's pivot mounting, which would be bolted fast during launch, in case the automatic deployment mechanisms failed.

Jimmy grabbed a protrusion on one edge of the pallet, curled his booted feet up against the wall, and pulled. Nothing moved. "Is that me, or the widget?"

"Hold still, Jimmy." Melinda was floating close beside him. She crowded in and reached under his knees to push at the recalcitrant toggle. It folded, and the dummy satellite suddenly swung smoothly on its mounting.

"How did you do that?"

"I spit on my hands," she said.

The instructor's voice sounded in their helmets. "Let's break off here. We're hauling you two out."

"Isn't it a little early for lunch?" Melinda asked.

"Commander Braide's orders."

The frogmen moved in and, unencumbered by spacesuits and maneuvering units, tied off the dummy probe. Each took an astronaut by the elbow and swam upward, rising toward the narrow, shimmering surface of the pool far above their heads.

The astronauts' padded white helmets emerged from the water, bulbous as the bronze pots worn by deep-sea divers. Around them, the surface of the pool took up a third of the floor space in a round steel building as big as a hangar. A crane lowered a wide swing into the water. Melinda and Jimmy climbed ponderously aboard and were lifted to the edge.

Robin was standing nearby on the wet cement, waiting for the helmets to come off. "What's up, boss?" asked Jimmy. His voice echoed in the hollow building, mingling with the reverberating slap of wavelets.

"The deployment procedure is being modified—no point in practicing this. You get the morning off, Melinda. Jimmy, I need to talk a few things over with you when you're dressed. I'll bring my car around."

Outside the WETF, the sunlight on the green grass and the white buildings was painfully bright; Houston's humidity was doing its best to drown the locals in their own sweat. Jimmy dashed across the soft asphalt of the parking lot and slipped into the Porsche, where Robin was waiting with the turbine whining and the air conditioner on arctic.

"Hold on," she muttered, and he braced himself reflexively as she popped the clutch and laid rubber in reverse. He was still scrabbling with his seat belt as they left the parking lot in a cloud of tire smoke.

It was a straight kilometer of empty blacktop to the nearest gate, and Robin hit well over 200 klicks before she stood on the brake. The tires wailed a long chord in a minor key. The exceptionally stable little car was still pointing straight ahead when it jerked to a stop beside the guardhouse.

"Blowing out the carbon," she said to the guard.

"Yeah. Not on the public highway, astronaut," said the guard.

"Wilco." The Porsche leaped away from the guardhouse with a rubbery burp, but Robin held its speed down. Soon she joined the traffic on NASA Road One, the speed-controlled skyway heading west, and put the car in Greyhound mode. She took her hands from the wheel but continued to stare straight ahead.

"You're either in a very good mood or a very bad one," said Jimmy, when the silence began to stretch.

"Right the second time." She looked away from the hazy, featureless green horizon and into Jimmy's eyes. "I'm about to do one of the hardest things I've ever done."

"Oh? Don't we usually have this conversation in a bar?"

"I'm not talking about you and me. Not directly. Although that goes down with the wreck." Her throat was dry, her voice husky. "I'm talking about you and the crew. You're off."

He laughed. Not that he thought she was joking—it was just that the news was so comically unexpected. His face started to tingle, and he realized that all the blood had drained out of it, and he couldn't think of anything to say.

She was talking again. "It *is* you and me, actually. Those weeks in space with a hard job to do. The rest of them sitting on top of us like a bunch of teenagers. We won't be able to stay away from each other—"

"I didn't expect we would."

"—and we won't be able to hide it—"

"I didn't think we could."

"—and I'm . . . not willing to be compromised that way. My authority undermined. My attention distracted by . . . by personal considerations."

"This doesn't sound like you, Robin."

"You know something? In the days of sailing ships women were Jonahs. I resented that when I read about it, but I understood the problem. You're the Jonah on this trip, Jimmy."

"We've talked about this—how many times? It's not the twentieth century, you know."

"That's beside the—"

"So were you lying before, when you said we could handle it?"

"I wasn't lying to you. I was lying to myself."

"Jesus Christ." He looked away from her out the window, and tears came into his eyes. The Porsche was locked in loose formation with other autopiloted cars, all proceeding west along the skyway at precisely ninety kilometers per hour. A woman in a Sybo coupe looked at Jimmy curiously. He turned away. "I think I want to get back to the office."

Robin punched keys on the console. "We'll turn around at the interchange."

"I think I want to file a protest."

"I've already discussed it with Stith."

"I can still file a protest."

"And make it harder on all of us. Yes"—she sighed wearily—"you can probably make a discrimination charge stick. Even harassment. So if you want, you can keep me off this mission. And the others with me. Is that what you want?"

"I want to be a part of a mission I've devoted half my working life to achieve. That I won't get another chance at."

"You can't be a part of it." The voice was tired; the words were iron.

The Porsche automatically negotiated the interchange loop at I-45 and headed east again. They did not speak during the rest of the trip, even when Robin drove into the parking lot near the astronaut offices and rolled to a stop. Jimmy got out and walked away from the car without looking back.

Robin sat in the immobile Porsche and let the air conditioner vent cold air on her burning face, watching Jimmy's square, compact body march stiffly across the grass. She had lied to him, lied as best she could. A hell of a way to break it off, Jimmy. But someday we had to break it off.

Meanwhile, this Travis Over-the-Hill. Something else to break: his ass.

"I'll file a protest," she had said to Stith. "The asteroid rendezvous—great. But Travis Hill, for all the respect I have for him—that everybody in the corps has for him—is not an asset to our crew."

"You may file a protest."

"Taylor . . . I don't want to do that. Because I think I can make it stick."

"Maybe. Indeed, it's not unlikely. I would come out of it looking very bad indeed." Stith rubbed his hands over his eyes. "Meanwhile, it will take time. Dick Crease's crew will be assigned to the mission, while the various review boards straighten things out."

"You're telling me—"

He snapped at her bitterly. "No, *you're* telling *me*—that it's either you or him. That's your two-bit ultimatum, Commander Braide. Well let me just warn you, don't overestimate yourself. It's him *and* you. Or you don't go. No matter what happens to me."

"God, Taylor, somebody must be leaning on you so hard—"

"You are out of line!" Stith turned away from her, trying to hide more distress than she had ever seen in him. Not that he was noted for grace under pressure. "That's all we have to discuss for now. Call my secretary when you want to see me again. . . ."

Had Taylor Stith not had all those tortured second thoughts after his lunch with Jack Fassio, had he not dawdled and sweat, had he made his mind up one week earlier, he could have nipped Travis's wavering ambitions in the bud—caught him in Mexico with alcohol still in his system, entertaining severe doubts of his own worth. But he waited too long.

Always, the hard part is making up your mind. But Taylor

was a good enough administrator to know that once you've decided to do it, you do it fast. Otherwise it's blood all over the walls and ceiling. That's why he hit Robin hard. That's why Robin—it only took her half an hour to make up *her* mind—hit Jimmy hard, and why she announced the decision to the rest of her startled crew the same afternoon.

Taylor had to scramble to catch up with her. He released the revised mission profile first. That gave the science-news people something to play with—STARFIRE TO RENDEZVOUS WITH ASTEROID—and the next day he named two astronaut scientists in addition to Travis Hill as candidates for addition to the crew. He and Robin were the only ones who knew they didn't have a chance, unless Travis obliged them all by publicly screwing up.

Harriet Richards had her sharp white teeth in a story. She went in to see her news editor, an ex-fax man who still harbored the notion that print was superior to moving pictures. Although he didn't do much about this conviction except hang out at the press club bar, wearing galluses and polka-dot bow ties in an attempt to blend in with the other old hands, occasionally he would go out of his way to bring good fax reporters like Harriet into the viddie biz.

Harriet's priorities were different. In her opinion, a minute or two of hard-hitting video was worth five or six columns of meandering faxese. Length was not the determinant of quality; putting the significant facts in the right order was.

She consulted a list of notes she'd whispered into her wordwriter. "Item: Travis Hill wants to go back into space. Item: Travis Hill's uncle is a senator from Texas. Item: the other senator from Texas heads the committee that oversees NASA. Item: the NASA administrator is rumored to be retiring. Item: the Texas senator who oversees NASA was seen taking a long lunch with the director of the Johnson Space Center, a man who hates Travis Hill's guts. Item: two weeks after this cozy lunch the guy that hates Travis Hill's guts names him to the crew of *Starfire*."

Her boss heard her out, then asked, "So what?"

"So *what?*" She was fired up this morning, ready to go to the mat. "So, if you want to give me time for background and color, I can make a case that Travis Hill's mother practically bribed the governor of Texas to put Albert Kreuger in office, that Kreuger had made some kind of deal with Jack Fassio, supporting positions Kreuger opposed when he was a state legislator, and that—get this—Travis Hill comes back from two weeks in a ritzy Mexican hideaway drying out from too much booze a few days before he gets invited to join the crew of one of the most important space missions of the century."

Her boss tugged his impressively gray-streaked black beard. "So what does all this suggest to you?"

"I really have to spell it out?"

"I think you'd better."

"Bribes, bribes, bribes. Travis Hill's mother bribed the governor to make Al Kreuger a senator, with her money. Al Kreuger bribed Jack Fassio to get behind Travis Hill, with his political support. Jack Fassio bribed Taylor Stith to assign Travis Hill to *Starfire,* by promising to get Stith named administrator of NASA."

"What if the current administrator doesn't want to resign?"

"What if the president wants to fire him?"

"What makes you think so?"

"I hear the current administrator thinks that himself."

"You got *anybody* that will give you independent confirmation? Somebody on the White House staff, for example?"

Harriet was silent.

"Harriet, I heard that rumor too—when the administrator's office called *me* to deny it. Then the president's media secretary called me to deny it. It's been denied to every fax and video outfit in the country."

"And that doesn't send a message?"

"Maybe, but what message? Look at what you've got: a couple of senators do each other favors. So? Astronauts and NASA administrators don't like each other. So? Some astronauts are drunks; Washington is full of rumors. So? So? Harriet, if any of this seems like news to you, you're younger than I thought."

"I think the public has a right to—"

He waved her to silence. "Save that tired speech. Maybe commercial video puts coincidence and rumor on the cables, but here at NPV, we don't." He rocked back in his chair and snapped his galluses. "Just keep on it."

Try as they might—which was not that hard, in fact, for many reporters owed Travis Hill a colorful quote or two—the commercial feeds couldn't nail down enough facts to field a story either. Thus, attended only by friendly news reports, Travis went through the mill that had been an aspiring astronaut's lot since the beginning, the perverse tests that had seemingly been selected for the amusement of NASA's hired medicos. They poked things down his throat and into his nose and ears and up his urethra and colon, stuck him full of needles, leaned weights on his eyeballs and flashed lasers at him, injected him with nauseating and disorienting drugs, scanned him by PET and CAT and NMR, made him talk to robots and psychiatrists for hours at a time, shook him and whirled him and bounced him up and down and plunged him into cold water, took samples of everything he circulated or excreted. He'd done all this before. He knew when to keep his mouth shut, when to open his bladder.

At last they found him to be a robust male human in his mid-thirties, with no obvious deficits. He wasn't quite as fit as a robust male human in his mid-twenties, but they couldn't find any a priori reason to keep him out of astronaut training.

Among other things, they made him learn how to put on a spacesuit. He knew how to put on a spacesuit. They made him learn how to use a parachute. He knew how to use a parachute. They made him learn how to deploy a life raft and climb aboard it; he pointed out some potential problems they'd overlooked.

The day Stith confirmed Travis's assignment Robin got nervous. She started to do then what she would have done with any other candidate six months earlier: she tried to find out who he really was. But beneath his bred-in propensity to say "sir" and "ma'am," Travis had grown stringier and rawer and more reticent than ever.

THE
MISSION

Among the clustered, now mostly abandoned domes of the observatory on Kitt Peak in southern Arizona stood one odd telescope unaffected by the spreading lights of civilization, one that still benefited from the usually clear air of the desert mountains. This quaint telescope was not housed in a dome. Its only visible moving part was a gimballed mirror, mounted where two white metal towers met at an odd angle above a spur of rock—the vertical tower of the two, over thirty meters tall, supported a diagonal tube that angled off to the south for 140 meters, burrowing deep into the rock for much of that distance, exactly parallel to the Earth's axis of rotation.

Each morning, before dawn, three lonely astronomers drove their station wagon up the mountain to the ruins of the great observatory and entered the subterranean chamber below the leaning tower, where they programmed the mirror to catch the rising sun—the only star this telescope was built to see. Until the heated air of midday rendered the atmosphere too turbulent for good seeing, they could study the image caught and reflected down the tube by the tracking heliostat: like a luminescent jellyfish laid out for dissection, the almost meter-wide solar disk writhed in silent agony on a table in the observation room, its granular photosphere seething in filtered light. Peering through welders' glasses, the astronomers saw a solar surface frequently pocked with sunspot lesions, sometimes breaking into rashes of prominence, occasionally ruptured by pustulent flares.

This day the astronomers had arrived even earlier than usual, leading a second vehicle, a van driven by a NASA technician and filled with communications gear. The basic equipment needed to establish a video link to JSC had been installed in the preceding days, but several hours of nervous tweaking remained. All morning the voice of a NASA public affairs officer reverberated in the underground room, and as the minutes ticked past, the astronomers stopped trying to get any work of their own done. They stood back and quietly watched as the NASA engineers took over.

". . . the launch director has given the go to pick up the count and proceed to launch," said the NASA PAO's voice on the audio feed. "The launch events are now being controlled by the orbital launch sequencer here on Archimedes Station, and will be from now until the T minus twenty-five-second point, when we'll switch to the on board redundantly set launch sequencer. The computers on board are checking primary propulsion systems, capacitors, fuel injectors, and so forth, and all launch requirements are in proper mode. And the launch countdown proceeds toward an on-time launch at ten-fifty-five Houston time, at T minus two minutes. . . ."

The solar astronomers had put their telescope at NASA's service in hopes of catching a rare spectacle. The resulting video images would have more publicity value than scientific value, but then the budgets of all the agencies concerned—not just NASA, but the NSF, the DOE, the DOD, even the Office of Education—depended on public enthusiasm.

In the confined space the NASA PAO's drone was constant, time-filling: "Pilot Spin Calder is performing the auxiliary power unit prestart, which consists of positioning a number of switches and verifying that they are in the proper position. . . ."

But as local noon approached on this particularly hot July

day, the watchers saw what they had been waiting for: across the bright wavering disk of the sun the black shadow of a dart-shaped object was slowly drifting: *Starfire.*

"There she is," one of the technicians breathed, "right on schedule. That's wonderful, right on schedule, we're actually going to catch this after all. Christ, I hope the video circuits don't fail us now."

"They won't. Let's just hope there's no hold in the count."

"Yeah, we're stuck in this hole and half of North America is out there looking at the sky."

"If the count goes all the way, we've got the best view on the planet."

The black silhouette fell in a smooth curve, angling upward across the boiling disk—

"Turn up the audio feed, will you?"

"Four . . ."

"Three . . ."

—until the sleek dart was almost centered, still sliding in its inexorable orbit.

"Two . . ."

"One . . ."

It happened, but for the radio, in eerie silence—

"Power."

"Ignition."

—a terrific stream of punctuated fire bursting from *Starfire*'s magnetic blast nozzle, the ship drawing a molten wire across the noonday sun.

"Oww, what a ride!" a technician shouted.

The telescope lost sight of *Starfire* within seconds; the recorded image would join the nation's archives.

In space, the brilliant glow of *Starfire*'s exhaust, brighter than the sun, glared through the heavily filtered windows of Archimedes Station. The only sound in the launch control room was the clicking of recorders and the muted cascade of numbers read off by robot voices, speaking from a dozen radio receivers. As control of the flight passed to the Johnson Space Center in Houston, the suave commentary of JSC's public affairs officer fed the aether: "Still at fifteen percent of rated thrust, and the spacecraft's bright exhaust of unfused hydrogen and lithium ions, perfectly collimated by the main engine, is plainly visible here in the western hemisphere on Earth, even at midday. Engine performance nominal at twenty seconds into the flight. . . ."

Starfire pulsed and tingled with life. Its black radiator wings glowed dull red, fast brightening to orange. No one would ever hear the unimaginable racket of the reactor's hundreds of thermonuclear explosions each second, for that repetitive holocaust was occurring in perfect vacuum. But the engine screamed with the efforts of high-speed pumps and centrifuges and nozzles and valves to keep vital fluids circulating through the ship's fiery heart. To those on board, the noise was astonishing, a mad audio engineer's mix of Niagara Falls with a cageful of hungry tigers. Slow beats of interfering high-frequency vibrations rolled through the crew module. On the flight deck the reflected images of glowing green and red instrument displays phased in and out of multiple exposure on the clear faceplate of Robin's flight helmet.

Her face, a mask of trembling lights, was projected on the rightmost of the three giant screens in Houston's mission control room. Mission controllers at their banked consoles were transfixed by that iconic mask like worshipers before an idol.

The Capcom spoke into his microphone: "*Starfire,* Houston. You are go for throttle up."

Robin's voice, loud on the speakers, carried the ship's vibration into mission control: "Roggger, go attt throtttle up. . . ."

A remote-imaging data relay satellite caught the gleaming steel ship, its incandescent wings swiftly brightening to pearly pink, falling toward the camera like a hot coal tossed from a cliff; the flaming apparition flashed past in an eye-blink.

The screen in the center of the wall at mission control diagrammed the ship's extreme path, bending toward the sun. "Launched at its own high noon—also noon here in the center of North America, by deliberate arrangement—*Starfire* is moving clockwise in the plane of the ecliptic, getting a minor boost from its orbital velocity around Earth to oppose Earth's orbital velocity around the sun. . . ."

". . . and Houston, we have a solid burn at eighty percent."

A wave of high-spirited emotion swept the room, shouts mixed with scattered applause that twice started and died away—

—for not enough of the controllers felt like cheering; long, tense minutes stretched ahead before anyone could say that all was well.

"*Starfire*'s engine is now operating at eighty percent maximum rated power, which is its optimal efficiency," said the PAO. "Acceleration is now six gees, six times that of Earth's gravity"—a brutal acceleration, although the PAO did not say so, which would continue for almost twelve minutes before the ship had shed Earth's orbital speed and vectored toward the path of 2021 XA. When at last the bright fire of its engine died, *Starfire* would have flown one-tenth the distance to the moon.

Seconds crawled. At mission control, controllers' heads bent to their consoles, but their eyes continually glanced upward: none could resist the pull of the giant image of Robin Braide on screen, the vibration less violent now, the reflections in her clear mask stabilized, making her features clearly visible—revealing her flesh, its weight multiplied, flowing down over her skull like melting wax.

In the row of consoles nearest the wall screens, farthest to the right, sat Prop, the controller in charge of monitoring propulsion systems. The woman on duty there suddenly twisted her head to look back toward the top of the room, whispering urgently into her microphone: "Flight, we're showing a serious loss of—"

"Attention. Attention," said the robot voice of *Starfire*'s master computer.

Robin's tight-beamed voice overrode it. "Seeing a high N-two H-four rate, much higher than . . . damn that . . ."

Meanwhile, the Capcom was conveying the message: "*Starfire*, Prop says we are showing an unrestricted crossover in . . ."

Again Robin's time-delayed and weight-deepened voice broke in: "Must have jiggled a valve open in MS-two."

"Copy excess MS-two rate. Hit that crossover on panel R-two for MS-one . . ."

". . . to MS-one. Oh, roger, Houston, we caught that already."

The silence in the room was complete.

"Attention," said the ship. "Attention."

Robin spoke again. "Think we got a little fire here."

Unseen by anyone, in the maze of spherical tanks and pipes that nestled below the crew module, in the guts of *Starfire*'s maneuvering system, an open vent was expelling a stream of self-oxidizing fuel all over the plumbing and wiring—

—where a random spark had burst it into lurid purple flames. A huge fiery bloom writhed in the airless sextuple gravity, taking the shape of a diseased orchid, consuming fuel at a rate of thousands of kilograms a minute, threatening to melt heat-sensitive control circuits.

On consoles in Houston and aboard *Starfire*, on the flight deck, in propulsion control, crimson emergency lights were winking.

"There is an anomalous consumption of hydrazine in the reaction control system fuel storage area," the PAO said calmly.

The flight deck was a wave of colored lights in front of

Robin's heavy eyes. She strained against her vast weight to hit a row of switches under the ruby lights on her panel. Beside her, Spin slugged at complementary switches.

In the service module the leaking vent snapped shut. White aerosol filled the compartment, snuffing the last lick of flame.

On the flight deck red lights flickered to green and amber. "Fire's out," said Robin. "Bled hydrazine all over—nominal now. Green board, mostly."

In Houston the controllers murmured as they exchanged glances. The flight director bent in solemn conversation with the Consumables controller, then leaned across the central aisle to whisper in the Capcom's ear.

Capcom said, "*Starfire,* you are advised of a unit decrement in MS consumables. Emphasizing this is a discretionary."

Capcom's words went out over the broadcast feed, but the public affairs officer, a white-haired gentleman whose desk overlooked the Capcom's from the rear of the control room, swiftly translated them for media consumption: "Flight director getting a go/no go from the control team and getting a go from them at the discretion of *Starfire*'s commander." What the PAO did not say was that "unit decrement" was a code phrase, indicating a change in the underlying assumptions upon which the mission profile was based, a change not sufficient for a mandatory abort at a critical moment, but sufficient to allow the commander to scrub the mission with cause. Full translation: *Starfire* is in good shape but heading into a long mission with a significant loss of maneuvering system fuel.

"Roger, Houston. Discretionary declined."

"Copy," said Capcom. "Concur there's no immediate problem on that."

"Mission control and mission commander Robin Braide have confirmed that there is no danger to the mission from the hydrazine decrement," said the PAO. "The spacecraft is carrying forward with its mission, now at five minutes into its flight, two thousand six hundred kilometers from Earth. All console positions in the control room are very quiet. No anomaly calls by any of their positions at this time."

Capcom said, "Want to give us some pictures, Robin?"

"Coming at you. . . ."

Robin's face on the right-hand wall screen sagged and disappeared in a snowy blitz, to be replaced by successive low-resolution images of the other crew members. "We appear to be nominal on the biomeds," said Robin, her voice low and slow. "And here's living proof. Spin's taking a nap. Isn't he cute? . . . Whooops, guess I woke him up." *Click*. "Melinda actually looks mildly interested in the proceedings." *Click*. "Linwood too; he must be amused by *something*. Who knows, probably rewriting his software." *Click*. "But looky here. Professor Hill's showing a pulse."

"Copy," said the Capcom. All on board *Starfire* were "showing a pulse," its commander included. Capcom hoped Hill knew she was being funny. "Biomeds nominal, confirmed, and everybody looks as good as could be expected. You guys'll be happy to turn off that torch."

"That's a roger."

"To the excellent reports the flight surgeon has received from the biomedical sensors, mission commander Robin Braide has added her own observations of the crew's attitude," said the PAO, putting a smile into his voice.

"MECO minus one minute twenty seconds."

"Capcom has advised the crew that main engine cutoff will occur on schedule. Now at ten minutes twenty seconds into the flight *Starfire*'s velocity has exceeded thirty-five kilometers per second, greater than the velocity of the Earth in its orbit around the sun."

Aboard *Starfire*, Spin was querying the system; below him, Linwood was doing the same and sweating, six-times-heavy beads of sweat landing on his cheeks like BBs.

"Thirty to the mark," said the Capcom.

Robin extended her massive hand to preset a row of switches registering concurrence with what the computers were about to do. "Copy," she said.

One of the two clocks on Capcom's console was busily compensating for the increasing time to communicate with the ship as *Starfire* fled his radio signal. "Ten seconds," said Capcom.

Robin waited for her own clock to hit its preset red line. "Heat transaction enabled, over."

As the roar of the pumps was sucked into thin vacuum— "MECO, mark," said Capcom.

—a silent puff of glowing plasma left the suddenly darkened blast nozzle, and *Starfire*'s wings immediately began to cool to gray. Aboard *Starfire*, five astronauts who a second ago had weighed almost half a tonne found themselves weighing nothing.

Robin said, "Houston, we read MECO at T plus ten . . . make that eleven . . . forty-four point seven, over."

"Copy eleven forty-four point seven. Good work, Robin."

The PAO's voice was rich with satisfaction. "An optimal MECO timed at optimal power with crew in good shape, ship in good shape, trajectory vector optimal. MOCR team concurs we have a damn fine spaceship here. Inbound for the sun."

Travis was showing a pulse, all right. While he lay in the dark crevice of his mission specialist's den, a surge of exultation had washed over him as the core of him realized that the sun had risen on the ultimate burning desert, and he was riding into it. The way he felt just then, he didn't care if he never came back.

Beyond the moon, fifty times farther away, a jagged object as big as a mountain and as black as a lump of coal was also falling freely toward the sun. Over the course of the next two days, if all went as planned, the gently curving trajectories of the two falling bodies would ineluctably converge.

A profusion of blueprint-style diagrams flickered past on a large pixel array screen. "You're looking at the most complex propulsion and maneuvering system that ever flew, Colonel. Controlled by one of the most complicated control programs ever written."

"Save the commercials."

A damn fine spaceship, the PAO had called it, in a vigorous affirmation for public consumption. And true. Unfortunately there was a bug in the damn fine ship. Within half an hour of launch Taylor Stith had assembled a tiger team of engineers and astronauts, assigning them in pairs to each critical branch in the logic tree of maneuvering-system hardware and software.

The image on the engineer's screen froze on a detail, parallel lines of pipe crossing and bending in tight formation around steel spheres, like shiny meatballs embedded in some weird spaghetti. "We know *where* it's happening," said the engineer.

"So do we," said the astronaut.

"Hardware, we're pretty sure. These valve triggers are accumulating an unfortunate history of randomized misbehavior under certain sets of microconditions. On the other hand, the software that attends to those sets—"

"You don't have a clue," said the astronaut.

"Sometimes it's difficult, initially, to narrow down the—"

"It could happen again."

"Look, Colonel . . ." These astronauts tended to be damnably straightforward, the engineer reminded himself, but this one acts like he's got a chip on his shoulder. On this little exercise the traditional rival professions were paired not so much to help each other solve problems as to keep each other honest, but random insults weren't going to aid that. "Let's just try to get along, okay? We'll go faster that way."

"I'll want one of these desks here with a terminal that can access this stuff"—the astronaut waved at the screen—"plus the entire code for the propulsion and control system, documented. However many hundreds of lines."

"Thousands," the engineer said.

"Good, you know what I want."

"Our own department team is on this specific problem already. Frankly, it's going to take time to get you up to speed."

"Worry about your own work. I'll ask if I need help."

"Fine. We'll get to it right away."

"I'll wait here."

The engineer blinked. "You mean now?"

"I mean now."

He had his desk and his documents in thirty-five minutes; the fellow who was ousted from it was thus publicly labeled as lowest on the local totem pole, and an entire roomful of engineers at their CADD terminals became nervous and resentful. Well, Jimmy Giles had been there before them, to that place called humiliation; he ignored their stares. He took off his jacket, loosened his tie, rolled up his sleeves, and sat down to open the first volume of code. Let the engineering side leap to their diagnostics and tapeworms; he preferred to read first. He flipped the loose-leaf pages back and forth for a couple of minutes before emitting the first low, unhappy grunt. . . .

Programs could be written in appropriate machine or assembly language or in a dozen or so useful higher languages, even in circuitry, but writing one wasn't the end of coding, only the beginning. Individual *styles* within those languages were immensely varied, and to the person fluent in a programming language, the style of that language could be read off the printed page without ever running the program—grasped better, if the program was at all coherent.

There were programs that were written with such grace and spare power that they evoked in the native speaker a thrill of comprehension and emotion akin to the reading of a poem of John Donne's, one of Jimmy's favorite poets. But there were tried and operative programs, widely used, that were the stylistic equivalent of a Pentagon press release read aloud by Donald Duck—impacted quacking, with operative phrases so recondite that loops within loops of definition and inference were required for the program itself to figure out how to do what it was supposed to, and running it was the only way for a user to figure out what it was actually doing.

The program Jimmy now perused was a ripe example. In three minutes he recognized that glitches in this software would be hidden in the programmatic equivalent of misconstruable phrases, grammatical inversions, deliberate obfuscations. His intuition told him the FUBAR was somewhere in these volumes of software, and it was up to him to find it. On the other hand, he hoped his colleagues who were leaning on the valve manufacturers could prove bad hardware design, because that proof, if it existed, was likely to come much more quickly.

Either way, the important thing was to prove the *existence* of a problem, one likely to recur, one with a cause to match its effects. Against the blind probability of accident there was no defense but prayer.

Jimmy was no stranger to prayer as defense. Jimmy had prayed often and passionately in the past year, pleading for understanding of his own unpredictable angers, too well suppressed, and his predictable lusts, too well indulged. He had added conventional prayers for the safety of his colleagues, of course, but beyond that he did not ask God to do anything for him but forgive him.

Jimmy refused to believe that his hopes for *Starfire* had been denied as a punishment; God was personal, but not petty. God didn't intervene in wars or football games, and in Jimmy's thin book those who asked God to do so were blasphemers. But the thought crept into his mind that he had been denied *Starfire* not as a punishment but for his life's sake. He tried to push the idea away but couldn't. He bent to his work, determined to prevent emergent reality from proving him right.

"This is mission control in Houston, mission elapsed time nine hours and fifty minutes. All nominal in the control room and on the ship and it's pretty dark outside in Houston, so our night control team is about to take over here in MOCR. Commander Braide and the crew will be getting into their sleep restraints on schedule, at ten hours after launch. *Starfire*'s day slides a little out of sync as the spacecraft gets farther away from Earth. Nothing fancy like relativity, just that the round-trip signal time increases and will increase to just about five minutes at farthest separation, so where mission control here is specifying time-critical aspects, we have to take into account that uplink has to go early. Flight team tonight is going to be very busy with a big data dump from launch, otherwise it is going to be a quiet night."

Jimmy Giles was still at his desk when the sun rose over Houston. He tuned his earphone radio to the public relations feed from mission control: ". . . read on the monitors down here that the crew was already out of the sack, they had begun their day, so we called up a little early and asked if they would go to work early for us on the RCS repatch. Thereafter the attitude, the position of the ship with respect to Earth for communication purposes, will be a little easier for them to handle. . . ."

Linwood Deveraux switched channels on his comm monitor to find the picture that was feeding to Houston: it appeared to be the negative image of a spiral galaxy. Over it the Capcom's voice emerged from the tiny comm speaker, denatured of its lower frequencies. "*In re* those RCS repatches, here's the best we can come up with right now, *Starfire*. When you're ready."

On closer inspection of the monitor, the spiral galaxy revealed itself as whorls of stiff black hair against a pale scalp; the monitoring camera at the pilot's position was looking down at the crown of Spin Calder's head as Spin studied his checkpad.

"Okay, Houston," Spin said on the comm. "Could you just verbally tell us what you'd like to do, what kind of interconnect you want?"

The delay in Houston's answer stretched to almost twelve seconds. "Yes, the interconnect will be the one-twenty MS to RCS per the new procedure on message twenty-three."

"It may be five minutes before I find the procedure in this thing." The spiral galaxy was bobbing with Spin's effort.

After the delay, the Capcom said, "I'll tell you what instead—if you want to go to the attitude control file, page twenty-eight-dash-three, I'll just tell you what's changed there and Linwood can write in the rest later."

"Go ahead, Houston," Spin looked up, relieved. "Give you something to do down there besides watch, eh Linwood?"

Linwood hummed thoughtfully. "Mmm, I shall be eternally—"

"Okay, step three there," Capcom began, "where you . . . Say again, *Starfire*?"

"—grateful," Linwood finished.

"Proceed, Houston," said Spin.

For a quarter of a minute everybody waited for everyone else. Then Capcom resumed. "Okay, fellows, at step three, where you check that the one-twenty MS tank ISOLs-two are open, delete that, and in place of it . . ."

The list was long, but for Linwood it held no surprises. He was finishing entering the changes on his checkpad when, from the corridor, the glass snout of a handheld video camera intruded into his cramped workstation.

"And how's the little creeper-peeper doing this morning?" asked its operator, indentifiable only by her curls.

Linwood stared at it, momentarily nonplussed. "Are you addressing me?"

She wasn't. The Capcom, delayed, replied to Melinda's question from the speakers. "That's a very good likeness of Linwood doing his famous Basil Rathbone imitation."

"Roger." Only now did Melinda speak to Linwood, but without raising her right eye from her vidcam. "Since this is for the record, I'll demand an explanation of what's going on here in propulsion control. Take it away, Linwood. The whole world is watching."

It was the sort of remark calculated to give him acute stage fright. He thought for a long moment before he began. "Essentially, as you know, a safety pressure valve in the one-twenty reaction control system—that is, the fuel supply to the steering verniers positioned at the one-hundred-and-twenty-degree position on the—"

"Speed it up, Linwood, they're all going to sleep."

"Mm, yes, certainly." Linwood was sweating with the effort to make his explanation both succinct and accurate, but he refused to alter his deliberate pace. "The maneuvering system fuel lines are to be repatched to circumvent the failed valve, according to standard procedures developed in training in advance. When time permits, the valve can be removed and inspected, perhaps even repaired. Meanwhile, there is no deleterious effect on system operation." He allowed himself to smile. "Indeed, it is almost comforting when this manageable sort of glitch occurs."

"Some comfort," said Melinda from behind her camera.

Linwood's eyebrows lifted at her impropriety, but he said nothing. The world was watching.

Melinda started to giggle. Twelve seconds later, Capcom's chuckle came over the speakers. "That should do fine for the portable video test, Melinda."

Melinda let the vidcam drift away. "Don't worry, Linwood, I'll warn you when it's really real."

As she swam away up the corridor, he shrugged and went back to work. He wasn't bothered. Linwood had his own sense of humor, although he always had been the sort who had to have other people's jokes explained to him. Maybe that's why they had so much fun pulling his leg.

Tired, but determined not to show it, Taylor Stith studied the sober faces of the tiger team assembled around his conference table. The mood in the room was mixed: an I-told-you-so smirk was pasted to the faces of half of those assembled, while the others betrayed varying degrees of apprehension and resentment as they stared wearily into the depths of their Styrofoam coffee cups. The trouble had been defined, but the blame was yet to be handed out.

On this first morning of the mission Taylor was feeling a peculiarly inverted sort of political pressure, peculiar because it was wholly self-induced. Rosie had evidently decided he was in no hurry to retire from NASA's top spot after all, and had vehemently denied rumors to that effect, which indeed had subsided in months past. Senator Fassio had hastened to reassure Taylor that this was proof in itself of Rosie's desire to leave, but that matters might be delayed a bit because the man was protecting his flanks against suggestions that he was being forced out. All of which left Taylor in limbo. He had to do his job as cautiously as he could—Rosie was looking over his shoulder. But he also had to do it as boldly as he dared, because Fassio was looking over his other shoulder. Wearily, Taylor reflected that keeping your ear to the ground sometimes gets you nothing but an earful of mud.

"We've had all night to work on this," he said, suppressing a yawn. "Let's have a progress report."

The head of the team was a dour, gawky Minnesota Swede from the *Starfire* flight control planning team. He glared at Taylor from under eyebrows stiff as straw. "The majority feel it's definitely hardware. We've duplicated the system, made it fail, torn it apart, rebuilt it, made it fail again." He held up a high-pressure valve and actuator assembly, sections of its metal housing cut neatly away to reveal its inner workings. He poked into it with the tip of his pen. "This actuator has now several times failed in the open position after extended vibration at high gees. Huntsville was already alerted to this possibility following the initial flight test, and they had done some redesign, which previously tested fine."

"Not fine enough, apparently," said Taylor, twisting the screws a little, for the record.

"We might not have had this problem occur when it did, except the eight-minute high-gee initial burn in the original mission plan was extended to almost twelve."

"Come on, *Starfire*'s rated for worse punishment, Bob. Why is a crucial actuator a piece of junk?"

"Possibly it's more temperamental than it should be, however it's not junk." The engineer was miffed. "And while I don't expect Arthur to agree with me on this"—the Swede's eyebrows twitched in the direction of a beefy, shirt-sleeved man immediately across the table from him—"my office thinks we can document an unauthorized design change in the actuator sensors."

"Damn right I object to that statement," said the man, his veined face turning the color of liver. He was the valve manufacturer's delegate to NASA. "That part is to Marshall's last specs. We made every requested change and no others, and I can prove it."

"All that comes later," said Taylor. "I want to reach a decision before we leave this room. Do we go for repairs? Or do we scrub right now?"

"We don't have perfect consensus on this, but the majority don't see any reason to abort," said the Swede. "It's easy to fix the stuck valve and do a little preventive maintenance on the others. The majority feel the problem will not recur. For one thing, there are no more long eighty-percent burns in the flight profile."

"What's it take to do the fix?"

"A short IVA. Pending your approval, we've got the procedure written up and ready to send."

"In a minute. I want to hear the dissents. Speak up, people."

"I guess I'm a dissenter," said a woman, a bony redhead who was a hired consultant in systems analysis. "The continued failure of these particular valve types suggests a systemic etiology."

"Say again?"

"A disease, if you will. Mr. Langschuld suggests we fix the valve and get on with it. That's fine, as far as it goes. But I suspect the repeated failure has to do with more than simple vibration."

"Okay, what do you think it is?"

The woman said, "I don't know. In a system this complex, there are combinatorial possibilities. This is like having a disease where you don't even know if it's caused by a virus and still trying to develop a vaccine."

Taylor looked at her wearily. "Okay, most of them think it's a bad valve, you think it's . . . a disease, or whatever. Any other dissenters?"

Jimmy Giles spoke into the uncomfortable silence. "I agree with Dr. Cruz, Taylor. This could happen again."

"Why do you think so?"

"If I had to vote, I would not say hardware is the real villain, I'd say software," Jimmy said. "Some of us hypothesize the flow sensor is getting phony reset signals, but we haven't been able to trace the bug. It's in work. But I'm more concerned about the significant RCS fuel loss we've already incurred."

Taylor pulled at his neck flesh. "Okay. Dale, you want to answer that for Consumables?"

The planning flight team's controller for consumables was still rattling his hard copies and clearing his throat when Jimmy interrupted him. "Excuse me, I already know the numbers, and agreed, they're marginally within rated parameters. That's not my point."

"So what's your point?" Taylor was edgy now, letting his impatience show to warn the others that whatever their opinions, they'd better be prepared to spit them out succinctly, dammit.

"*Starfire*'s got no significant reserve," said Jimmy. "I mean if anything else goes wrong. They wasted too much RCS propellant, which is of course also shared with the main MS system."

"The maneuvering system is not really where it's at, Colonel," the Swede put in. "The main engine is functioning perfectly. The gyros and reaction wheels are functioning perfectly. MS propellant is chiefly going to be consumed in operations at the asteroid rendezvous."

Jimmy pounced on it. "Now *that* is my point."

"You're suggesting we don't let Professor Hill get out on his rock?" Taylor smiled as he said it, but nobody laughed.

"One thing goes wrong, *Starfire*'s okay. Two things go wrong . . ."

"You were eager to be on that mission, Jimmy." Taylor wasn't smiling now, but he was still affable—the thing to do, he figured, was to be serious yet sympathetic. "I would have been, too. In your position."

"This is not a personal matter, sir. I think we ought to maintain the asteroid EVA on a contingency opportunity status."

"You're on the other side now, but if you were down there with them you'd be begging us to let you take this type of minor risk."

Jimmy expelled quick breath—not so much a sigh as an irritated whiffle. "You're right, Taylor. Sir. Maybe. But if I did that, I would have been mistaken. We on the ground have a mandated responsibility—"

"Your responsibility is mandated by me, Colonel." Well, hell, Taylor had lost it; his buttons had been pushed. His face glowed. "*My* responsibility is mandated by my superiors and by the Congress and administration of the United States."

Taylor on his high horse—which pushed Jimmy's buttons. "We are all well aware of Professor Hill's congressional affiliations—"

And that, for Taylor, was too much to bear. "Not a personal matter, Colonel Giles?" he screamed. "Bullshit! You want to rewrite the mission plan? Present evidence, not your festering resent—"

"When did you *ever* before let goddamn politics come between you and the safety of a crew?" Giles shouted back at him.

Everybody else at the conference table, all eight of them, were now unanimous in their ponderous, disapproving expressions, wearing the fixed stares of people who fervently wanted to be somewhere else.

Taylor stared back at them, raking his gaze around the table. Those who happened to be looking at him suddenly found the wall more interesting.

Jimmy, his tie loose about his soiled collar, had the haggard look of a man fighting a battle nobody wanted to join. "Simply urging the point, despite the gung-ho attitude here, that even with the system fixed, the mission is down on MS propellant."

"Yes. You made that point well." Taylor turned away from him. "Okay, we're all tired. Tempers . . . and so forth. Okay. We've got disagreement. With no imputation of merit, we're putting asteroid EVA on contingency status. Pending reassessment when they match orbits. Now let's look at this repair procedure."

"Mission control, Houston. This afternoon we are looking at an attempt to repair the malfunctioning vent in the one-twenty maneuvering rocket system and do a little preventive maintenance on the other vents in the system. The repair exercise will require an IVA, an 'internal EVA' entry to the service module, that module not being pressurized, and so the astronaut will have to suit up, but the astronaut will not go outside the hull. Commander Braide has specified propulsion specialist Linwood Deveraux for the IVA."

*   *   *

The repair message was sent to *Starfire* as text, with accompanying diagrams. Robin and Linwood huddled in front of a glowing schematic on Linwood's screen in PROP.

"Dick Crease ran it in the water this morning and he says there's plenty of room to maneuver if you don't try to turn around in there," she said.

"It seems straightforward. I'll commence at once."

"Straightforward, yeah." Robin grinned. "Don't forget your monkey wrench."

The text of the repair message read:

1. Diagram accompanying is detail of MSVFO valve and actuator assembly. Location RCS 120 pressure system is shown in MS schematics file, diagram 143.4, location M6.
2. Code (*) indicates six bolt heads on flange of actuator/valve juntion. Code (+) indicates target bolt head.
3. Diagnostic procedures have indicated piston hangups can be freed by mechanically shocking the piston housing.
4. Recommended procedure is to strike the MSVFO housing at the point (+) indicated in the diagram. Tests indicate that you cannot hit the MSVFO hard enough to damage it.

Translation: try banging on the pipes.

Some time later, the PAO conveyed *Starfire*'s report: "Mission control, Houston. Today at mission elapsed time one day nine hours twenty-seven minutes, Linwood Deveraux completed repairs on the MS system and spacecraft reports system test bursts nominal, system nominal. . . ."

Translation: it worked. Some things go routinely, even in space.

*   *   *

Aboard *Starfire,* dinner was at eight. Hardly a formal affair: the flight plan allowed but did not mandate time for everyone to eat together, a privilege mission control would readily have trespassed upon had not Commander Braide fiercely guarded it.

Melinda, the first to arrive this evening, was already sucking on a plastic bag of vichyssoise when Travis entered the wardroom. He nodded a friendly nod and set about assembling his own dinner tray from the pantry, conscious of her close but silent attention. Tonight's choice of entrées was veal piccata or smoked turkey, with assorted vegetables. In a spirit of detached curiosity bordering on optimism, Travis took plastic envelopes of veal, broccoli au gratin, creamed corn. He pulled the package tabs for instant heating, then floated to a different corner of the room.

Spin flew in from the ceiling and headed straight for the pantry. Melinda brightened at the sight of him. "Finally build up an appetite, sport?"

"Yeah. Futzing with the high gain for two hours. Thought that was your job category."

"Oh, they only call on me when it has to be right the first time."

Spin never won these verbal exchanges with Melinda, so he busied himself with smoked turkey and a handful of condiment packages. He reluctantly added corn because he knew regulations, and Robin said he had to eat his vegetables.

"How come you don't like corn, Spin? Your ancestors invented it, didn't they?" Melinda seemed intent on needling him; the rosy glow of her skin underneath her freckles was evidence of her high excitement.

"You're as much Indian as I am," Spin grumbled. "So you say."

"Come on," she sneered. "Half the people in America claim a Cherokee great-grandmother—mine's a myth, I bet.

But you're an honest-to-God Mohawk, right? A U.S. government-certified one-quarter Indian."

Spin addressed himself to his turkey and corn.

"You're a Mohawk?" Travis asked him, surprised and curious. "The ones that build bridges?"

"Some of 'em used to," Spin muttered.

"His mother's father was in high steel," Melinda said brightly. "He told me his grandfather worked on the World Trade Center."

"Tallest buildings in the world, in those days," Travis said. Spin didn't answer. "Maybe that's why you're not afraid of high places," Travis mumbled, masticating his broccoli.

"Exactly what my mom used to say."

Travis looked up and was surprised to find Spin glaring at him in naked anger. Travis shrugged. "Hey, I didn't—"

"Forget it," Spin said.

Travis was glad to.

Linwood entered the room. A few seconds later, Robin joined them. Waiting for Linwood to assemble his dinner, which he was doing silently and deliberately, Robin turned to Travis. "Looked to me like you got in some good observation runs today."

"Oh, we'll drown 'em down there in tonight's data dump."

Melinda peered at him. "I've been studying the spectra associated with the two hemispheres of the asteroid," she said, too casually. "Which as you've frequently briefed us is one of its problematic features. I was wondering if you have an explanation yet, Professor?"

Travis cocked an eyebrow. Most of his instrument readings could be monitored from the bridge and from NAV-COM, but he didn't know Melinda was tuned in. "Kinda soon to pick one explanation."

"Impact ejecta," she said firmly. "Looks pretty obvious."

"Well, that's certainly a good possibility."

"Want to bet on it?" I-can-do-anything-better-than-you-can, said her smirk, including your job.

"If you'll handicap me," Travis said.

"What?"

"Define your terms. Are you really betting that the color difference is due solely to matter from a foreign object distributed over the surface?"

"Sure. Except for the one pole, we're looking at a classic carbonaceous chondritic albedo and spectrum. . . ."

"One hemisphere matches the classic C1 meteorite curve," Travis agreed. "And the other's a little redder, more like what we see in the Trojan asteroids. Are you sure this thing is a rock? Maybe it's a ball of ice covered with organic sludge, or a pile of loose gravel left over from a burnt-out comet. What about that odd trajectory—where did the thing come from? Is it from the inner solar system or the outer?"

Melinda opened her mouth, but no sound came out.

"Assume it's an ordinary carbonaceous chondritic asteroid," Travis continued, ticking off the possibilities. "Nobody's ever seen the inside of one, you know. No one dug holes on Phobos and Deimos. If the red stuff isn't from an impacting foreign body, could it be due to subsurface material distributed by the impact? Or partially to subsurface material *exposed* by the impact, perhaps—red ice, for example? Or to a molten flow following impact—red lava, for example? Or to outgassing of some internal substance? Some of the above? All of the above? Make a choice, you got a bet."

Melinda stared at Travis. The rest of the crew stared at her, seeing a rare sight: Melinda slowly turning the color of a brick. Spin was so fascinated he left a sphere of barbecue sauce he'd just squeezed out of its package tumbling in space above the smoked turkey he was intending to smear it on.

"No bet." Her laugh was low and dry. "Okay, ya got the drop on me, cowboy."

Travis kept watching her. "Very few people without professional training would've shown enough interest in the spectrographic data to make a sensible guess," he said.

Her color deepened further, to claret. "Back off. I'll survive without the patronizing remarks."

"Hell with that. I'm sayin', since you and me are the EVA team to the surface, I'm delighted to find I'm going down there with somebody who's interested."

Into the silence, Robin said quietly, "I was going to bring the EVA up myself, you guys. Houston is being a little pissy about it because of our consumables loss. They just officially put EVA on contingency, pending a reassess after our burn to inclination tomorrow."

Travis munched on his wet-cardboard veal for a second. "Yeah. Or maybe we could save even more consumables by goin' home right now." Goddam it, he had let it slip out: the anger, the want. He focused his attention on the curious color of his broccoli.

"There are a few other reasons for being out here," Robin said. She was studying him, as she had been studying him throughout his little joust with Melinda.

"Dumb remark," he mumbled. "Sorry."

She let it go at that.

"Mission control, Houston. A full day for the *Starfire* crew, getting a bite of chow now before nearing the end of their wake period and heading into their sleep period preparatory to tomorrow's maneuver to inclination. . . ."

The evening summer sun came in low through the live oaks, projecting copper shafts through the blue smoke that drifted toward the river from the chimneys of whitewashed cement-block ovens. Inside the long ovens, slabs of beef and pork and goat ribs, slathered in thick vinegary sauce, baked over oak and mesquite coals. The smoke was sweet incense. . . .

Deep in the darkness of *Starfire,* Travis was half asleep,

half awake, wrapped in his sleep restraint like a butterfly in a cocoon.

In the final days before he and the rest of the crew had ridden the shuttle from Kennedy to Archimedes Station, there had been bon voyage parties. He'd gone to a couple of backyard barbecues in Houston—Linwood's was the most congenial, even if the Doc still insisted upon addressing him as "Professor Hill." And his mother had thrown a barbecue bash of her own, out on the ranch. Not terribly convenient to NASA, but very convenient to the state capital. A couple of hundred good friends of Edna May Kreuger Hill and her brother, Albert, were chatting and laughing, rattling the ice in their tall glasses, roaming the wide springy lawn beneath the crooked oaks and cedars, already well fortified for the fund-raising pitch that would come after dinner. Travis, the supposed guest of honor, kept inside himself, smiling and mumbling and sipping sparkling water with a chunk of lime in it and watched them crowding to the patio tables like cows to a water tank, guzzling champagne and feeding on toast and caviar and mounds of oysters and prawns and cracked crawdads arranged upon an ice sculpture of Pegasus, which had been hacked out by the hired chef with a chain saw twenty minutes before the party began. This Austin catering service did its share of cowboy-and-astronaut affairs—Pegasus was in their repertoire.

For his going-away party there were an astonishing number of people Travis did not know—ranchers and bankers and various political hangers-on. But real people came too: Sam and Bonnie, and Don and Doris and Ruben from the Asteroid Resource Center, even Irenie Su with her slick new boyfriend, whom she'd met at her new job in the state senate—which she'd found when it became clear that Travis would not be interrupting his training in Houston for frequent visits to Austin. Oh, and Uncle Al sent his congratulations and regrets, decining to make a personal appearance, which was discreet of him.

Bonnie, heartbreaking with her flaming blond tresses, wearing a lacy white dress virtually transparent when the orange setting sun was behind her, carefully avoided him, staying close at her husband's, his brother's, elbow. But he caught her throwing icy blue looks from across the lawn, full of hurt and confusion. He averted his gaze as quickly as she did. It was hard to look her in the eye, she still wondering how she could have misread him so badly and he with no way to explain it to her.

To Travis's surprise his skinny kid brother appeared, looking intensely uncomfortable, with his wife at his side. Brother Jim's internship was completed and he was back in Austin, making waves at the university hospital. Manuela was as coolly charming as ever, a Castilian queen in a long gown of something black and clingy, her glossy black hair elegantly braided with pearls; Jim, with his gaunt beak thrusting from a penguin suit of white tie and tails, looked exactly like what he was—a bright young surgeon climbing as fast as he could.

"Sorry we can't stay, Trav"—Jim's first words, skipping hello—"big charity fund raiser in town, Manuela's on the board, but we did want to wish you the best."

"Hey! Pleased to see you, Manuela. Jim. Real nice surprise."

"In any event I would not have missed seeing you before you left," Manuela said in her rich contralto.

"Manuela, you honor me."

"Say, this is the big one for you," Jim said jovially. His mind was already back in his car, heading into town.

"Could be the last one," Travis said. "Except for the kids on the crew, most of us could be too hot to go back up."

"Five years from now—maybe less—that will all change," the young doctor pronounced; the remark had evidently triggered a programmed response. "The progress we're making with customized smart antibodies, we'll be able to go in and clean out radiation-damaged cells, aging cells, tumors, you name it."

"They always said I was ahead of my time," Travis remarked. He got a knowing smile from Manuela, although Jim didn't see the joke.

"Mark my words, it's going to be a new world. Listen, we must run."

"Not without saying hello to your mother," Manuela prompted.

"Yes, of course." Mother was already approaching. If Manuela was an Iberian queen, Edna May was the empress of India, in raw silk and yellow diamonds. Jim couldn't suppress his wince. He could barely tolerate Edna May's condescension to his wife, whose family had been Texans before Texas was a state—or even, briefly, a nation.

Manuela never gave a sign that she noticed Edna May's attitude, accepting her sugary compliments as heartfelt—like tonight's, "My, but aren't you just the loveliest thing, and don't you have just the right kind of hair to do that clever business with pearls?"

Travis watched that exchange and sucked his soda water. He couldn't really blame Jim for staying away from the family as much as he did.

What was significant about the party was not so much that Jim and Manuela came—Manuela had put Jim up to it, a fact Travis fully appreciated—but that none of the astronauts came except Robin. Which was okay, because at his insistence, in a minor confrontation with his ma, his invitations to his mates had been strictly informal, over the phone, made at the last minute. And Austin really was a long way from Houston.

Robin actually made the trip. She showed up to meet Edna May. Slim and athletic in a bold print dress, she was not competing for royal rank; both women knew what Edna May had done to put Travis on *Starfire*'s crew, and presumably Robin felt this was an opportunity she couldn't refuse, to gain insight into her wild-card crew member. After making the introductions, Travis made himself scarce, but he managed to lurk close enough to hear the gist of their conversation. To his surprise, it seemed to be about roses. Where did Robin find time to know a damn thing about roses?

Despite the minor point of contact, it was one of the briefer social encounters Travis had witnessed. If asked, he would have confessed himself simply amazed at how much social life seemed to be centered in the hill country tonight, for after about five minutes Robin, just like his brother Jim, moved on to a pressing prior engagement. Meanwhile Travis watched and smiled and wondered what, besides certain emotional and financial debts for which amends must be made, was connecting him to all these people. . . .

"Mission control, at MET one day twenty-two hours fifteen minutes. After a successful burn this morning to match the three-degree inclination of the asteroid with respect to Earth's orbital plane, the crew now looks forward to obtaining good visuals of 2021 XA on *Starfire*'s imaging systems. . . ."

The solar astronomers on Kitt Peak, since obtaining their spectacularly successful pictures of *Starfire*'s launch against the sun, had taken a personal interest in *Starfire*. For the third morning they were listening to the audio feed from NASA as they worked, when something on the image of the solar disk seized their attention.

"That spot has fissioned since yesterday. There must be a dozen little ones now."

"Well, that's not so odd."

"I think we're getting a flare right now," the younger man said, excited. "Look there."

They watched through their welders' glasses as the black spots heaved out bright flame, persisting for several seconds.

"We're supposed to be in a minimum!" said the young man.

"It's all statistical, you know," said the elder. "That flare wasn't much, as they go. Some activity here and there isn't all that strange."

"You don't think we're growing a complex magnetic region here?"

"Oh, I don't know. Let's just wait and see, shall we?"

Aboard *Starfire,* the sun already seemed a little closer, a little brighter.

Travis locked off his spectroscope eyepiece. The asteroid was demonstrably there, a speckled blotch enhanced in the computer-processed display, but not yet directly accessible to the human senses. After tapping his observations into his notepad, Travis wriggled out of the cramped work space into the corridor and headed for the exercise room. It was a little pie-wedge corner of the deck just below the wardroom, thickly padded and equipped with isometric gadgets to which each astronaut owed an hour of torture a day. Without exercise—which was much less pleasant in space than on the ground—you'd get back to Earth with the muscle tone of a sponge.

He slipped into the gym, shed his jacket, and harnessed himself to the treadmill with the rubber bungee cords that substituted for gravity and forced him to support his own mass. He set his watch and started to walk, pushing against the friction of the treadmill's rubber belt.

It hurt. All your bodily fluids rapidly redistribute themselves in microgee, your legs get skinny and your face puffs up, and your blood doesn't feed your extremities quite so readily. Without good circulation the acids that cause muscle soreness build up rapidly and don't disperse. You live with that for the duration, exercise or not. And during exercise there's the constant irritation of sweat, which doesn't fall away but tends to pool in cupfuls in the middle of your chest, on top of your head, under your arms, in your groin.

But Travis had that little masochistic trick of his. He embraced the discomfort, entered the pain, went for the personal hair-shirt record.

Two days out, and what had been clear enough on the

STARFIRE 179

ground was now a pressing fact of life. Thing was, Travis
wasn't one of them. They knew it, he knew it, and the way
they all dealt with it had a long tradition: they were polite to
him, and he kept out of their way. No jokes, no cama-
raderie, no backslapping. *Starfire* was their ship. Travis was
a mission specialist.

Travis knew it was to his advantage, in the beginning, to
maintain the separation, to play the quiet tourist. The resentment that came his way because he had bounced their
teammate—Giles had been a mission specialist too, but over
time he'd become one of them—was delicately balanced by
the clinging aura of Travis's once-upon-a-time astronaut heroics. And Travis figured that anything that made him more
human made him less of a hero, more open to their resentment.

Beneath the mythical cowboy hero he presented to the
world, beneath the cool manipulator the world was able to
see, there was a Travis he had not figured out how to reveal.
An existentialist, maybe . . . yet he lacked the central article
of existentialist faith, the notion that nothing mattered except his own values. Yes, he accepted personal responsibility
for the situation in which he found himself, but he was enthralled by—there must be a better phrase for it, he
thought—he was enthralled by a sense of destiny. A destiny
somewhere out there beyond the last sunset. . . .

He never put it to himself that he had a destiny. What he
had was a job to do, people to pay off—the making of
amends, as it was phrased in some circles. But when that job
was done, there was nothing he could put his finger on. In
reality, maybe there was nothing at all. Maybe destiny was
nothing at all.

He glanced up to see Linwood Deveraux floating into the
gym.

"Doc," he muttered—the minimal acknowledgment, if
not quite so minimal as Linwood's grunt in reply.

Linwood strapped himself to the wall at right angles to

Travis and proceeded to yank rhythmically at a spring-loaded chest pull—pumping iron over Travis's head. The two men went on for some minutes, the silence between them broken only by occasional groans escaping through clenched teeth.

Travis liked Linwood better than the others, although he was not sure why. He liked them all well enough, but there was something about Linwood. The Doc was very difficult to talk to; he took everything you said to him literally, and he thought about his answers. So a "Howya' doin'?" didn't get an automatic "Great, and you?" It got a considered response about what was on Linwood's mind. Sometimes that response was a joke, but it took someone on Linwood's wavelength, or a person who'd known him a long time, to realize it was a joke.

"Doc . . . I was wonderin' . . . if you've given any thought . . . to the name of this rock."

Silence for several seconds, broken at last. "No."

"Yeah. I hear the IAU wants to call it . . . Horace. . . . I got a cousin named Horace. . . . Why'd they name an asteroid *Horace*?"

Linwood thought about that while he tugged on his springs. "Horus—H-O-R-U-S—was the Egyptian hawk-headed god . . . a manifestation of the sun. . . . Therefore an appropriate name for an Apollo object. However . . . I believe that name is already taken." Linwood paused, thinking a bit more. "Or perhaps you were joking."

"I was thinking we could call it Everest."

Linwood said nothing. He probably wouldn't say anything until Travis asked him another question.

Travis didn't want to ask him another question. Especially not another fake question. (His cousin Horace, indeed.) He was wondering if Linwood would get interested. "Roughly the same size . . . about the highest mountain peak anybody's tried to climb."

Linwood was quiet a long time, pulling on his springs, the

sweat collecting on his sinewy chest. Then he said, "You've always been a climber, Professor Hill?"

Aha, the Doc's turn for a joke. "You mean, have I always been a politicking, video-milking, hand-shaking, arm-twisting overachiever?"

"Did I say all that?"

"Doc, you don't say much of anything. But when you do, you make your point."

Linwood stopped working the chest pull and stowed it against the wall with Velcro flaps. He pulled a cloth towel from a dispenser and carefully began toweling the pooled sweat from his body; the wet towel would go into the Automated Laundry Device, which would recycle both the sweat and the wash water back into consumables.

Meanwhile Travis kept marching. He'd made a joke. Linwood had made a joke. Time to drop it. Perversely, Travis didn't want to drop it. "How long have I been officially part of this team, Doc? Year and what, couple of weeks?"

"Since a year ago last May."

"Yeah. Met your grandkids at the beach." He blew globules of sweat off his lip. "They were diggin' somethin' out of the sand, ugliest thing I ever saw, a clam or somethin' . . . asked me if I thought it was an alien."

"Oh?" Linwood was interested at last. Probably the mention of his grandsons. "And what did you tell them?"

"Can't remember, exactly. . . . Do remember thinkin' some of the stuff on the beach is probably weirder . . . than anything we'll ever run into out here."

"I disagree, Professor Hill," Linwood said firmly. "As the twentieth-century biologist J. B. S. Haldane noted, the universe is not only stranger than we imagine—"

"Right, it is stranger than—"

"—we *can* imagine," Linwood finished, with determination.

"Yep," said Travis. He could kick himself for interrupting, even if everybody knew the hoary quote. Hell, Travis had used it himself, on that guy Cartwright on that video show—thought it might goose him a little, Haldane being a notorious commie. Which cut no ice with the Doc, one way or the other.

Travis changed the subject. "Wearin' myself out . . . fifteen more seconds, break my personal best—seventeen thousand eight hundred kilometers in ten minutes . . . little help from orbital mechanics . . ."—blowing sweat and blowing his cool; why was he trying so hard with this guy?—"Goin' for the four-minute light-year"—the Lone Ranger act getting too hard to maintain?

For fifteen more seconds Travis trundled in silence, except for his panting. Linwood continued to towel himself with great care and precision.

"So what do you think of the name?" Travis demanded. "Everest?"

"My specialty is propulsion, Professor Hill."

Travis quit walking. "Okay. Your turn." He unclipped himself from the treadmill and took the fresh towel that Linwood handed down to him. He got out of the way, swiping the towel over his glistening skin, watching quietly as Linwood flipped over and began strapping himself into the walker. Travis finished with the towel and shoved it into the receptacle of the ALD. "I was thinking, Doc. Since we've known each other a year ago May, you could call me Travis. If you wanted to."

Linwood looked up at him, painfully trudging against the treadmill's friction. He didn't say anything.

Well, Travis didn't really expect an answer; he hadn't asked a question. So when Linwood said nothing, Travis just gave him a big grin and pushed himself out of the cramped room.

"Mission control. *Starfire* now closing on 2021 XA, with shipboard computers doing almost all of the work; here at Houston we are keeping our hand in with an occasional position check, useful by virtue of Earth's extreme separation from the spacecraft. Nice to have two points of view, when you want to know where you are out there. . . ."

Robin's voice came over the comm. "We've acquired a visual of the target. Anyone interested in a really crisp picture, join us on the flight deck."

Travis was first in line, soaring up the corridor toward the flight deck, almost colliding with eager Melinda on the way. Linwood pushed in behind them.

The main screen was a packed field of stars, crowded unbinking points of silver against matte black and bright dust—the view from the optical telescope feeding the video circuit. The sun was somewhere off-screen to the left, but its unfiltered light struck an obstacle at dead center: a knobby black thing, pitted and scarred, perceptibly crawling across the star field.

The five astronauts studied it wordlessly.

Linwood, quite uncharacteristically, was the first to break the silence. "In view of the object's eight-point-seven-kilometer length along the major axis, Professor Hill has suggested we refer to it as Everest." He paused. "The name would be unofficial, of course, since the privilege of naming is given to the discoverer, subject to the approval of the International Astronomical Union. However, as a convenience, I—"

"Gee, I always thought 2021 XA had a kind of catchy ring to it," said Melinda.

"—I, for one, have no objection," Linwood finished.

Travis peered at Linwood over his shoulder, but Linwood avoided his eye. He appeared to be absorbed in the image on the screen.

"You like it, Spin?" asked Robin. "Everest?"

"Sure."

"Okay. Everest, here we come," said Robin.

*   *   *

Taylor Stith gave the knot of his tie and the line of his tweedy lapels a brief, happy adjustment. "Thanks, people," he said. "The MS worked flawlessly during the inclination maneuver, better than a hundred percent efficiency. Thanks for a quick fix and a good one."

The members of his tiger team looked equally fresh and cheerful, happy to be demobilized. All but the manufacturer's rep, who would be spending the rest of the mission waiting for his valves to misbehave.

And grim-faced Jimmy Giles, of course. "Registering continuing concern with the overall MS consumables status," he said in a monotone. "And I'm not satisfied that we're not generating anomalies in the MS software. I'd like to keep working with Dr. Cruz on it."

One of us, at least, is generating anomalies, Taylor thought.

Dolores Cruz, the red-headed analyst, caught Taylor's sour glance as she was chewing the fingernail of her right pinkie. She took her finger out of her mouth. "It would be reassuring to eliminate the software question," she said quietly.

A safe enough answer; it was what she was hired to do. Taylor thought about it a second more and concluded that it wouldn't be such a bad idea to lose Colonel Giles in some endless maze of software. Keep him out of everybody else's hair. "Okay, Jimmy, I'll have a word with the astronaut office." He stood up. "Now the rest of you people can get back to your regular jobs."

Dinner time again. Travis was backed into his favorite wardroom corner, contemplating his cauliflower w/cheese and wishing Melinda would stop looking at him. That little girl is spoiling for a fight, he thought, and I sure wish she'd pick on somebody else.

Across the room Robin was chasing a chunk of floating

chicken tetrazzini with what seemed like a very dull fork. A crackle of noise burst from the comm speaker: "Starfire, this is Houston, transmitting at UT twenty-seven hours twenty-three thirty." Robin looked up angrily as the Capcom's cheery voice plowed on. "Sorry to interrupt your dinner, know how you feel about that, but this one we thought you'd like to hear. Flight has completed the MS consumables reassess, with the result that you are confirmed go for MMU EVA by the original numbers. . . ."

"Hey, how about that?" said Robin, her frown vanishing.

"Hot doggie," said Spin, and Linwood cleared his throat in a manner denoting satisfaction.

Travis in his corner and Melinda in hers caught themselves sneaking peeks at each other in the midst of their grins, and each knew what the other was thinking—that this was it, the real thing, and is he/she going to hold up his/her end of it?

"When we hear from you that you are ready to receive . . ." The Capcom's voice was swallowed in a blast of searing static.

Spin, abandoning his dinner, leaped to turn down the speaker volume. "I don't much like the goop tonight anyway," he said to Robin. "Okay with you, I'll go up and tell Houston to send whatever they want to now."

"Your privilege," she said. "Don't get too far behind on your calories, Spin."

"Yeah, okay." He flipped his tray in the trash and was gone, swimming upward through the hole in the ceiling.

"Good news," said Robin. "Too bad it's lousy reception."

"Sounds like the sun's in our side lobes," Melinda said. "Early for that."

"The sun is unusually active for this phase of the sunspot cycle," said Linwood brightly. "I have several rather good snaps in the hydrogen-alpha of an interesting complex of new spots."

"I don't think I want to think about sunspots," Travis

said. Silence greeted him. Damn again. Why had he said
that? A none-too-subtle reminder of his adventures with solar flares, raising the hero's shield he'd let slip earlier? He
peered at his watch. "Am I wrong or did that last message
take half a minute to get here?"

Melinda glanced at her watch and said, "Yes, you're
wrong. Twenty-five point nine seconds, in fact, if we're
where we're supposed to be. Which we are."

The comm speaker stopped frying, and the Capcom could
be heard saying, ". . . updates for Professor Hill, Science
would like a verbal confirm after he has had a chance to
study. Over."

Spin was upstairs now, his reply coming over the comm.
"Houston, this is *Starfire* at UT twenty-seven twenty-four
forty on board, copy we are go for tomorrow's EVA, and
you have messages for the Prof, but we lost a piece in the
middle, will you say again, over?"

Travis bent to his cauliflower w/cheese. Trusting
Melinda's numbers—she was never wrong in these matters—it would be fifty-one point eight seconds, at least, before Houston said again.

"A long way from home, cowboy." Melinda's words came
out so low they were almost a growl. "So if you want to
reach out and touch someone, it'll have to be someone in the
neighborhood."

Now what the hell did she mean by that?

"This is mission control, Houston. Day two, eleven hours.
Starfire's crew is in the sack. Two of the astronauts, Wooster
and Hill, are in the sack inside their spacesuits and sleeping
inside the air lock, where at the appropriate time the computer will switch them over and begin feeding in the pure
oxygen suit environment, the gradual prebreathe necessary
to ensure against the bends. . . ."

Dawn. The solar telescope on Kitt Peak looked at the rising sun through clear still air and discovered a complex mosaic of minor sunspots. A cautionary word was sent to NASA, but orbiting solar monitors detected no unusual x-ray activity in the region. Within an hour three diminutive flares had burst from the region before, strangely, it began to shrink again.

Inside their suits Travis and Melinda hung like possums from a branch, their knees relaxed, their arms raised, their gloved hands draped at the wrists. Inside each clear helmet was a round, sleeping face, snug in its Snoopy hat.

Through their earphones flowed Mozart's Sinfonia Concertante.

"Good morning, campers. Your prebreathe is complete, your bloodstreams are fully purged of useless N-two." Robin's voice on the comm channel was loving, a mother coaxing her children to wash and dress in time to catch the school bus. "Would you like to take a little walk?"

Travis opened his eyes and rolled them toward Melinda, who was already staring at the padded white wall of the air lock. He closed his eyes again. Mozart, rich and complex, filled his mental space. One more moment—

"Melinda?"

"Roger."

"Uh, Travis?" When he didn't instantly reply, Robin faded the Mozart.

His eyes flew open. Suddenly his heart was pounding. "Roger, commander. Unconsciousness termination achieved."

She had the grace to laugh at that. "Okay. Let's do this by the numbers. Official comm check on you, EV-one."

"EV-one comm check, receiving you loud and clear." To Travis's ears, Melinda's enthusiasm bordered on the obscene.

"And your biomeds read nominal."

"I read my biomeds better than nominal," Melinda said.

"Have it your way. You, EV-two?"

"Fine, good. Comm's good."

"Copy, and your biomeds are looking good," said Robin. "Stand by, we're going to set up a clock. . . . Okay, you guys are go for battery."

They unplugged themselves from the wall and switched to suit power. Melinda said, "We're in battery, let's get our water on."

More switches. "Boy, I'm getting cold in a hurry," said Travis, reaching to reset his heaters.

They inspected each other for loose straps and other oversights. Gazing deep into Melinda's eyes, Travis said, "You know, I just now fully realized that I'm gonna miss breakfast."

"Breakfast, ugh." Melinda ran her tongue over her teeth. "I just wish I could brush my teeth. . . . We're nominal, Robin."

"Roger, I'm pulling you down," said Robin. Pumps throbbed in the wall of the air lock, sucking away the air. "Want to give me a rundown? Melinda?"

"EV-one suit P is thirty point four kp. O-two pressure is five nine three. Battery voltage twenty point seven, r.p.m. eleven point eight, water temp seven six, gas pressure one oh five point five, water pressure one oh three."

Spin's face appeared at the small round window in the air lock's inner hatch. "Air lock coming down," he said, his voice picked up by the mike beside the hatch. "I read air lock pressure down to thirty-five eight."

Robin said, "Copy. EV-two, give me your numbers, please."

"Suit pressure twenty-nine six kp, O-two pressure five nine eight, r.p.m. nineteen point seven. CO-two is one point two, water temp seventy-one, water pressure. . . . Scratch that. Gas pressure is one seventeen, uh, one eighteen."

"Copy all."

"Air lock at twenty-six two," said Spin.

"Okay, Spin, whenever they're ready," Robin said. "Remember to keep breathing, guys."

Travis and Melinda grabbed steel staples in the wall. The round outer hatch unseated. The remaining air in the chamber rushed out with a whisper, taking all the thuds and bumps and pump throbbings with it, into the starry universe.

"I want to be out when you come out," said Melinda.

"Then you get the tethers," Travis said. He grabbed her well-padded butt as she reached out through the outer hatch and retrieved a yellow nylon safety tether, pulled it in, and snapped it to a ring on her suit front. She reached out again and found a tether for Travis.

"Okay, I'm hooked up," he said.

Melinda maneuvered carefully through the opening and floated away, until the safety line was almost taut. With one hand she unholstered her portable video recorder. She turned slowly and raised the camera. "You have a picture, *Starfire*?"

"Roger, Melinda," Robin replied on their headsets. "And we are sending it on to Houston."

"Okay, cowboy, come on out. The whole world is watching."

"Roger." Travis moved through the hatch cautiously and stood on the skin of the ship, perpendicular to Melinda, his eyes still on the interior of the air lock. Then he raised his head. He was standing on the back of a stainless steel whale, plowing smoothly through clear seas of incandescent plankton.

"Whoo*eee!*" His heart was thudding again, not with fear but with exultation. Travis had never been farther from Earth than low orbit, had never been in the farther reaches of outer space where a planet did not fill half the sky. In this shining darkness there were only stars; even the polished skin of the ship reflected the stars.

"Hoo Eee? Is that a cowboy expression? Like Yah Hah?"

Travis ignored her. "*Starfire,* how far away are we from the rock—I mean Everest?"

"Spin snuck up on it while you were asleep," Robin said. "I don't want to spoil the surprise."

"Well, let's get these MMUs on and go look."

The ship's three cargo bays were positioned along the length of the hull below the main air lock. Two large bays held the solar probe satellites. The smallest bay, nearest the air lock, was crowded with a miscellany of equipment: experiment packages to be placed on the surface of the asteroid, folding solar panels, an extensive tool kit with spare parts and handy extras like rolls of shiny Mylar and reels of electrical cable, and three backpack maneuvering units.

"Want to try a dolly shot, camera person?" Travis asked.

"If you'd be so kind," Melinda replied.

Floating to the lip of the cargo bay with Melinda's tether in hand, Travis turned and reeled her steadily in while she recorded the view. Robin had already opened the cargo bay doors from the flight deck. The MMUs were stored against the floor, looking like white-painted armchairs with the seat and legs missing. Like everything else in the cargo bay, they were securely bolted to the floor. Travis let go of Melinda's tether and floated into the bay, turning to back himself into the unit that bore the painted numeral "2."

"Houston wants to tell you they are getting some nice pictures in between breakup, Melinda," said Robin.

"Copy. It's going on auto for a minute." Melinda tugged herself into the bay and snapped the recorder to a bracket on the maneuvering unit labeled "MMU 1."

"Okay," said Travis. "Let's release the . . . well, let me think here, I'm not getting any reading on this."

"Check your TD-one is open to flow fully clockwise," Melinda said flatly.

"That's verified."

"Okay, open your GN-two supply valve."

"Somehow I don't think this QD is on yet. . . . Close the flow fully which way?"

"Clockwise . . . no, the *other* clockwise."

"Shoot. You been born left-handed, you'd understand."

Her reply was full of scorn. "You're not left-handed, cowboy."

"Ma claimed she trained it out of me. . . . Uh, that camera's probably going to interfere with you."

She locked herself fast to her MMU and deftly freed the recorder, aiming it at him. "No sweat."

"Hell, it looks easy when you do it."

"Okay, and my launch bolts are out, how about you?"

"All the launch bolts came out."

"You say the launch bolts are out?" Robin asked.

"That's an affirmative for both of us," said Travis. He and Melinda unsnapped their safety tethers.

"Okay, you got circuit breakers, one and two?" Robin asked.

"Sure, we got the circuit breakers," Melinda said.

"Okay, power's going internal. Disconnect the power cable. It'll take me a couple of seconds and then you can close those things."

"We got 'em out," said Travis.

"Okay, a final word," said Robin. "Houston's concerned

that when you're down there trying to match spins, that your attitude hold could be on, continuing to send fire commands to the jets and we might overheat something. What we'd like you to do is, while you still have the attitude hold on, turn the THC ISOL valves to isolate, and then—"

"Isn't that already on the checkpad?" Travis asked.

"It is, except we want the cycling—"

Melinda abruptly interrupted. "*Starfire,* copy we want to ensure that we do not have attitude hold commands firing jets that don't have any GN-two supply to them. Copy, copy, copy."

"Copy you said you understand," Robin said. "I show all systems on MMU batteries. Mark."

"After you, hotshot," Travis said.

"I'm cutting loose." Melinda triggered a puff of nitrogen from the MMU's thrusters and flew out of the cargo bay, toward the stars. She rapidly got farther away; the stars did not move. With three more expert puffs she wheeled herself to face Travis. Again she raised her camera.

His exit from the cargo bay was only a little less expert. It had been awhile, but some skills, like riding a bicycle, never really desert you. Cautiously he wheeled, then fired the thrusters to raise him above the flat steel horizon of *Starfire*.

As he rose above the ship, Everest rose into view.

"Dear God."

It wasn't a planet. It was something much more immediate, more pressing. Almost nine kilometers of crumpled black rock fell away beneath the shining ship. Every inch of its surface was cratered, craters within craters within craters, receding to invisibility—overlapping circles reaching a limb that was much nearer than a moon's or a planet's and yet impressively far away. Seen thus, the rock was much, much bigger than Mount Everest, for its height was viewed not from altitude but all at once, entire.

In this immensity there were radiating fractures, and crevasses, and rays of little craters like fumaroles, and the sharp rims of fresher craters not yet eroded by the constant sand-papering of micrometeorites. And all of this gnarled, ancient, brutally battered landscape was perceptibly rolling beneath the ship, its clarity undiffused by the lightest veil of atmosphere.

"You say something, cowboy?" Melinda's voice seemed unnaturally loud in his ears.

"Uh, I was thinking, if I get braver, this'll be easy."

He hit the triggers and moved away from *Starfire*, flying slowly toward the rock. He had a momentary picture of himself in a flimsy hang glider, desperately attempting to land on a ledge on some awesome cliff in the Himalayas even as a steady downdraft kept pushing him away from his target.

It was not quite that tricky. They could inch their way in, stop, wait to see where the crater rims slid past, move in again, match speed, make their landing.

Tricky enough.

They were helped by the fact that Everest's rotation was not a wholly unruly tumble but more like that of a wobbling top: the oblong body turned slowly on an axis through its center, but its two poles also described lazy circles about another imaginary axis in space. Near the poles the relative motion was at a minimum.

They headed for the north pole. Melinda flew past Travis, leading the way. Their jets gently, invisibly outgassed as they descended the curve in space; the miniature computers in the MMUs did most of the work, keeping the two astronauts slowly spiraling inward in a universe of spirals, closing on the nearer, redder hemisphere, its color that of coal dust mixed with rust.

With a final extra burst Melinda hit dirt, bounced soggily like a half-flat beach ball, then quickly stabilized herself on the surface. Her voice came gleefully over the radio. "That's one small step for a woman."

"Easy for you to say." Travis, from Melinda's perspective, was a white cross against the arcing stars. "How'm I doin'?"

"Twenty meters out—but it looks like you're starting to lose it." From where she stood, he was coming closer but sailing farther and farther to the side, like a whirling rock on a lengthening string. "Crank in a little Y."

His gas jets puffed. "That should do it."

"Yeah, not bad. Hold on, I want to get out of your way." Moving with tiny bunny hops, she cautiously retreated from the pole. Like any mass the asteroid had its gravitational field, but Everest's escape velocity was not much more than a meter per second, and too vigorous a step would have launched Melinda back into space. She turned and aimed the tiny camera at Travis, tracking him in. "Come on down. Gently, gently. Got the bunting ready?"

"A sec." Travis tugged at a long thigh pocket and withdrew a shiny plastic cylinder. "Okay, say when."

"Gently, Travis! Pay attention to—"

"Whoops!" Travis hit the surface hard. His knees bent and he fell forward; his knees unbent and he took off, rolling into a spectacular forward somersault with enough energy to send him careening into space feet first and flailing. Body memory came to his rescue—he'd been *here* before, too—so without taking time to calculate he squirted his MMU jets . . . and again . . . and touched surface at last. Gently.

"What's your condition, EV-two?" Robin asked curtly.

"All in one piece, Commander." Travis's voice was an embarrassed growl. "The old buzzard has landed."

"Copy."

"You got out of that good," Melinda said, "considering you got in it. Still holding on to the scarf trick?"

"It's tied to me," he said. "Like my head."

"Whenever you're ready."

"Here goes. . . ." Travis manipulated a catch on the side of the plastic cylinder. A twist of fabric shot out, opening like an umbrella to reveal a plastic American flag, bright

red, white, and blue. Travis pulled the flag out and planted
its thin wire "pole" into the pole of Everest; it stuck out
sideways, stiff as starch. Then he fiddled with the catch
again, and the flag of the United Nations similarly unfurled.
He planted it beside Old Glory.

He stood back carefully and saluted. "Got that on
video?"

"Yeah. And I got your nifty landing, too."

"I knew you'd say that."

That night most of the video channels on Earth carried the
scene. In the warmth of their Clear Lake home, Jimmy and
Eleanor Giles watched on National Public Video: ". . . earlier today, when astronauts Melinda Wooster and Travis Hill
became the first humans to set foot on an asteroid."

The recorded image frequently broke into senseless noise,
but its elements were clear: the image of a space-suited astronaut, intensely white against the reddish black dust of the
asteroid, saluting the flags of the United States and the
United Nations. After a few seconds a second astronaut appeared, also saluting—Melinda had suspended her camera at
eye level, letting it fall as slowly as a mote of dust in air, and
jumped in to join Travis in the picture.

"Tomorrow *Starfire*'s crew begins a detailed geological
and seismological survey of the asteroid. Reporting from
Houston, Harriet Richards. . . ."

Jimmy punched the remote, searching for a rerun on another channel. He and Eleanor were sitting at opposite ends
of the floral-patterned Hide-a-Bed in the family room,
watching the flat video screen mounted on the antique brick
wall beside the fireplace. Meanwhile their daughters passed
back and forth through the room, telephones clapped to
their ears, eyeing the screen, whispering; "Oh, something on
the video about them landing on that asteroid—anyway, I
don't think she really wants to see him after what he said
about her to . . ."

Spitefully precise, Eleanor said, "The irrepressible Professor Hill. He seems to have succeeded in spite of you." She did not look at her husband.

"I have nothing against Hill." Jimmy sipped a cup of coffee. He was a coffee addict, but he was so wired from three nights of work that instant decaf was all he could risk.

"You've been so *concerned*—"

"Still am. There are inherent problems with this mission. Taylor wants desperately not to believe that."

"And you so desperately do." She eyed him. "And wouldn't you just love to fly off to her rescue?"

"What is that supposed to mean?"

"I'm not blind, Jimmy. Or deaf."

"I'm sure you're not, Eleanor," he said in a harsh whisper. He put down his coffee cup and glanced at the girls, who were talking, talking, oblivious, circling in the shadows of the room with phones growing out of their ears, their eyes transfixed by the video screen's glow.

"Stop trying to baby Robin Braide. She certainly doesn't need a father." Eleanor stared at the screen, where Jimmy had found a video channel that was flashing back to comic relief: Travis, landing on the asteroid, doing his fantastical spatial ballet.

Jimmy stood. "Eleanor, let me tell you something, I've pulled a lot of duty as Capcom, and the first time I realized we were really in the space age was the first time I was communicating—supposed to be communicating—with a mission that was so far away, it took so long even at the speed of light just to talk to them, that we couldn't make their decisions for them." Like Eleanor, he was studying the screen, standing the sofa's length away from her. "Rescue, for your information, is impossible. They come back on their own, or they don't come back."

She didn't hesitate. "For which I suppose I should be thankful," she said tartly.

"I'm going back to the office," he said, and walked out.

"This is mission control, Houston, mission elapsed time three days twenty hours thirty minutes, and it is eight-thirty in the morning on *Starfire,* the crew has breakfasted and is going to work. After yesterday's historic EVA by astronauts Melinda Wooster and Travis Hill, that team is preparing for a second EVA to visit the opposite end of the asteroid and take samples and place seismometers as they did yesterday. The crew has been calling the one end, which they partially explored yesterday, the red hemisphere and the one they will visit today the black hemisphere, which is a reference to the difference in spectral signatures from those surfaces. . . .

"Also, we learned yesterday when Capcom queried the crew about their frequent references to 'Everest,' that that is the informal nickname the crew has adopted for the asteroid. Capcom was pleased to uplink the text of a faxgram a few minutes ago that we received here in Mission Control during the night. The fax was from Roy Rouse and Nora Kline at Mauna Kea observatory in Hawaii, the team of astronomers that first spotted the asteroid, and it read, 'Today we have proposed to the International Astronomical Union that asteroid 2021 XA officially be named Everest. Godspeed to all aboard *Starfire*. . . .'"

Jimmy listened to the PAO on his radio earphone. Far from JSC's mission operations control room, Jimmy's desk was a lonely workstation, even though the big, windowless, neon-lit room in which he sat was full of busy engineers. Haggard and tense, he had just learned that his only ally in the search for a software bug, the red-haired systems consultant Dolores Cruz, had been pressed into service on other matters by her contractor boss.

Well, he would do it himself if he had to. Jimmy had soon learned all he could by the quixotic method of eyeballing the written code; his instinct had quickly led him to suspect sensor input to the maneuvering system's position estimator.

Numerous sensors reported the position, attitude, acceleration, and instantaneous velocity of the spacecraft; the temperatures and pressures in the fuel tanks and lines; the mass distribution of fuel and other components—all the variables. These sensors were redundant and smart, equipped to perform validity tests thousands of times each second—Do I make sense? Am I telling the truth?—but their reports had to be integrated before the main computers could use them to control the ship's steering thrusters; the collation was done by the estimator.

Jimmy had been running simulations for the last two days, simulations that tested the estimator subroutines during main engine burns—straight burns at various throttle settings or burns with excess vibration and vibrational interference, every plausible set of conditions. He ran the same tests repeatedly and compared the runs side by side, searching for any small inconsistency in program performance from one test to the next.

In two days he had found no flaw in the estimator subroutines. If asked to justify his persistence he would have replied, a bit sourly, a bit less than seriously, with a quote from another of his favorite Catholic poets:

> We shall not cease from exploration
> And the end of all our exploring

> Will be to arrive where we started
> And know the place for the first time.

He was prepared to take a very long time. Seriously. So it was with some surprise, even suspicion, that on the morning of the fourth day he greeted the first tangible hint of the nature of the problem.

When it appeared on his screen he pulled the radio out of his ear and picked up the phone. "Dolores? This is Jimmy Giles. I think I've found it. It looks a lot like a trap door."

Cruz was with him in the time it took her to get across the campus. On the big graphics screen he put up the schematic of the maneuvering system; the smaller screen beside it displayed the alphanumerics of the code. He ran the key sections: simulated launch at high gees and sustained vibrational interference.

"In the first couple of dozen runs, nothing happened. In this one, this vent is getting a phony overpressure reading. It's not the same vent that went out in the real incident, but that's probably a random thing. If I keep running this, I'd probably get them all to fail."

"But it closed again instantly," Cruz said. She was frowning at the screen.

"In the simulation. The real valve pistons were sticky."

"Where's this so-called trap door?"

"An unassigned character combination in the estimator. There may be more than one. The clock stacks up the sensor readings to the estimator, and if you look here"—he scrolled the lines of code on the small screen and froze at a locus by now familiar to him—"the code specifies a character block for this sequence from the PE CCW that is an unassigned block for any other sequence."

"If it comes in the wrong sequence, the estimator should ignore it."

"Yes, but it doesn't. It interprets it as overpressure from a different sensor and opens the vent."

Cruz studied the characters on Jimmy's screen. He watched her, waiting. As she concentrated, her freckles darkened and the wrinkles above her nose multiplied; the lacquered nail of her right hand's middle finger tore at the flesh in the corner of her thumb. She was an attractive woman, Jimmy thought, but her hands were not her best feature.

"Okay, you're right," she said at last.

"But now you're going to say that if the hardware is fixed, it doesn't matter that much."

"We're not getting off that easy, I think. We have a rogue character block in the MS program. Okay, we can uplink a rewrite. But this is massively parallel hardware—massive opportunities for unpredictable decision paths. What if there are other unassigned blocks sitting there like hungry little parasites, not only in the MS estimator but in other key ganglions? We're going to have to run through a lot of combinations and permutations."

Jimmy nodded. "Support me in that, and we'll get a team."

"Oh, we'll need one."

"Mission control, Houston. Day four three hours twenty minutes. Hill and Wooster are back on board, and there will be a series of tests and experiments. . . ."

Starfire, gleaming in the brightening sun, lay off the rolling flank of Everest like a whaler closing on its prey. A fiery harpoon streaked from the ship, plunging into the asteroid's flank with a soundless flash.

On the flight-deck screen, a cone of shattered rock was seen to spew from the wound—a sheet of debris like a flower unfolding from Everest's shadow into full sunlight, blowing away toward space in absolute silence.

Travis, watching over Robin's shoulder, let out an enthusiastic yip.

Melinda was squeezed in behind Spin. "You know something, cowboy? You sound like you're starting to have fun."

"Ever since I was a little kid I loved to blow things up," he replied.

"I know that feeling." Linwood had emerged from the corridor behind them. "I got over it," he said quietly.

Travis eyed him, but Linwood was studying the screen, neither expecting nor wanting a reply. Funny thing to say.

Melinda's NAVCOM computer had the best graphics capability on the ship; there they did the first-approximation seismographic work. But NAVCOM was cramped, so most of Travis's body was hanging into the central corridor as he pushed his head in beside Melinda's, craning his neck at the screen.

The screen displayed a synthesized image of Everest as a white translucent solid, its interior cloudy in some regions, bright in others, with hazy dark inclusions deep in its core. The surface was scattered with half a dozen pinpricks of light: from the newest bright spot, waves of light still pulsed through the translucent body, bouncing off those pinpricks, interfering with one another, sharpening and refining the internal structure already evident.

"If we had one more shot . . ." Travis murmured.

"We've hit it from every orientation," Melinda said irritably. "Six times. How much more seismic data do we need anyway?" Impatiently she wiggled the joy sticks on the console. The lumpy shape rolled in computer space.

"Go slow, go slow. Don't get all nervous just when we're about to learn somthin'."

She scowled, took her hands off the joy sticks, and stuffed them into her armpits. This was something new: men who called her on her act had usually already lost their tempers.

Linwood had joined them in the corridor, coming from Travis's geology laboratory below.

"Doc, you got a platinum ratio for the black hemisphere yet?"

Linwood looked faintly sheepish. "Perhaps I should go over this with you again, Professor Hill. I confess I could have contaminated the sample—unless a ratio almost three thousand percent higher seems plausible."

"Wow." Melinda forgot to sulk. "Can we take it with us?"

"I'll bet the difference is real, Doc. There's gotta be some damn interestin' geology down inside there. Now just look at that," said Travis, indicating a plane of differing textures that cleaved the breadth of the asteroid. "That's beautiful.

The ice and the carbon, divided as clear as can be. And these fissures from impact. Probably reheated the interior ice, and gas flowed—gave rise to these little chains of craters."

"The sky was crowded a couple of billion years ago," Melinda growled.

"Oh my yeah. Now what do you suppose those black places are?" Resonating waves from the last charge continued to sharpen the image of the black areas deep in the interior; they had become smaller, more focused.

"That says low density, maybe even hollow," she replied shortly.

"Hollow, you say?" Travis rubbed the bridge of his nose. "Interestin' to know what's in 'em, wouldn't you say?"

The sun was going down somewhere to the left of Taylor Stith's picture window. "Let me get this straight," Stith said. He was slouched in the chair behind his desk, peering at Jimmy Giles and Dolores Cruz across the joints of his knitted fingers, which were supporting his nose—a posture that rendered his voice less than clear. "It's your contention that a programming error induced the MS one-twenty vent excursion. You concede that the mechanical repairs already effected make recurrence improbable, plus we've just uplinked a program rewrite to remove the glitch. But you think there are more glitches."

"We think it's likely, yes," said Jimmy.

"Because of the nature of the problem," said Cruz. "Sloppy programming."

Stith eyed her. "*You* can say that—"

"NASA pays my employer for me to say things like that, sir."

He grunted, dismissing her. "It took you people, what, two days to find that glitch? Which in itself would have been insignificant without a fortuitous . . . well, that's not the right word . . . but an *accidental* correspondence with a hardware hang-up. You want to roam through a few million lines of code looking for other things that might conceivably go wrong." He unknitted his fingers and straightened himself. "In four days *Starfire* burns for Venus. You want me to assign some people to sift through six or eight million lines of code hoping to find some more little fuck-ups? Okay, sure, I'll do that. Maybe you'll be lucky and get another chance to say nyah-nyah before they get back to Earth."

"Our sense is that the mission should return to Earth with the minimum exercise of the program," said Giles.

"Leave the asteroid now," Cruz emphasized. "Before getting closer to the sun."

Stith ignored her. "Your ex-companions will love you for that, Colonel."

"For the record."

"Oh yes indeed. It's on the record. And for the record, you'll get your team of programmers. And for the record, if they come up with anything valid, it will be implemented at a moment's notice."

"Well thank you very much, Taylor." It was not a polite remark.

"Get lost."

"Mission control, Houston. Elapsed time six days twenty hours. An early start for the *Starfire* crew. After yesterday's extensive exploration of the surface and deployment of surface instrumentation, crew will bore a shaft in the asteroid preparatory to implanting of subsurface instrumentation. . . ."

Travis and Melinda were on the surface again; the stars arced in complex curves above their heads, too slowly for them to follow, and the bulging sun described barely perceptible wobbles on the horizon. They had spent much of the previous day deploying solar power arrays, unfolding the flimsy metal panels like giant paper fans. Three of the huge sun-catching arrays now bracketed the waist of Everest.

The solar panels produced much more power than required for the instruments and antennas *Starfire* would leave behind. Indeed, the panels themselves would perish, flaring like wisps of paper, if left to the mercy of the sun anywhere within Mercury's orbit. Their power was needed for a more immediate task.

In the days before perigee, all sides of the asteroid would receive a thorough roasting. But as Everest turned lazily about its own axis, one side would lean over the imaginary curve that was its orbit around the sun, and for some hours before and after the asteroid passed closest to the boiling photosphere, that side would take the heat, while the side opposite would be effectively shielded.

The astronauts worked half a day to lay cables from the solar arrays to a wide crater on the asteroid's rugged, irregular equator, for calculations indicated that this was the spot most likely to be facing away from the sun at perigee.

In the crater sat a strange device: a wide flat metal cone like a Chinese hat tipped awry, perched on a wide tripod—the whole resembling a cartoon flying saucer that had just suffered an outer-space fender bender and had made a forced landing on the nearest asteroid. A squat cylinder projected downward through the center of the cone.

Travis leaned over the tripod base and fired a recoilless gun with a silent, sharp thump, driving a steel bolt into the friable rock, fixing the tripod leg. The gun wasn't entirely recoilless. Travis bounced off the surface but didn't travel far; to save propellant in the MMUs, he and Melinda had pinned themselves to the rock at the ends of yellow tethers.

"We should have power," said Travis. "Let's set coordinates."

Melinda floated above the shield, reaching to flip the cover on the side of the barrel-shaped device; she queried its computer. She punched keys and the massive barrel rocked in its cradle, adjusting itself. "Okay."

"*Starfire*, we're ready to drill," said Travis.

"Copy," said Robin's voice.

"You pull the trigger. I'll take your picture." Travis held out a remote switch, and Melissa traded him her video camera.

They stood back a good thirty meters, to the length of their tethers. Melissa pushed a button on the remote control and a beam of white light issued from the tripod-mounted barrel, aimed straight at the ground. A centimeter-wide hole immediately opened in the rusty black ground, and the surrounding rock began to flow like lava, cherry red.

"Half a meter?"

"Should be enough," said Travis.

The barrel spiraled slowly outward on an eccentric cam; the pulsing laser beam carved a widening cylindrical hole in the asteroid. The pressure of rock vaporizing at the bottom of the shaft blew molten magma back out of the hole, where it was deflected to one side by the curved shield. Some of the glowing stuff puddled in the crater bottom, some kept on flying to splatter against the far rim or to sail into space. Asteroid's blood.

"Hey, it works," she said, feigning surprise.

"I hold the patent, y'know."

"Yeah, you told us. A couple of times. How many'd you say you sold?"

"Hmm. Five, at least. Including this one."

"Terrific investment."

"Remember Velcro! Remember Tang! Hell, when we get back to Earth, everybody'll want one of these."

Bursts of steam spurted from the wide shaft, and gouts of incandescent solid matter bounced off the debris shield; the beam had cut its way through a thick rind of reddish-black rock and was encountering a mix of ice-glued gravel. Almost ten minutes passed before the laser abruptly went dark and the artificial volcano fell still.

"Circuitry says we're there," Travis reported to *Starfire*. "We've still got a mighty hot hole here."

Robin's dry voice came over the static-clogged radio. "Well, don't stick anything in there you don't want to lose."

Melinda burst out laughing.

"Commander, I didn't think you cared," Travis drawled.

Perhaps she didn't; no emotion was detectable in her reply. "Your clocks look good if you want to set up for the second shaft."

"Roger."

It took them an hour to reposition the drill, for they had to fly it almost halfway around the asteroid. Their target was the largest of the hollow areas revealed in the seismographs, a dark node lying on a deep fault plane between the hemispheres.

After another hour to re-rig the cables, they drilled. It was a deeper shaft than the first, and the laser cut through ice and rock for forty minutes before blinking out.

Travis and Melinda cleared the drill rig from the mouth of the shaft and abandoned it. The consumables in their MMUs were quivering on red lines.

Linwood was eager to display his new laboratory results: the ruddy matter that coated one hemisphere of Everest was rich in primitive organics, including some amino acids found in living things on Earth; the black hemisphere, in addition to its tarry carbonaceous deposits, was a treasury of metal ores. There was no doubt that Everest was the product of an anomalously gentle collison between two quite different objects: one typical of the inner solar system, one of the outer. But the conjoining had occurred early in Everest's history; since then it had been pounded by a great many smaller objects at much higher velocities—hammer blows against malleable metal, elemental carbon, deep-frozen ice—melting and folding and driving the gases from the raw billet.

Dinner time. By now each crew member had staked out a favorite patch of weightless turf in the wardroom; Travis's was in a cranny farthest from the pantry. He and Melinda and Linwood had already started eating when Robin and Spin dropped in through the ceiling. They assembled their trays of corned beef and asparagus and went to their own corners, perching lightly in midair.

After a few moments of quiet slurping and crunching, Travis said hesitantly, "Commander . . . Melinda and I were talking . . ."

When nothing more was forthcoming, she said, "Glad to hear it."

"We think you should fly the EVA tomorrow," Melinda briskly explained. "Instead of me."

"That's a guidance specialist rating," said Robin. "I haven't practiced it."

"Nothing much to practice. Just take pictures and pick up rocks."

"Thanks for the thought. Another time."

The room was quiet a moment. Travis said, "Smell the roses, Commander." The words hung like a challenge in the air.

She didn't reply. Nobody talked much during the rest of dinner.

But later, before they climbed into their suits for another night of prebreathing, Robin stopped Melinda in the corridor outside the air lock. "I've rethought. Let's discuss it."

"Mission control, Houston. As we head into day seven, transmissions to and from the spacecraft have been interrupted by an unusual amount of solar activity. Video from the spacecraft is of generally poor quality. Audio continues fair despite intermittent LOS. The round-trip communications lag, limited by the speed of light, is now almost three minutes and twenty seconds. As to the mission time line, there's been some creativity on the part of the crew in redesigning their EVA. . . ."

Melinda was a guest in the commander's couch, watching the flight deck's big screen, where two white MMUs descended toward the black waist of Everest like radiant angels in the sunlight. To her right, Spin did the work.

"On video again," said Robin's voice. "Got a picture?"

"Trying again," said Spin. The main screen splintered into a tearing, jagged image. "We do have your feed. Quality not great—not your problem. We're forwarding what we've got to Houston. Maybe they can patch it back together."

The intermittent view from Robin's handheld camera showed that part of the wide crater where the temporarily abandoned pulse drill stood; nearby was the opening of a shaft that reached deep into the core of the rock. Below the camera a blob of white—Travis in his MMU—spiraled steadily downward.

"*Starfire,* we're about at the crater rim, so I'll call this sea level."

"Okay, Travis," Melinda replied.

"Video any better?" Robin asked.

"Not much," said Spin. "You'll be shielded from the sun when you get in there. Maybe that'll help. Helmet lights, please."

"Roger."

Pools of light illuminated the crater bottom, coming up steadily. Travis briefly hovered above the black opening of the shaft, then disappeared into it. The subjective view from Robin's camera betrayed a moment of hesitation, adjustment to the motion of the asteroid, before she followed Travis into the hole.

Melinda and Spin stared hard at the high-resolution monitor, trying to make out a coherent image in its erratic patterns. Evidently the narrow shaft was full of dust and congealed droplets of lava which had been floating, neither sinking nor rising, since the laser had stopped drilling the day before. Occasionally, when the picture stabilized, they could make out bars of light from Travis's and Robin's helmets cutting through the murk at oblique angles, as if they were swimming under water in heavy silt.

Her voice revealed excitement, nervousness. "Amazing walls. We went past about two meters of reddish gunk, all melted together—looks like what comes out of your crankcase when you haven't changed your oil for too long—and now these slick walls of ice. Perfectly smooth, like glass—which is from the laser. But right under the ice there's black gravel. It's like a silo full of frozen raisins. Can't see a damn thing below me except for a big white blur that's Travis." She paused. "Shouldn't complain, though. This is better than Carlsbad Caverns—not that I've ever been to Carlsbad Caverns."

"There's the bottom," said Travis. "Maybe twenty meters."

"For that matter, I've never been out of the country!" Robin said. She laughed. "My first trip away from home. Not counting orbit."

Melinda traded glances with Spin across the firefly darkness of the flight deck. "Her biomeds are good," he reassured her. "It's not hypoxia, she's just having fun."

"I guess that's the purpose of the exercise."

"Can you see this, *Starfire*?" Travis asked on radio.

"No, EV-two," said Spin. "Okay, now we see something. Some movement." On the big screen, bars of light swayed, and glowing dust particles swirled. "I'm getting dizzy," Spin complained.

Linwood had risen through the corridor opening to join Spin and Melinda on the flight deck. "Rather chaotic picture."

"I can see the bottom now," Travis said. "About four meters. My sweet Lord—"

Robin's voice broke in. "What's that? What is that?"

"This is unbeliev . . ." Travis's voice was swallowed in a blast of static—the picture jerked into zebra stripes. ". . . confirm that, over."

"Say again, EV-two?" Melinda's voice was sharp, eager.

Robin again: "My God. Are those really d . . ." All noise.

"Dammit, you guys, talk to us. Keep talking to us." Melinda turned to Spin, her mouth pursed with chagrin. "I think I goofed. *I* could be down there. . . ."

Inside the asteroid Travis had come gently to rest in the hollow space toward which the shaft had been accurately directed. Light blazed around him as Robin slowly descended, brightening his green eyes, spotlighting the smile that stretched the lines of his face.

They had entered a giant geode, its crudely spherical walls encrusted with crystals—not, they suspected, crystals of silicon oxide, but crystals of carbon. The floating dust was diamond dust, refracting every color of the spectrum. Frosty stones tumbled around their heads, weightless and lazy: diamonds. Extravagant nodes of crystal were embedded in the walls of the chamber: knots and clusters of diamonds.

"Starfire," he said, "we're swimming in diamonds."

For a moment the radio space between them was filled with a crackling nothing. Then Robin said to Travis, "You knew it. That's why you talked me into coming." A child given the run of a toy store would have worn Robin's expression: her stern and touching concentration, her effort not to be overwhelmed.

"I thought we might find a little bitty industrial-grade diamond or two," he admitted. "There's precedent. In Meteor Crater in Arizona, on Phobos, some others. Not this, though. This must have been the face of the anvil when the two halves of Everest came together. Later the ice in these pockets escaped as gas."

"It's wonderful," she whispered.

"It was Melinda's idea, bringing you here." His voice had changed from what it was a moment before: it was oddly drained of enthusiasm. For a time he silently inspected the walls of the geode with his hand lamp. "I'll fill the sample bags. Make me a good record."

She trained the video camera on him as he took a mallet and a bronze chisel from his thigh pocket, braced himself, and drove the chisel into a thick node of crystals. Gems exploded from the wall.

"The last samples."

Four of the crew were hovering in the corridor, peering into Travis's tiny geology laboratory, while Travis himself peered into the barrel of a microscope. "All industrial-grade, or worse," he muttered.

"Thus, in addition to several kilos of low-grade diamonds," Linwood said, without a hint of humor, "we have catalogued a mere hundred and twelve fine gems bigger than anything in the collection of the Smithsonian Institution."

"*This* we can take with us," said Melinda, issuing a throaty purr. "God, think of all the other hollow places in this rock. D'you think they're all like this?"

Linwood cleared his own throat. "The rarity of diamonds on Earth has been somewhat exaggerated," he said. "Indeed, it has been suggested that diamond prices have been maintained at ?n artificially high level."

"South Africa won't want to be our friend?" Melinda asked.

"Breaks my heart," muttered Spin.

"I believe Linwood means that we have accomplished our scientific objectives," said Robin. "After Travis and Melinda have positioned the experimental packages tomorrow morning, there will be no further modifications in the flight plan—merely to stuff our pockets with trinkets."

"I got that message," Travis said irritably. "I already got it before the speech."

What was bothering him suddenly became clear to them all. They had almost finished their mission on the asteroid—

—and once they left it, Travis, in his own mind, was baggage. True, there were a couple of satellites to launch. Terrific. Super. Anyone could push buttons.

"Please see me on the flight deck," Robin said to him, turning away, pushing herself up the corridor.

He crawled out of the laboratory. The others moved aside, trying to avoid staring at his weathered face, as bleak as they had seen it.

Robin turned to face him as he rose onto the deck. Their eyes locked.

"I'm not . . . used to this much formality," he said at last. "I guess I was a civilian too long."

"That's not your problem, Travis. You're not a team player. You're used to having it all your own way. Your own company. Your own senator. Your own mission. Maybe you'd like to be out here all by yourself."

"I don't think that way, ma'am."

"There will be no heroics on this trip. No one-man stands. Learn to play with this team or you *will* go it alone, all the way."

He was quiet. He'd heard these lyrics before; it was the theme of his life: either you're with us or against us—hang together or hang, period. For Robin was threatening not legal action but something simpler, far more devastating— six weeks in Coventry. He would work by himself. Eat by himself. Sleep in some separate part of the ship. No one would talk to him or listen to him except in an actual emergency.

Of course it was the presence of the others that made it a threat. By himself, he was plenty of company for himself. Only other people could make him be alone.

The struggle behind his pale green eyes was manifest. What was it in him that polarized him to every group he associated himself with? Must he always invite this black-mail? "I apologize," he said at last, hoarsely.

"You are a creative and resourceful crew member. Your suggestions are welcome."

"I appreciate your saying so, Commander."

"There will be no more insubordination."

He nodded.

But she lingered, pondering, until finally she said, "I accept your apology." She held out her hand and he shook it.

His diamond name bracelet sparkled in the colored light. Seeing it, her mouth softened into a half smile. "Maybe NASA will let you keep a souvenir—to add to that."

"Enhance my colorful reputation." He turned away from her, then caught himself at the lip of the corridor, on the verge of leaving the deck. His look back at her was quizzical, plaintive. "I thought maybe you had some fun today, Robin."

Her features softened, although she did not smile. "Yes. I realized something. I realized I'd never been anywhere but straight up. There I was. In a cement mixer in space. A rock named for a mountain on Earth I saw once—from three hundred kilometers *straight up*." She paused, and a nervous smile tugged at her mouth. Whatever she was trying to put into words, the words weren't cooperating. She sighed. "Crazy."

"Sometimes you gotta go a little crazy to have fun."

That night, inside his sleep restraint, he thought about everything that didn't get said in that encounter. Impossible not to cast her in the role of den mother. That's what some of them in the corps called her behind her back: Ma Braide. Lucky for Travis it was so public, so obvious to everybody. Lucky he didn't have to discover it for himself. Else he might not have caught himself in time.

Christ, but they were crazy, putting him on this mission; any half-decent psychiatrist would have known it. The way Travis felt sometimes, he could have gotten stressed and confused and done something really dumb by now.

But it was over, just about over. He'd made his amends— he'd made it all the way to the asteroid. Hey, the trophy's yours, Ma. And here's a little souvenir, this bracelet with the name of your son spelled out in diamonds.

He didn't owe anybody anything anymore, except to keep quiet and do his job until they were home. But for the first time in months he was conscious of a powerful thirst, an awful craving for oblivion.

In Austin that night, Edna May Hill was making phone calls. "Darrell, this is Edna May. Now don't let me interrupt your dinner, but I had to pass on the news. Albert just called me from the capital to say the president is personally going to address my boy Travis and the *Starfire* astronauts tomorrow morning when they leave that asteroid of his. Isn't that something to make a mother proud? . . . Now you be sure and watch, you hear?"

"Ladies and gentlemen, the president of the United States."

On comm screens in each of *Starfire*'s workstations the president's sunny face appeared above the presidential seal—tugged and smeared into a cartoon by the interference.

"My fellow citizens, people of the world. It is with great pleasure that I address, on behalf of us all, the brave men and women of the crew of *Starfire,* who have established beyond doubt the great potential of aster . . ." A blast of static swept away the high voice and the picture that went with it.

"We're not going to get a whole lot of this," said Robin. "Will you give me the MFS pad update, Melinda?"

Melinda glanced up at Robin on the screen. "I have Houston's numbers, but the star tracker failed to lock up."

"Copy, it needs a warm-up. Uh-oh, here he comes again."

". . . fulfilling the promise of our forefathers—and foremothers—when they . . ." Then static swallowed the president again, more quickly this time.

Robin said, "Melinda, I'm going to record a reply, and when you decipher good signal evidence that the president has finished, you beam it back for me, okay?"

"Roger, Commander."

"No disrespect, but we need to get on with our work."

Melinda flipped record switches. "I'm set to record."

"Here goes: Mr. President, on behalf of the crew of *Starfire* and all the folks at NASA, we, uh . . . we thank you. We intend to carry out our mission to the best of our abilities. Over."

"Stirring stuff, Commander."

"Well, I'm afraid to say more. How do I know what *he*'s saying?"

"Roger, I'll send it as is. Listen, I can lock this up so it goes on its own when he stops talking."

"Excellent, do it. And when you can, give me some firm aim-point numbers?"

Melinda tapped a moment, then turned to the computer screen. "Numbers coming at you. MFS burns at oh nine ten and all balls. Aim is X minus zero point two five seven, Y minus point two five seven oh, Z plus point oh oh nine."

"Copy MFS burn at nine ten, aim X minus zero point two five seven, Y minus point two five seven oh, Z minus point oh oh nine."

"Roger, except Z *plus* point oh oh nine."

"My pencil slipped." On the comm monitor Robin bent to her work. "Okay, everybody's here, I think. Let's count off."

"Ready!" Spin said gleefully, abandoning his script. Houston, after all, was so far away that mission control was serving in a merely advisory capacity.

"Ready in NAVCOM," said Melinda.

"PROP ready," said Linwood.

"The mission specialist is ready for lunch," said Travis.

"I think you mean launch."

"Whichever comes first," he drawled.

"We'll try not to keep you waiting," Robin said. "Let's give it to the robots."

She set the automatic launch sequencer by hand. At some point the president stopped talking and *Starfire*'s reply was sent beaming back to him through the static. For most of an hour the astronauts were bent to their redundant tasks, setting and resetting switches, checking the positions of those switches.

"T minus fifteen minutes and counting." The voice was the gentle coloratura of *Starfire*'s own robot, replacing a too-distant launch control director. Although the ship's computers routinely communicated some messages by synthesized voice and could be programmed to understand voice commands, humans reserved most voice communications to themselves. It wouldn't do for the ship's robot brain to take some offhand remark seriously. Like, "Get lost."

Pumps spun up; the ship began to tremble. In the banks of capacitors inconceivable hordes of electrons were poised, ready to spill current into the lasers, igniting the beam.

The minutes ticked away until only one was left.

"Attention," said the ship. "Attention."

"I've got a light here," said Linwood.

"Damn! I've got it. Spin?"

"No. I show a green board. Talk to me."

Linwood said, "Negative coolant flow to radiator one. It's the sensor at LB-four."

"No. Four's okay but five is negative on my board," said Robin.

"I show no problem," said Spin. "We've got about forty-five seconds to go/no go."

"Running a system check," said Linwood.

"T minus fifty seconds and counting," said the ship.

After a long silence, Linwood said, "Well, arbitrator would have us believe it's a soft bit in computer four."

"T minus thirty seconds and counting," said the ship.

Spin said, "Worst that can happen is auto-shutdown. We're not going to melt anything."

"Tell me something I don't know. What do you show for coolant flow pressure?"

"Under batteries, four hundred ninety," he said.

"Copy," Robin said. "Same here."

"T minus twenty seconds and counting," said the ship.

"Auto-shutdown can have consequences," said Linwood.

"Linwood, are you making a recommendation for a hold?" Robin demanded. "We have the time."

"My life will get awfully complicated," Melinda volunteered, "if I have to recalculate the solar probe launches all by myself."

"Cut the chatter, please," said Robin. "We have time for a good decision here."

Linwood said, "No, Commander. I'll go with the arbitrator."

Robin's voice was firm. "Go for enable."

Spin said, "Capacitors at rated V, LL pressurized, LD pressurized, LT pressurized, lasers locked, system locked—"

"Now the damn light went off," said Robin.

"Not mine," said Linwood.

"T minus ten seconds," said the ship. "Nine, eight . . ."

"Now mine's off," said Linwood, relieved.

"Three . . ."

"Two . . ."

"One . . ."

"Power."

"Ignition."

The ship moved. The astronauts sank deep into their couches. The great wings began to glow.

"Attention," said the ship. "Attention."

"Showing failure to achieve rated power," said Robin.

"Showing no coolant flow to wing one," Spin said. "It's a wash."

"We're in auto-shutdown," said Robin.

Panels turned from green to red; a great shudder and groan went through the ship.

"There it goes, oh there it goes," said Spin. The ship's pain was his own.

Everybody was weightless again.

"Coolant override?" Robin asked.

"Negative, that kicked in."

"Copy," said Robin. "Damage report."

"The safeties appear to have functioned nominally," said Linwood.

"Well, it was a clean power down," said Spin.

"I show no anomalies," said Melinda. "Total delta-vees only about seventy meters per second. Want a position check?"

"In a minute." Robin's voice was remarkably calm. "All right, everybody take a deep breath."

Everybody did; then they took another.

"Looks like lunch it is," said Travis.

Perverse, but it struck them all funny.

At that moment the alert went out, from Sacramento Peak, from Kitt Peak, from Palehua, from wherever the solar observatories could see the sun. Within the previous hours a chain of small positive and negative sunspots had re-formed around the persistent members of the decaying sunspot group; a complicated mosaic of magnetic fields had knit itself among the spots; minor protoflares had burst from within the cluster.

Now, suddenly visible in the orbiting x-ray monitors, a bright loop of gas had snapped like a rubber band; electromagnetic radiation flooded the sky across the full spectrum.

Bulletins flashed to the National Oceanic and Atmospheric Administration, to the Air Weather Service, to NASA. This was a real flare, a big one. Too soon to know how big. It had escaped the forecasting net; it was even now in progress, growing and feeding on magnetic energy, spewing photon radiation and energetic particles into space.

On *Starfire* they still were debating what to do next when Linwood uncharacteristically interrupted his own lecture.

"Urgent report, Commander," said Linwood. "Significant radiation readings."

"Message from Houston, Commander," said Melinda.

"Can it for five minutes, Melinda," said Robin.

"Recording gamma-ray bursts and hard x-ray bursts at short intervals from the sun," Linwood continued.

"Can't wait, Robin," said Melinda. "Urgent situation."

"What situation, dammit?"

"Houston says life-threatening solar flare radiation due to arrive our position—well, already."

"Yaw thirty degrees left," she ordered. "On manual."

"Roger," said Spin. "X thirty left." His fingers flickered over the board. "Now."

Forward and rear thrusters exploded in sustained fury, a cannonade. *Starfire* slowly slid end for end against the stars. Thrusters erupted again. The ship presented its stern to the sun.

"Linwood, what's your ES?"

Linwood had switched on the audio feed from the Geiger counters. A crackle, sounding at first like crumpling cellophane, was quickly building to the sound of frying meat. "The useful numbers in the alert suggest solar protons with energies of well over fifty MeV will arrive within two minutes. Very high energy levels could be sustained indefinitely." He cleared his throat, even at this moment speaking as carefully as if he were addressing a class. "I fear the mass in our fuel tanks is insufficient to shield us from a lethal dose in the event of prolonged exposure. The superconductive magnets of the main engine will doubtless deflect many charged particles; unfortunately, to maintain attitude—"

Robin interrupted. "On the MS, Spin. Back to Everest. Melinda, vectors please, straight to the robot."

Melinda called up the numbers on the NAVCOM computer and fed them directly to the main computers. Lights blinked; Spin's fingers hit the buttons; cannons boomed.

On stern thrusters alone, *Starfire* limped toward Everest.

"I'm seeing stars," said Travis. Little prickles of white light were dancing in his vision.

"You're seeing protons," said Melinda. They all were. And in the process they were all losing bits of their retinas.

Already, sleeting protons were drilling holes through the ship, smashing its atoms to chunks and driving the debris forward to do more damage—invisible subatomic dumdums slamming through the brains and bones and soft tissues of the crew.

"No time to turn around," Robin said. "Stand by to take negative gees."

They had regained somewhat less than half the distance to Everest. To avoid overshooting the target they had to decelerate. Forward thrusters exploded.

Robin and Spin fell headfirst into their harnesses. Checkpads fell over their heads and recoiled on their cables, and pens and penlights and Swiss army knives fell out of their pockets and clattered on the ceiling.

Melinda fell into her harness; Travis fell into his. They endured a hard rain of bric-a-brac.

Linwood fell into his harness. He escaped the pelting of his own debris, for he kept a taut ship; everything in Linwood's workstation was taped or Velcroed down. But a stabbing pain seized him, an involuntary groan escaped his lips—to be swallowed in the forest-fire howl of his Geiger counters.

The hammering roar of the ship's thrusters ceased. They were weightless again. On the flight deck screen the gnarled black surface of Everest rolled up under the ship.

"Do it by hand," Robin ordered. She watched Spin grab the stick. Never had he seemed more a part of the ship, sensing as it sensed, moving as it moved. Under the gentler thrust of vernier jets, *Starfire* sidled into the asteroid's shadow.

In Linwood's workstation the howling white noise of the

Geiger counters rapidly fell off to random clicks. Linwood reached to switch off the counter's audio. "We appear . . . to be adequately shielded by Everest, Commander."

"Your biomeds indicate a slow pulse, Linwood."

"Must have been taking it easy, Commander." He tried a laugh, uncharacteristic of him.

"Irregular pulse," she said.

"I'll attend to it."

"Okay. What do our consumables look like?"

"Precisely, unh . . . perhaps you will give me a moment. Presently I would say that we are somewhat below nominal lines for this stage of the mission."

Robin took a breath. "Well, it's a different mission."

"This is Mission Control. Intermittent LOS continues. We are aware that *Starfire* suffered an MFS failure due to a malfunctioning radiator. We are aware that *Starfire* attempted to shelter from flare radiation in the shadow of the asteroid. We cannot presently confirm that they were successful in this attempt; however, we are receiving fragments of communication and telemetry, which are being deciphered in an attempt to clarify them. The press conference scheduled for nine P.M. has been cancelled, repeat cancelled. . . ."

The flare on the sun persisted for four hours and in that time released half a million times the energy the United States consumes in a year. Twenty minutes after the flare was detected on Earth the first accelerated protons arrived; forty-six hours later the shock wave collided with the Earth's magnetosphere and triggered a magnetic storm. The sunspots continued to swarm; after the first flare subsided, new flares continued to bloom at short intervals.

Fax dailies and video news shows waxed lurid with purest speculation concerning the fate of *Starfire*. For two days NASA issued only prepared statements to the media, until at last a press conference was scheduled. As it got under way, the magnetic storm was at its height.

The big auditorium in JSC's Building Two was packed, the air thick and hot with uproar. A table draped with blue felt was set up on the stage; the dignitaries straggled in to take their seats behind it, about as eagerly as suspects in a police line-up. Taylor Stith was first; the chief flight director joined him, then the commander of the alternate crew, Dick Crease; then two flight planners. Then the public affairs officer. Then Jimmy Giles. Glumly they faced the press.

The reporters restively tolerated the opening statements—then suddenly, sensing a pause in the prepared text, they were screaming at the panelists, interrupting each other's questions, interrupting the answers.

". . . two days ago, and you say don't even know where they *are*?"

"No sir, we know where they are, I said we don't know—"

"Why haven't they *contacted* you?" The questioner was a woman this time.

"As we explained, ma'am, communication has been extremely difficult due to solar activity. Our DSN, uh, deep space network has been out of commission for most of the past two days. As you're aware, no doubt, major areas of northern Europe suffered power outages earlier this morning as a direct result of the phenomenon, which will give you some indication—"

"What's to keep us from assuming they're all dead?" Another woman.

"Uh, well, all deep-space communications have been affected by this flare, this unusual solar activity . . ." The planner paused, floundering.

Stith helped out. "They have their own warning systems. We have every confidence that *Starfire* is sitting it out in the shelter of Everest."

A man: "How long can they afford to wait?"

"They have ample supplies of consumables, that is, air, food, water. And we are constantly computing and updating likely return trajectories in preparation for reacquiring signal," said Stith.

A snarl of objections arose. One voice cut through, from a young woman with spiky black hair. "A question for Colonel Giles." It was the first question anyone had directed to Jimmy; nobody seemed to know why he was there. "Harriet Richards of NPV, Colonel Giles. Word is you know the cause of the engine failure."

Within seconds, the auditorium fell silent.

"We have identified the cause, yes," said Jimmy. "The cause appears to have been, we are virtually certain of this, a misinterpretation by the ship's computers of signals from sensors in the radiative cooling system—"

Stridently, Richards broke in. "That's in the handout, sir, for those of my colleagues who bother to read it. My question—I mean you identified the cause, you located it almost before it happened, I believe. You are a software expert, originally you were on this crew. If you were on it now, maybe they wouldn't be in trouble. Why aren't you on it?"

Jimmy blinked. "Well, I would say that that is a question of balancing contin. . . Uh, NASA has to do what it thinks—"

"Why did you get bumped?" she demanded.

Stith glared at Crease, the back-up commander, who quickly fingered his microphone. "Each member of the *Starfire* crew was chosen after extensive test and review," he said. "On every mission many other astronauts stand by, fully capable. I don't see that this type of Monday morning quarterbacking is of use."

"Mr. Administrator. . . !"

"Mr. Stith, sir!"

West of Kitt Peak the sun was about to set; Venus was a shimmering lamp on the horizon. The northeast horizon was even now glowing with the lights of greater Tucson.

Two astronomers walked to their cars in the parking lot of the solar telescope. To the north, the desert sky was hung with veils of pale green light.

The younger of the two paused at the door of his car to study the aurora borealis. "Beautiful. Ever seen it this far south?"

The older man shook his head. He looked to the west, to Venus, squinting against the blaze of the sinking sun. "They're right about there now. Just above the horizon."

"How long can they live in that?"

"In it? Oh, they couldn't do that."

Mission control was quiet, its screens a silent jumble of static. At every post there was a controller, but otherwise the place was empty—there were no hangers-on, no one in the big room who didn't have to be there. The glassed-in booth behind the consoles with its rows of comfortable seats, dependably filled to capacity with VIPs on days of big launches, was deserted now.

Except for Jimmy Giles, who stood back in the shadows, watching the bright senseless screens through the glass. Had he been a day or two earlier, had he found the glitch before it disabled them . . . Jimmy refused to succumb to despair, that sin against the Holy Spirit, but only the slenderest of reeds supported his faith: in times past, Robin had been at her best when all seemed lost. Indeed, she was famous for it. Of the off-duty exploits that had endeared her to the media, one incident stood out amidst her race-car driving and gambling sprees and general hell raising, the time she had disappeared on a solo cross-country ski trip out of Carson Pass in the Sierra Nevada and showed up a week later with a half-starved, three-quarters-frozen family of four in tow.

Robin did not go to places like Tahoe for the scenery; something in her put off direct confrontations with the landscape. From the window of her suite twenty stories up in the hotel she could appreciate the ice-littered blue lake and its ring of snowy mountains—she wasn't tempted to get any closer, and she rarely went sailing anymore, even in summer—but the action she wanted was right downstairs, in the gilt and plush of the casino. It was one way to spend a Christmas vacation, between marriages.

Robin spent her nights at the tables and an occasional afternoon on the slopes of the big downhill resorts. Her outlook was social, and she had no trouble making new friends, indoors and out. But too much fun can be like too much triple chocolate torte; someone told her there were long bare ridges in Carson Pass, not much more than half an hour's drive south of the lake, flat and open to the sky, a cross-country skier's paradise, if all that skier wanted to do was stretch her legs in a hard all-out run for the horizon, strictly by herself. She rented a set of funny shoes and skinny skis, put her lunch and a few prudent odds and ends in a day pack, and went south on a warm Wednesday morning, as last week's accumulated snow fell from the branches of the ponderosas in fat wet dollops on the road in front of her.

She parked her Porsche near the wind-carved ridge line and set out under a bright sun. She didn't do any hard running; instead she spent two strenuous hours attempting to master the unfamiliar skis, which she could not seem to turn in the deep snow without falling over or twisting her toes out of the bindings, the heels being unattached. But she got plenty of exercise anyway, far more than she could get sliding down a hard-packed slope in the middle of a crowd of college kids and suburban dentists.

By the time she finished her lunch, seated on a folded space blanket, the sky had clouded over. If any hint of an earlier sunny day turned to disaster entered her mind, it did so only subconsciously; one cannot take every change in the weather as an omen. She was only a couple of miles from her car, and she headed back unhurriedly. Meanwhile, the landscape of twisted glacial valleys to the west slowly whited out; soon snow was falling in lazy thick flakes and the visibility was down to perhaps a quarter of a mile. Her deep tracks were blurred with new snow but still plain, and even if she should lose them, she only needed to follow the ridge to find the highway. She heard a man shout, his voice curiously flat, all its strength and resonance absorbed by the falling snow, its desperation plain. He shouted repeatedly. Then she heard other, feebler voices.

They were in an alder-choked draw well down the slope, the man and woman in their late thirties, sleekly dressed in fashionable cross-country gear, by the look of them not accustomed to much exertion. The two children, a twelve-year-old boy and a ten-year-old girl, were equally brightly dressed and even more obviously overweight. The man had fallen into a stream, sat down in it apparently, for he was soaked to his armpits. Panicking when snow started to fall, the family had tried to ski out without stopping to build a fire to dry the man. Now he was shivering uncontrollably, his strength wasted. The snow was coming thicker, the wind rising, the temperature dropping fast.

Within seconds Robin knew where she would be spending the night. A hundred meters downslope there was a stand of dwarfed and twisted aspens; they struggled to the place, she and the wife supporting the man between them. Among their joint supplies were plastic ground cloths, rubber pads, the space blanket. The pads and blanket went onto the snow, the tarps were hung against the wind on upright skis. Robin made them strip the man and wrap him with their own clothed bodies while she gathered wood. She hastened the fire along by using what paper she could find in her pockets and pack, even her rental contracts. She had to work like a demon to keep ahead of the fire, scavenging the aspen trees of their dry lower branches.

The man stopped shivering, but his clothes, hung on crossed skis, weren't getting much drier: the fire was melting the falling snow almost as fast as it steamed away the moisture. Robin told the boy to keep the fire going while she turned her efforts to more lasting shelter. It took her an hour to dig a cave in the nearest snow bank. They got the man and his wife inside and moved the fire. Robin dug another cave for herself and the children. It was dark now, well below freezing; only the wind spared them, coming in gusts but never developing into a steady gale. It was the last bit of luck they had for a long time.

Sierra skiers have learned to expect storms that last a couple of days, separated by two or three days of sparkling weather. But on so fine a scale no weather pattern can be regarded as typical. Robin and her charges were caught in a series of Pacific storms that piled into the mountains one after the other without ceasing, dumping many feet of snow on the ridges, closing the passes even to plows, grounding aircraft. Robin had left word of her destination with the hotel, but searchers had to wait a day for the least break in the weather. They found the remains of the first night's camp three days after they started looking, and the note that said "We went that way."

At first, Robin's strategy had been to do things by the book: stay put, build a signal fire, keep warm. Although the man, whose name was Doug, had escaped serious injury, the toes on his right foot were numb, possibly frostbitten, and it didn't seem wise to try for the road. But the break in the weather lasted hardly more than an hour, and no one saw the smoke from the fire. By the time the next break in the weather rolled around, they had eaten the last scraps of their bygone picnics, and Robin knew they could not afford to wait any longer. In three hours they got a mile before the weather closed in again. They could hear a distant airplane engine somewhere far behind them. Dinner was bark tea, brewed in the tin ice bucket that Robin had stuck into her pack the morning she'd left the hotel, along with adhesive tape and matches and bouillon cubes she picked up at the ski rental shop, making an impromptu survival kit; the bouillon had lasted a day.

Doug was a San Jose contractor who'd only recently come into a little money and decided to take up a stylish new sport. He and his wife, Mary, and little Hank and Amy stored plenty of extra energy in their fat, but they were on the edge of panic the whole time. Robin kept them going on her knowledge of what it would really take to kill them—how easy it was to freeze, how hard it was to starve. She told a lot of astronaut stories to keep their courage up; she wheedled and growled and shamelessly flattered them and kept them moving down the long ridges. All five of them were amateurs floundering on narrow, awkward skis that readily sank edgewise, bringing them to their knees in fluffy new powder, but she kept them going in a straight line, more or less, that after three more nights—again immobilized by falling snow—and one long last desperate day under skies cloudless at last, brought them stumbling onto the buried highway eight miles below the summit, moments before a roaring plow almost ran them over.

All this happened long before Jimmy met Robin. She didn't mind telling him about it, and when he asked her if she'd ever had doubts about whether she was going to be able to pull the family through, she said no, never. She told him a secret. "Everybody has a fantasy, don't they? Starring themselves as hero. I got mine from reading *Mutiny on the Bounty*, but I have to admit I didn't much sympathy with the mutineers—but Bligh! He brought the ones who stayed loyal most of the way across the Pacific in an open boat, more than three thousand miles. He was a son of a bitch, but he saved their lives. When I was a kid, I daydreamed about doing something like that—except being a nicer person, of course. And that was my chance."

Jimmy stood in the darkness and stared at the blowing electronic snow on the screens in mission control, a sign of *Starfire*'s isolation. He remembered Taylor Stith's last words at the press conference: "We have a number of solid options remaining. We haven't given up on *Starfire*, ladies and gentlemen." But in truth, Houston had no options at all. *Starfire* was adrift on the emptiest ocean of them all.

Linwood was banging on the pipes again, this time assisted by a fidgety Travis. Both men were wearing pressure suits reserved for work on the radioactive structures of the ship— bright yellow suits lined with lead. Linwood's wrench, and his other more specialized tools, were of titanium; ordinary steel tools were dangerous near the engine's immense superconducting magnets, liable to fly out of an astronaut's grip at critical moments.

Repeated queries to *Starfire*'s computers had given contradictory reports on the plumbing that connected the reactor's lithium cooling blanket to the radiator wings. Linwood had concluded that the computer was untrustworthy: the heat pipes through which the highly corrosive—and by now highly radioactive—metal flowed would have to be inspected at first hand. For each of the three wings, the crucial plumbing had to be flushed, the lithium shunted to reservoirs, the key valves disconnected.

For Linwood and Travis this was the second IVA of the day, and they'd spent most of the previous day in the same predicament; for although the core of the fusion reactor was no bigger than the standard soccer ball whose geometry it mimicked, getting anywhere near it meant threading a maze of pipes and struts and electrical buses and coils and magnets and cylinders of lasing glass. The work took tedious hours. . . .

"If it starts to falter give it a quarter turn and maybe more, but wait, okay?"

"We are within half an hour of the limit on this IVA, Professor Hill—"

"Call me Travis, Doc, why don'tcha?"

"I suggest we temporarily abandon the effort to reassemble this junction in favor of continuing diagnostic procedures."

"Heck, if I don't put it back together now, I won't know where everything goes."

"I assure you—"

"You wouldn't want any leftover bolts lying around in your fusion engine, would you?"

"—I *know* where everything *goes,*" Linwood finished. After a pause, he added, "I suppose you were joking."

"Doc." Before Travis could shake his head he had to withdraw it from inside a mass of shiny pipes so oddly entwined they suggested the freeze-dried intestines of a giant alien. "Okay, we'll finish this later. Number three next?"

"An excellent deduction."

"Oh? Oh, you mean it's the only one left." Travis carefully freed a wrist strap from a protruding U-bolt. "Why don't you climb around over there first? I have this tendency to tangle myself in the plumbing."

The heat-transfer couplings to two of the radiators had shown themselves to be in good condition; one had been fully reassembled. But the third still needed inspection, and making a start on it would be the last work they would do that day.

In NAVCOM, Melinda was putting orbital graphics on her screen; Robin, hovering in the corridor, peered over her shoulder. "Could be bad news."

"What do you mean, could be? How long do we have?"

"If we can launch within twelve hours, we can still do the whole mission—retroburn, launch the satellites, burn for Venus. Beyond twelve hours, it's gonna be hard to put those satellites in tight solar orbit. We'll be going too fast."

"We'll give that to mission control when the UHF stops making like frying rice. Could be the attitude control systems on the satellites can salvage something for them, even if we're already headed for Venus."

"That window's not too wide either."

"How wide?"

Melinda turned to look at Robin's anxious face. "Robin, if we don't burn in fifteen hours, we're sailing right past Venus."

"I guess we have to start counting our delta-vees."

Melinda nodded. "Even getting home is gonna be challenging."

Not even the comm systems were free of the static that plagued all attempts to communicate. "You guys"—noise interrupted Melinda—"down there? What's taking so long?"

"Next time call Roto-Rooter," Travis said.

"Calling Roto-Rooter-one. RR-one, come in please."

Travis looked at Linwood. "Hard to get the last word in with that woman."

"I heard tha . . ." Static intervened.

"I think she heard that."

"Melinda, please tell the commander that we will make a full report within a few minutes. We are returning to the crew module."

"Copy you are coming in, Linwood."

Travis, like a curious bird sensing a worm, cocked his head at Linwood. He hadn't known they were that close to a diagnosis. "What's the answer, Doc?"

"It is evident that one or more downstream filters in the number three transfer system have been corroded, possibly during emergency shutdown. In principle, the situation is easily remedied."

"Great."

"Unfortunately, it will take time."

"Yeah? How much time?"

"Perhaps forty-eight hours."

The four of them hung in midair in the wardroom, trading deadlines. In the midst of their conversation a quick hiss of the verniers nudged them momentarily sideways—on the flight deck, Spin had fired thrusters to prevent the ship from drifting out of Everest's shadow into the full rush of the solar wind.

"Priority is to repair the heat-transfer couplings, no matter what else," said Robin. "We'll worry about the solar satellites later. We may have to take them home with us and try again later."

"What of the gravity boost from Venus?" Linwood asked.

"We will have to wait to assess until you pronounce the MFS reliable. We have lots of delta-vees stored. Obviously, the longer we fall toward the sun, the more of 'em we eat up."

Linwood nodded slowly. "In that event it seems we had better go back to work tonight. Can you help me, Professor Hill?"

"Sure, Doc."

"It's my turn," said Melinda. "I need a change of scene."

"Hey," Travis protested, "I'm already familiarized—"

"I agree, Melinda" said Robin, interrupting him. "You're going to encounter fatigue, Linwood. We can't help that—you're indispensable. But at least the people helping you can be fresh."

Travis suspected he was being tested. He kept his mouth shut.

"Mission control, Houston. This afternoon at UT twenty hours DSN established positive contact with the crew of *Starfire*. Continued interference from solar activity plus a round-trip signal delay of some five minutes creates . . . that is, there are some communications difficulties, however commander reports all aboard are well. The ship is station-keeping in the shadow of asteroid 2021 XA. There is a functional problem with one heat-transfer unit but that looks to be repaired shortly. There is some concern about potential return trajectories and our mission planning staff here is at work on possible alternatives. . . ."

Whatever Houston was busying itself with, *Starfire* knew nothing of it.

Fast work in space is impossible; every maneuver takes thought. Without Earth's gravity to keep things grounded, every twist of a wrench or heft of a tool produces as much force on the worker as on the workpiece, pushing them apart. A spacesuit can't be worn at normal atmospheric pressure or it would be a rigid balloon; even at its most flexible it is a mass of cloth and metal to be dragged around, fogged up, sweated and shivered in, farted and pissed in, sometimes cursed at.

Robin had rigged the crew module to eliminate time lost in prebreathing for EVA. Inside the ship, just as inside the suits, the atmosphere was now pure oxygen at low pressure. Until they got used to it the fear of sparks made them nervous every time they flipped a switch. That didn't last. Strangely, humans manage to accustom themselves to any danger that remains constant.

They rejoined each other for dinner. Linwood had not slept for thirty-eight hours, had not taken time to shave, had barely taken time to eat. He pushed syrupy fruit cocktail into his mouth with weary desperation. The bags under his eyes and the white stubble on the jaw he normally kept so meticulously smooth made him look older than his years. It was not his dirtiness and fatigue that discouraged him; it was the nature of his job.

"It now appears we will be unable to complete the reassembly of the unit in less than seventy-two hours," he announced. "That estimate allows four hours rest in every twenty-four for myself. It's unlikely I can do with less."

The four other faces in the wardroom were as glum as his.

"Good-bye, Venus," Melinda muttered.

"Assuming seventy-two hours, where would that put us in terms of MFS propellant?" Robin asked.

"Well, we're not going to make Earth on a straight trajectory," Melinda answered.

"Stripped?"

Melinda said, "Say we dump all the excess mass—about fifty thousand kg of solar satellites, reactors and all, and maybe another ten thousand kg with all the drilling gear and everything—we still come up short of delta-vees. In seventy-two hours our velocity relative to Earth is going to be approaching seventy kilometers per second." She sighed, a short, angry expulsion of breath. "Easier to keep on going to Jupiter."

"We'd get hungry before then," Robin said. Hungry. Thirsty. Out of air. Individually freeze-dried.

"Mercury's out?" Spin asked. "Isn't it pretty massive? For its size?"

"In seventy-two hours Mercury will still be on the wrong side of the sun"—Melinda was patient; Spin always had flown by the seat of his pants and always would—"and when it rises, it'll be behind us."

"I been thinkin'"—Travis spoke as if the thought had only recently occurred to him—"what if we went right on around? Came up on Mercury from behind?"

"I haven't actually run that scenario." Melinda still managed to control herself, but this time the effort showed. "I haven't run it, seeing as how we would melt first."

"Uh, what I had in mind—"

"You propose rounding the sun in the shadow of Everest?" Robin asked.

He nodded. "If we can stay a couple of kilometers from the surface of the rock we'll be in the shadow cone, even at perigee."

"We'll also be inside the corona. Temperatures in the mill . . ." Melinda caught herself too late. "Scratch that, temperature isn't heat."

He nodded. "We'll be flyin' through a very hot, very thin plasma, but we'll be ninety-nine percent shielded if we stay out of direct sunlight."

Melinda, her face aflame with embarrassment, said, "But Everest is going to burn."

"There will be outgassing. The surface will ablate, maybe as much as twenty or thirty meters—we've calculated that. Still be lots of mountain left."

"We've got no prop," said Spin, and his words came close to ending the discussion. Flying even a few meters closer to the sun, Everest would be spinning deeper in the sun's whirlpool of gravity, traveling faster; to stay in its shadow *Starfire* would constantly have to overtake the asteroid, and the scant remaining propellant in the maneuvering system could not provide the necessary difference in velocity.

"So that's that," said Robin. "The sooner we leave Everest, the better."

"No," Travis said abruptly, a little too loudly. "Scuse me, I think it's too soon—"

"Maybe you should drop it," Robin suggested.

"I'm droppin' it. I agree—without prop we can't stay in the shadow."

"Okay, then—"

"We can bury the ship."

For a moment the only movements in the room were nervous adjustments of clothing—suppressed but obvious attempts to sidle away from Travis—efforts made faintly comic by lack of weight.

In the lengthening silence Linwood was the first to speak. "One or two questions occur to me." He let them all wait while he arranged his words. "I do not include mere matters of scale, for example that *Starfire* is almost one hundred meters in length, with a wing-tip diameter of some thirty meters—or that for thermal protection it must be buried at least thirty meters beneath the surface, by your estimate, Professor Hill, with perhaps twice that depth being more prudent—"

"Thanks for not burdenin' us with the inconsequentials, Doc," Travis muttered.

"—because these matters may be resolved by calculation. For example, do we have enough available mechanical energy and physical labor to do the job in the time remaining? This is a matter of calculation. I should suppose we would have to bury the ship soon after we cross the orbit of Mercury, which is, I believe . . ."

"A week from now," said Melinda. "Give or take a few hours."

"Yes, thank you. During that period we would be well advised to continue work on the heat-transfer coupling, so that we will be prepared to launch from Everest after rounding the sun. All these are matters of calculation." He paused again; they did not interrupt his silence. "Let us suppose the calculations are favorable; then my question is simple enough," he said at last, weariness reducing his voice to a whisper. "Do we have the courage to try it? Oh, it's a desperate course, even if we are lucky. Still, if the numbers are with us, logic tells me it's our only hope."

They gaped at him.

He went on. "I'll put it as bluntly as I can. Do we have the good will to work together, all of us? Are we willing to get ourselves out of this fix—or die trying?"

Melinda began to cry. And when Travis tried to speak, he found to his shock that his throat was tight and his own eyes were brimming with tears.

Travis and Spin were laboring in constricted icy darkness, floating at odd angles in the deep shaft. In slow motion Spin swung a cage of steel strutwork toward Travis. "Grab this."

The steel cage housed a laser interferometer, an exquisite instrument of science and artistry; Travis grappled with it and steered it, cables trailing, out of the shaft. He watched it fly slowly away, dwindling to blackness among the barely visible stars at the top of the shaft. The experiments Travis and Melinda had buried here in frozen gravel, forty meters below the surface—buried to preserve them when Everest buzzed the sun—were so much jetsam for the moment. Perhaps they could be redeployed, circumstances permitting. . . .

"I made a horse's ass of myself," Travis said.

"Guys cry sometimes. Like when they lose a game."

"No, he made me feel like a kid again. Like my dad sayin', 'Got the guts, son?'"

Spin grunted. "Your dad say that a lot?"

"Once. Maybe twice. That's all it takes to make an impression—when you're a kid."

"Yeah, I know."

"Do you?" Travis drew a deep lungful of recharged oxygen. "You're so damn quiet, Spin. So cool."

"Hell with that. Typical Travis Hill asshole remark." Spin

stopped what he was doing and glared at Travis, holding himself back. "You know why I don't like you, cowboy?" Spin's sudden vehemence, his unexpected loquacity, put Travis on guard. "It's not that you're a fucking know-it-all. It's not that you're a tin-plate hero, or that you bumped a guy we were all getting along with pretty good."

"No?" Travis coughed. "Then I guess it's because I got us into this."

"*This?*" Spin's hand lamp flickered over the slick surface of the eerie pit. He laughed. "Don't take too much credit."

"I mean I proposed this mi—"

"This isn't your asteroid. This isn't your ship. Maybe the mission was your idea; okay, it was a good idea. We would have been happy to do it without you."

For several moments they worked in silence, disassembling the delicate instruments, sending them out the shaft.

"The reason I never liked you, cowboy, is 'cause you don't need anybody. Not just us—if you don't want to be a team player, that's your business. I get the feeling you don't need anybody on the ground, either."

"And you do?"

"I wouldn't mind letting my mom set eyes on me one more time," Spin murmured sadly.

"Why are you telling me this?"

"Help me here." They disconnected heavy cables from a massive cylinder the size of a milk can—a radioisotope thermal generator, a container of hot fissioning plutonium 238 which had been intended to power the buried experiments for a century or two. "Watch the fins—okay. Let's heave it." Gently they sent it floating out the shaft.

For a long time after that, Spin ignored Travis's discomfort and said nothing else. When the pit was finally empty and they began placing the charges, Travis said, "That's bullshit. About me not needing anybody."

Spin sighed. "Quit trying so hard, will you?"

*   *   *

In the tangled guts of *Starfire*'s fusion reactor, Linwood and Melinda were curled around the third heat-transfer assembly.

"A little more and then we can go down and left. Let's go down," he said.

"The main thing is to—I got to squeeze it in between the three-sixty and the little dingy. . . ."

"Go forward and left."

"Watch it, Linwood!" A bracket sprang free and sailed away. Melinda lunged and caught it, quick as a fish, a split second later banging her shoulder painfully into the strutwork. When she handed him the curved bit of metal, she looked through the glass of his helmet and saw the clenched anguish around his closed eyes. "You all right?"

"Oh yes." His eyes opened. "That was a nice catch."

She watched his face. "We're pushing you too hard."

"Thank you for a fine sentiment, Melinda," he said quietly. "But it really is all or nothing."

She nodded. "I understand. I'm saying that we don't have to get this thing patched by day after tomorrow. We've already established that."

"There are so many other things to be done."

"They'll get done; there's time."

His gaze faltered; he looked down at the shiny piece of plumbing he held in his yellow glove. "Let's close this up before we quit. Then perhaps I'll take a nap."

Spin and Travis were out of the experiment shaft. With the pulse drill they were drilling a ring of new shafts around it, a ring thirty-five meters in diameter—a little more than *Starfire*'s diameter from wing tip to wing tip. These new shafts were narrow, not much wider than the fiery beam that bored through them, and they reached deep into the icy rock. Once the drill was positioned, each bore went quickly, but each subsequent repositioning of the drill, followed by a repositioning of the astronauts, was exhausting and did not go quickly at all.

"Spin, Travis, come in now. Your clocks are winding down." Robin's voice was a thin thread of meaning in the static.

Wearily they flew back to *Starfire*. The ship's bright metal was lit only by the stars; no longer a proud predator, it was now a shy pilot fish swimming nervously in the shadow of Everest.

Shed of their MMUs, safe inside the air lock waiting for the pressure to come up, Travis and Spin still avoided each other's eyes.

"Okay, we're at twenty-six kp," Robin said, her voice loud in the earphones of their Snoopy hats. "You can unsuit."

They helped each other out of the soiled and worn suits. "Well, hell," Spin said. "You're okay, Travis. For a middle-aged guy."

"What?"

"I was trying to shake you up."

Travis looked at him, surprised. "Why?"

"Whether you feel like it or not, you're part of the team, man. Time you admitted it to yourself. Pull on this, will you?"

Travis lifted the top half of Spin's suit over his head as the inner air lock door swung open.

Spin said, "What Melinda sees in you, I don't know."

What she had seen in him at first was a challenge, another big smart guy to be put in his place, a hero to be knocked off his pedestal. The way he'd muscled his way onto their crew with his money and his connections and his media charm, just casually brushing aside their teammate who'd been in his way. . . .

Not that she'd really liked Jimmy Giles all that well as a person. He was a sufferer and a preacher, a solemn prig who knew how to save the world and was eager to tell you. Melinda wasn't a Bible reader, but a line she'd heard in Sunday school at age ten or so had stuck in her head—it was such an odd figure of speech—about not trying to pluck the mote out of somebody else's eye until you'd cast the beam out of your own. Imagine going around with a two-by-four through your head. Anyway, Jimmy was a Bible reader, he probably knew that verse, he should have taken the advice.

And there was something going on between Jimmy and Robin, she hated to think what; it gave her the queasy feeling she got whenever she tried to imagine her parents having sex. Or worse, her mother having sex with anyone but her father.

So Jimmy was no great loss in himself, if you wanted Melinda's opinion. Still, what got her steamed was Travis's attitude, or what she'd supposed his attitude to be, that he could just push his way onto their team.

But when he got on, he'd stayed out of their way, he hadn't messed with them, he hadn't tried to hog the limelight, he hadn't seemed to care about anything but his big fat asteroid. Being part of their team didn't seem to matter to him. And that was worse.

He wouldn't fight. Challenge him on the facts, and he'd answer—and usually be right, dammit—but it wasn't a contest. Challenge him physically, in space—this was the only guy who ever bailed out of orbit and lived to tell the tale—and he'd fuck up, get stuff backwards, crash into things, and laugh about it. Oh, he cared enough to be embarrassed, but not enough to be humiliated. So you couldn't beat him at that, either.

And the wisecracks. Melinda loved to get in the last word; she frankly savored the "gotcha" when the other guy was left standing there with his mouth open. With Travis around, half the time it was her with her mouth open. And he didn't care about that, either. He didn't rub it in, and when you'd zing him he'd just laugh again, as if to say, "Hey look, isn't that great? She did it again, she got in the last word"—which made her feel like a kid.

He'd even topped her at crying, not one of her specialties, but an area she had thought off limits to men.

She could have been punching a bag full of Styrofoam. Her frustration had been building throughout the year's training on Earth—especially because so much of what there was to learn about the asteroid was taught by Travis himself—and it finally peaked when they landed on Everest. She'd set him up to make an ass of himself with his little flags, and he'd obliged. But he'd looked good doing it.

When the frustration finally peaked, it vanished. She was astonished to find herself feeling differently about him. She realized that she'd devoted a disproportionate amount of attention to this man, this hard, scarred, green-eyed man with the cool ways and the hole through his core.

Feisty Melinda, always spying, always listening, always

lurking with her creeper-peeper, did not lack empathy; she had been quick to realize, even before he let the mask slip, that Travis's apparent not caring was rooted in profound despair, some devastation more sere than Jimmy Giles's wet guilt, and perhaps more honest.

Was she the only one to see it? Spin couldn't, Robin didn't have a handle on Travis at all, and Linwood never talked about other people. But Melinda knew: Travis cared, all right. He wanted Linwood's respect, he wanted Spin's friendship, he wanted Robin's commendation. He wanted to do his job, do it right, be technically and socially competent, be acknowledged for it. Enthusiasms and ambitions welled up errantly from whatever part of his soul, of himself, that he was trying to excise.

But Melinda, or so it seemed to her, was irrelevant to his goals. From her he wanted nothing.

In the darkness of the sleep compartment clockwise from Melinda's, Spin was trying to coax his weary muscles to relax. That exchange with Travis had set him to worrying an old ache: he was thinking about his father, long gone from the family and now dead as well, a fat little middle manager at General Electric who'd had Spin pumped full of growth hormones before he was old enough to understand what was going on, much less have a say in it. For fifteen years, ever since he'd found out why he was so tall, Spin had been secretly convinced he was some kind of freak of science. Although his mother and his coaches and subsequently teams of NASA doctors had assured him that his reflexes owed nothing to artificial growth factor, that they were his own genetic legacy, he had not trusted any of them. Through no fault of his own, life had cast him in the role of the fastest android on Earth, he thought, and he had studied the part assiduously. He'd been good at it, handling aircraft and spacecraft as if he were a thinking extension of the hardware.

Lately he had begun to ponder the nature of machines, of the shiny spaceship of which he felt so much a part, which had proven so vulnerable to errors of logic; of the clockwork solar system with its inherent uncertainties; of the counterintuitive ability of humans to nudge fate. He had begun to wonder what his life might be like if things didn't always go according to someone else's plans. Maybe that's what made him want to see his mother again, to tell her that he'd finally gotten the message he hadn't wanted to accept from her before, that he was human after all.

Along with his awakened human curiosity, he had discovered an unfamiliar zest for what each new day would bring. As he drifted into sleep, he found himself already eager for tomorrow.

Clockwise from Spin, Robin too was trying to sleep. Her duties this day had been light, monitoring the ship, keeping track of the work parties, attempting to communicate with ever-more-distant Earth through repeated violent solar disturbances.

She knew all the ship's measurable dimensions in "readiness space" to several places past the decimal, so she could stow that worry. Her thoughts were on her crew.

On Linwood, under increasing physical stress.

On Spin, with his blossoming desire to be a person instead of a machine, something he had discovered for himself yesterday or the day before, it seemed, although his hope had been discernible to Robin long before that.

On Travis, still torn between the urge for companionship and the need to be utterly alone, emerging painfully and with unpredictable starts and stops from his fibrous emotional cocoon.

On Melinda. She was in love, and it hurt to watch.

"In love," detestable phrase, but the condition it described was serious. Melinda watched Travis all the time he was visible, challenged him, provoked him, made jokes, bid for his attention. And he carefully avoided her.

Robin, if she had known Travis well enough, might have been able to intervene with some subtlety. But she knew Melinda much better than she knew Travis, knew her whole *vita:* Punahou School, Carnegie-Mellon, MIT—valedictorian, *cum laude, summa cum laude*—NASA research grant, group achievement award, desperate achiever, addicted winner. Double-bound by her entrepreneur father, the billionaire video capitalist and superjock amateur racer, the master of sarcasm, the perfect asshole, that father of hers without an untrimmed line or a hemorrhoid or a visible emotion.

Melinda's striving for perfection never acknowledged by her father, not once—always dismissed with a sneering "How nice, what a surprise, such a sweet little girl"—her serious, determined striving for perfection, never once acknowledged by her father. What extraordinary calm she exhibited, sliding through NASA's psychiatric review, letting the desire show, disguising the need. How many questions must she have endured on the subject of her older brother, driven to suicide—"driven" not too strong a word, despite whatever nastiness her brother may have been nursing in his own hothouse psyche—driven to suicide by their father's demand for perfection.

And so we all support Melinda, Robin reflected, and respect her for all the things she does so well, and find ourselves helpless on her account when she comes up against the wall.

Melinda. Travis. Not as old as he pretended, or even as old as he looked, but worn and experienced enough to have a good opinion worth her coveting. She craving that final gold star. He pretending, for what reason Robin did not know, that love was foreign to him, and thus pretending that Melinda did not exist.

Perfectly suited to break each other's hearts, if by some miracle they survived the passage of the sun.

Clockwise from Robin, sleepless Travis tried to concentrate on the engineering problems that faced them, the excavations, the planting of charges, the tricky matter of removing 225,000 cubic meters of debris from a hole big enough to swallow a rocketship. His imagination ran instead to Melinda's curly hair, her freckled nose, her muscular legs and arms in the shorts and T-shirt she often wore around the cabin. . . .

Turning his head, he could just glimpse, past the edge of the curtain, a wedge of Melinda's sleeping form, upside down across the corridor. Her hair was floating around her head; her arms were raised like an operatic sleepwalker's.

He tried the mind-emptying trick, the one where you say "One . . . one . . . one . . ." over and over, with the intention of discarding any coherent thoughts that arise in the process. Great trick, but it never did work.

He sighed and stared at the white canvas padding of his sleeping compartment, a few centimeters away from where he floated in his sleep restraint. He stopped struggling. He would either go to sleep or he wouldn't.

He turned his head again and peeked across the corridor.

In the last of the sleeping compartments, Linwood's sleep was deep and dreamless.

In the slow dark days that followed, *Starfire* remained in the line of sight of Earth, still enjoying the shelter of the black mountain that rolled beneath the ship a little less than once in half a day. Even with anomalously high levels of solar activity and the sun shining fully into the Earth's antennas, the ship was able to maintain sketchy communications with NASA—communications, however, that were more successful for high-speed, highly redundant streams of telemetry than for ordinary voice communication. So Houston and *Starfire* gave up talking to each other, except for perfunctory daily words of mutual encouragement.

Sent as telemetry, Jimmy Giles's software corrections were received and written into the ship's programs by Melinda and Linwood a day after the two of them finished reassembling the heat-transfer unit. They queried the computers: according to *Starfire,* the ship was ready to fly. Had not a deep suspicion of *Starfire*'s software infected the astronauts, the word might have been more reassuring.

In any event it was too late to take the easy way home. All the mass-energy remaining in the hydrogen and lithium tanks could not have lifted *Starfire* from the whirlpool of the sun's gravitational field by main force.

The sun drew closer and shone brighter; on the surface of Everest the temperature continued to rise. Long a stranger to the inner solar system, the asteroid at its heart was frozen to within a few dozen degrees of absolute zero. The chill rock was approaching the sun so swiftly that warmth had penetrated no more than a few centimeters of its husk, but already the astronauts were daily entertained by luminous jets of glowing gas on the near horizon, plumes of vapor sublimed from watery pockets in Everest's red hemisphere.

After three days of work Travis and Spin had drilled all their holes and planted all their charges. They returned to the ship. Travis watched over Spin's shoulder as the flight deck screens displayed the asteroid rolling slowly under the ship. The target inched up below them. Spin pushed a button. There was a jolt, a confused slurry of rock and dust outlining a wide circle, debris floating above the surface in a slowly sifting cloud. Much of it would take days to disperse.

They climbed back into their stinking spacesuits and went down to the surface again.

The good results were confirmed: with well-placed charges they had cut a plug in the crumbling coal-and-ice side of Everest thirty meters across, and a hundred and fifty meters deep—a plug of frozen rock longer by half than a football field, fitted into the side of the asteroid like a cork in a bottle. Force would be needed to pop that cork: a powerful explosion from beneath or a long, slow, steady pull from above.

They opted for the steady pull. Although they still had high explosives in their seismographic kit, they would need them later, beyond the sun. Their corkscrew was a solar probe, one of the two satellites *Starfire* should have launched days earlier, satellites that were looking more like NASA surplus with each passing hour.

The probes had been intended to orbit close to the sun, where they would have been constantly buffeted by unpredictable shock waves in the corona. Throughout their useful life they would have had to point their carbon-carbon heat shields at the sun's center with great precision—so close to the sun they could not deviate from true vertical by even two degrees without burning out their instruments. In order to maintain stability in the seething solar environment, each probe was equipped with neutral-beam ion thrusters, their power supplied by compact nuclear reactors intended to operate for a decade.

Now it was apparent that those clever thruster systems would never see duty around the sun. But they could still lift a mass of rock from the side of Everest.

One probe was enough. Travis and Spin ditched its heat shield, settled it in the center of the plug, spiked it to the ground; they brought its reactor to critical, reprogrammed it, set its X- and Y-thrusters to compensate for the asteroid's lazy spin, set its Z-thrusters to spewing neutralized ions in a steady, undeviating stream. Lifted on this persistent thrust, the cork slowly emerged from the bottle. Where corners of the massive plug hung up, Travis and Spin aimed bursts of laser-drill fire to free them. They slaved at the task for two days.

After final hours of sweat-drenching labor, Travis was able to stand lightly on the surface of Everest and look up as a rough cylinder of frozen water and blackened stone finally eased clear of Everest, to hang in space like a flying acropolis in a Magritte painting. Beneath that soaring hill, a blacker well had opened in Everest, surrounded by a hazy cloud of detritus. Through the debris *Starfire* must descend and then pull down a blanket of stones over its head, to cover it against the fire to come.

Melinda and Robin had their heads together in NAVCOM.

"Adjusted orbital data from NASA," Melinda said. "If Everest is falling the way they say it is"—on the screen the orange line looped in and past the sun—"we're in trouble."

"What's the difference from before?"

"Not much in delta-vees. Maybe only a hundred meters per second or so. The problem is the shape of the curve."

"Show it to me again," Robin said.

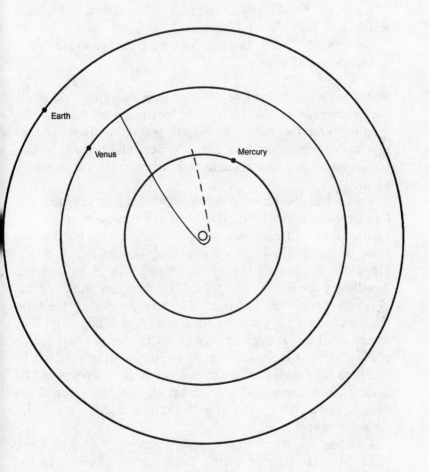

Approximate position of planets at perigee, August 15, 2023.

"Here. On a pass this tight our last window for Mercury is seven hours past perigee. At that point we're only six solar radiuses from the sun. We can't come out of Everest—we'd melt."

"Once more," Robin said.

Again the trajectories unspooled on the screen as Melinda watched. "Yes, it's a problem."

Robin said, "Well, the numbers may change again."

Melinda said nothing.

The word went around. By dinner time everyone had made the pilgrimage to the NAVCOM computer to look at the graphics and the data runstreams for themselves. Dinner that night—choice of beef steak w/rice pilaf or beef w/barbecue sauce and green beans w/mushrooms—was a dreary affair.

Travis had the cleanup detail. With his feet snugged into loops on the floor, he deftly fished the trays out of the discard basket and carefully scraped them under the suction hood of the disposal, before inserting them in the sterilizer. He was conscious of Melinda watching him as he worked, dawdling over her dinner plate. His thoughts were not exclusively upon her, however. He was pondering their dilemma: even if they survived the sun, it now appeared they would not have enough energy to catch Mercury and use its gravity to steer themselves back to Earth—Earth, which by the time they could afford to emerge from hiding would be fleeing from them, halfway across the solar system. They needed extra energy. His thoughts returned to the sturdy little solar probes. . . .

Crossing the wardroom with her plate of abandoned rice pilaf, Melinda tangled with a floating seat cushion; as she batted at it, the rice scattered like sticky shrapnel—all over Travis. "Oh, God dammit!"

He turned and made a nasty face.

"You think it's funny?" she cried. When he grinned, all

teeth, her embarrassment flamed into rage. "Clean it up yourself, then."

Nodding solemnly, he unlatched the vacuum hose and started carefully sucking the mess off himself and out of the air. She relented and tried to help. His solemnity didn't last; he couldn't keep from laughing.

"Damn you, Travis." She launched herself out of the room.

She sought refuge in NAVCOM, only to find Robin there ahead of her, running numbers on the computer. Linwood, across the corridor, was deep in thought. She tried to excuse herself, but Robin stopped her. "Don't go."

"I didn't really have anything to—"

"Melinda, stay here. Talk to me."

Melinda stayed, taking it as an order, trying to hide her tears. Linwood glanced up and Robin glared at him; he coughed discreetly and extracted himself from PROP. Robin glanced at the comm screen; Spin was on the flight deck, staring at the big screen, a plug in his ear, listening to an audio chip. He had taken to living up there, communing with the ship.

"Will you talk to me?" Robin asked softly.

For a long time Melinda didn't want to say anything. Tears were pressing at the back of her eyelids, words were pressing at her throat, but she hated what they would sound like. Why make herself naked? "We're going to die," she said.

"You mean because we can't go home?" asked Robin, speaking quietly, distinctly. "Because we're going to bury ourselves in this rock, and this rock is going to burn to a cinder?"

Melinda laughed through her tears, startled, offended. "Yeah."

"And. . . ?"

"And that's not the worst of it," Melinda said, bobbing her head.

"What's the worst of it?"

Melinda turned away, rubbing at her forehead.

Robin persisted. "That over-the-hill cowboy doesn't know you're alive? Is that the worst of it?" She flicked the comm screen to the wardroom, where Travis was stowing the last of the dishes.

"Fucking ludicrous," Melinda agreed, crying harder.

Robin let Melinda float into the comfort of her embrace. Melinda's breath came in constricted heaves; after a moment the sighs flowed, the groans issued—

—and then she was giggling again. "Jesus, let's talk about something minimally significant."

"Okay," said Robin. "How about this: we aren't going to die."

Melinda sniffed. "I wish . . . I wish I didn't know better."

"I mean it," Robin said. "I've been studying the runstreams. . . ."

Travis was about to leave the wardroom when Linwood appeared. "Say, Doc, there's somethin' I'd like—"

"Later, please. I'm trying to think this through."

"Oh, okay. Sure." Be that way, Travis thought. He pushed himself into the corridor and moved upward.

He rose to the level of NAVCOM. "Say, Robin," Travis began, "there's somethin'—" In the indirect light it took him a moment to realize he was interrupting a private conversation. "Guess this is a bad time."

Melinda freed herself from Robin and smiled at him. Her face was smeared with tears that had no place to fall. "Go ahead. We had our talk."

Travis was already drifting away. He stopped himself. "Well, in that case—Robin, I've been thinkin' about this potential delta-vee situation. . . ."

"Do me a favor and sit on it a few minutes," she said. She flicked a switch on the comm panel, sending her voice throughout the ship. "Spin, Linwood, we need a meeting right now. In the wardroom."

Robin maneuvered past Travis and moved down the corridor. Travis and Melinda were left staring at each other. Her eyes were red above her pink and freckled nose. This time the look she gave him held no challenge. "I'm sorry I made such a mess. With the food, and . . ."

"Hey." He plucked at his sweat-soaked, soil-stiffened jacket. "Time I took this outfit to the cleaners anyway."

"We've all had a look at the data Houston sent up. The orbital corrections are minor, based on the refined mass estimates we gave them. The consequences for us, however, are significant. We can't wait until two days past perigee to leave Everest, as we'd assumed. It looks like our last opportunity is going to be seven hours, maybe pushing eight hours, past perihelion. Exposed, that close, only the engine structures and the radiators will be able to withstand incident radiation—and how efficient the radiators would be . . ." She let the sentence dangle. "No matter. The solar disk will still take up some fifteen angular degrees in the sky. Even perfectly aligned, end on to the sun, the tanks"—and, as she did not have to remind them, everything above the tanks, including the crew module—"will be above the shadow cone." She smiled. "So we've got this minor technical problem: at P plus eight, we can't come out of our hole."

Linwood said, "I have been giving the matter some thought." Then he paused, as he customarily did, to marshall his sentences.

Into the pregnant silence Robin said, "I'll be interested to know if—"

But Travis, whose eyes had been growing brighter throughout her speech, could not sit on it any longer. "Folks, there's a hell of a lot of energy stowed on this ship that we haven't *thought* of yet."

"Propulsion is your department, Linwood," Robin said.

"Hm, well," Linwood said, "it has occurred to me that the solar probe satellites are equipped with nuclear-powered ion-drive attitude stabilization systems."

"Hell," muttered Travis, chagrined. "I guess we did."

Spin and Melinda glanced at each other. Satellites? So?

"Now, in the short time remaining to us," Linwood continued, "the ion drives are of insufficient thrust to impart the necessary incremental velocity change to Everest. . . ."

Spin and Melinda looked at each other again. Delta-vees to *Everest*?

". . . however, the reactors themselves are fueled by the fissile isotope of uranium, U 235."

Melinda said, "Fissile!" Spin's eyebrows were still raised.

"I calculate that, given appropriate processing and assembly, a device with a yield of perhaps forty kilotons may be fabricated," Linwood continued.

Melinda said, "Three Hiroshimas."

"Mm, well, hmm," said Linwood. "That's one way of putting it. A device on that order."

"A device?" Spin asked. "An atomic *bomb*? Won't that tend to bend our rear end?"

"Placement will be a challenge, but I should imagine we'll be quite safe," Linwood said. "Given ablation and internal collapse of the asteroid, we should be able to arrange things so that our instantaneous acceleration is less than one gee."

"See, we don't blow ourselves up, we blow up the rock," Melinda reassured Spin.

Travis grinned. "You know, Doc, when I was a kid on the ranch, I used to love to tie two firecrackers together and stick 'em in the end of a lead pipe, light 'em both and shoot one out with the other—"

"Yes, Professor Hill, that is the general idea. The essential concept is to steer a portion of the asteroid. By ejecting a significant mass near the sun, the remaining mass—which includes ourselves—will be thrown into a higher orbit, allowing us to achieve rendezvous with Mercury without emerging from hiding."

"Simple," Robin said soberly, avoiding Spin's eye.

"I *know* it'll work, Doc, I just know it," Travis said.

Linwood bent his weighty gaze on the enthusiastic astronaut. "Professor Hill, there is something I've considered saying for some months now. Please forgive me if this is an inappropriate moment."

"Hell no, Doc. What is it?"

"I *hate* being called Doc."

Early in the morning, Linwood and Robin went into the cargo bay and ripped open the remaining solar probe. It took them only an hour to remove the fuel assemblies from its reactor; with their moderators still in place, the steel-sheathed rods were not warm, not even dangerously radioactive. Robin and Linwood spent another hour scavenging the instrument platform for useful electronics, then carried their booty inside the ship. Linwood, commandeering the geology lab, went to work tearing the uranium fuel assemblies apart. He had four days to build an atomic bomb.

Everest had given birth to a satellite, a plug of rock and ice orbiting at a thousand meters altitude, kept in position above the hole in the asteroid's side by the thrusters of the shackled first solar probe. Melinda and Travis were in the bottom of that hole. They had redeployed the solar panels above and rigged the laser pulse drill to sink a narrow shaft deep into the heart of Everest, wide enough to permit the passage of the bomb that Linwood was building.

For two hours they hovered nervously above a chaos of splattered lava that coagulated on the walls and floor and occasionally threw up globes of molten rock that Travis and Melinda had to dodge. In the midst of the inferno the squat and ugly drill persisted, like a plumber in a flooding basement, until finally its beam went dark.

"We make it to depth?" Melinda asked.

"That's what the numbers say."

"Nifty gadget," she said. "I hope you sell lots of 'em."

"Thanks. Let's get some lunch; I hear it's ground beef wi' pickle sauce today."

"Hey, hey."

"When we get back to Houston it's beef Wellington. Baby carrots, Belgian endive, whatever, all that fancy stuff. And all the champagne you can drink. I'm buyin'."

"Cowboy, you've got a date."

Over the horizon, *Starfire* crept from hiding in Everest's shadow. The excavation site that they hoped would be in shadow during the crucial hours of perigee was presently sidelong to the sun. Slowly the ship wheeled, aiming itself with bursts of fire until it was pointed backwards at the gaping hole—poised between the asteroid and its satellite like a billet of shining metal between anvil and hammer.

Sunside, every surface blazed; shadowside, only a lack of stars rendered outlines visible. Everest was a day past the orbit of Mercury; the temperature at its surface had risen to 400 degrees Kelvin, not yet as hot as noon on slow-rolling Mercury, not yet hot enough to melt lead, but getting there fast.

Spin was on the flight deck, sweating. "Twenty meters, did I hear?"

Melinda's shredded reply came over the comm: ". . . enty meters, rog . . . clos . . ."

"I wouldn't mind some pad numbers," Spin growled at Robin, beside him on the flight deck.

"Four-niner over forty. RCS downmode on the maneuver pad."

"A braking pattern, please," he said to Robin. Her fingers jabbed at keys while he rocked the joy stick.

Melinda was riding above the engine exhaust coils, sheltered from the sun on the shadowside of the ship. She trained her

video camera on the scene that unfolded below her: the maw
of the pit opening beneath an obscuring mist of water vapor.
Far above her, little attitude jets constantly puffed from the
side of *Starfire,* rocking the ship gently into the depths of the
great hole.

"Okay, we're at sea level. We're inside the hole,"
Melinda said. "Repeat, wing tips are below sea level. We are
inside. Clearance nominal."

Below the mist the vacuum was thick with floating gravel
and glittering chips of ice. The debris bounced off the delicate carbon wings of the ship as they edged past the walls.
Melinda switched on her helmet lamp and called numbers
for many minutes until, finally—

"Ten meters and closing," said Melinda.

". . . opy ten," said Spin's voice in her Snoopy hat. The
jets spewed vapor, and the column of steel imperceptibly
slowed.

"Five meters," said Melinda.

"Fi . . ." Spin never sounded tense, even when he had
reason to be. Now his tension was evident. If one radiator
wing scraped and sustained significant damage, if the magnetic coils of the main engine exhaust slammed into the
floor—well, never mind flaming suns and A-bombs.

Melinda watched as the delicate engine coils approached
the shaft's shocked and frozen bottom.

Steering jets intermittently outgassed, playing an intricate
tune on a soundless calliope. The massive ship continued to
slow, but its inertia was that of an ocean liner drifting into a
pier. Finally it stopped, floating mere centimeters from the
bottom of the shaft.

"Jesus, Spin."

The dogged, ugly laser pulse drill squatted below the ship,
fixed in gelid slurry.

". . . ay again?"

"Clearance approximately one-half meter," she said.
"One-half meter from the bottom of the shaft. Hold it there.

We will proceed to secure the ship. Just don't let 'er move, buddy."

On the flight deck, Spin let a nostril-flaring grin stretch his face. "Ain't I hot shit, though?"

"Yes, you is." Robin smiled.

"Whoo*eee!*"

Travis was descending hand over hand, headfirst down a steel cable, the spark of his helmet lamp marking his passage. A dozen similar cables, scavenged from the solar arrays, draped down *Starfire*'s sides, almost invisible in the dark. Toggle bolts were sunk into the sides of the shaft. Melinda and Travis laced the cables through the bolts, cradling the ship in a cat's cradle of wire. The work went on a long time. A small bright cloud of sunlit mist hung forty-five stories over their heads.

When it was over Travis played a hand lamp over the flimsy web that suspended the ship in the shaft. He shook his head dubiously. "Like tryin' to hog-tie a shark with ten-pound test."

Spin and Robin took the next shift. They moved out of the main air lock, drifting cautiously upward through the tangle of cables and the dense floating debris.

They swam upward toward the light. They passed through a cloud of subliming water. The burgeoning sun flooded the scene with a harsh yellow glare: all around them the surface of Everest was glowing with escaping gas. They immediately adjusted the water flow in their suits and flew on into space, until they reached the far side of the plug that hung in space above *Starfire*.

From here they could have looked down upon the whole of the mighty mountain silhouetted against the sun, but they ignored it, laboring instead at the clumsy task of inverting the massive solar probe. Its Z-thrusters had been designed to work in only one direction, "upward"—now they needed the probe to push "downward." Before they got it rerigged, the air conditioners in their suits were starting to fail. They barely finished the job before fleeing to the shadow of the pit.

From *Starfire*'s flight deck they reactivated the probe's thrusters. Slowly the ragged plug nosed back into the hole. They sent a radio signal through the mass of rock to turn off the probe's thrusters; crumbling and sliding, the plug sank thirty meters before fracturing and jamming fast. *Starfire* was sealed into the cold and airless pit.

Robin repressurized the ship with a mixture of nitrogen and oxygen approximating air, for what Linwood was doing could not be done in pure oxygen.

Some home-brew nukes are easy to build, some are not. Using material from Travis's geology kit—solvents, an intense little furnace, a high-speed centrifuge, clever slicers and grinders and polishers, a store of high explosives—Linwood could have tackled any one of several designs, but the more difficult would have taken more time than he could spare. To a man of Linwood's talents, however, "easy" did not mean unsophisticated.

He considered himself lucky to be working with highly enriched fuel from the solar probe's small, hot, high-efficiency reactor. Inside its cladding, the fuel was cast in rods of uranium-zirconium hydride. The trick was to burn off the hydrogen, then dissolve the zirconium without dissolving the uranium; a solution of sodium hydroxide did the job, with barium nitrate added to precipitate the uranium. After the hydrogen was cooked out in the furnace, the rest of the six-hour operation was done in a centrifuge at low gees—necessary to keep the reactions going in weightlessness, in the absence of convective currents. The final separation of the heavy uranium from dissolved zirconium took another half-hour of centrifuging, at high gees.

After forty-six hours—four hours off for sleep—Linwood had the pure, enriched uranium he needed. He didn't need anywhere near the so-called classical amount, the twenty kilos that, when found missing from the inventories of uranium fabrication plants, make their administrators nervous. There were tricks to building an efficient bomb, and Linwood knew them by heart.

His design was classical in its own right, with tropes. Start by holding two subcritical masses of fissile material separated, then drive them rapidly together at the moment of detonation. With Little Boy they did it by firing a subcritical plug from one end of the bomb into a hole in a subcritical donut at the other; the bomb casing was hardly more than a gun barrel.

So sure were the Manhattan Project scientists that the gun-barrel scheme would work that they never bothered to test it; they just shipped it off to Japan. The test they conducted in the sage flats of the Jornada del Muerto, three weeks before Hiroshima, was of a far trickier implosion design, using plutonium, not uranium. It worked too. Curiosity or possibly sheer technical exuberance, masquerading as politics, inspired them to test it again, three days after Hiroshima, on Nagasaki.

Linwood had no intention of building anything so chancy as a pure implosion bomb. It was possible to combine the best features of the gun-barrel and implosion designs, to combine ruggedness, reliability, and moderately good yield. The idea was to bring together two subcritical masses of uranium and at the same time crush efficient neutron reflectors around them. He'd done this sort of thing before, though never in quite such a free-hand fashion.

After Linwood had his shaped masses of uranium—each about half the size of an orange—he set about machining the steel reflectors. That was a bit trickier, for reasons having to do with melting points and shock waves and the shapes that shaped charges take as they are hurled into their targets.

Afterward there would be the kneading of the explosives, the welding of the casing—a couple of surplus satellite fuel tanks should do for that—and detonators to be wired, and the synchronizer circuits to be etched and soldered, to ensure that everything went off at once. . . .

His hands were quite happy with this work. He felt he understood what drove sculptors and carvers and ceramicists—the luxury of combining abstract thought with the pleasures of touch, the rush of muscular flexing as well as the tingle of fine manipulation. One might arrange the arts on a scale of sensuousness, he thought. Were dancers starved for ideas? Were photographers starved for touch? No wonder poets loved their pencils, their only point of contact with the material world. The myth of Pygmalion had originated in the seductions of the marble itself, he was sure. All those tales of artists and models . . . the tension of the intellect which held opposites at a distance snapping in an instant—dichotomy lost, fire in the womb, criticality.

Some children are born with fear; they will not taste, they will not touch, they will not dare. Some are born indomitable; pain for them is instructive, not a deterrent—like Jean and Marcel, his grandchildren, grubbing in the sand after strange creatures. Suggesting that marine biologists are the adult forms of fearless children who would stick their hands into any dark hole, who were cut and nipped and stung repeatedly but were not deterred. And suggesting that bomb makers are the adult forms of fearless children who played with matches and caps and firecrackers, who were blistered and burned, who lost fingers, perhaps, or eardrums, even eyes, but who were not deterred.

Such children, in the adult form, still do not understand deterrence; individually they lead us to discovery, and in groups they lead us to the brink of extinction. Jean and Marcel had inherited perhaps too many of the wrong kind of Linwood's genes, although certainly their fearlessness had been transmitted by their mother, his daughter, without notably affecting any aspect of *her* life. Let sociobiology, that pseudoscience, straighten it out if it could; for his part, Linwood had come late to the realization that it was not his right to keep blowing things up and shooting things down because he would not be deterred from having fun.

Sooner or later we adult forms must learn to channel our enthusiasms, he thought. Channel, not eradicate—and only in a limited way for the sake of our progeny, since evidently the world will continue full of dangers. Still, if it came to that, Linwood would rather Jean and Marcel were eaten by sharks than vaporized in war games.

Ahead of all those considerations, Linwood wanted to see his grandchildren again, to discuss their newest discoveries with them. Ahead of that he wanted to take Jeri in his arms. And if he had to build another damn bomb to get home, well . . .

Besides, it *was* fun.

They had no communication with Earth, not even telemetry; no signal from Earth penetrated the increasing solar interference. Two days from the sun the cameras and antennas they had left on the surface burned out, but not before they had seen the surface of Everest seethe, not before flaming chunks of it had spun off into space and a veil of incandescent haze had been drawn across the stars. Through that haze the sun rose twice in a ship's day, a gargantuan disk of flame, rapidly enlarging. Then the big screens went dark.

Linwood, seeking a moment's respite from his lonely work, floated into the wardroom. Travis and Melinda were there, he curled into his corner, she into hers, both of them watching Melinda's recording of the descent into the shaft. Travis called it her how-to video: how to put a ship in a bottle. Linwood glanced around the cluttered space. The ferns with which the place had been cheerily decorated had withered from neglect, but a tiny lithops, Linwood's contribution, still thrived.

Melinda looked up at his haggard face. "Anything we can do?"

He shook his head. He occupied himself prying a package of orange drink out of the pantry, while on the big screen, a shining *Starfire* slid into the pit, a sword into a stone.

"We humorin' ourselves, Linwood?" Travis asked. "Is this gonna work?"

"Mmm"—Linwood yawned—"'scuse me. The answer is yes. The techniques are well established."

Travis chuckled. "Shoot, you're just tryin' to make it sound like you're havin' fun."

From Linwood's studied expression, they knew he was about to deliver himself of a statement. "It *is* fun, you see," he said. "I think that no one who has not sat in on that peculiar game of dares could understand. It used to be a great deal of fun. Making them bigger. Making them smaller. Enhancing neutrons, or x rays, or . . . just making them do tricks. Making fools of Congress and everyone else who objected. . . ." Linwood rubbed his reddened eyes.

Travis said quietly, "I guess I never understood what you—"

"One day I realized what they were for." He fought off another yawn. "Then I changed specialties."

Twelve hours later Linwood tightened the last bolt. The "device," a steel egg the size of a big garbage can, filled most of the corridor. Both its ends bristled with protrusions resembling spark plugs—the detonators for the hand-molded explosives inside the casing. The thing had to be put together in the corridor because it was too big for the laboratory.

"Hope it can squeeze through the air lock," Spin muttered.

"Uh-oh. Anyone measured it?" Travis asked sharply.

"Oh my goodness gracious." Linwood looked stricken. *Why hadn't he thought of that?*

If a pin could have dropped . . .

Linwood smiled a slow, sly smile.

They had to dismantle the laser drill to get access to the shaft. Spin and Melinda and Travis guided the bomb into the shaft. She went first, the bomb went next, and Travis followed, pulling a wire behind him that Spin payed out from the cargo bay. Spin had fixed connectors to the ends of separate spools of cable, scavenged from antenna leads, and sometimes he brought Travis up short while he snapped them together.

The shaft reached deep, to the fault plane that divided Everest—a shaft narrow and dark and exceedingly long, but perfectly straight. So they had no need of maneuvering units; a gentle shove from the edge of the shaft, and inertia carried them through a suspension of ice crystals, steadily on toward the bottom more than one kilometer away. For most of the distance the walls were the familiar frozen-gravel mixture, but they passed seams of pure recrystallized iron, layers of dense black basaltlike stone, and inclusions of compressed ice that had not seen light for a billion years, or four billion. . . .

"Okay, *Starfire,* we're here."

". . . opy," the radio hissed.

Melinda slowed her descent by pushing against the walls. She drifted into the natural chamber near the end of the shaft and shone her lamp over its walls. "Golly." It was a hollow on the fault plane, and like the geode explored by Travis and Robin, it was a cave lined with diamonds. "I'm glad I didn't miss this."

"Comin' at ya," Travis warned.

The spike-headed bomb slid out of the shaft. Standing on diamonds, Melinda cushioned its descent.

They maneuvered the bomb to one side of the irregular cave. They wanted no gamma rays, no prompt neutrons flying up the pipe toward *Starfire* before the shaft was melted and crushed.

They sank bolts between clusters of diamonds and strapped the bomb to the rock with steel cables. They fastened electrical connectors to the detonators, connected the detonators to the synchronizer, connected the synchronizer to the cable from the main bus. After an hour of close, patient work, when they were ready to return—

—the asteroid trembled. The violent shaking went on for

half a minute. Travis and Melinda bounced from the walls, collided with each other, ricocheted off the walls again. The soundless tremor stopped abruptly, but it took the astronauts another half a minute to stabilize themselves. Unintelligible voices squawked in their headsets.

"We must be burning for real," Travis said. "Like riding on a Roman candle."

Chunks of diamonds were bouncing around them, but the steel tub they had implanted in the gravid crystalline uterus was still strapped securely in place.

"This will get worse, won't it?" Within the flickering shadows of her helmet Melinda's eyes were wide.

"Safe bet."

"In that case"—she reached up and plucked a bright gem rolling in the vacuum—"for the memories."

Two more quakes rattled the shaft before Travis and Melinda rejoined Spin outside the air lock.

"Why don't you look happier?" Travis demanded.

"There's a dozen splices in that cable," Spin said. "If we'd needed any more I would have been tearing out the internal wiring."

"We let a lot of cable burn on the surface," Travis said. "Stupid. Waste not, want not."

"Your dad say that?"

"My ma. More than once or twice."

They clambered in through the open outer hatch. Spin hit the buttons to bring the steel door down and seal it behind them.

"I had some friends in San Francisco," Melinda said as they waited for the lock to pressurize. "They bought an old house, and they were remodeling, and when they opened the walls to get at the wiring, there wasn't a piece of wire more than a foot long in there. It was all twisted together, a piece at a time, copper and iron—some of it was even barbed wire, fence wire—because the house was built the year after

the earthquake and you couldn't buy enough good wire anywhere."

They pondered that a moment. "Lucky it never burned
down," Spin said.

The pressure came up, and they pulled off their helmets
as the inner hatch opened. Robin was waiting in the corridor. Her expression was sober.

"Melinda, when you're out of that thing, Linwood needs
your help."

"Sure, what's he need?"

The ship rattled and shook.

"Help with the detonation program."

"Program? I thought we just pulled the trigger."

"He'll explain."

Melinda found Linwood asleep, floating loosely in the webbing of his acceleration couch in PROP. Reluctantly she
shook his shoulder. He didn't respond.

Dirt was etched into the crevices on his forehead and
around his eyes; his white-streaked beard was three days
old. His mouth was open, but his breathing was inaudible.
She shook him harder.

His eyes came open, but for a moment he seemed lost.

"You wanted help with something, Linwood?"

He turned to Melinda and took another second to recognize her. "Oh, yes. Sorry to bother you with more work," he
whispered. He struggled to free himself from his webbing.
"If you would be good enough to call up the seismographic
plot . . ."

Motioning her ahead of him, he drifted across to NAV-
COM. She slid into her seat in front of the computer and
brought up the stored graphics.

He yawned and shook his head. "Now when we detonate
the device, it will cut Everest in two," he said, his voice
recovering something of its dry strength. "Our goal is not to
accelerate ourselves, but to change the mass, and thus the

trajectory, of our piece of the asteroid. To change it with sufficient precision to encounter Mercury, we need to know the relative masses of the two pieces we intend to sever. Moreover, we must relate these variables to Everest's position."

"But we've already calculated all tha—"

"Perhaps, but—"

A severe tremor rocked *Starfire* in its hammock of webbing.

"Yes, that illustrates the point nicely." Linwood nodded, as if he'd arranged a demonstration. "Everest is ablating. We have no way of knowing in advance precisely how much mass it will lose or where. We must monitor the changes continuously and program the device to detonate within some reasonable interval—say within five minutes of the optimum launch window."

"Five minutes?"

"Do you think that's too much?" he asked anxiously.

"Too much? No, I wasn't thinking that," she said, and sighed. "You're probably right—we haven't got the option to steer anything until we dig ourselves out. Where do we get the data?"

"We shall place gravimeters salvaged from the solar probes at our own position and at that of the device. Their data combined with our own inertial systems will drive the detonation program."

"Which we gotta write now—"

"Which we must now begin to write."

"—since we hit perigee in about twenty-four hours."

They split up the program and worked separately, across the corridor from each other. Two hours passed in concentrated labor, amid continual tremors. Then Melinda said, "Linwood, this doesn't look to be unmanageable. Why don't we take a break?" Getting no answer, she peered more closely into his cubicle. He was asleep.

She left her post and swam down to the wardroom.

Robin and Travis had recently returned from placing gravimeters outside the ship. They were hungrily shoving peas
w/mushrooms into their mouths.

"Linwood's been working too hard," Melinda announced.
"He won't hit the sack, but he keeps nodding off anyway."

The others peered at her. Robin swallowed a mouthful of
peas, with effort. "You have something in mind?"

"Dr. Deveraux, this is the commander. Report to the wardroom on the double. Mandatory briefing."

Linwood stirred and opened his eyes. His confusion lasted
longer this time—the dreams had been getting more vivid,
and this one had been particularly rich and persuasive. He
had been trudging the sand with Jeri as the sun came up in
the Gulf, brighter and brighter, the reflection of it piercing
his eyes with a dagger of light across the water.

From the clocks on his console he realized he'd been
asleep for five hours. They must have been waiting for him
to wake up, watching him on the comm.

"Now, Linwood," the tinny speaker insisted.

His heart began to pound. He pushed himself into the corridor and downward toward the wardroom.

As he emerged head downward through the ceiling, the
first thing that met his eye was a smeared lump he recognized as a cake—a symbolic cake, anyway—floating in space
in front of him. It bore a crude picture, a mushroom cloud, a
flock of five-pointed stars, sketched out with something like
icing.

"Who fabricated that?" he growled.

"Actually the design program was quite complex,"
Melinda began, in her best Linwoodese.

"Three weeks of cupcake rations stuck together," he interrupted, "and that looks like—"

"Toothpaste," Spin said. "Your regular, your peppermint,
and your whatever you call that blue goo."

Linwood righted himself, avoiding the drifting cake. "You could be joking," he muttered. "But somehow I think not. . . ."

Melinda launched herself at him and planted a fat kiss on his cheek. Robin and Spin and Travis applauded raucously.

"Yes, well," Linwood said, flustered. "Is there to be a briefing? Perhaps I might add a few items to the agenda. . . ."

"Are you kidding, Linwood?" Travis was aghast. "This is a *party*. Here, have a drink. You're a big orange man, I believe?" He thrust a plastic bottle into Linwood's hand. "Look, we even made decorations."

A strip of paper towels in one corner bore the legend "Goodbye Sun, Hello Earth." Over the screen of the big monitor more towels had been taped, with a movie-style title drawn in colored marker pens: *Flash Deveraux and the Rocketeers of the Lost Diamond Asteroid. Chapter One.*

"So you have." He sucked at his orange drink. "What are we celebrating?"

Travis, at a loss, shrugged. "Sort of a pre–device-ignition party, I guess."

"Really, this is premature," Linwood said stiffly.

"You mean it might not work?" Spin asked, wide-eyed.

Linwood was offended. "As I have said repeatedly, there is no question of its not . . ." They watched solemnly, cheeks quivering, as he got it. "I mean . . . I meant to say, this has not been anyone's personal project." His voice softened. "We're together."

"And we'll stay together," Robin said fervently.

"I'll drink to that," said Melinda.

"*Salud,*" said Travis, and he and Melinda gleefully thunked their plastic bottles together so hard they both rebounded and ricocheted from the walls.

While everyone was laughing Linwood eyed the drifting cake. "Do you suppose if I dug into that from underneath I could salvage some of my personal cupcake ration?"

*   *   *

The party ended an hour later, a bit awkwardly, with everyone fake drunk on fatigue and silliness. Linwood, whose eyes kept closing in the middle of his long sentences, said he wanted to go back to work. Melinda insisted that the program was almost complete, that what remained was routine work, that the optimum time to detonate the bomb would fall beyond perigee, somewhere within a window that was still a full day away. Robin finally ordered Linwood to his bunk, firmly enough that he took her seriously.

Travis volunteered for cleanup, and Melinda offered to join him. Robin glanced at Spin, who was already sleeping where he floated. "Calder, wake up," Robin barked. He did so instantly. "You're hitting the sack, *now*. And so am I." They left the wardroom without looking back.

There was not all that much mess to clean up. Travis and Melinda did what had to be done and turned down the lights.

"Well . . ."

"Yep."

She turned to go and found he had her by the ankle. She rolled and floated perpendicular to him. His right hand was around her ankle, the wrist with its bracelet of sparkling diamonds exposed beneath the soiled cuff of his jacket. He looked at her, and the green eyes in the shadowed face might have been saying anything, but she knew what they were saying.

"Hey, cowboy, you be holdin' on to my foot."

"Yep."

"What's the matter, the shoelace got you stumped?"

His face wrinkled up and he started to laugh, without a sound.

When the last of their clothes came off, the diamonds spilled from her pockets and went tumbling through the half-light, pouring spectral webs of rainbow over their bodies.

"I've never done this," he said.

"Tell me another tall one."

"I mean, like this."

"I hear they've run it in WETF. Results nominal." She was trying to make him laugh again, but tears were pooling in her eyes.

Later they crept into their own sleeping compartments. Everyone around them snored energetically. They watched each other awhile, peeking from their sleep restraints across the dark corridor. Finally her shining eyes closed, and Travis allowed his gaze to drift to the white quilted padding of the wall.

Damnedest thing . . . across the textured canvas a little black ant was crawling. An ant, for God's sake.

"Mission control, Houston. Asteroid 2021 XA has passed behind the sun. There has been no futher communication with the crew of *Starfire*. . . ."

The dreams came swarming just ahead of consciousness. Travis knew where he was, wrapped in nylon in a steel tube in a black pit, so by a trick of half-sleepy logic he was convinced that his dream of Earth was real. His mother and Bonnie were in the rose garden. His mother lifted her shears to the stem beneath a hard scarlet bud.

"Not yet," said Bonnie. "It's just opening."

"It will open on the wall."

"You mean in the glass."

"Of course."

The blades severed the stem, leaving a clear green drop to ooze from the stump. Travis laughed in his sleep. His mother was so dramatic.

Taylor Stith arrived, tugging at his blood-colored wool tie and straightening the lapels of his tweed jacket, to announce that he was ready to go to work.

"We didn't expect you until next week," said Bonnie.

"The roses are wilted already. I don't have anything to do this week," Stith explained.

"When it gets dark he can clean up after Riptide," said Sam. "He'll have to put on a different uniform."

Travis was not happy about Sam casually making dispositions for his horse. He reached out of his sleep restraint and rapped on the glass doors to get their attention, but they ignored him.

Then the sun rose. Bonnie took all the clothes off her glowing body as quickly as she could, but it was too late: everyone shriveled and burned away. Only Travis could watch, by letting the sun eat his eyes, eating as it was eaten with lizard tongues of flame, seething with granules of fire like a pot of boiling oatmeal. Something crawled over it, an ant on a quilt—Everest, rolling in crazed desperation, but not fast enough. Everest flickered and vanished. Only the textured fire remained.

"Linwood is dead."

He looked away from the fiery quilt to see Melinda's face a few centimeters away.

"What?"

"He died in his sleep." She was close, sweating, her oily hair clinging to her head, every freckle brown against blue white skin. "She found him . . . Robin, I mean."

Travis peered at her. She really was real.

"His heart, she thinks. Could you. . . ?"

He struggled with the Velcro tabs of his sleep restraint and pulled himself out of it, wearing only his shorts.

Robin was at Linwood's side. His face was composed, his eyes half open, downcast, looking thoughtfully at nothing. Travis touched the cool eyelids, but while they gave a little under his touch, they did not move.

"He's been dead several hours," Robin said.

"We need to get him home," Travis said. Too loud; it sounded crazy.

But Robin understood. "Yes. Would you help Spin? Cargo bay one would be best."

He looked at her, gaunt, apologetic. "I haven't done this. I—I forgot where we keep the bags."

"I'll show you, Travis."

*   *   *

The ship vibrated all the time now, a hum in the wires transmitted from the withering asteroid, burning steadily as a coal.

They did the quick version of the prebreathe, compensating by pumping up the pressure in their suits. In the inflated suits they were as awkward and roly-poly as marshmallow men. The stark beams of their helmet lamps cut through the ice-swarming darkness. They eased themselves down the tethers to the open bay, carrying their near weightless burden.

The cargo bay doors were open, the bay empty but for the MMUs. They waited while the ship trembled through another quake—the glowing coal throwing off unseen sparks. Then they guided Linwood's body into an empty equipment locker and closed the lid.

They floated above it for a moment. "He was a Christian," Spin said. "Some kind of Protestant."

"I don't have a goddam thing to say," Travis rasped.

"We can talk about it later," Spin said.

"Damned old son of a bitch."

Robin was at the air lock to let them in.

"Where's Melinda?" he demanded, pulling off his helmet.

"She's busy, Travis. She's got a program to write."

The men shucked their suits and crawled inside. Robin sealed the inner hatch solidly behind them.

Everest shuddered again. *Starfire* swayed in its cradle.

They had nothing to say to each other and not much to do but wait. Robin and Spin stayed together and kept on going, drifting naturally toward the flight deck.

Travis drifted to the wardroom. His head and his heart were full, but he had no way to express the swelling pain; the thought of writing or dictating anything at this moment struck him as repellent.

There were movies and books on file. He could have improved his Texican Spanish or tried to learn French or Russian or Japanese. He could have played chess with the ship. Instead he dug out the chip Melinda had been assembling in her spare time, her video documentary of the mission.

The opening scene on the chip was file stuff, hardly as daring as Melinda's own camera work. There on the stage of JSC 2 the original *Starfire* five were sitting behind long tables draped in blue felt—Robin, Spin, Melinda, Linwood, and Jimmy Giles, whom he'd never met—fielding questions from the press.

". . . an exceptional career, Commander Braide, and a reputation as a no-nonsense, by-the-book career astronaut. How does that professional reputation square with your well-publicized private lifestyle."

"Don't believe everything you read in *Us People,* Hugh." The crowd of reporters tittered, but clearly they were hungry for more. "Hugh, since I'm not eager to go into the details of my private life, let me put it this way"—the image on the screen suddenly jittered into quick cuts, grainy fax blowups: Robin in a bikini beside a pool, flanked by muscle boys; Robin in a sequined gown at a craps table; Robin in fireproofs at the wheel of a sticker-plastered Porsche—"I think of Houston as the place I vacation. Space is where I live. I spend way too much time on vacation."

Suddenly Melinda's image came on the screen, speaking into the camera. "So here's an intimate view of Robin Braide at home."

The screen displayed Melinda's point of view as she floated through *Starfire*'s corridor, which looked both bigger and darker on screen than it was in reality. The camera discovered Robin, hunched over, pulling at something in the wall. Melinda's low voice-over explained, "Here you'll recognize our commander changing the lithium hydroxide air filters. In space, everybody pitches in to do her share."

Robin looked up at the camera. "Want a demonstration?"

"We were actually here to get something more personal," said Melinda's off-screen voice.

"Come back when the crapper breaks. And it will."

Melinda's face reappeared, distorted by the wide-angle lens of the camera she was pointing at herself. "The commander seems unwilling to talk while the whole world is watching, so we'll have to wait till she's off guard. Next, let's introduce the boy who once referred to himself, in a moment of drunken abandon, as the world's fastest android. . . ."

The scene switched back to the press conference, as the camera was zooming in on Spin.

Travis switched it off. The chip was what the video people called, by tradition, a jolly reel—in-jokes and outtakes, something for wrap parties, not for public consumption. Maybe someday he'd find it amusing.

He pushed the heels of his hands into his weary eyes. Gently he settled toward the floor.

Perigee. With no eye to watch, Everest streaked through the sun's corona at the astonishing velocity of 300 kilometers per second. The terrifying ball of flame filled fully twenty-eight angular degrees of sky. The surface of Everest was white-hot, dissolving, where it faced the sun—the dull red of banked ashes where it was turned away.

"Commander, the window program is in the launch sequence." Melinda's voice was quivering with exhaustion as she keyed in the last loops, completing the work she had expected to share with Linwood.

"Thanks, Melinda. Time you got suited up."

Melinda encountered Travis outside his bunk, squeezing into his cooling and ventilation suit. The two of them were on standby for EVA. "Travis, Linwood . . ."

He turned away from her, his eyes puffy. "Died trying, didn't he? Like he said. Guess he had the best of it."

"You liked him a lot. I didn't know that about you, until a little while ago. How much you care."

Still he avoided her eyes.

"Second thoughts about me, cowboy?" she asked.

"Hell, no." He glanced at her sidelong. "Hate for you to see me looking like this."

"Like what?"

"Old."

"Your imagination. I think I love you, Travis."

"Maybe I love you, too."

Their kiss was silly and awkward and brief.

"Guess we'll have to go into it later," she said. "In more depth. I mean at greater length. . . ."

"Cut it out!" He was sheepish now. "I think you really mean, over time."

"Yeah, that's what I mean. Thanks."

Travis was strapped into Linwood's couch, peering at the unfamiliar console in PROP and hoping he wouldn't have to do anything with it, when Melinda slid into NAVCOM opposite. A tremor rattled the ship, but they paid it no attention. He watched her hungrily as she climbed into her couch. She turned her head and winked at him.

"Everybody secure?" Robin asked on comm.

"Roger."

"Roger."

"All right, we just sit here about an hour and wait until this thing decides to kick us in the butt."

The computer constantly updated its calculations. At any moment within the optimum launch window the program could decide that the mass balance in the asteroid was satisfactory, or as good as it was likely to get. The bomb would detonate. Simultaneously, inside the narrow cave, *Starfire's* thrusters would fire for a few seconds, providing enough thrust to balance the instantaneous acceleration of the bomb and keep the ship from falling to the floor.

"Listen, I don't want anybody getting up and wandering around until this is over. After the time we've spent up here, one gee even for a few seconds is going to feel like ten. Let's not have any twisted ankles."

They let her nervousness pass without comment, except for obligatory mumbled "rogers."

"I've got T minus forty-five and counting," Spin said. "To computer's best guess."

"Wish I was doing the counting," Robin grumbled.

"Attention. Attention," said the ship.

"Robin," Travis said. "Commander . . ."

"I see it." A red light was blinking on their boards. "If it's another goddam flaky sensor I say screw the computer, we'll play this by ear."

"No, it's in the shot cable," Travis said. "A break, maybe a bad connection."

"You and Travis, Melinda," Robin said. "By the book. Spin at the air lock. Emergency air."

"Copy, wilco."

"Wilco."

They went to the air lock. Spin helped them into their suits. "We've got time. You can breathe fifteen minutes; we can ease the pressure down some."

"If I can't move in this thing I'm going straight to twenty-six," said Melinda.

"You're not gonna move at all if you get the bends," Travis said. "Do it by the book, like the woman says."

Spin closed the inner door and started evacuating the air lock. After ten minutes of waiting Melinda's weary impatience got the best of her. "I'm popping this door if you don't, Spin. I'll breathe on the way down."

"Okay, okay. Grab hold." The outer hatch unseated, and residual air rushed out.

Outside, Travis and Melinda pulled themselves awkwardly

down the tethers, fighting against their overinflated suits.
They reached the service module, where the bomb's power
cable issued from an access panel.

"I'm going deep," she said.

"You're pretty tired, maybe I—"

"By the book, cowboy."

"Yeah, roger."

She pulled herself away from him, heading down past the
tanks, past the dark wings and the engine, her dingy white
suit fading out in the thick gloom. He watched the play of
her helmet light a brief moment, then turned to examine the
connector where the thick black cable left the hull.

"Hull connection looks good," he said.

". . . opy," Robin's scratchy voice said in his ear.

On the flight deck, Robin watched her board, her clock, her
monitors. She had a monitor on the air lock, and cameras
outside the ship picked up Travis's head lamp erratically
darting over the lower part of the hull, but beyond that she
was blind.

. . . fway to the bot . . ." Melinda said.

"Copy, Melinda," said Robin.

". . . one's g. . . ?" Travis inquired.

"Negative, Travis. No change."

In the blurry scene on the monitor, ice chips shaken from
the quivering walls gleamed like swarming plankton. Travis's
light dwindled as he headed down toward the next cable connector, and she lost sight of him altogether.

Melinda arrived in the geode. Diamonds shaken from the
walls filled the hollow space, but back in its crevice the bomb
and all its thoroughly taped detonators seemed secure.

"I'm at the bomb. No obvious problems."

". . . opy."

She moved closer and steered the beam from her helmet
lamp slowly over each taped nipple. All neat, but neat as it

was, it was still patchwork. In the time she had, with the limited flexibility of her suit, she would not be able to check and reconnect even half the detonators; the mathematics of probability said leave them, move on up the cable, check the connectors that were easiest to check.

She started up the shaft again. Squeezed into the passage in a stiffened suit, she took a moment to consciously suppress her rising panic. She came to the first cable splice.

"I'm at the first connection."

"Copy."

She unscrewed the knurled ring that locked the male and female plugs and unsnapped the connection. She inspected the pins and sockets, then snapped the plug together again.

"Reconnected here. Got anything?"

"No change. That's not it. Do you rea. . . ?"

"Copy no change. I'm moving up, over."

Far above her, Travis was moving down into the shaft. "What about that one?"

". . . egative. Still red," said Robin.

His helmet lights caught standing waves in the icy dust, set up by the steady tremor of Everest.

He heard Melinda on the radio, her voice excited: "Hey, Robin, this one looks loose! Could be . . ." She was washed out by static. ". . . putting it back together. What say?

"Negative, repeat negative, Robin. Spin, I nee . . ." The static seemed to be getting worse; the shaft was a waveguide, and they were on the wrong frequency. ". . . nversion tables. Travis, can you see Melin. . . ?"

"Negative. Pretty thick dust in here."

". . . barely read . . . switch over to RF . . . switch your . . ."

"Okay, I'm in RF," he said.

"Any bett. . . ?"

"Not much." He had grabbed another cable junction,

twisted it apart, and reconnected it. "Does this one do anything for you, Robin?"

"No change. Getting tired of the color red."

Travis was getting plain tired, fighting his stiff suit. He
resisted the temptation to lower the oxygen pressure.

On the flight deck, the clock was winding down. When the
window opened, the bomb could go at any moment unless
Robin chose to override the program.

"T minus seventeen minutes thirty. We need both of you
in the air lock in twelve."

Melinda's voice crackled from the radio: "No use . . . out
bomb."

"Copy that, but you will be in the air lock in twelve minutes." If the damn bomb doesn't work, we'll just have to
think of something else, Robin thought. But she didn't say
it. She didn't figure it would play.

Melinda was moving up through the shaft. Far above her,
Travis's helmet lamp was bouncing light from the icy walls.
She heard him say, "I'm connecting. . . ," and a moment
later Robin replying, ". . . egative."

"I'm at number five junction," Melinda said. She grasped
the connector and twisted it. She peered through her faceplate, inspecting the interior of the socket half—nothing.
Then the other half, with the pins.

Bent pin.

Cursing her clumsy ballooning gloves, she bullied the pin
back into vertical. She tried the connection again.

"Robin?"

". . . irmative! I've got . . . een light! Repeat . . ." Static
washed her away, but the message was clear.

"Copy you have a green light. I'm locking this turkey.
Travis, get your ass out of the way"—she twisted the locking

ring, which was oddly loose in her hands—"'cause I'm comin' up."

Travis pawed at the walls, boosting himself with his finger-tips. He flew from the shaft, tugged himself up the length of *Starfire* toward the circle of yellow light that was the open air lock. He flew into the lock. Behind the inner window, Spin's face was a haggard mask in the worklight.

Travis turned to face the outer hatch. In the yellow light, ice plankton swarmed.

"T minus three minutes forty-five seconds," said Robin. "Where's everybody?"

"Travis is in the lock," Spin said.

Melinda's voice came through static: ". . . see the lock."

Melinda rose smiling into the misty golden light, framed by the circle of the open hatch. She moved toward the lock.

"She's in," Spin said, exultant. "Ready to seal."

A violent tremor swung the ship.

"We have a flickering red light," said Robin. "I am over-riding the ignition sequence."

Melinda did a somersault and hooked her boots against the upper rim of the hatch. She dived out of sight.

Spin slammed the hatch switches. The hatch swung to-ward Travis as, off balance, he tried to exit.

"Damn you," Travis shouted, yanking at the interior air lock control with no result; Spin was overriding him. "She needs help."

"I don't need . . . cking help," said Melinda's voice on the radio.

"She doesn't need your help," Spin said. "It's a job for one." The hatch was down and sealed. The air lock filled with a whistle and crescendo of air. "Get out of that suit, Travis. You're blocking the air lock."

The inner hatch popped up and away. Travis hesitated, but Spin had left him no choice. He unlatched his helmet. Spin moved in to help him shuck the suit. They returned to the inner corridor, and Spin slammed the inner hatch down and turned on the pumps to evacuate the air lock.

Melinda's voice came over the comm system. "Okay, at five, see the prob . . . got to tape this togeth . . ."

Robin said, "Melinda, I can override for two or three minutes before Everest's attitude is completely fucked. After that we lose the window. Repeat, you have a maximum of three minutes."

". . . oger, let me just get this tape . . ."

"Travis, be seated," Robin demanded.

Spin pushed his face at Travis's. "You're loose cargo, cowboy. Tie yourself down."

Robin's voice boomed from the speakers. "We have a green light and it's holding. Come aboard, Melinda. Repeat, come aboard. Travis, go sit down, dammit. Spin, find a flat place."

"You think you can do this job better than I can?" Spin demanded of Travis.

Melinda's voice cut through the silence. "A-OK, clear the decks, I'm com . . ."

Still Travis didn't move. He couldn't explain his reluctance to leave the air lock, to strap himself down, to wait passively while Melinda conducted her own affairs—except that his heart cried to see her again.

"What the hell is it with you?" Spin yelled at him. "You think you're the only one who cares?"

Travis looked at Spin and saw him rattled. The sight shook him.

The only one who cared about her? The only one who loved her? Travis shook his head. He turned away and pulled himself up the long corridor. The ship bounced wildly in its wiry cradle, then settled down to growling vibration.

Spin turned to the air lock window and saw nothing but an empty room, its round door open to murky swirling night. He looked back up the corridor and saw Travis pulling himself into PROP, high above.

"Spin, I will enable the ignition sequence when Melinda is

in the air lock. Give me immediate word. Melinda, what's your status? Do you read?"

"Okay, Robin, I'm at the air . . . coming inside. Repeat, I'm coming inside."

"Welcome aboard. As soon as you are in, put yourself on the floor. Spin?"

But Spin was staring at an empty air lock. "Uhh . . ."

"Confirm that she is in and secure."

"I'm in, Robin. Just get . . . suit off."

Spin was looking at an air lock as empty as a blown egg.

"Repeat, I'm in," said Melinda. "Suit out of the way. Thanks, Spin . . . out of the cold."

"Uh, roger, Melinda," Spin said, the words searing his tongue. "And copy you, Robin, she's in good shape, uh, she's inside . . ."

There was no one in the air lock.

Robin knew it, because the monitor showed an empty air lock. The monitors showed Spin still in the corridor beside the empty air lock and Travis yanking at his straps as he tied himself into the unfamiliar couch in PROP. The monitors showed an otherwise empty ship. The monitors showed nothing outside the ship but drifting debris.

Robin knew all there was to know, then. She knew why. She stared, frozen, at the empty air lock. "Spin, find a flat place, right now. We are in the window." Spin lifted his head and peered bleakly at her, through the monitor camera over his head. "Spin . . ." Robin had not yet reset the switches she had disabled. But Spin began to move, to swim up the corridor, and his action relieved her paralysis; she reached for the switches—"Ignition sequence enabled. Repeat, ignition sequence enabled"—but even though she had just said she did, still she did not throw the switches. She told herself that she knew what she must do and that she would do it, but she would just wait the ten or twenty seconds it would take Spin to reach the flight deck.

*   *   *

Melinda was in the shaft, her knees pulled up and jammed against the walls, braced against the asteroid's shuddering. She held the two halves of the cable connector tightly together. She had run out of tape.

"Okay, we're in and sealed, everything is A-OK, I'm real comfortable. Let's get the hell out of here." There were arguments on both sides of this, and Melinda was still running them in her mind. She really resented having been rushed into a situation that begged more thought.

Only one of the monitors in PROP was patched into the comm channels; on it, Spin was seen swimming up the corridor. After Travis strapped himself in, he reached up and jabbed at the channel selector. *Click*. Nobody in the wardroom. *Click*. Nobody in the bunk area. To his left Spin moved past him toward the flight deck—Travis already knew nobody was in NAV-COM. *Click*. The air lock was open and empty.

"Spin, dammit . . .!" Robin's voice splintered the audio.

Perhaps the tears, pooling weightless in front of his eyes, distorted his vision, for at the lip of the flight deck Spin inexplicably missed his grip; as his arm shot past, the back of his wrist brushed a fire-suppression nozzle—a trivial slip, but for the fact that his expandable steel watch band slipped over the nozzle and entangled itself. Momentarily adrift, he jerked hard but failed to rip himself free. His head slammed against the wall.

One second before, Robin had set the ignition sequence switches. "Travis, grab him, save him!" she screamed. "He'll fall!"

Travis had struggled to get out of his harness, the primitive thoughless part of his brain reacting to the realization that Melinda was not in the ship. As he yanked himself into the corridor, Robin's plea smashed into his consciousness. He grabbed for Spin's tumbling body, immediately above him.

There was the fragmentary beginning of a thought that he would pull Spin into PROP with him, a thought that was never fully formed and that afterward he did not even remem—

The white light reached Melinda ahead of the charged particles, well ahead of the heat. The shaft crumpled around her and she never completed her considerations about whether this was a reasonable sacrifice in view of the fact that she had not had time to thoroughly review the altern—

The white light and the other photons got through the shaft before it sealed. The light seared the cameras that watched the outside of *Starfire*'s hull, spraying amplified radiation from the monitors inside—

The white light emerged laterally along the plane of the collision fault. For an instant Everest was circled by a ring of perfect light, whiter than the intense yellow sun that filled a quarter of the sky behind it. The middle of the icy rock dissolved in plasma; its top and bottom parted; the lower half instantly began a long spiral into the sun. The fireball swallowed all—

A battery of cannons boomed:*Starfire*'s ignition sequence had kicked in thrusters to offset the instant acceleration—

The acceleration was only a single Earth gravity, but Travis and Spin happened not to be holding onto anything at the moment it was applied, and they were at the top of a ten-meter shaft which had suddenly become vertical. At that moment Travis was underneath Spin, in the act of grabbing him around the waist with his left arm. Spin's watch was torn from his wrist. They fell together, four and half meters in the first second, colliding randomly with the walls as they fell. Desperately Travis grabbed for a ladder rung—it wrenched itself out of his grasp. *Starfire* had already stopped accelerating when they slammed into the bulkhead, side by side. Travis hit feet first.

On the flight deck, Robin tore at the throat of her uniform, opened it, twisted the chain of the platinum cross in her hand, and yanked it hard. The chain cut her neck. She threw the weightless cross against the wall.

". . . with today's disclosure that the asteroid apparently disintegrated during its closest approach to the sun. The loss of *Starfire* and its crew, which for more than a week NASA sources have privately held to be inevitable, has now been publicly admitted. This morning the White House announced that President Purvis will name a commission to inquire into the causes of the disaster. Meanwhile, a number of high-ranking NASA officials have submitted their resignations, among them the agency's administrator, T. Whitney Rosenthal, and the director of the Johnson Space Center, Taylor Stith. For National Public Video, this is Harriet Richards reporting."

A crumb of glowing carbon tumbled away from the sun. Inside it there were people.

Spin was there, stretched in midair in the wardroom, rigged in a shock-absorbing hammock as elaborate as that which restrained *Starfire* inside its sealed cave. His head and body were taped to rigid splints of aluminum spars; he was medicated and fed through his veins by pressurized tubes; his wastes were removed by other tubes; ribbed, hissing gas bladders, in imitation of peristalsis, continually stimulated his circulation; an oxygen mask rested over his nose and mouth; his unseeing eyes—their pupils oddly dilated, the right slightly wider than the left—stared in the direction of the life-support electronics that monitored the ebb and flow of his life. His back was broken; possibly his skull was fractured. It was, perhaps, a miracle that he remained alive, a miracle of automation.

Travis and Robin were there, although they had not seen much of each other in three days, not since the centripetal moment when Travis, stunned and disoriented, found Spin flopping beside him at the bottom of the corridor, weirdly limp and insensate, and in the same moment knew fire in his own shoulder and the bite of a crushed ankle, and simultaneously felt his heart crumple under the shock of knowing what had become of Melinda. He would have screamed, but he was an imploded man, unable to expell so much as a call for help without gasping for breath.

Travis recovered, or seemed to, at once. His ankle and torn shoulder were of little concern so long as the ship remained weightless. Within moments, he and Robin had addressed themselves to the business at hand. Working desperately, they immobilized Spin, diagnosed him, plugged him in. Then Robin patched up Travis. When that emergency work was done, they collapsed in pained and exhausted sleep.

In the next days they did necessary things, like repairing the cameras, replacing eroded lenses and fried circuitry, and constructing a cradle for Spin that they hoped would protect him from the acceleration still to come—breaking off to sleep only when they had exhausted themselves again. When the necessary things were done they did useful things, like tidying the ship and stowing what would not be needed. Then they did meaningless things, like replacing the instrument package in the shaft below the ship—meaningless because if they survived, the fragment of asteroid they must soon separate themselves from could not. But perhaps they would not survive; perhaps their calculations had been in error and they would miss Mercury: then, at least, the subsequent travels of the smashed asteroid, Melinda's grave, would be recorded on those mute instruments forever, until someday someone chose to recover them.

Now Travis was in the wardroom studying Spin, studying the steady pulsing march of the waveforms across the monitors, the rhythmic hiss and sigh of the pumps and bladders. The monitors indicated a steady pulse and respiration, stable blood pressure. . . .

Only to Spin had flying *Starfire* been an end in itself. To Travis, *Starfire* had been a means, a magnificent tool but subordinate to his purpose of re-entering the void. Robin's stance toward the ship was different, more complex, but he thought it no less operational than his own; Melinda and Linwood had been proud of their vessel, but their pride was uncomplicated, or so it seemed to Travis. Spin, in his great modesty, had not thought of himself as a controller, had not thought of the machine as an instrument of his will or an extension of his power. Indeed, his most exalted moments came when he felt himself an extension of the machine. Spin's passion for the ship had struck Travis as merely odd at first, but eventually it had come to seem worthy of respect. Far from robbing Spin of humanity, the symbiosis had infused *Starfire* with soul. Now the ship kept Spin alive. At any place within its massively parallel submicrocircuitry, did it sense its own striving?

On the flight deck, Robin watched the bright meters and dials and monitors, straining her senses to the rhythm of the ship. One monitor showed Spin's impassive face. Above it, the big screens were black. As the rock flew on, Robin struggled with loss.

Her loss had begun before the mission. Since the day she fired him, she had not betrayed a hint of what she felt for Jimmy Giles—not to him, not to her bosses, not to her crew. What she felt was a rip in her side, a stone on her heart, hot sand beneath her eyelids. And guilt at her own relief. Her decisiveness, her laughter, her excitement, her rational calm since the moment she had made the decision—all had been at best a momentary diversion, at worst a disguise, an overlay on the truth. The intensity of her double-edged pain had never abated.

She knew what the rest of them thought of Jimmy, of course. Linwood had been involved in an ongoing and occasionally acid debate with him; Spin had never taken him very seriously; Melinda had never liked him at all. He was prissy and self-involved and politically as unsubtle as most men of his rank. No matter. If Jimmy could have disentangled himself from his guilt—not to mention from his wife and children—none of it would have mattered, so she thought. But maybe she was wrong. Maybe the impossibility of loving him made it possible for her to love him. Not anymore. Any possibility of love for him had died on Everest.

What Robin struggled with now was the possibility of her own life, in the face of loss she could no longer deny. Like a ghost rising from the deep, Melinda's face appeared on one of the monitors, speaking to her—

—but it was only Travis, in the wardroom, playing Melinda's jolly reel. He had played and played it; he kept returning to a scrap of conversation: Melinda at the press conference.

". . . two or three kids someday. Sure. But not until after I've got my own command."

"Sounds like a busy life," said a reporter.

"I've got time. I've got a head start."

And the audience laughed.

Had she been mostly crushed, Travis wondered, or mostly burned? Or in the best case, simply vaporized? While the ship was so near her the question would haunt him, and perhaps for long after. There was more than the simple loss of her. She posed a question trembling on the brink of an answer, residing there in death, embedded in some form in the rocky matrix. Those who survived her were no less inextricably embedded in the matrices of the repetitive patterns of their lives.

Three days out from the sun, as the color of the hot rock's glow was cooling from apricot to mere brick, it suddenly expelled a cloud of fiery rubble. The last of the chemical explosives had gone to blow the cork out of *Starfire*'s bottle.

Nursing his strained shoulder and broken ankle, Travis worked beside Robin a long slow time, freeing the ship from its tangle of cables, which snared it and the two of them like the snakes that crushed Laocoon and his sons. When they had cut free of the last of the black cables, Robin returned to the flight deck. Travis stayed outside the ship to talk to her through the floating debris. Verniers puffed again and again. With agonizing slowness the ship eased out through orbiting ice and black gravel. Travis pulled himself into the air lock just as the ship's black fins sliced into the glowing haze above the horizon of the ruined asteroid.

"Aim point numbers, please."

Travis was in NAVCOM now, peering at Melinda's computer screen. He sucked a lungful of air. "X plus oh point oh one one seven, Y minus oh point four six one four, Z minus oh point oh three eight five."

"Copy X plus oh point oh one one seven, Y minus oh point four six one four, Z minus oh point oh three eight five."

"Roger."

"Stand by." Robin pushed the buttons. The maneuvering thrusters spurted, and *Starfire* translated itself into a minimally different orbit about the sun. Slowly—so slowly their separation would not become evident for hours—the ship and the flake of rock began to part company.

"Thank you, Travis."

He said nothing. The numbers weren't his.

*   *   *

Later he joined her on the flight deck. Mercury was visible now on the screens, a bright spark growing brighter against a dazzling field of stars. Soon the planet would resolve itself into a ball as bleak and cratered as the moon.

Travis let his gaze slip sidelong from the starry screen to peer at Robin. Her clear white skin was luminous in translated starlight, showing a fine network of lines around the eyes and mouth that reminded him that she was, after all, as old as he was, older. The enigma and challenge of her presented itself in light that to him was new.

She caught him looking. "Hey, cowboy."

He forced a grin. "Hey, Cap'n."

They looked away, and the silence threatened to stretch into its old intransigence. Neither wanted that to happen.

"It was easy for you, Travis," she said, her voice husky.

"What?"

"It was easy for you to do the right thing."

"The right thing?"

"Save Spin."

"*Save* him!" He was too surprised for anger.

"Because you wanted to, even without thinking about it. And because I ordered you to."

"Without me gettin' in his way he might've done better."

"Whenever you're ready to look at the chip, I'll prove to you that you saved him. Without you he would have broken his neck."

"What's the point of this?" he said impatiently.

"You did what you could. I did what I had to." Her hand went absently to her throat, and finding it bare, went to her brow, to shade her eyes against the stars.

He was quiet a long time before he said, "No, Robin." His reply, when it finally came rasping from his throat, surprised him as much as her. "You made the choice, when you'd just as soon we all died. In the face of that you did what was right." After another pause he continued, with effort. "Robin, people say I'm real good at talkin' about stuff that doesn't mean much. Talkin' people into things, sellin' 'em things. But why we bother to stay alive . . . well, maybe I've never been too sure myself. You ever feel that way?"

She studied him. "Do you mean the feeling that my life is a lie?"

"Yes."

"I put a lot of energy into not thinking about that."

"But then you find yourself right there staring it in the face. The ones you were supposed to save die on you, or want to kill themselves so you can live. And if you don't push the button, you're sayin' all our lives, theirs too, are lies—or worse, just dirty jokes."

"What if that's the truth?" she whispered. "And I simply lacked the guts to admit it."

"I don't know that it's not true," he rasped. "I don't know one way or the other. I wanted to be dead the second I realized what Melinda did. And right now, if it weren't for Spin, maybe I still would. Maybe it's an open question." He fell silent, worrying the thought. "But I don't think so," he said. "I don't think it's open for me anymore. It's not just Spin; it *is* her, but it's more than her. She died for us, who had more life than any of us. It's not so much that I owe her as . . . that I can't see the choice as trivial anymore."

Robin heard the thoughts he couldn't find words for—that he would live and embrace life because it was a gift and not a burden, because it was a gift he had not earned. She wished she could be as accepting. "We're a fine pair of heroes," she said wearily.

"Heroes!" Suddenly he laughed, surprising her—not a cynical laugh but a bubbling up of enjoyment, the revelation that comes with the punch line of a good joke. "Hell, Robin, we've been there before. We should know the difference."

"The difference?"

"Between what we know and what *they* want to think.

This time it's gonna take more guts to play the part than to do the deed." He smiled. "You up to it?"

She studied him. "You never let me see this in you, Travis. You never let anybody see it."

"I didn't have anything to show. Until maybe a couple of days ago."

She reached out her right hand and stretched across the yawning mouth of the central corridor. "Thanks for showing it now."

He leaned across and stretched out his right, the diamonds sparkling on his wrist. "You know something, I still owe you a mai tai." His voice, stronger now, was still husky. He wondered if it would ever again be clear. "This time I won't forget." They shook hands.

In the screens little Mercury, dense and massive, swelled like a stony balloon. They were diving at its bright limb, rushing at its baked stone with appalling velocity; within seconds they would add another bull's eye to its splattered surface—

—then they were soaring mere kilometers above its ragged scarps and ridges, painted in ink on gleaming silver. They plunged into shadow; at that instant lobate fire erupted silently below them, streaking across the gnarled landscape on a track precisely parallel to their own, flooding the darkness with lurid light. All that was left of Everest had impacted with the planet.

Mercury's gravity tugged and bent the worldline of Starfire; the starry sky tilted—

—and they were flying not away from Earth but on a course that in a month's time would bend across that planet's bows.

"T minus ten seconds," said the ship.

"I have an all-green board," said Travis, seated in PROP. "Copy."

"Three," said the ship.

"Two . . ."

"One . . ."
"Power."
"Ignition."

The fat red sun was sliding toward the long curve of the dunes; the desultory surf was the color of blood. Jimmy ran toward the sinking sun, jogged along the beach past picknickers packing up their baskets, and fishers stowing their gear, and sunbathers wrapping themselves against the cool of approaching evening.

He was running against his anger, against his frustration, running to drain the energy he might otherwise have vented on his colleagues and superiors. This morning he'd quite unexpectedly received orders. He'd been promoted—wonderful! He was a full bird colonel now, not a light colonel anymore, which was a bit overdue in fact, at his age—

—and with the rank came a new job. Jimmy Giles discovered that he wasn't an astronaut anymore. The Air Force was transferring him to Colorado Springs, to an administrative post at Headquarters Space Command. Effective immediately. Put on your uniform and get out there, space available on the next plane. Wife and minor dependents and household goods to follow.

So he drove to the Galveston beaches and ran. He couldn't quite get over the suspicion that they were distancing him as rapidly as they could from the *Starfire* debacle. Maybe even letting him know it hadn't been politic to let himself become so visible in the first place . . . though how was he supposed to have controlled *that*?

Suspicion, hell. Don't ever let anyone tell you Personnel doesn't read the dailies. Anyway, thanks for the promotion, fellows. Join the Air Force and fly a desk.

Running, he tried to ignore the people around him, until it entered his hot consciousness that their fitful attention was turning with him as he ran. Their attention was not tuned to Jimmy, however—

The bloody sun oozed toward the dunes. Below and to the left of it, Venus hung like a bare bulb in the blue gray sky; farther to the left and higher, a needle of white light scratched the sky.

People were pointing at that peculiar streak of light, too straight and bright to be a cloud or a contrail or a comet. Jimmy stumbled to a halt in the sand, gaping. He knew the light for what it was.

Jimmy flashed his badge and pushed his way into mission control. A lot of other people had recently been squeezing past the guards; the skeleton crew in mission control left to monitor *Starfire* suddenly found itself with more help than it wanted.

Jimmy went straight to the flight director. "What's their status?"

"It's all guesswork, Colonel, but we think maybe they tried to brake around Mercury."

"Christ and Mary, they did that, did they?" The flight director was too busy to answer rhetorical questions. "What about communication?" Jimmy demanded.

"Nothing so far," said Flight. "We're doing our best."

"What about the VLA?"

"Yeah, New Mexico's pitching in. Nothing so far."

Jimmy stared over Flight's shoulder at the barren screens. "Maybe they just don't want to talk."

"What?" Flight was getting irritated.

"They got this far without us."

The wings glowed and the engine poured blazing hydrogen and lithium into space. The trail of fire cut across the sun's disk, gently curving backward toward distant Mercury. The ship was a firebird plumed in flame.

Then, with a silent puff of plasma, the fiery stream evaporated, and the wings, a fading rainbow, began to cool.

Travis went down to the wardroom to look at Spin. His

life-support systems had functioned superbly through the crushing acceleration; his pupils were regular now, and as Travis watched, his eyelids gently closed. On the monitor his brain waves had assumed an encouragingly regular pattern. Travis climbed to the flight deck and settled himself into Spin's couch.

"Looks like he's doing okay," Travis said.

They studied the screens, searching the stars for the cool point that was Earth.

"We've been receiving signals from Houston," she said. "I haven't . . . had time to answer."

He smiled. "Maybe we should keep on good terms," he said.

"You think so?"

"I'm already gettin' the itch to ride this thing again. Don't you think it would be amusin' to walk on one more planet, before we call it quits?"

"Yes," she said, turning to him, "I do think that would be amusing. How many asteroids did you say were out there?"

"Can't hardly count 'em all," he said, grinning. "Plus a few billion comets. Not to mention a few dozen interesting moons. And a star or two, just might be in reach."

"Well, keep your ass in that right-hand seat long enough, cowboy, and I'll teach you how to do more than ride this thing. I'll teach you how to make it fly."

Back on Earth the engineers were already calling up the plans, the drawings that a week ago had seemed destined for limbo—the plans that took a hot-rod rocket engine and mounted it on a longer frame, with bigger tanks and bigger bays and more room for more people to live longer; the plans for a ship that would lift an expedition to Titan, that would make a journey to the stars; the plans for a ship whose designation did not begin with X—because that X-ship, that hot rod, that engine with wings, had done its job.

Starfire was falling up now, out of the deep well of the

sun, sliding up and over the sheer slick wall of gravity's maelstrom, slowing as she rose, curving as she rose, the arc of her ascent bowing gracefully past Venus, to meet the curve of distant Earth. She was a firebird, yes, a seared and battered firebird, blackened with the dust of a vanished worldlet that could never blow away—

—and she soared.

AFTERWORD

Gary Gutierrez—shortly after he directed the special effects for *The Right Stuff* and shortly before he did the same for *Top Gun*—suggested to me that we ought to make a realistic, documentary-style film about a future space mission, a film in the spirit of *Destination Moon* using the tools available to filmmakers today. Producer Lynda Obst encouraged us as our story evolved over many months, a story I privately nicknamed *Destination Sun*. Alas, we realized that an uncomfortably hefty budget would be required to make the kind of movie we wanted—not to achieve spectacle (that's easy) but to achieve its opposite, a convincing portrayal of everyday life in microgravity. So with Gary's blessing I've turned our ideas into this novel, which owes much to Gary's originality and hard work; indeed, some of my favorite images and bits of conversation are Gary's. Gary also read the first draft of the book and made pointed and valuable suggestions. Many thanks, good friend.

Freeman Dyson crucially instructed me on the acceleration of extended structures. Brian O'Leary shared his work on the potential resources of the asteroids. Don Dixon gave me the benefit of his home-brew Earth-orbital program. Andrew Fraknoi let me play freely for hours with the Astronomical Society of the Pacific's computers and programs, including the versatile MacStronomy by Etion Software. Terry White and his fine staff at the Johnson Space Center extended every courtesy; we mined the transcript of shuttle mission 41-C for gems, ditto the design study of the Solar Probe mission sent to us by Dr. D. S. Spicer of NASA headquarters. Gilbert Shapiro gave me a microcourse in fissile materials. Sincere thanks to them all.

Special thanks to William K. Hartmann. Bill's own ground-breaking research on the small bodies of the solar system, his books and stirring paintings, and our many talks have long inspired me.

All of these people were gracious and helpful, but none are responsible for what I have done with their suggestions. The goofs are all mine.

David Hartwell was again this writer's essential editor, a creative partner in the enterprise. Tom Doherty and Beth Meacham and their colleagues at Tor make for a wonderfully supportive publisher. They know how much I appreciate them.